NAOMI'S JOY

NAOMI'S JOY

by
Cynthia Davis

FOOTPRINTS FROM THE BIBLE

CROSSINGS BOOK CLUB
Garden City, New York

Published by Crossings Book Club, 501 Franklin Avenue, Garden City, New York 11530

Book design by Christos Peterson

ISBN: 978-1-58288-257-4

Printed in the United States of America

✎ Prologue ✎

THREE WOMEN SAT TOGETHER. Prayers of dedication drifted from the next room. They were very different in appearance and manner. The youngest was dressed in a simple gown. The straight, neatly braided, dusky hair framed a small-heart shaped face. Her gray eyes attracted and held attention. They seemed to be deep, clouded pools of mystery as she watched the archway between the two rooms. When a baby's cry sounded, the young woman flinched and caught her lower lip between her teeth.

Seeing the reaction, the taller of her companions bent close. Nearly white hair could just be glimpsed beneath the widow's veil Rahab had worn for five years, though a few strands of red still lingered. Despite her age, there was a grace and peace about the woman that spoke of a great inner beauty and faith.

"It is the price we women pay to abide by the covenant of Abraham. We feel the pain when our sons cry. He will soon forget," the old woman sighed in sympathy.

"It seems cruel." For a moment, it looked like Ruth would cry.

"My dearest daughter," the third occupant of the room said. Her comforting hand covered Ruth's twisting fingers. "Better the pain now than when they are older. My own sons were not circumcised until the entire congregation of Israel camped at Gilgal. They were in agony for weeks afterward."

A grimace crossed the deeply lined face. The tragedies of life left their mark in each crevasse. On her lips a serene smile was visible although faded brown eyes sparkled with tears of memory. Naomi, too, wore a widow's veil over her grey hair. The old woman had buried her children and her husband in a distant land.

"Behold the newest of the Sons of Israel. Obed, son of Boaz bar Salma, is an inheritor of the promises to Abraham, Isaac, and Jacob!" From the main room came the triumphant proclamation over the cries of the infant.

Proudly, a tall man entered the room. Tenderly, he held his child. Ruth reached out to take her baby then drew back her arms when she saw Naomi stretch out eager hands.

"My grandson," the old woman cradled the small body. "I never thought I would hold an infant again."

"Obed is indeed a blessing," Rahab, mother to the child's father, agreed with a smile. She bent over the infant to rub his cheek gently with one finger. "The Holy One has given you an heir in place of the sons you lost."

The widow of Salma, spy of Israel, did not add what many in Bethlehem whispered privately. "Naomi is better served by her daughter-in-law Ruth than she ever was by her feeble sons and stern husband. Even though the girl is a foreigner, she is loyal and honorable and serves the God of Israel."

Naomi smiled down at the baby now hiccupping in her arms. "It is fitting that you are named Obed. You will be a mighty man and serve the Lord our God."

From her seat, Ruth smiled at the pair of elderly women hovering over her son. Her heart expanded with love for the grandmothers. Surreptitiously she wiped damp eyes with the corner of her veil.

"My love, why do you weep?" A low-voiced question came from the tall, auburn-haired man now leaning close to his wife.

The young woman looked up and smiled through her tears.

"They are so happy." A slight movement of her hand indicated the still-adoring grandmothers.

"Yes." A broad smile appeared. "I am not sure who is more proud, my mother or Naomi. You will need to be vigilant, or my son will be spoiled."

"No, Obed will not become a spoiled weakling. My son will be a strong man like his father," the young mother insisted and nodded decisively.

Boaz kissed the wisps of hair on his wife's brow.

"God is gracious," the man stated in a musing tone.

Across the room, Naomi looked up. "Yes, the Lord is indeed gracious. I never believed I could ever claim such a promise."

"My mother." Ruth tilted her head and smiled at the old woman. She leaned against her husband. "Your God has given me all that I desire."

"I have learned the One God does indeed answer prayers and heal pain," Naomi stated as she looked at the young woman. "It was a long journey for me. I was so bitter. The hand of God seemed always raised against me. From the time my father died in the desert, I feared that the Holy One would strike me down for some indiscretion. I struggled to do all that was required and never dared believe that God would care about me. Not even the signs and wonders I saw could convince me that the Almighty cherished the Children of Israel. All I saw were the laws to be obeyed. I dreaded the punishment that I was sure would come."

Naomi looked down at the small bundle in her arms. There was just a hint of red in the fuzz that covered the tiny head. She bent to kiss the infant.

"My child, you will never know the special food God sent each morning. We called it manna, for no one knew what the substance really was. It tasted slightly sweet, but unless ground or mixed with other ingredients, it melted by midmorning. No one dared store any overnight because then it crawled with horrid worms."

Ruth shuddered at the thought.

"Even in Jericho, we heard of the manna and of the pillar of cloud and fire. You are blessed to have seen the power of the Living God among you during the time in the wilderness." Rahab looked almost wistful.

"It is true." Naomi smiled ruefully. "I grew up knowing that the God of Sinai was present. What I did not learn was that **I AM** was among us with love. As a child it was impossible to not be aware of the pillar that everyone knew was the presence of the Holy One. Despite the stories of Miriam, I was afraid of the Holy One. My belief centered on avoiding the terrors and plagues, rather than on the loving care we experienced in our wanderings."

"It must have been amazing to know that you were freed by the hand of God." Rahab sounded awed.

"The tribes of Israel left Egypt ten years before I was even born. My mother was a child of eight when Pharaoh bowed to the God of Moses and freed the sons of Jacob. I never knew a life of slavery. It was a vague anecdote remembered by the adults. Sometimes Father told me about his work on the monuments for the King before the Exodus. 'We dragged huge blocks of limestone into place over logs and sand,' he said. 'They were larger than the entire tabernacle.' I could easily imagine rocks that large. All around were the stony mountains of the wilderness. They loomed over us every day. A life of whips and taskmasters I could not understand."

Naomi rocked from side to side with the infant in her arms. He dozed. Her companions were silent.

"The mighty acts of *I AM* to punish those who rebelled were what I remembered. My own father died in the Wilderness of Shur." The gray-haired woman took a deep breath. Her family leaned forward when she softly began to remember the past.

❧ 1 ☙

EVERY YEAR WE CELEBRATED Passover at the foot of Sinai. We herded the sheep from pasture to pasture in the wilderness just as Abraham did long ago. Our travels brought us back every year to the sacred mountain where Moses received the Law of the One God. Our covenant with the Almighty was renewed with sacred foods and ceremonies. We were exhorted to be unswerving in our obedience to the ways of *I AM.*

"By the blood of the lamb on our doors, the Angel of Death passed over the homes of the faithful children. You must never forget that God brought you out with a strong hand." Moses always reminded us that the death of every firstborn son in Egypt was our ransom. "The Holy One will fulfill the promise to Abraham, Isaac, and Jacob. We will have a homeland."

Despite the yearly promise, we remained nomads in the desert. Abital, my mother, tended to our food and clothing when she was not bearing children. My brother Isaac was two years younger than me. Leah was born when I was six and Hephzibah, three years later. Mattan, our father, worked among the sheep. All of Israel herded their flocks together. The fleece was marked with a sign of ownership. Each man took his turn tending the animals. It was my duty to watch my siblings when we moved from camp to camp. They preferred to wander away to look for lizards and inspect interesting rock formations rather than walk with me. I grew tired of chasing after the children.

"Will we ever stop traveling and live in a house?" I was twelve when I approached my father. "It would be easier to keep Hephzibah and Leah out of trouble if we were not always traveling."

"God will fulfill the promise," the man responded gruffly.

"But—" My impending argument was cut short.

"Do not question the ways of the Lord. The God of Israel punishes those who rebel. The graves at Kibroth-hattaavah are proof."
My father was stern. "Remember how the fierce anger of Moses and
his God sent plague along with the quail. You have seen the forbidden place at the foot of the holy mountain where the ground swallowed the rebels who built a golden calf."

I lowered my head and hurried away to help Mother. The reminder of the chasm near the Sinai terrified me. I dared not ask any
more questions. However, not many weeks later, I overheard my father in discussion with other men. They voiced the same question I
was scolded for asking.

"Even my daughter is tired of the endless traveling." The man's
words made me pause to listen.

"My wife wants a home."

"We have been promised a homeland."

"I do not think we will ever get there."

"Let us confront Moses and demand answers."

The coalition defied Moses in the Wilderness of Shur. The
Prophet of God stood just outside the camp. His antagonists faced
him. My father was with them. They lined the higher ground.

"What do you ask of God?" Our white-haired leader did not appear intimidated even with the mob facing him.

From the camp, everyone watched the drama. Mother stood beside me. Her face was white.

Nearby one of the youngest Levites snorted his contempt at the
display: "Fools."

"What do you mean?" several voices asked at once.

I inched closer to hear the answer.

"Have you still not learned that Moses is chosen of God? This
confrontation can only lead to death." The reply was unmixed with
any compassion.

My intake of breath was lost amid the collective gasp of fear.
Voices erupted in denial and rage.

"No!"

"How can you say such things?"

"What will happen?"

"It cannot be."

Terrified, I rushed back to my family. My heart pounded with anguish. It was my complaining that brought us danger.

"Mattan," Mother spoke my father's name. The whisper was full of terror for her husband.

"What do you ask of God?" Again the steady voice of the Deliverer was heard.

All eyes turned to the hillside. Everyone strained to see what was happening. Abital stretched on tiptoe. She was trying to see past our milling neighbors. After some shuffling and what appeared to be arguing one man stepped forward.

"Why have you brought us to wander and die in this wilderness?" Loudly the spokesman snarled. He leaned forward; a vicious look twisted his face. "We are no closer to the Promised Land than twenty years ago."

With great patience, the leader repeated what we had heard over and over again. "The God of Israel is forming the Chosen People into a great nation. At the appointed time we will enter the land promised to Abraham, Isaac and Jacob."

"It is not enough," another voice spoke from somewhere in the mob. "We had houses in Egypt and recognizable gods. There was meat and fruit instead of this endless manna."

The last word almost sounded like a curse.

"My brothers," the leader tried to reason with his opponents.

"You do not know the way to bring us to this Promised Land," another shouted challenge interrupted him.

"Give us a sign that your God is real!"

"Yes, a sign!"

"Where is the God of Moses?"

Shouting and stamping, the men appeared ready to attack. From the corner of my eye, I saw something frightening. The pillar outside the camp seemed to be increasing in height. To my eyes, it appeared to loom angrily over the camp.

"Mother, look!" I tugged the woman's arm and pointed to the object.

"Mattan," I heard Mother whisper in despair. Although he could not hear her, she moaned softly, "Come away."

Almost simultaneously, Moses cried out, "Living God, have mercy."

His words were drowned by sudden screams from the mass of men on the hill.

"Snakes!"

"Nehushtan is among us!"

"*I AM* will have vengeance!"

"I am bitten!"

"Run!"

Men began to race up the hill, as well as toward the camp. In their panic, they ran into one another. With curses and fists, each man sought to escape from the death that crawled at his feet. Those on the edges of the rabble charged into camp. Some of the vipers had fastened onto clothing and now slithered among the tents.

"My baby is bitten!" Our first warning of the invasion was a young mother's scream.

Panic ensued as everyone in the camp began to flee hysterically in all directions. Mother stood frozen. Her eyes searched for my father in the crowd dispersing on the hillside.

"What can we do?" I tugged the woman's arm. "Snakes are in the camp."

In a dazed voice came an ineffective answer: "Your father will know, Mattan will tell us what to do."

"We have to get way from the danger." I tugged her limp hand.

Amid the shouts and screams, I heard someone say, "Snakes cannot swim. We will be safe across the water."

With all my desperate, twelve-year-old strength, I tried to pull my mother toward the stream that meandered past the camp. When she stubbornly refused to budge, I snatched Leah from her arms. Isaac and Hephzibah stood frozen beside our mother.

"Come on! Hurry!" I shouted.

By shoving my siblings with my shoulder and free hand, I made them move. We dodged between the adults who did not seem to know where to turn. After splashing through the shallow stream, we joined a small group already there.

"Wait here." I handed the baby to my brother. "I will get Mother."

Back through the chilly water I rushed. More of the men had

reached the camp. Most wore an expression of anguished hopeless-ness. They stumbled and staggered blindly. Blood dripped from an-kles or arms where a serpent had left venom. Keening started when one man and then another dropped to the ground. The poison acted rapidly, especially among the older men.

"Mother!" I scanned the area for the woman.

Finally I saw my parents. My father sat beside our fire. At first I thought he was unharmed. Then I saw the bite on his forearm.

"I fell," the man was explaining in a dazed mumble. "If I had not fallen . . ."

He seemed fascinated by the twin puncture wounds, staring at them even as he continued to speak.

"We should not have doubted." It sounded like a confession.

"Father." I rushed forward to grab the man's uninjured arm. It hung unresponsive at his side.

"Naomi, let me look at you," my father mumbled, trying to fo-cus on my face.

I realized that the poison was stealing my father.

"No!" My scream rang in my ears when a convulsion rocked the man.

He struggled for breath. Then all was silent. Too late I heard the voice of Moses cut across the cries in the camp.

"The Lord has provided healing. Let all who are bitten look upon the bronze serpent and live."

I swung around to see the leader flanked as always, by Aaron and Joshua, holding up the staff of God. On the top was a snake hastily formed of beaten and twisted bronze.

"Father, you will be well!" Excitedly I turned back to the man.

"He cannot look," in a numb tone Abital informed me.

"Father, see the serpent Moses holds!" Vainly, I lifted my father's head.

There was no longer life in the man. He could not hear my pleas or feel my hands.

"My husband is gone," the toneless words from my mother frightened me more than the realization that I held a dead body.

"You are too late." Whether I spoke to God or Moses, I was never sure.

The Prophet heard my accusation. The old man stopped in his traverse of the camp. He turned to face me.

"I am sorry." Such grief was etched on the deeply lined face that I was slightly comforted. "Mattan was a good man. You will be cared for."

With that promise, the Deliverer moved on.

"We have lost many good men today," the voice of our leader was low and mournful.

Moses fell silent, and Aaron took up the chant, "Look toward the snake. Those bitten may live if they look upon the serpent."

Some were saved by that bronze image. Still, for many more, like my father, it was too late. We left their graves behind when we moved on.

"It is my fault," despair and grief welled up inside me as I accepted the blame. "If I had not asked for a house, Father would not be dead."

Care of my siblings fell to me. My mother was too broken by her grief to tend us. Even though I never dared tell anyone my secret, I knew that the hand of God was against me. I would have to spend my life atoning for my father's rebellion by perfect obedience to the laws of Moses and his God.

❦ 2 ❧

MOTHER CONTINUED TO GRIEVE. She took no interest in the changes of seasons or new campsites.

"Widows and orphans are cared for. It is enough." Her resignation tore at my heart.

"When I am a woman, I will marry a man to care for us. Then you will not have to endure the pity of others."

"My daughter, we are fortunate to have the Law of Moses. In Egypt, a woman with no husband is outcast and destitute," Mother chided me. "We must be glad of the law and obey what we are commanded. It is our protection."

I did not need to be reminded to obey. Assiduously I observed each of the laws set out by the priests. In all my prayers, I sought to propitiate the Deity that I feared.

"Remember to pray to God that we are not at fault in our actions," I ordered my siblings. It became part of my daily litany along with, "Hephzibah and Leah, let me braid your hair. Isaac, change your tunic."

Each feast day and Sabbath added extra responsibility.

"You cannot play with the blocks of wood or those small stones. It is the Holy Day," I reminded the children.

"You are mean," my sister whined when I removed the toys. "Father let us play even on the Sabbath."

"Father is not here. We must follow all that God commands. The Sabbath is a day of rest from all things." I spoke sternly and ignored the tears the welled up in the child's eyes.

"Obedience will not bring Father back," Isaac's insight made me angry.

"You do not understand," I blazed at my brother. "It is to prevent any more sorrow that I insist you abide by every bit of the law."

The boy frowned and shook his head.

"It is not fair." He turned to his mother.

"Your sister is right." Mother surprised me with her support of
my discipline. "We must obey or God will send a greater punishment on us."

I could not imagine what price could be greater than the loss of
my father, but did not tell the grieving woman my thoughts. She
kept herself wrapped in the widow's shawl and only went from tent
to oasis or stream for water. Other tasks were left to me.

As the fall chill settled over the land, I faced my eleven-year-old
brother. "You must represent the family at the sacrifice of atonement." "Soon it will be time for each household to offer a sacrifice
for the sins of this year."

I shuddered when I thought of the offense that Mattan had already paid for with his life.

"I am not old enough." the argument was expected.

"You are the oldest male," I answered swiftly. "Besides, you are
almost of the age to be known as a man. Soon you will be an adult
and welcomed at the counsels of the men."

The boy looked astonished. Then he straightened his back. For
just a moment he resembled the man he would soon become.

"Why do I have to do it now?" His petulant question spoiled the
moment.

Exasperated, I repeated my answer. "You are the only male."
"You must do this. No one else can. Even if I wanted to, I cannot."

"You are not even a woman." The boy turned on his heel after
rudely reminding me that in the eyes of the world I, too was still a
child.

"I will be a woman soon," I whispered reassurance to myself.

Other girls my age and younger welcomed their maturity with
feasts and dancing. I was fourteen before my cycles began.

"Mother, mother, wake up," I roused the woman one autumn
night, two years after the death of Mattan.

"What is it, Naomi? It is still dark." There was enough light from the full moon to show that her eyes were open, even though she lay on her pallet.

Almost in tears, I shared my news. "I have pain in my belly."

The cramping agony had awakened me. It seemed to have gone on for hours, although the moon had not made much progress toward the horizon in the time I lay debating whether to disturb my mother.

My mother sat up to feel my forehead. "Pain . . . are you ill?"

"No, I do not feel sick. It just hurts." A little sob escaped with the explanation. I bent over clutching my belly.

Fully awake, Abital scrambled up and led me out of the tent. The darkness was cold. I shivered and the woman hastily grabbed a blanket. I hunched over the banked fire, clutching my midsection. The movement did not ease the pain.

When Mother draped the warm wool around me, I whispered my fear. "Will I die?"

"My daughter, we have reason to rejoice." The woman was cheerful. "You will not die."

She set about stirring the fire to life. A kettle was filled with water and placed over the small blaze. Mother disappeared into the tent. A moment later, she was back with a pouch.

"I will brew you herbs to ease the cramping. The first time I felt them, we had been away from Egypt for five years." There was a pause while she measured the amount. "Your grandmother rejoiced that I was a woman. She had despaired of my age although I was a year younger than you are now. We will celebrate this day."

"I do not want to be a woman." In agony, I clutched my belly. "It hurts."

"Here, this will ease the pain." A cup of tea was thrust into my hand. "You will learn that to be a woman is to endure much hurt. It is the price of being able to bring life into the world."

"It is not fair," I whined with a sniff.

"God has blessed women with the power of new life." Mother explained patiently. "The cost is the pain of our cycles and of childbirth. It is in this way that all of life is balanced. My mother told me that in Egypt this balance is called *maat*."

I sipped the hot liquid. It tasted surprisingly good.

"You will be able to wed." Abital was bubbling with plans. She had not spoken so much since my father died. "When it is known that you are a woman, I am sure that many of the young men will speak to me. Mattan would have rejoiced to see this day."

Mention of my father sobered me and silenced my mother. Slowly dawn arrived. I crouched beside our fire sipping the herbs. Mother was clearly excited by the event. As soon as it was light enough to see our way, she gave me my outer cloak.

"Come, Daughter, we will go to the Tent of the Women," she announced proudly.

She took my hand and led me across the slowly awakening camp. A quiver of anticipation ran through me at the idea of entering the secret tent. The next week passed swiftly. It was a time of sisterhood and camaraderie. All the women seemed sincerely delighted that I was a woman. Almost regretfully I left the haven at the end of the week. Several women joined me in the procession to the tabernacle.

"You will offer the prayers and sacrifice due to God for cleansing," Mother gave me two pigeons.

I took the birds. They were light and soft in my hands.

"Give them to the priest," she whispered. A small shove set me on my way.

"God of Israel, behold and bless this daughter who offers the sacrifice for her cleansing. Give to her a strong husband and sons for your glory and the strength of your people." Rapidly the Levite repeated words said many times a year.

A swift move dispatched the birds. I watched in horrified awe as flames consumed the sacrifice. Never before had I been so close to the sacred altar.

"Go my child, the Holy One accepts your offering." The bored statement signaled the end of the ceremony.

Mother turned away. "Come, Naomi."

In silence, I followed. Our tent and fire seemed no different than a week earlier.

Hephzibah caught my hand. "What was it like?"

Before I had a chance to reply, my mother answered, "You will find out when it is time."

The little girl looked so downcast that I bent close to whisper, "It is hard to explain. Someday you will understand."

My words did not mollify the child.

"At least now I will not have to do all the work." The petulant whine from my little sister brought a smile to my lips.

With a pout she stamped away. I thought my mother hid a grin by biting her lip. We bent together over the meal preparation.

"Your sisters missed you," she said softly.

"Or hated having to do the work," I replied with a half smile, glad that the woman was entering the conversation.

I hoped she was leaving her grief behind but the next day Abital resumed her solitary role. Again, I shouldered care of my brother and sisters. Many days she seemed lost in the past. Other women in the camp treated me as an equal, but my siblings did not care about my new status.

"Braid my hair," Leah greeted me with a tangled mess of black curls in the morning.

"I am glad you are here." I thought Isaac might mean the words until he added, "I am tired of collecting the manna."

"Daughter, you are a woman," dreamily Mother mentioned the fact one cold winter night. "We must ask the God of Moses to provide you with a husband."

"Almighty One, send me a husband." My new plea was raised nightly even before Abital's prompting.

If I married, a man would care for the family. Two more moon turnings came and went before it appeared that God heard me.

"It is spring." I told my mother, trying to interest her in the new life all around. "Sheep are grazing near the camp. There are the first new blades of grass breaking through the ground. See how green it is."

She barely looked up from her endless spinning. We had piles of yarn. Hephzibah, Leah and I could never use it all. We worked to make blankets whenever we could set up the looms. These we traded when we met traveling merchants or at Sinai for the Passover foods.

"Go and gather some fresh plants for our meals," I suggested to my siblings. "Leah can help you. I am sure that there will be some in the sunny areas amid the rocks."

Glad for the excuse to do something different, the trio hurried away. I glanced at my mother. She was now mending an old tunic that had belonged to my father.

"Is that for Isaac?" I asked.

"Does he need it?" My mother was oblivious to the needs of her children.

"Yes," I nodded. "He is outgrowing all the clothing he has. Your son is becoming tall."

The woman frowned slightly and stroked the homespun garment. "I am not sure that I want him wearing anything of Mattan's."

With teeth gritted against an angry reply, I turned to knead the bread dough violently. When I looked up a few minutes later, I saw clouds gathering over the cliffs.

Dread tapped me on the shoulder. "I am going to find Isaac and the girls."

Spring storms could flood low-lying wadis rapidly. Without waiting for an answer, I set out to look for my sisters and brother. I hurried away from the camp scanning the hills for the three children. Soon I heard familiar voices raised in conflict.

"Leah, come back here. You are not supposed to be in the wadi," Hephzibah screeched at her sister.

"I am not in it," came the defiant reply. "Isaac is."

The words chilled my heart. I began to run. In a moment I saw that my brother was deep in the gully. Leah was watching from partway down the side while Hephzibah jumped up and down at the top. None of the youngsters saw me until I spoke.

"What are you doing?" My sharp voice made my younger sister whirl around.

"Isaac went into the wadi," Hephzibah could not wait to tattle on her siblings. "So has Leah."

With an effort, I kept my tone calm. "I see. Leah come here now."

The little girl shook her head stubbornly.

"Come on," I leaned forward and held out my hand in case the little girl needed help.

It was then that I saw the reason for the children's presence in the ravine. A ewe lay on her side near the bottom. Beside her was a newborn lamb. Isaac was trying to get the animal to stand. Bare feet were braced in the dirt at the bottom of the ditch. His shoulders bunched as he struggled to roll the sheep over.

"Oh dear." A quick look around showed no help in sight.

The gray cloud that gathered over the nearby hills was building in size. I heard pitiful baaing from the ewe. I could not tell if the lamb was even alive. Concern for the trio in the wadi overrode the wisdom of staying out of gullies when rain threatened.

"Stay here." I swung Leah out of the ditch as I slid down the incline.

"She will not get up." Isaac's face was red from exertion. Tears of frustration gleamed in his brown eyes.

"I will help." Closer now, I could see that the lamb was weakly breathing. A sense of urgency gripped me. "We have to get them out. The lamb will not last long without milk from his mother."

Together, Isaac and I shoved against the pile of wool.

"What if we roll her down the hill onto her feet?" I suggested when we paused and stood panting.

"I tried that," grumbled the boy. "She just rolled all the way over to here."

Sudden inspiration dawned. "You stay on this side to steady her."

The first drops of rain began to pelt us.

"Hurry!" I did not need the scream from Hephzibah to remind me of the danger that increased every second we wasted in the bottom of the ditch.

Uphill from the animal, I dug my hands into her fleece and heaved upward. Desperation must have given me strength. I felt movement and dragged the animal to her feet.

"Now," I panted.

Isaac shoved a slender shoulder into her side when the ewe tottered. A bleat of discontent came from the creature. Clearly, she was happy to die in the water that was beginning to dampen our feet.

"Put your belt around her neck." I released one hand from the wool to untie my own woven belt and wrap it around the wooly neck.

Almost afraid to let go, I asked my brother, "Can you hold her while I get the lamb?"

Staunchly the boy nodded. He frowned as he braced against the flank. Rain fell harder, and the water at our feet rose to our ankles.

Rapidly, I snatched up the lamb by the loose skin at his neck. He made a weak cry. For the first time, the ewe raised her head.

"Did you see that? She heard him." Her interest gave me hope.

With a soggy lamb over one arm and my hand dragging on the two belts, I started up the now slippery side of the gully.

"Push her," I urged my brother.

He was already alternately shoving and beating the animal forward. Whether it was the intermittent cries from her baby or the combined efforts of Isaac and me, the sheep began to climb. With her four hooves, she had an easier time than we did. My feet kept slipping. After a few steps, it was the sheep that helped us up the side instead of the other way around.

"Hurry!" Hephzibah kept screaming encouragement while we struggled.

I wanted to shout at my sister to be quiet, but all my concentration was needed to clamber up the wadi.

Near the top, I handed the belts to my sisters. "Take these and pull."

Another step and we were all safe. Panting in great heaving breaths, I dropped to the muddy ground. The desert storm would soon be over, but for now, the rain poured down.

"Look." Awe and fear were in the one word Isaac spoke.

We looked into the gully as a rolling wave of muddy water and debris from the nearby heights rushed through where we recently stood. The waves flooded halfway up the side, washing away our footprints.

The boy drew close to me with eyes wide in realization of the danger. "Sister."

My own shiver was not so much from cold as from the knowledge that we came very close to death. Mesmerized, I watched the raging torrent. A faint baa reminded me that our rescue was only half done.

"Come here, baby," I coaxed as I picked up the sodden lamb.

"Look, it is your lamb." The ewe sniffed at the body and at my hands.

Mud covered us both. I guessed we smelled alike so she did not refuse her lamb.

"We will have to squeeze milk into his mouth. Who would like to help?" I looked at my sisters because Isaac still stared at the pounding water.

"I will," Leah offered eagerly.

Both little girls crouched beside me. Leah attempted to draw milk from the swollen udder. Nothing happened.

Hephzibah pushed her aside. "Let me do it."

I thought Leah would scream. Her lip thrust out threateningly, but she did not cry.

A moment later the older girl squealed in triumph. "I did it!"

I held the lamb close to the nipple. With my thumb, I held his jaw open. Milk trickled into the little mouth. My free hand stroked the skinny throat until I felt a swallowing motion. Some of the nourishment was going into the newborn's stomach.

"He is swallowing on his own," I barely dared whisper the good news a few moments later.

When I held the lamb close to the udder, he even closed his lips on it.

"He is drinking!" Leah jumped up and down in delight.

"Yes, he is," I nodded.

Relief helped me ignore the cramping in my arms from holding the little animal close to his mother.

"The rain has stopped." At Isaac's comment, we all looked around.

It was true. Clouds moved off to the north, leaving behind a soaked landscape.

Responsibility returned with the rays of daylight peeking through the departing clouds. "We need to get back to camp."

The roundly distended stomach of the lamb was evidence that he was full. He shivered in my arms.

"We need to get dry clothes for you all and something to warm this lamb."

Standing up, I began to urge my siblings toward our tent. Another shiver from my small burden concerned me. Leah gaped when I stuffed the lamb inside my clothing. The cold wool felt coarse against my skin. We walked rapidly to the camp.

"I remember Father once put a lamb inside his tunic for warmth during a late snow storm." The little girl frowned while I explained. "It was when you were still a baby."

My little burden bleated weakly. Behind us, the rescued ewe followed the sound of her lamb. I thought he shivered less against my skin and hoped that my body heat would warm him.

"Lambs are very easily chilled," I told the child.

I tried to remember what else Mattan did.

"The first ewe's milk is very important," he said many times. "Lambs need to be dried and fed as soon as they are born."

We reached our tent in a short time. Mother was just emerging after the rain.

"Where have you been? Naomi, look at you. How did you get so muddy?" Our bedraggled appearance made her frown. Sight of the ewe trailing behind caused the woman to raise her eyebrows. "Why is there a sheep in camp?"

I had no chance to reply because the children burst into explanations.

"There was a sheep . . ."

"Isaac rescued . . ."

". . . was hungry . . ."

"Flooded wadi . . ."

While Isaac, Leah and Hephzibah all spoke, I hurried to the tent for an old torn blanket. Beside the fire I set about rubbing the lamb to get him dry and warm. Fearful of the fire, the ewe stood at a distance away and bleated pitifully. The sound brought many neighbors from their tents. Elimelech of Judah was one.

"What is this?" the man strode forward.

At his loud voice my siblings became quiet.

"What is an animal of my flock doing in the midst of the camp? Why is my ewe at the tent of Mattan?" As he questioned, the man inspected his mud-spattered sheep.

She continued to bleat. I was surprised and relieved when the lamb in my arms suddenly responded with his own weak cry. He was almost dry and the shivering was hardly visible.

Still I rubbed the little creature. "There, there, you can have more milk soon."

"Is that my lamb?" With a frown, the shepherd moved toward me.

Isaac leapt forward to confront our neighbor.

"Naomi saved your sheep! The ewe gave birth in the wadi." My brother gestured. I noticed his hand shake from excitement or anxiety. "She would not get up. I went down to help. Then it started to rain. Naomi found us there. We got the sheep on her feet. The sides were slippery. My sister had to carry the lamb. She pulled your sheep. Then the water rushed through."

The explanation poured out in a staccato flood. I heard Mother gasp when she realized that we were in a gully when the storm started.

"Naomi." The woman turned angrily to me. "You know better than to go into a wadi."

Again Isaac came to my defense. "It was my fault. She would not have gone in, but I would not come out."

"I see that thanks are due," Elimelech stood near me, mollified.

"Here is your lamb," I held up the dry and almost fluffy creature.

"You have done a good job of getting him dry. The only question is; will the ewe accept him now?" The shepherd cuddled the bleating animal with one arm.

He turned to the ewe. She inched as close as she dared to the fire and her lamb.

"Here is your baby." A gentle, coaxing tone entered the man's voice. "See? He is dry now."

I held my breath.

"Sometimes a ewe will refuse a lamb handled by a human," I whispered my worry to Isaac.

The sheep seemed to recognize Elimelech. She allowed him to approach. A black nose stretched out to sniff the lamb. When the man lowered four little feet to the ground, the tiny creature staggered forward.

"That is good. Come on baby." The coaxing whisper from the man warmed my heart.

The lamb nosed at the udder. It only took a small amount of guidance by Elimelech for the lamb to begin to suckle. I gave a sigh of relief and released my tightly gripped hands. Around me watchers also relaxed and began to chat as they dispersed.

"How exciting!"

"It is good to save a life."

"Foolish children."

"Elimelech is sure to be grateful."

Watching the man with his sheep gave me a feeling of contentment. I found myself admiring the broad shoulders and thick hair that curled at the nape of his neck. Big hands gently stroking the ewe gave me a shiver of some intense feeling.

"Naomi." Mother's stern voice broke into my dreaming. "You know better than to go into a wadi."

"I could not leave the ewe." It was a feeble defense.

"It was my fault," Isaac interrupted. He reiterated his part in the story. "I went down into the wadi and was too stubborn to leave, even when Naomi called me."

Suddenly, Abital reached out and drew us both into her embrace. "You are very lucky. I hope Elimelech is grateful."

The man turned from his animals to bow in our direction. "Thank you both for saving part of my flock."

I dropped my gaze when our neighbor stared at me for a long moment. Color and heat rushed to my cheeks. I could make no response.

"You are welcome," Isaac answered for both of us.

I was relieved when the shepherd led his ewe away. He carried the now content lamb. My eyes followed his long strides until he was out of sight.

Later I lay on my mat and pondered my reaction to Elimelech. The man was not unknown. He was ten years older than me and usually set his tent not far from ours when we camped. I could not understand why I was suddenly so conscious of the man.

"I will speak to Mother," after tossing and turning, I finally achieved some peace with the decision. However there did not seem to be a good time to approach the woman.

"Help me gather manna," I ordered my sister. In the morning twice as much covered the ground.

"Tomorrow we rest. Today we work harder," Hephzibah grumbled while stirring the round balls that looked like hail into water for porridge.

I bent over the bread dough and ignored the complaints.

"Leah, cut these vegetables," I gave the little girl a handful of carrots to chop.

I did not see Elimelech. That did not stop me from thinking about him.

"I wonder how the lamb is." Isaac's question gave me an excuse to bring up the subject.

"Can we go and find out?" I begged. "The mixing and chopping are done."

Rather than the hoped-for permission, new tasks were assigned. "You should shake out our blankets and sleeping rugs."

I sighed dramatically. It did not affect the woman who chose this day to behave like a mother.

"Isaac may run to the flock. Hurry back." Her slight relenting did not appease me.

"I will," the boy said and shouted as he dashed off.

Angrily, I flounced to the tent. Never had our blankets been so roughly shaken.

Smoldering with rage, I snapped the wool coverings so that dust flew out. "It is not fair for Isaac to go while I have to work."

The thick woven rugs used to make the ground more comfortable received the same treatment. Before Isaac returned, the tent was clean and each bed in its place. I was preparing to get water for the Sabbath when male voices approached.

The man bowed to my mother. "I am the richer by two, thanks to your daughter."

"Naomi is a special girl," Abital responded softly.

"It is true. I have watched her grow from child to woman." Elimelech looked at me as he spoke.

My face blazed with embarrassment. I felt a thrill and weakness that I could not account for. It made me uncomfortable. I dropped the water jar. It spilled but did not break.

"Naomi, go find your sisters and bring fresh water." I was relieved when Mother indicated the jar.

Leah and Hephzibah were easy to locate. They were on the hill in plain sight. I was not in a hurry to return to our tent.

"Meet me at the oasis," I told the pair. "Finish filling your basket first."

Beside the water, I let my hand rest below the surface. The sensation of the cool water against my wrist eased the feeling of heat in my blood when I thought of the way my mother and Elimelech discussed me. I did not dare let myself hope that the man looked at me as a possible bride.

"Are you ready?" Hephzibah's overly loud voice broke into my musings.

"Do you have fresh greens for our meal?" I countered.

"See?" Leah held up the basket piled high.

"Then let us go." With a deep breath, I picked up the full water jar.

My sisters swung the basket between them in happy disregard for the concerns that weighed my own steps. Elimelech was gone when we arrived.

"The lamb is thriving," Isaac reported even though I forgot to ask.

Mother said nothing to me. Once again she had wrapped the widow's veil around her body to shut out her family. I guessed that she missed my father most on the Sabbath days when he would have led our prayers.

"Blessed be the Almighty, the great *I AM*," began Isaac.

Now at thirteen, he preened because he was old enough to attend the men's prayers.

"Soon I will be able to provide for you, my mother," the oft-repeated promise brought a smile to the woman's face.

"Yes, my son," she affirmed.

Another Sabbath came. My brother went to pray as the law required. The boy wore a grin when he returned. He looked at our mother sitting with head bowed outside the tent.

"Elimelech wants to talk to Mother," Isaac's words made my heart skip a beat.

"About what?" My heart resumed pounding so loudly I feared it would be heard.

The boy lifted his chin proudly. "He has spoken to me, man to man. What he has to say is for our mother now."

"What does he want to talk about?" I resisted the urge to shake my brother.

"When it is time, you will know." My brother wore a smug expression.

His superior attitude almost earned the boy a slap. Only the presence of Abital saved him.

"Isaac says that Elimelech wants to talk to you," I took my mother's hands in mine. Nervousness made the words tumble over each other.

"My son, what is this about? Is something wrong?" Too easily the woman assumed the worst.

"Elimelech spoke to me as a man." While the words sounded mature, I was privy to the teasing thrust out tongue that betrayed his youth. "The man wants to discuss an important matter."

"Will you be there?" Her sudden dependence on the boy almost angered me.

"Yes, my mother." A reassuring answer calmed her.

With a nod, Mother signified her agreement. "Then I will speak to Elimelech. He is a good man."

"We will go in the morning," Isaac decided. "This is not a discussion for the Sabbath."

In the morning, I watched, seething, as mother and son crossed out of my view into Elimelech's tent. Isaac refused to even hint at the topic to be discussed. Hopes and fears danced in my head until I was dizzy. I frowned after the pair until I was interrupted.

"Where did Isaac go?"

"Why did Mother go with him?"

Almost identical questions came from my sisters.

"They went to see Elimelech." I was satisfied that my calm voice did not betray my inner turmoil.

"Why?" Together, the girls requested further information.

"You can ask when they come back," I replied, short and sharp. "Now you can help me grind the grain Hannah brought us."

Anticipation of the rare treat of real grain in the bread helped distract my sisters. For me the minutes dragged by. My nervous energy made short work of the barley. It seemed hours later when Isaac and Abital returned. The grain was finely ground and stored in a covered basket before they stepped out of the nearby tent.

"Where did you go?" chorused my helpers.

Abital ignored the little girls to embrace me. "My daughter, it is settled. You are to be a bride."

While my mouth hung open, Leah and Hephzibah began to dance around me.

"A bride!"

"Will Naomi get a new dress?"

"Are you excited?"

Mother smiled benignly. "Your father would have been pleased!"

Finally I found my voice, "Elimelech . . . me." The two stammered words were all I could force out.

"Yes, Elimelech spoke to me after the Sabbath prayers," Isaac could no longer contain the secret. "He said, 'Your sister is of an age to marry, is she not?' You know he is a very cautious man. It probably took him days to decide to approach me."

"What else did he say?" I was impatient to hear more.

"Well," the young man drawled. "I am not sure I should tell you."

"Tell us!" Unknowingly my sisters came to my aid.

"Why not?" Without hesitation, the boy continued. "When I assured him that Naomi was indeed marriageable, he asked me for permission to become betrothed. 'Your sister is a faithful daughter of Israel. I have watched her obedience to the Law of Moses,' he said. 'She will bear strong sons.' Only after I agreed did he also ask to talk to Mother."

My brother again straightened and turned into the man I glimpsed once before. With a tinge of sorrow I recognized that he was no longer my baby brother.

"The betrothal will be sealed this Sabbath," Mother interjected. "After the Passover we will hold the marriage feast."

"So soon?" The question was breathless. My life was changing too rapidly.

"It is a shorter betrothal than many," acknowledged the woman. "The man is lonely. He has admired you since before you rescued his sheep."

Elimelech will be responsible for my family, My thought was not spoken aloud. Instead I nodded, "It is good."

"We must arrange for your betrothal feast." Abital happily began planning the details.

It was as if the past years of mourning were erased by this event. She even spoke of Mattan without retreating into grief.

"Naomi, you must wear the necklace that I wore to make my vows with your father. In all our travels I have kept it safe." She hurried into the tent.

In a moment the woman was back. She sat on the hide stool. In her hand was a small leather case that we were never allowed to touch.

"Here it is." Proudly the tarnished chain with oddly shaped ornaments was produced. "Your grandmother wore this in Egypt. Now you will wear it!"

On closer inspection, I realized that the charms were tiny bells. They barely gave off a sound. The slight tinkling was like the whispering of birds. It was very soothing.

"I will be happy to wear this," I was honestly delighted.

"We will clean it, of course," Mother took the jewelry back.

The Sabbath arrived almost before I was ready. Everyone in camp already knew the news. Many hands helped prepare food for the celebration.

In my freshly washed gown and wearing the tiny bells around my neck, I let Isaac escort me to the tabernacle. Elimelech greeted me with a stare. Immediately I wondered if my face was dirty. I was thankful that it was not Aaron who spoke the words of betrothal. The ceremony was uncomfortable enough without the intimidating presence of the ancient priest.

"Therefore you will be considered as one yet separate until the marriage. Should Elimelech die, Naomi will be considered a widow. Should Naomi die, Elimelech will be as a widower. The rights of dowry and bride price are exchanged. Honor her as your own." I barely listened to the intoning of the law.

The Levite droned on and on. I quivered beside the man who filled my dreams but seemed a stranger on this day.

"Now may the Holy God of Israel bless you and keep you faithful to one another in this betrothal." The man held his hands up in benediction.

At last the ceremony was over. Elimelech led me through the camp to our tent where the feast was spread. After the Passover, he would take me to his tent. The feasting would be great then as well.

"Naomi, I can hardly wait until we are truly husband and wife." Under cover of the music, laughter, and talk, the man's words startled me.

I looked up. A warm light in the dark eyes eased some of the nervousness I felt. That night I relived that moment so that I would not forget. For many nights, I fell asleep treasuring the promise in the longing statement, and in my daydreams, I imagined how Elimelech's kisses would feel.

⋯ 3 ⋯

"WE LEAVE FOR SINAI," Isaac announced when the moon began to wane. "Elimelech has offered to travel with us."

"It is good," Abital smiled in my direction. "He is a thoughtful man."

Mother started to blossom again now that she felt secure in the protection of son and son-in-law. Even her grief appeared to be less intense. I rarely heard sobs in the night. The lengthening days and approaching feast made me nervous about the day when I would be a bride.

"It is a blessing that you are able to get to know Elimelech," more than one woman in the camp encouraged me. "You will be more comfortable with your husband."

Before the moon of Passover we reached Mt. Sinai. The clouds hovering over the summit were always awe inspiring. Every year I was reminded of the story of how Moses went up into the cloud on the heights to receive the Law of God.

Elimelech warmed my heart when he approached Abital on the night we arrived at Sinai. "I consider you already my mother and ask permission to provide the lamb for our Passover meal."

"Elimelech, truly the One God has blessed my daughter with such a considerate husband," the woman glowed. "You ease my mind with your offer. We will eat the Passover with you."

My soon-to-be husband smiled in my direction. "This year and every year."

A flush came to my cheeks. The man had a way of crinkling his eyes when he grinned that made mundane words seem very intimate.

"We will prepare the herbs and breads. Isaac can help you with the lamb," Mother was her old self as she gave directions.

I heaved a sigh of relief and bent to uncover a basket.

"You are happy, my Naomi?" Elimelech covered my busy hands with his big tanned ones. My blood tingled at the caress and nearness of the man.

"Yes." When I nodded, my hair tangled in his brown beard.

"I have many reasons to thank the Living Lord." The man spoke so softly that only I could hear. "My pleasant and sweet Naomi is soon to be my wife. Her mother is as dear to me as my own would be if she were alive. Isaac is the brother I have longed for. Leah and Hephzibah will be as my sisters. Surely the God of Moses is a gracious God."

Tears welled in my eyes at the recitation. I was amazed that my betrothed would feel such love for my family. A lump formed in my throat. After a moment, Elimelech stroked my hair free of his beard and stepped back. I looked up, slightly chilled by his departure from my side.

"We will soon be wed. Then I will have the right . . ."

The man took a deep breath. He appeared to be harboring some intense emotion. Another heaving intake of air seemed to give him more control.

"I will try to be a good wife and please you." I hoped my shy promise would bring back the smile I loved.

The grin that appeared was my reward. "Innocent, sweet Naomi. You cannot fail to make me happy."

One broad hand reached out to tuck a strand of hair behind my ear. Briefly—very briefly—the fingers lingered on my cheek. Then the man turned away.

"Isaac, let us go to find the best lamb in my flock. We will honor the God of Israel in keeping the commandments."

I stared after the pair. My brother had a companion, maybe even a brother in Elimelech.

Mother, too, watched the pair. "It is good. Isaac has missed his father's company."

When the men were out of sight, the woman turned to me.

"We have much to do. Leah, you go with the other girls to find

herbs. Hephzibah, it is your job to bring the water. Naom[
go to the traders for grain to make our bread."

We scattered to our tasks. I picked up the pile of ne___,
blankets to barter. Every year a caravan of Midianite traders awaited
our arrival at Sinai.

I could still hear my father's explanation from years earlier. "It
was Jethro, father-in-law of Moses that started the arrangement. As
nomads, we cannot grow crops as we did in Egypt. We are forced to
buy grain from foreigners for the Passover bread."

"But are not the people of Midian related to the Children of Israel?" My hesitant argument was based on a vague recollection of
something in the sagas of Miriam, sister to the Deliverer.

"It is the only reason we are allowed to buy from them. The de-
scendents of Esau are not the chosen ones, but they are sons of Abraham the Patriarch," my father answered and gave a dismissive shrug.

As we walked to the bazaar, Mother instructed me in details of
bartering for our grain. It was the same lecture every year. I could
have repeated the tirade myself.

"Never take the first price. Merchants always set the cost high.
Only the gullible pay so much. There are many booths. It is best to
visit them all before deciding on an honest face. Then you can offer
a low price. The trader will bring his down a little. You raise your
offer and the game is on until both are satisfied." The woman stared
at me until I nodded. "This is important, Naomi. You do not want to
be cheated. I will do the first purchase. Then you must try. We have
many things to buy for both Passover and for your wedding feast."

Again I nodded. This was not my first trip to the traders' camp.
Every year I accompanied Abital. Still the sights and smells and bustle were so different from our usual days that I found myself almost
dizzy from trying to see everything. Hides normally pitched as tents
were used to create booths. From these each man shouted his wares.

"Fine grain from the Delta."

"Spices from the East."

"Linen woven in Egypt."

"Dried fruits from the hills of Lebanon."

Everywhere I turned, another voice vied for my attention.
Mother shook my shoulder.

"Naomi, we must obtain the grain and spices for Passover and some fruit if possible. For the wedding, I want to purchase a length of material to make a new veil for you. We cannot afford enough cloth for a dress, but my daughter will have a linen veil. Extra grain and some wine must be obtained for the wedding, as well."

I nodded as the woman ticked off the items needed. When I looked at the mound of soft woolen blankets we had for trade, I hoped we had enough. My sisters and I had woven many from the yarn Abital spun every day. The first stop was with the caravan master. It was he who determined the value of our items.

"These are the finest wool blankets you will see today," Mother appeared calm.

My own heart was thudding when the black bearded man fingered the work of our hands.

"Not too bad," he mumbled. "The colors are good and design is unique. However this edge is a little ragged."

I held my breath while the trader began to find something wrong with each one of the items.

"Please, sir, have pity on me. I am a widow with four children. This is the work of my youngest daughter. She wept over the cloth in her eagerness to get it right," wheedling and clasping her hands in supplication, Mother offered an excuse.

"Your husband died, did he?" An almost suspicious frown appeared. "Many claim that."

"Many died." I had to insert the comment. "The Living God punishes those who rebel."

I cast a glance at the mountain nearby. At the foot of the incline the ark and tabernacle sat. God's pillar loomed between Sinai and the camp. The trader followed my gaze.

"The One you follow is very demanding. I shall gain no profit in dealing with all these widows," the man grumbled. "Still, I would not want to incur wrath from the God of Sinai. Here is your tally."

A notched stick was given to us. Each mark symbolized an amount of credit. As items were purchased, the stick would get shorter as each merchant cut off the right number. Later he would exchange the pieces for his profit.

"It is good," Mother seemed satisfied.

She made the same comment when we walked back to our tent with a basket full of supplies. It was midmorning. I was exhausted from haggling with each merchant. However, I was thrilled with the length of fine, almost transparent linen we had obtained for only three notches. The creamy color would accent my brown hair. I hoped Elimelech would find me lovely in it. The final notch was used to purchase a tiny vial of scented oil.

Just before we left the camp of traders, Mother made her decision. "We have enough to get perfume for your wedding night."

Rapturously I sniffed several bottles before selecting one with an exotic floral hint. The prize was clutched tightly in one hand. Carefully I wrapped the perfume in an outgrown tunic when we arrived at the tent. Gently I tucked the bundle into a corner of a leather trunk.

"Thank you, Mother." I hugged the woman.

"You did well. Soon you will be able bargain as I do," Abital smiled back. She lifted the wooden mixing bowl. "There is much to be done. I wonder where the girls are."

"They should be here soon," I looked around.

A group of children could be seen making their way toward the camp. Although I could not hear, I knew that there was much laughter as the boys and girls ran back and forth in their play. We completed mixing the wheat flour with milk before Hephzibah and Leah arrived. Their cheeks were rosy from the exercise.

"Here are the herbs," Leah carried a full basket.

"I have the water," Hephzibah balanced the jar on one shoulder.

At eight, my sister was already admirably graceful. Sometimes I felt large and clumsy beside the dainty child. She was strong, too, I noticed, when she carefully lowered the full jar to the ground. Many men would seek her as wife.

"Hephzibah, here are apples to chop," Mother's instructions interrupted my thoughts. "Leah, wash the herbs. They must be ready when Elimelech and Isaac return with the lamb."

I cringed at the reminder of the sacrifice. All morning, the men of the congregation had been praying before the ark. Now the bleating of many sheep replaced the chanting. Family by family, an unblemished lamb was slain. I hoped the lamb I saved in the wadi had not been chosen.

Later we all sat around our fire. Elimelech recited the story of the first Passover to our family group. All around the camp the same scene played out.

"I was the oldest son in my family," the man remarked after the saga was complete. "My mother used to say that she spent that night in terrified anguish holding me close and listening to my breathing. I do not remember Egypt. Even what my parents told me seems a distant dream."

"It was long ago," Abital mused. "All I can remember are huge monuments and statues. They seemed enormous to me. I wonder if they would look as large now."

"We will build our own monuments in Canaan." Isaac had grand plans.

A sigh came from my mother. "If we ever reach that place."

"God will be faithful if we follow the commandments ordained," Elimelech asserted confidently. "This family will keep the statutes of the Holy One. My sons will live in the Promised Land!"

Teeth gleamed in the firelight as the man smiled at me. His eyes crinkled, and I felt warm for some reason. I knew that the darkness hid the flush on my cheeks but bent my head anyway.

Almost before I was ready, the Passover week ended.

"Come, my daughter." Abital took my hand. "We must prepare for your wedding."

After sundown, my mother and sisters with two friends, led me to the stream that rolled down from Sinai's summit. By moonlight, they bathed me. Even my hair was unbraided and washed. The perfumed oil anointed my body. In the early morning, a clean linen tunic was dropped over my head.

"You will go to your husband cleansed of the past," Mother told me.

My friend Abigail surprised me with a simple wool gown. At first I shook my head.

"You should save this for your own wedding," I remonstrated.

"I have never worn it," she explained. "If you wear it, I will be honored. When the Holy One grants me a husband, there will be time enough to have a new gown."

"Naomi is pretty." Hephzibah sounded surprised, but I was too happy to take offense.

"My daughter is a bride." Emotion choked Abital.

She held me close. Tears dampened my shoulder. When the woman drew back she tied the necklace of tiny bells around my throat. All my attendants smoothed the fine linen veil into place.

"Your father has not left you entirely without a dowry," my mother lifted a wide chain from her private basket.

With another hug and kiss she added the dowry chain to my neck.

"It is enough," she whispered. I saw tears in her eyes.

Leah held out the bridal headdress used by all the brides. Each tribe had their own that had been used since the time of the patriarchs. It was passed from bride to bride. The little girl carefully separated each dangling charm that offered protection and fertility to a bride. I looked at myself in the small bronze mirror and barely recognized the woman standing there.

"I am a bride," my words sounded so amazed that my sisters giggled. They did not hear my whispered question. "Will Elimelech find me desirable?"

"Elimelech is a fortunate man," Abigail smiled at my worry. "May you bear many sons."

The wish was repeated again and again throughout the day. From the priestly blessing to each expressed wish for our happiness the desire for strong sons prevailed.

"God of Abraham, Isaac, and Jacob please open my womb." The prayer was my own as well.

In the dark privacy of the marriage tent, Elimelech gently introduced me to love between a man and a woman.

"My sweet Naomi, you smell of flowers." At my husband's delighted surprise, I was glad that we had purchased the perfumed oil.

We were both shy and fumbling until passion consumed us. For a week, the man and I reveled in one another while life in the camp continued to swirl around us. When we rejoined the daily routine, Elimelech moved my few things into his tent. It was erected close to the one that still housed my mother and siblings.

"I will help care for Abital as my own mother." His promise was rewarded by a lingering kiss.

Spring showers brought fleeting green to the desert. Each moon turning, I left my husband to reside in the women's tent when my time was upon me. All the women had suggestions for becoming pregnant.

"Try drinking tea from this herb."

"Relax during the union."

"Bathe in the full of the moon."

"Sleep on a pillow of lavender."

The Feast of Atonement arrived. We gathered at the tabernacle. Old Aaron stood with all the Levites. The jeweled breastplate and ornamented turban signified that the priest spoke for all the people. He led a long prayer in which we acknowledged our transgression of every command given on Sinai. We stood in silent recognition of our guilt.

"Do not hold my failures against me," I begged in an anxious whisper thinking of the times I knew I had failed to keep all the law. Fear that God would strike me down for the times I was impatient with my mother or coveted Hephzibah's graceful figure made me cringe.

A bull and goat were killed. Their blood was sprinkled on the altar and then on each tribal leader to symbolize the cleansing of us all. Then a second goat was led forward.

"May *I AM* accept this goat of atonement. He is for Azazel, the scapegoat for the transgressions of the people." Aaron laid his hand on the beast chosen to bear all our sins into the wilderness. "Upon this animal is laid the guilt of the Children of Israel. The chosen people are cleansed by the exile of this goat from our midst."

The beast was driven from the camp by two of Aaron's grandsons. The boys were already in training to be Levites although they were not even Isaac's age. In the silence, we could hear the shouts of the boys fading into the distance.

"God has accepted the scapegoat. All our sins are removed." The priest made the announcement when we could no longer see the boys or hear the shouts.

"Amen, Alleluia, El Elohim Israel," we all shouted in relief.

"This sacrifice is a new beginning. The Living Lord has cleansed you all," Aaron and the other Levites removed their robes and cast them into the fire.

Moses pronounced the blessing at the end of the ceremony. "*I AM* will bless us for our faithfulness."

Again we shouted the response, "Amen, Alleluia, El Elohim Israel!"

For a time, my heart felt lighter. I hoped that the One God had accepted my contrition and would send a child. After another moon turning, I realized that no monthly flow had come. When a second moon cycle passed, I shared my secret with Elimelech. The man lounged comfortably near the fire after we finished our evening meal.

"My husband, God has removed my shame," I blurted.

At my statement, the man sat upright.

"Your shame? Can it be true? Are you with child?" He moved from confusion to understanding to excitement.

"I think so," I barely had time to nod before I found myself swooped off the ground into a hug. "God has heard my prayers."

"Truly the Living Lord has heard our prayers." My husband was ecstatic.

Our hearts beat together as Elimelech held me tight against his chest.

"My wife will bear a son. . . ." Into my hair, the man repeated the words again and again.

"We will have a son," I agreed when we finally drew apart. "He will be born after the summer's heat."

"It is good!" A kiss sealed our joy.

"I will offer the sacrifice required to ensure a healthy pregnancy." My husband shared the news with everyone in the camp the next day.

"God is gracious!"

"Pray you have a son."

"Blessings on you, Naomi."

I was content in my pregnancy. Even the slight queasiness soon passed.

"I am pleased for you," my mother smiled. "It will be exciting to be a grandmother."

"I will be an aunt!" Hephzibah was delighted.

"Will I get to play with the baby?" Leah wanted to know.

"I am sure that Naomi will let you help when the baby is born," Mother reassured her daughters.

"Of course," I nodded. "You will be the best aunts my son could have."

That they would be the only aunts I did not need to add. Elimelech had no kin. The hardships of the desert had stolen his parents, as well as his younger twin sister and brother a year after I was born. As a boy, he took on the responsibility for his father's herd. I guessed that was why he was so willing to allow Isaac to work with him. The two herds now mingled. I wondered how any equitable division could be made when my brother decided to start his own family.

Optimistically my husband answered my query. "That is several years away. By then we will be in the Promised Land. Our son will not lose his inheritance; nor will Isaac."

I was content and did not really care if the sheep grazed together. Both Elimelech and I rejoiced in my rounding belly.

"My Naomi is lovelier than ever." Without shyness, my husband proclaimed his pleasure.

During the heat of the summer, I welcomed the cooler high pastures. My ever-increasing belly made me slow, and I became easily tired.

"Let me carry your water," Hephzibah offered.

"Thank you," I was grateful. It meant I would not have to hike to the stream and back up the hill to the level place where the encampment was pitched.

One night I lay in our tent. "When will this heat end?"

Elimelech stroked my belly. His delight in the stirring of life that rolled across the skin made me smile and briefly forget my swollen feet and sweaty body.

"The rains should begin soon," the man tried to comfort me. "Our son will be born after that."

I nodded and fell asleep lulled by his stroking of my hair and belly. As the man promised, the days did cool when the rains began. I found that I had energy to gather clothes for the baby.

"Do not wear yourself out with preparations," Mother cautioned. "This burst of energy could mean that the baby will be born soon."

She was right. A week later, the twinges in my back turned into gripping, vise-like pains. All morning, I tried to ignore them. Leah went for the midwife when the sun was high. Before the moon rose, a son lay in my arms.

"A man child for the house of Elimelech," I rejoiced to hear the midwife's proclamation.

"My husband will be pleased." With a sigh of relief, I lay back and held the crying newborn to my breast.

His wails were interspersed with gasps as he struggled for air. I barely noticed the frown that passed between my mother and the midwife. All my attention was on trying to get the baby to suckle. When he continued to fuss, despite my efforts, both women came to my side.

"Sit up a little more." The midwife lifted me and piled pillows behind my back.

"Hold him so," Mother moved the baby into a different position.

At last, the child began to nurse. Even when he seemed satisfied, the infant continued to whimper until he dozed briefly. I slept to be roused by squirming, a gasp and a cry.

"There, there," I rocked the infant and offered my breast.

This time we were both more adept at the feeding. For a minute, he sucked only to pull back to wheeze and whimper.

"My son, what is it?" Feeling very helpless, I cuddled my baby.

The sobs stopped when the little mouth sought my breast again. Soon he dozed. His breathing sounded erratic. I told myself that it was from crying.

"I have a son!" Elimelech entered the tent grinning with delight. "Let me see my son!"

"He has fallen asleep," I cautioned, holding the newborn carefully so his father could see him.

The man dropped to his knees beside my pallet. One finger stroked the soft cheek. His hand looked huge next to the tiny head.

"You have given me a son," my reward was a kiss on the forehead.

I was happy. My husband sat beside me. Together we watched the sleeping baby.

"The great God is wonderful," at last the man spoke. "See how perfectly my son is made. I must offer the sacrifice of thanksgiving. Our son will be blessed."

"Yes," I nodded agreement.

Elimelech walked from the tent with a light step. I could not hear the words, but knew the man was being congratulated by his friends. My sisters arrived at midmorning.

"He is so cute!" Leah held a blanket. "I made this for your baby."

"It is lovely," I took the gift with a smile.

"Can I hold him?" Hephzibah eagerly held out her hands.

"You must be careful," I cautioned.

Gently my sister took her nephew. I hovered near, ready to snatch the baby away if I though he was in danger.

"What is wrong?" The girl almost thrust the infant at me when he began the now-familiar panting cry.

"He is hungry," I insisted, trying to believe my own words.

The next few days melded into an endless cycle of trying to ease the cries of my son.

"Wrap him more tightly," Mother suggested, noticing that the spindly arms and legs thrashed whenever the baby was not bundled securely in his blanket.

"Do you think he is growing?" I frowned at the small form.

Although he soon learned to suckle greedily, the wheezing struggle for air when he cried worried Elimelech, as well.

"Is the child ill?" A grimace of concern etched the bearded face.

"I do not know." I tried to reassure myself and the man, "Mother says he will grow out of this."

"Naomi, we will pray that God will strengthen Mahlon so that he will no longer be ill." His father nodded decisively as if prayer could solve all things.

"Must we name him Mahlon?" I argued against the name because it meant 'sickly.'

"It will remind God to heal the boy each time he is called by name," Mother sided with my husband.

I was too weary to argue. Every ounce of energy was spent on my son. I hid my real fear. In the darkness of the long nights, the thought lingered. *God is punishing me for some offense.* Even though I could not identify any failure of obedience, I was sure that my son's weakness was my fault.

"Let Leah and Hephzibah continue to carry water and gather the manna for you," Elimelech urged.

I agreed, even after the ritual sacrifices for my cleansing a moon cycle after the birth.

"Mahlon seems a little less weak and his breathing sounds better," I confessed to Abital hopefully after another moon turning passed. "He does not awaken in the night as often."

"That is good, Naomi," she agreed. "I have not heard the rasping breaths as often, either."

Other women offered a variety of advice.

"It is his stomach. Rub this on him."

"Steep this herb in water, and let him suck it through a cloth."

"Lay him facing north."

"Feed him just before sleep."

"Do not feed him too much at a time."

Only the advice of old Hannah seemed to help.

"Use this shawl to make a sling so your son will be close to your heart." The matriarch of the tribe of Judah showed me how to tie the cloth. "The child will be more content close to you."

With Mahlon in the sling, I could cook and weave with the child cradled near me. It made the work go more smoothly. The baby was more content, as well. The frightening episodes of gasping for air were fewer.

"My husband, forgive me," I begged the man one night when the child finally slept. I feared that Elimelech blamed me for the weakness of his son.

"Sweet Naomi, you are not responsible for the discontent of Mahlon. God has granted us a son. The Holy One will remember our faithfulness and make him strong."

I wished I could believe the soothing words. Ashamed of my doubts, I attempted to put on a happy smile. "You are too good to me."

"My wife, we have this time. Let us not spend it in repining." The man held out his hand. "Come to me."

With an almost guilty glance at the sleeping baby, I allowed my husband to embrace me. We lay side by side afterward. Elimelech's hand rested on my belly.

"The God of Jacob will send us another son. Mahlon will have a brother." The man kissed my cheek before rolling over to sleep.

I lay awake staring at the tent walls. They moved slightly in the early spring breezes. Soon it would be Passover again.

"Living God, will you open my womb when we camp at Sinai so that I may give my husband a strong son?" Even as I prayed, part of my mind was fearful that a second child would be as challenging as the baby who began to stir restlessly and whimper on his blankets. I added a final petition. "Please, God of Israel, strengthen Mahlon. Punish me, not my child."

In a moment, I had the six month old cuddled against my heart. He cried and then quieted at my breast.

We moved steadily toward Sinai as grazing permitted. I found that traveling with a baby was difficult even with Mahlon in his sling. My back often ached when we stopped for the night. I was glad when we reached the Mountain of God. Sinai was blanketed in gray. Even the Midianite traders eyed the low hanging clouds with misgiving.

"The God on Sinai stirs," I overheard the exclamation at the flour merchant's booth.

"The sooner we finish our business, the better," agreed his neighbor.

"We got great bargains this year." Mother was delighted. "The traders are fearful of the clouds on Sinai."

"I heard them talking," I agreed as we worked side by side to prepare the festal foods. "The clouds do look ominous. Some say that the Holy One is angry with us."

Elimelech arrived with Isaac in time to hear my comment. "Those that trust the Living God have nothing to fear."

"Aaron says we will be blessed this year, for *I AM* is close," Isaac stated.

My brother carried the lamb. For the first time since Mahlon's birth, I really looked at the boy. No longer a lanky child, a young man stood before me. With the sprouting beard, he looked like Mattan.

"Isaac, you are a man." My astonishment brought chuckles from Elimelech and Abital. Isaac turned red and scowled.

"What I mean is . . . you . . . are . . . I see Father in you." I was not sure why I felt I had to justify my exclamation.

"Naomi," Mother's voice was now choked with emotion. "You are right. I had not realized. I, too, see my husband in my son."

My brother squirmed when the woman caught him in a tight embrace. "I do not understand your fuss."

"I will take the lamb," Elimelech laughed and removed our dinner to safety. "Naomi, help me spit the meat."

I held the stick while my husband attached the small carcass.

"Leah, I think you are old enough to take a turn at the spit," the man announced and turned to the nearly nine-year old girl.

"Really?" My sister was delighted.

She, too, seemed to have grown up in the past months while I was caring for Mahlon. The chubby child was replaced by a much taller girl who showed the promise of surprising beauty with huge brown eyes and lustrous, matching curls. My gaze moved to my other sister. Hephzibah was beginning to have a woman's shape. Her smoothly braided hair accented high cheekbones. Wide set eyes and a prominent nose made her face striking and attractive.

"You and Isaac will soon need to find a husband for Hephzibah," I whispered to Elimelech as he adjusted the fire by banking it slightly so the lamb would not scorch.

"It is true," the man agreed without looking up.

"Naomi, tell my sister how to dice fruit," Hephzibah called out.

I was swept into the bustle of final preparations for the feast. Later, after the meal was consumed, Mahlon nursed comfortably.

"My son, so much has changed in my family." I rocked the child and thought about my siblings. "My sisters will soon be married women. Isaac cares for our mother. She is content now."

The baby boy gave no response. His eyes blinked once and then closed in sleep. Elimelech snored nearby. Quietly I moved to tuck Mahlon into the blanket nest where he slept.

"My family may not need me, but you do," I bent over my son and reassured myself. "I will protect you from becoming sick again. Perhaps the One God will send you a brother, too."

Comforted by my thoughts, I slept.

❧ 4 ❧

BEFORE THE NEXT PASSOVER, Hephzibah offered the sacrifice that announced to the congregation that she was a woman. I was not surprised to learn that the girl was sought after even with the small dowry Isaac provided. Her dark hair fell in braids past a slender waist. The graceful figure caused many young men to watch her progress through camp.

"Our sister will be wed at Sinai in the spring," Isaac told me after we moved to the cooler mountain pastures. "I have agreed to a union with Abrahim of Benjamin. The contract will be signed at the midsummer celebration."

"What do you know of Abrahim?" I was concerned. "None of our family is of Benjamin. Mother and Father are of Manassah. Elimelech is from Judah."

"Our sister will be well cared for," the young man assured me. "Elimelech and I have met with the family. It is not as though she is marrying a foreigner. We are all Children of Israel."

The girl was dreamy-eyed.

"Abrahim is handsome and strong. He can carry a sheep on each shoulder," she bragged. "None of the girls of Benjamin interested him. When he saw me at the oasis last Passover, his heart was struck."

"Abrahim is not the only man who sought Hephzibah as wife," my mother informed me. "Isaac wisely chose the man who can best provide a home for your sister when we reach the Promised Land. He is older than Hephzibah. His maturity will be good for her. Fifteen years is not that great of a difference. Like your husband, Abrahim was a child when we left Egypt."

Preparations for the wedding consumed Abital's attention. Even when I announced I was pregnant, she simply smiled.

"It will be good for Mahlon to have a brother," was her only comment. The next question was about my sister. "What do you think of this color embroidery for the edge of the veil? Hephzibah must wear your veil, but I will make it new with ornamentation."

I smoothed the material she held. "The veil will be my contribution to the festivities. I may not be able to attend my sister's marriage. My son will be born in the spring."

My labor began the night before the wedding. I heard the music, chanting, and cheers as I panted in my tent to bring forth life. Leah brought me a bowl of meat and bread from the marriage feast. I lay on my pallet, newly delivered of a second son.

"Hephzibah was beautiful," the ten-year old enthused. "Abrahim killed three sheep to show his delight in our sister. Nearly everyone in the camp stopped to offer congratulations."

Chilion began to fuss. I picked up the baby. Mahlon toddled over to stare at his brother.

"Ch . . . Chi . . . Chil'n." It was the closest my first-born could come to pronouncing the new arrival's name.

Like Mahlon, at first the infant was slow to thrive. He was lethargic and slept much of the time. Elimelech offered a goat as propitiation.

"It may be that we have sinned somehow," he pointed out, awakening my own fears. "God is punishing us with weak sons for our disobedience."

I wracked my brain for some trivial or large transgression. The only thing I could identify was my secret jealousy against my sisters.

"God of Israel, I am sorry that I have envied Hephzibah for her beauty and desirability." It was a private conversation with the clouds on Sinai just before the congregation moved on toward the summer pastures in the north.

I rejoiced with my husband only a moon turning later. "We can no longer claim Chilion is failing. Look how plump he is, Mahlon is stronger, too. God has heard me."

"Yes, my son will soon learn to tend the sheep." His father grinned. "He will be a good shepherd."

I was content, but not everyone felt the same.

"When do we enter the Promised Land?"

During the summer the question was raised again. Since the invasion of the serpents in the Wilderness of Shur, no one dared confront the Deliverer.

As always Moses replied, "The Holy God will tell us when the time is right."

It was not a satisfactory answer. Grumbling was heard.

"You have tried the patience of the Lord before," the white-haired leader reminded the congregation. He took a stand near the tabernacle. "From Meribah to Kibroth-hattaavah, you complained. The Living God provided water and manna and even meat for your cravings. You rebelled in the Wilderness of Shur and serpents came among you."

For several minutes, the prophet surveyed the people. We shifted nervously. Then the recitation continued.

"Twenty years ago we encamped at Mt. Hor, ready to enter the land. Fearful reports from all the scouts except Joshua and Caleb caused you to doubt the Holy One. Because of that disbelief none of the generation that knew Egypt will enter the Promised Land. Those who have left our midst to seek the land on their own are lost to the desert or to the swords of Canaan."

Around me, I felt a shudder of apprehension. I was sure that Moses was building up to some condemnation. Instead, the next words were conciliatory and almost pleading.

"Despite your hardness of heart, *I AM that I AM* has given us the laws and ordinances that make us a strong nation. The hand of our God is not shortened. Each day brings manna. Never has the guiding pillar failed from among us or led us astray. Even when we have faced battle against the Amalekites and other tribes, we have triumphed by the might of the Living God. You have not been forsaken. Do not turn your back on the One God."

Moses fell silent. In a raspy voice, Aaron spoke.

"From everlasting to everlasting God is God." The ancient priest seemed to gain strength as he intoned the words.

"We will serve the Lord God of Israel, El Elohim Israel," Joshua spoke from his position at Moses's right hand.

A few voices took up the chant, "Amen, Alleluia, El Elohim Israel."

More and more joined in. I was relieved that a crisis was averted and eagerly added my voice to the crowd.

When we moved on to Mt. Hor for the winter, I was not surprised that Aaron died. The old priest had aged greatly in the past few years. Long was the mourning for the brother of our leader. Two years later, Zipporah, wife of Moses, was buried on the heights of the mountain. Moses seemed to be bowed down with grief. Even his sister Miriam could not consol him.

The old man spent much time with his sister. The woman amazed us with her ability to write. In the special wood and bronze trunk that accompanied the ark were the sagas of the Children of Israel. They began with the tales of creation and included all the stories of Abraham and even Jacob and his sons. There were many tales. When I was a child, I looked forward to hearing Miriam, sister to the Deliverer, sing of the mighty works of the Holy One.

Every story began with the same affirmation. "God does not forget the Chosen People. Hear what love our Lord has for all."

When she ended the recital at sunset, the conclusion was always the same, "Remain faithful to the Living God and you will be blessed to be a blessing."

When my father died, I stopped joining the weekly gatherings of children.

My mother noticed that I no longer attended. "You used to love to hear the stories."

"I did like them. My favorite was the story of creation. We all said the refrain 'It is good'," I agreed. "Now I do not have time; I am no longer a child."

She did not argue with my decision. I never explained that I no longer believed that the God of Moses cared. My father was dead. Life was empty.

"Together, the laws and history will provide a framework for the nation," Moses intoned years earlier when the scrolls were placed in the oiled wrappings of leather. "They are written that generations to come may know the saving acts of the God of Israel. All will hear and learn of the deeds that the Living God has done for the sons of

Jacob. Children yet unborn will hear what the Holy One demands of the Children of Israel in response. The God of Sinai is a gracious God, forgiving those who are penitent, but *I AM* will visit the sins of the fathers to the third and fourth generation."

I could not believe that the God of Abraham, Isaac, and Jacob was gracious. To me, the Holy One was to be feared and obeyed, or punishment would follow. Elimelech taught our sons their responsibilities. I recited the stories as I remembered them from my childhood.

The years slid by in a similar cycle that began with Passover at Sinai. A summer of grazing from oasis to oasis brought us to Mt. Hor for the Feast of Atonement. Spring found us back at the Holy Mountain. Mahlon was twelve when the routine changed.

We camped at Mt. Hor as always. This time a rumor rippled through the camp.

"The spies are returning to the Promised Land!"

Excitement built when we realized it was true. A dozen men, including Caleb, Joshua's young aide, left camp. They were disguised as traders. A moon-turning later, they returned, bearing grapes and other produce of the land.

"Truly the land is rich!"

"The cities no longer intimidate us."

"Word of the favor of the Lord our God has spread among the people."

"We are already feared."

An assembly was called. Moses stood before us all.

"God has made us ready to enter the land promised to Abraham, Isaac, and Jacob. We will seek safe passage through Midian."

"Amen, Alleluia, El Elohim Israel!" The cheer rang off the mountains.

Word came a moon-turning later that our way was barred. It only slightly dimmed our enthusiasm. Vengeance on Midian was swift and thorough. The army returned to the camp at Mt. Hor.

Moses forbade travel south to Sinai for Passover. "Miriam is ill. We will not move from this spot."

She died before the festival week began. Her brother wept openly. Every woman and man grieved with the Deliverer. It was a subdued Passover. After the celebration ended, the leader called the congregation together.

"We will journey on toward the Promised Land." The old man offered good news to ease the grief that still clung to us all. "The spies who entered the land found it rich just as *I AM* has told us. Moab lies open before us. The people will not be able to stand against us."

"God will be with us to bring us into the Land of Abraham, Isaac, and Jacob." Joshua's words left no doubt. "From this mountain, we will journey east before we enter our homeland."

"Amen, Alleluia, El Elohim Israel!" Spontaneously the cheer rang out.

The Deliverer held up his hands in benediction. "We will pass through the people of Moab, cross the Jordan and march forward in the power of the Living God!"

Again and again, we chanted. "Amen, Alleluia, El Elohim Israel!" My throat was hoarse when we stopped.

Joshua grinned at the response. When the sound finally died down, our general turned to the elders.

"Bring sacrifices for each tribe. We will sanctify ourselves for this journey and conquest."

The man gestured to the animals penned nearby.

"Judah will be first as signified by our father Israel on his death bed," Eleazar announced.

Nashon, chief of Judah brought a lamb forward. An elder from Simeon, Reuben, and the rest of the leaders followed in turn. Priests dispatched each animal. Soon smoke from the sacrifices wafted up to mingle with the cloud of God.

"Look, the pillar is embracing the tabernacle." My awed whisper went unheard in the murmur of prayers and movement of many feet.

"Behold, God is with us," Eleazar shouted, gesturing toward the smoke and flame.

The ark, altar, and priests were overshadowed and engulfed by the mingled smoke, incense, and cloud. We could not see the men, but we could hear the chanted prayers of the Levites.

Chilion hid his face in my gown. "I am afraid."

"It is God," my own voice quavered.

"Have no fear, my son. We obey the laws of the Holy One. God will bless us." Elimelech patted the boy on his head.

"I am not afraid," Mahlon tossed his head. He pretended to have no fear, although his knuckles were white from clenching his fists.

"That is good. Those who follow the commands of the Living God need not be afraid." My husband gripped his son around the shoulder in a brief hug.

"Israel, prepare to enter the Land of Promise," Joshua emerged from the smoke to issue the order.

The congregation began dispersing. Small groups visited briefly before scattering to tents. All the sacrifices were complete. Only the priests remained to offer prayers for preservation and guidance until the cloud lifted.

A moment later Elimelech turned from the gathering. "Come, there is much to be done before we move on."

I stared at the hovering, engulfing fog. A great desire welled up in me to experience the intimacy with God that Joshua and the priests had. Without thinking, I took one step and then another toward the tabernacle area, I lifted one hand in wordless supplication toward the glow that seemed to beckon.

"Is God more than obedience to laws?" The surprising question appeared in my mind.

I stumbled on a stone. The spell was broken.

Mahlon tugged my arm. "Mother, Father says you must come. We need to be ready to break camp when Joshua gives the order."

"Yes." I swallowed a sudden surge of disappointment.

When I looked back toward the tabernacle from my tent, the linen curtains were visible. The presence of God had withdrawn from the ark. Only three Levites remained to clean the brazier after the flames died.

"Mahlon and I will gather the flock. Our goods need to be packed for the journey. Naomi, we will be entering the Promised Land!" Elimelech was like a child anticipating a gift. "A new life lies before us."

"Do we not have a long journey still?" I tried to insert rationality.

"Not as long as the trek we already have been on." A wide grin crossed his face. "The nations will fall before us. We will have our own home before my sons are a year older."

Although many in camp believed the same thing, it was longer than we expected before we came to the homes we all desired.

⮟ 5 ⮞

MOAB OFFERED LITTLE RESISTANCE. Each night we set up camp further into their territory. The men gathered near the ark to offer prayers of thanks for another day of safe travel.

"Not even those who serve the gods of this land can stand before the Almighty," Elimelech was jubilant one afternoon when he returned from the gathering.

"What do you mean?" I looked up from the stew I was stirring.

"Balak, chief of the land, sent for Balaam from the Land of the Two Rivers," the man grinned smugly. "The seer was supposed to curse us. Instead he offered blessing upon blessing."

"That must have made Balak angry," I could not understand why my husband was so delighted. "What if he sends out his armies against us?"

"The chief of Moab will not attack," Elimelech laughed. "The man has fled to Jericho for help. He will get nothing from the leaders there."

I shook my head, not convinced that we were in no danger. Joshua led us forward, deeper into the land of Moab. The leaders of Israel were right. There was no threat. The residents regarded us warily. Some overtures of friendship were offered. Other places closed their gates against us. After our years in the desert the towns were tempting. Even though much of the land was brown, small watered gardens and the fields close to the river were inviting.

"This is not the Land promised to Abraham, Isaac, and Jacob," Moses reminded the congregation.

"We have wandered far enough," Samuel bar Elizur of Reuben was heard to mutter when we crossed the River Arnon.

It was not long before a delegation approached Moses and Eleazar for permission to settle.

"This is what our father Jacob spoke against at Shechem," Joshua and the Levites pleaded. "Unless the people of Moab are willing to follow the covenants of the Lord, they must remain outside the congregation. We must not mingle with those who do not obey the Living God."

Proud defiance came from the chief of Reuben. "We have not forsaken God. What we seek is a safe home for our wives and little ones. This is a good land for flocks. Our herds will flourish. We will not desert our brothers. The tribe of Reuben will march at the head of the columns when we invade Canaan."

The argument went back and forth for a moon turning. My husband was disgruntled with his kin. He stood firm against the urging of his cousins.

"Samuel wants me to join them. My grandmother was born into the tribe of Reuben," he reminded, me adding with a contemptuous grunt, "These men are fools. They are satisfied with this when a richer homeland awaits."

"It would be nice to have a house," my longing whisper was brushed aside.

"Wife, the Living God is acting." My husband frowned at my yearning. "Soon we will enter the Promised Land."

I was sorry to learn that the Deliverer gave permission.

"Those of the tribes of Reuben and Gad who desire to remain in Moab may settle between the Arnon and Jabbok rivers. Any one of the sons of Manasseh who does not want to cross over will have to land north of the Jabbok toward Bashan." The old man seemed resigned. "Only remember your oath. Your families will stay here but you will help your brethren enter and settle the Land of Promise."

"We will." The vow was witnessed by the entire congregation one Sabbath.

Moses announced, "We will help you build homes for your families."

Muttering erupted and was only stilled when the leader added, "When our brothers are established with safe homes for their families, we will move toward Canaan."

The incentive was enough for many eager hands to help dig wells and erect new homes along the small stream that was called the Arnon.

"Some of the women and children are staying here," Elimelech admitted to me one evening. "If you want, you may remain."

"Do you want to leave me behind?" Before I thought, the question burst out. "Have I not pleased you? I have begged the One God for more sons."

I was immediately appalled by my outburst and clapped a hand over my mouth. Wide-eyed, I stared at my husband. My words surprised the man. He swung away from studying the newly constructed town to stare at me.

"Naomi." The tender way my name was pronounced made me blink back tears.

I turned my face away embarrassed by the emotion. Seeking to offer comfort, the man moved to my side. Tenderly he bent close.

"Naomi, I would rather you came with me. However, I want you to be comfortable. I know that you long for a home."

"I want a home with you!" I could not suppress the wail.

"Then you will come with me. I will have my brave wife and sons at my side." I found myself enclosed in warm, strong arms.

At last my doubts eased and I could offer kisses. "Do not leave me."

For the first time since we left the wilderness, I lay content in my husband's arms that night. Our love was tempestuous. I almost felt like a bride again, so deep were our embraces.

"We will enter the Promised Land together. Our sons will find a home in the Promised Land," Elimelech promised just before he began to snore. "What need do we have for this land of Moab? The new land will be richer even than the richest fields near the river."

"Perhaps God will give me another son in the Land of Promise." With budding hope, I, fell asleep.

In the morning, I collected the daily ration of manna. That routine was the same, but my heart was lighter. I knew that Elimelech still loved me.

"God of Sinai, let me please my husband and give him a new

son for the new land," I offered the quick prayer as I passed the tabernacle on my way to draw water from the recently dug well.

Mahlon and his brother spent their days with the other children including their cousin Eglah. Hephzibah's daughter was a year younger than Chilion. Already, at nine, she showed promise of a beauty similar to her mother. Hepzibah was pregnant again, which saddened Leah. She had wed Terah of Benjamin seven years earlier. Her first child had died as an infant. A second son, now five, was the joy of her heart. He was named for our father.

My own secret sorrow was that still neither of my sons was strong enough to take their turn as shepherds. Both were prone to fits of wheezing. Exertion too often brought on one of the frightening times when my sons struggled for breath. I was not sure if it was the work or the animals that affected the boys. I was sure that God was still punishing me for inciting my father to question Moses. Often I had to grit my teeth when the women gossiped about the boys.

"You should not spoil your sons."

"Weak boys grow into weak men."

"They do not know what it is like," I whispered vehemently to myself. "I must keep Mahlon and Chilion safe. God may strike them down if I allow them to act recklessly. One indiscretion is all that it will take for me to lose my children."

Even Elimelech refused to believe me, until Mahlon collapsed one afternoon after a short run trying to catch a lamb.

My husband was in an agony of fear when he carried the child to our tent. "Wife, see to your son."

My routine of pounding his back and rubbing his chest eventually eased the boy's breathing. The man did not ask again for his sons to join him with the flocks.

"When they are older and stronger," I promised both my husband and myself, "then our sons can join the shepherds."

Mahlon tried to pretend that the teasing of the other children did not bother him. Chilion however, ran to me every time the taunts started.

"The boys in town called me skinny and sick and stupid," the boy sobbed into my lap one afternoon, just before we set out toward the Jordan.

I dropped my sewing to cuddle the child close.

"They are just jealous of how much I love you." I wondered how much longer my son would accept my consoling words. "Do not cry. You will make yourself sick. Besides, it is not true. You are not skinny or stupid."

By rocking and soothing, I was able to avert an episode of the breathlessness I feared. The boy set out to find his brother after he had a piece of bread with a little honey.

Elimelech's arrival with news helped me forget the events of the afternoon.

"We will soon leave this place and travel north to the Jordan crossing," the man announced. "Joshua is gathering information about Canaan. Spies have been sent to Jericho. It is the largest of all the cities. When Jericho falls, the land will be open to us."

The congregation gathered with eager anticipation when the spies returned.

"The people of the land fear us. Jericho will fall to the armies of the Living God," Salma reported.

"It is true. Word of our victory over Midian and Moab makes us a feared enemy," Jamal, his associate, nodded in agreement. "The priests of Jericho offer incessant sacrifices to their gods for protection. Indeed, a temple harlot is paid to send word of any strangers in the city to the chief and priests."

I wondered why Salma frowned at his friend. His explanation was directed at Joshua although the general did not ask.

"The woman saved our lives," the young man spoke earnestly. "She showed more faith in the might of our God than some here. When soldiers came searching, she hid us on her roof amid the flax. Her life was forfeit if we were found. What she did took courage."

"Great is the God of Israel," our leader led the chant of victory.

"Amen, Alleluia, El Elohim Israel," we repeated as one.

"The Lord will go before us. Prepare to march, O Israel," Moses raised his staff in the air. "We await the command of *I AM*."

"Amen, Alleluia, El Elohim Israel," again the cheer rang out.

"We will enter the Promised Land!" Elimelech's delight knew no bounds. He swung me around and gave me a hearty kiss.

"When will we leave?" A little breathless, I asked the question.

"Joshua will give the order. We must obey and be ready." It was not an entirely satisfactory answer. I did not mind because my husband held me close in the night.

Less than a moon-cycle later, we set out to march to Mt. Nebo between the Arnon and the Plains of Moab, near the Jordan. I did not even notice that my monthly flow was absent. I was too busy with my sons and our belongings. After the respite in Moab, we were unused to the travel. It took us past nightfall to set up the first camp. By the second night, we were slipping into the routine of march and camp. We reached Mt. Nebo and made camp on the third day. Moses called the congregation together in the morning.

"You will enter the land in the power of the Most High. My people, I will not cross the Jordan. This is where I will remain," He saddened us when he unexpectedly bid us farewell.

"You must go with us," Joshua stared at the old man in consternation.

Slowly, the Deliverer shook his head. He leaned heavily on the staff that performed miracles a generation earlier in Egypt. I saw the Prophet turn his head so that he could survey the entire encampment.

"I have been angry with the people. *I AM* long ago showed me that I would not enter the Land of Promise."

A moan of distress interrupted the old man. With a sad smile, he looked around at our shocked faces.

"Joshua will lead you forward." Moses laid a hand on his general's shoulder. "He is chosen by the Living God. To him, I give the staff of the Lord. It is the symbol of his leadership."

Joshua fell prostrate before his mentor.

The old prophet held out his hand. "Rise, my son. The Spirit of God will be with you to lead the people."

The man shook his head. "I am not worthy. You must lead us."

"No," Moses was emphatic. "The task is yours."

Joshua bowed his head in acceptance and took the staff. I felt tears stinging my eyes. Women, and even men, sobbed without shame.

"My people," the Deliverer addressed the congregation. "Remember all that the Holy One of Israel has done. The law and writings are in your midst. Do not forsake the Lord. Behold the Living God will bring you into Canaan. It is a rich land, flowing with milk and honey. You must obey all that the God of Abraham, Isaac, and Jacob commands. Each man will live under his own vine. Only remember to follow the Lord God."

"We will observe all the commands. Amen, Alleluia, El Elohim Israel!" Our response was loud.

Before morning, Moses left the camp. We never saw him again. Even those who searched could find no sign of the Deliverer.

"God has taken him." Joshua's explanation was accepted by all.

Our mourning was sincere. Even to those who had opposed him, Moses was set apart by God. His relationship with *I AM* was one that no one, not even the priests, dared attempt to emulate.

"Will the God of Moses desert us now?"

"How can we continue without the Deliverer?"

"Who will speak to God?"

Many questions formed a sense of fear that might have destroyed the community. Joshua stopped the flood of concern. We gathered at the sound of the *shofar* even though it was not the Sabbath or a festival.

Our new leader stood before the tabernacle. Levites, all the sons of Aaron and their cousins, stood behind him. Eleazar wore the breastplate of the High Priest. The elders of each tribe were also present near the altar.

"People of Israel, chosen by the One Living God, have no fear." The general looked first at the tribal leaders. "The Holy One has not abandoned us. *I AM* is with us still."

"The pillar of the Presence of God remains with us. We will march in the might of the Living God!" Eleazar announced. "Bring forward sacrifices for our God."

"Amen, Alleluia, El Elohim Israel!" Our response gradually swelled.

Beyond the ark and tabernacle, the glowing smoke was clearly evident. I felt courage return as the billowing smoke over the altar merged with the fiery cloud not far away.

"God will be with us," the priest insisted as dark descended.

"Return to your tents, O Israel, and prepare for service to the Lord of All."

We slowly moved away to our fires. They seemed dim in comparison to the pillar.

"Will God cross the Jordan with us?" Mahlon asked his father while I spooned stew into wooden bowls.

"The Holy One remains with those who obey," the man nodded. "Do not fear. We are the chosen of God."

"When will we get to the River?" Chilion wanted details.

"We move north past Beth-peor and Shittim," their father responded. "The crossing is near Gilgal. Do not be afraid. The Almighty is with us. Ahead is the Land of Promise."

His words comforted me, even though I worried about the river we must cross and the cities that barred our way.

6

"WE WILL KEEP THE Passover in the Land of Promise." Joshua made the announcement to the congregation.

We stood before the tabernacle. Behind us, the rushing waters of the Jordan mocked such a boast. I was not the only one to cast a skeptical glance at the flood between us and Canaan. Even more intimidating was the sight of twin cities on the far shores. Lit by the sun reflecting on the walls, we could see them even though they were miles away.

"That is Jericho and Gilgal," I overheard the explanation Jamal gave to his wife when we made camp the night before.

"They are huge!" Fear and awe were in her response.

I saw the young woman tighten her arms around the baby she held. Jamal bent to pick up the water jar. Shamelessly, I dallied with filling my own jar to hear the reply.

"The One God has given them into our hand. Lamash, chief of Jericho, is terrified of our approach." With soothing words the man calmed her fears. "He knows that Gilgal is an ally. Her elders have maintained ties to the shrine of the God of Jacob at Bethel."

I remembered the young spy's words when the general spoke. Around me, muttered complaints echoed my concerns.

"How will we cross that river?"

"Bold words will not stop the flood."

"Even if we cross, those cities block our way."

"Sanctify yourselves." Joshua did not seem disturbed by the whispers. He conveyed such confidence I was ashamed of my doubts. "We will purify ourselves to enter the land promised to Abraham, Isaac, and Jacob. The God of Israel will honor our obedience and lead us to victory. In three days, we will enter the land. We will camp will in front of Gilgal. There the Passover of God will be remembered."

When the man ended his speech, we scattered to our tents.

"It is good to obey the commands of the Holy One." Elimelech seemed satisfied with the general's orders. "Each household will offer a sacrifice. Men are to keep from contact with women. Our weapons will lie before the ark and receive blessing for the invasion."

My husband appeared eager to begin. He was not alone. Every man in the camp joined in the three-day ceremony to sanctify the congregation. Time passed swiftly. There was much for the women to do.

"We should have clean clothing and blankets." No one knew who first suggested it, but many decided to wash dusty garments in the thundering river on the third morning.

Mother struggled to her feet. "It is a good idea."

"We will go together." I carried my own blankets, as well as my mother's.

I stared across the water. "I wonder what Canaan will be like."

"It looks a lot like here." Somewhat disappointed, Leah frowned at the brown land visible beyond the river. I had to agree with my sister.

"The mountains look green," inserted Beulah of the tribe of Dan as she caught her son by his belt just before he tumbled headfirst into the water.

"I can see fields on the hills," Chilion stated. His sharp child's eyes could see farther than mine. "There are trees, too."

"We have heard that it is a rich land." I squinted to see more of the details. It did not help.

Hephzibah sighed in frustration. "Anything is better than the endless traveling. I want to have a house for my children."

My sister had her hands full trying to wash blankets while cradling my nephew. The child was named Beriah. He was born only a little over a month earlier.

"Terah has promised me a home larger than the one we could have had in Moab. He insists that obedience to God will bring greater riches in the new land. I hope he is right," Leah sighed.

A moment later, she smiled and caught the namesake of our father by the hand.

"Come, Mattan, you carry this basket of tunics." My sister held a small basket to her son. "Let us see who can make it back to our tent without dropping anything."

I smiled as I watched my nephew frown in concentration. Step by careful step, he followed his mother.

From her small stool nearby Abital spoke. "My daughters are blessed. They have children and husbands who care for them. I have lived to see the Children of Israel enter the Promised Land. My son will find a bride and home among those hills."

"Yes, Mother, I am sure Isaac will at last find wife and raise sons," I crouched beside the old woman.

Her gray hair was neatly braided away from her face. My sisters and I took turns helping her plait the thinning strands. Gnarled hands made it difficult for her. Although she lived in Isaac's tent, we all shared the care of our mother.

"You will have a new home as well," I infused enthusiasm into my voice. "Elimelech or Isaac will build you a fine place."

Her wrinkled hand patted my face. "It is enough that I have seen the land. I only wish Mattan had been less impatient. We would have seen it together."

My throat tightened at the grief still evident in my mother's face and words. Gently I took her hands between my own. I could find no words to say.

"God has given me grandchildren in place of a husband." Brightening after a moment, the woman looked past me. "Here comes Chilion with Mattan."

"I carry bas'et," the little boy proudly told his grandmother.

"What a big boy you are!" Sorrow gone, Abital let the child kiss her.

"Father and Mahlon are at the tent," my son told to me.

"Help your grandmother." I left the boy to offer a strong arm to the old woman.

Rapidly I grabbed tunics and robes from the rocks. Then I hurried to meet my husband.

The man eyed the full river. "Tomorrow, we cross."

"How?" I looked at the water was surging dangerously south-ward. "It is not safe to enter the river. We will be swept away."

Elimelech shrugged. "Joshua orders us to trust God. He will have to be another Moses to cross such a torrent."

"You have all obeyed the commands. Surely God will be merci-ful," I offered hopefully.

"We will see." My husband frowned and entered the tent.

I was busy with preparation for our meal when Chilion arrived with Abital. Mahlon carried Mattan. The child ran to Leah when his cousin put him on the ground.

"Sit here." I placed a stool near the fire so the woman would be warm even in the waning light.

"Mahlon says we cross tomorrow." It was a flat statement from Mother.

"Yes, Elimelech told me," I agreed and added a handful of dates to the fruit platter.

"If Joshua can lead the people across, we will all know that God is with him." The old woman shook her head, as if doubtful that such a thing would happen.

The meal was eaten in silence. Elimelech faced the water and frowned. Mahlon and Chilion imitated their father. Mother slowly chewed a soft piece of manna bread soaked in goat milk. A couple of bites of boiled apple followed. It was her usual diet. Hard fruits were more that she could chew now that most of her teeth were gone.

All around the camp, talk was subdued as each family surveyed the river we were to cross in the morning. I slept restlessly, dream-ing that my mother and sons were swept away from me. The ram's horn rescued me from the nightmare. We assembled near where the ark waited. The curtains, poles, and altars of the tabernacle were al-ready loaded onto the Levite's wagons.

"Watch for the intervention of our God!" Joshua stood beside the ark, a look of anticipation on his face.

Priests waited in their places, ready to lift the golden box that bore holy things. There was a bustle in the camp as we folded tents and arrayed ourselves into the normal line of march.

"We go forth in the name of God," shouted the general. "Amen, Alleluia, El Elohim Israel!"

The priests echoed, "Amen, Alleluia, El Elohim Israel!"

We all joined the shouting, "Amen, Alleluia, El Elohim Israel!"

Only then did the priests bend and lift the ark. They moved toward the river. Our shouts ebbed to silence as the priests approached the water.

"God of Israel, we obey your commands; will you save us?" My heart thudded with a desperate prayer.

Confidently the white robed figures continued to walk forward. Another step and they would be in the flood. Not a sound came from the congregation. Then a communal gasp broke the silence. When the first of the priests stepped into the river the water vanished. Nothing roared through the channel from the north. It drained away to disappear to the south.

"Amen, Alleluia, El Elohim Israel!" Eleazar burst out in exultation.

"Mother, the river stopped!" Mahlon grabbed my hand. Excitement made him gasp for air.

"Yes, I see." My reply was panted as astonishment and awe chocked off my words.

All around, excited babble broke out.

"It is like the shores of the sea."

"God has opened the waters again."

"Surely the Lord is with us still."

My own attention turned from the dry riverbed to my son. Chilion pounded his brother's back. The boy was still struggling to breathe.

"Look at me." I crouched and took the contorted face in my hands. "Breathe slowly, like this."

Gradually, the harsh gasping eased.

"I am better now," the boy finally spoke normally.

"Then let us join the march." Elimelech pulled me to my feet.

We joined the somewhat hesitant march through what had been a raging river. There was no water to be seen in either direction. The Levites remained standing calmly in the center of the riverbed. Families hurried to the western shore between the stones and boulders that a few minutes earlier broke the flow of the water. Smooth rocks now stood slowly drying in the sun. It took all morning for everyone to reach our first footfall in the Promised Land. On the western side of the river, we milled around, uncertain of our direction. Sheep and other animals were driven beyond us to herd together between the river and the cities of Canaan.

"A representative from each tribe shall bring a stone from the riverbed," Joshua ordered.

Most of the people stared at the leader, then at the priests, still stationary in the center of the Jordan. Some squinted to the north, wondering if the water would sweep down and drown the bearers of the Holy Ark. A few glanced apprehensively to the west. No fighting men emerged from either of the cities.

Our leader expanded his plan. "We will build an altar to the Most High. When generations to come ask how we came to this land, we will show them the altar built of stones from the dry bed of the Jordan River."

A dozen men hurried to the river. Huge rocks were pried loose and hefted onto broad shoulders. Each man acted like a boy in a competition, trying to find the largest stone for the altar. An irregular monument stood on the shore a short time later.

"It is good." Eleazar's words were a signal.

The quartet of priests bearing the ark marched out of the river. Barely did they begin to climb up the incline when a trickle and then a rushing flood filled the river as though it had never been dry. The men took their stand beside the altar. One of the younger priests kindled a fire.

"We will offer thanks to our God," Eleazar proclaimed.

The elders moved to stand before the new altar. Each man carried a sheep as sacrifice for his tribe. The rest of us gathered silently to watch.

"Did you see the river fill the banks?" Leah whispered to me. "I was terrified that the priests would be swept away."

"It was powerful," I agreed. "Only our mighty God could have stopped such a flood."

"Hush," Hephzibah hissed. "I want to hear."

"We are consecrated by this thank offering. The God of Israel brought us from bondage as slaves to the homeland promised to Abraham, Isaac, and Jacob. By this, we know that we are a chosen people. The Almighty has set us apart. All are sealed by obedience to the laws and covenants given us by God through the great Prophet Moses. Obey the Lord your God so that you may live long in the land."

On and on, the priest harangued the congregation. Each sacrifice brought more prayers and warnings.

"We obey the Lord," we responded after each one.

It was easy to promise to follow the One who had acted in such a powerful way.

Finally the priest ended with an admonition, "Reuben, Gad, & Manassah you will go before your brethren to settle the land. Remember the oath you swore in Moab."

The chiefs responded with a low bow to Eleazar and the altar. "As we have sworn, so will we do."

"We will sleep beside the altar this night," Joshua announced when the prayers and sacrifices were concluded. "Tomorrow, you will eat of the bounty of this land."

No tents were erected. We slept wrapped in blankets on the ground. A guard was posted out of fear of the inhabitants of Jericho. The city loomed not so far away. In the night, the torches on the walls seemed like new stars low along the horizon. A little further to the north the city called Gilgal also flickered against the hills.

I slept restlessly, waking often to check my sons and to be sure my mother was still warmly covered. Before dawn, I gave up the pretense of sleep. I crept past the sleeping camp to the river. Starlight glinted on the little waves bouncing off the rocks we walked past earlier. An occasional splash signaled the presence of a fish or frog. The scene appeared normal. I knelt down to dip a hand into the cold water.

"How could so great a river be stopped?" I did not expect an answer to my question.

"The hand of the Living God who brought us from Egypt has acted." I turned with a start.

I was not alone. Sarai, wife of Caleb, sat on a nearby rock.

"I could not sleep either," she confessed. "When the Holy One acts in such an impressive way, I must sit in awe."

Slightly defensive, I tried to explain my own confusion. "I know

God brought us safely here. All my life, I have seen the pillar and eaten the manna and obeyed the law of Moses. None of that explains why God would stop the flow of a river for us to cross."

"The Living One accomplishes what is promised. God cares for us like a shepherd." The woman made it sound so simple. "Now is the time when the Children of Israel are ready to claim the promise to Abraham, Isaac, and Jacob. The river was a sign to all that *I AM* is with us."

"What if we fail to obey the law?" Almost angrily, I interrupted the triumphant proclamation. "We will be struck down and erased from the face of the earth."

"Naomi, I cannot believe that the One God has brought us so far to destroy us." Her sympathetic hand took mine. "The law is a guide for our community, not a whip. You give your sons rules. It means you love them and do not want them to be hurt. So it is with the commandments."

Shaking my head, I insisted, "God does punish those who rebel. My father died because he confronted Moses."

"I cannot explain every action of the God of Sinai," the woman admitted. "What I do remember is that there was a bronze serpent to provide healing—"

"For those who were still alive to see it," I interrupted as anger rose in me.

Roughly, I pulled my hands out of the gentle grasp and rushed away from the river. My guilt and grief felt as fresh as when I had watched my father die.

"Naomi." I ignored the concerned calling of my name.

In a dense thicket of brush, I hid from the wife of Caleb. Anguished tears slid down my cheeks. Miserably, I sobbed. "It was my fault. I caused the death of my father by my desire for a home. My sons must be kept safe. I must not let them break any of the Laws of Moses."

Later, I avoided looking at Sarai when we met near the river. All the women were filling water jars for the next phase of our journey. No one seemed to be sure where we were going.

"We turn northwest," Elimelech told me when I returned with my jar. "Our camp will be by the walls of Gilgal. The chief has made an alliance with Joshua. We will be safe there and can trade for food, as well."

"That is good," I was relieved to hear the news. "There was manna this morning, but no one knows how long it will continue."

"Joshua told us that the manna would end when we celebrate Passover in the Promised Land," the man explained, although he looked around with a doubting frown. "We will eat of the fruits of the land from now on. The scouts have guaranteed a rich land of vines and fields and pastures. I will believe their report when I see these riches."

Hopefully, I pointed to the tilled area between Jericho and Gilgal. "There are fields and the hills are green."

"We will see," my husband shrugged and turned away to tighten a leather strap on the pack.

Further conversation was interrupted by the *shofar* sounding the signal to march. As we had for endless days and years, each man and woman shouldered their pack and set out after the priests bearing the ark. Our journey did not take long. Each step took us closer to the imposing walls protecting Gilgal. By the time the sun was high, we had arrived.

The *shofar* called again. This time, it was answered by a bronze trumpet from the city. A delegation of men strode out of the gates. There was a shifting in the ranks of Israel. Men loosened swords and daggers. The weapons were not needed.

"Welcome, Joshua son of Nun," an imposing man in a chariot shouted, loudly enough for us all to hear.

"That must be the chief," I whispered to my mother and sons.

The trio found seats when we stopped. Abital unfolded her ever-present leather stool. Chilion and Mahlon flopped down onto their packs. By stretching on my toes, I could see the meeting between the leaders of Gilgal and the general of Israel.

"We come in peace to the land promised to Abraham, Isaac, and Jacob," Joshua offered a *salaam* and held out his hands.

I guessed that they were empty of weapons to indicate our peaceable intentions. The chariot rolled forward a few steps to stop not far from where Joshua stood with the priests. Attendants bowed when the man stepped out of his chariot. Both leaders offered a *salaam* I could see that Joshua towered over the man from Gilgal by a cubit when they faced each other.

"My people remember the stories of Jacob called Israel and those of his grandfather, Abraham the Wanderer." The chief of the city spoke loudly. "Pray that your God will give blessing and protection to my people."

"The Living God will bless you for your hospitality," the successor to Moses replied firmly.

"Joshua and the chief of Gilgal have embraced," I reported a moment later to my small audience.

"The Children of Israel are welcome here," the official announced and gestured with his hand. "Set up your camp here between Gilgal on the west, the brook to the north, and the highway to the south."

"We will have a large encampment," I eagerly told my mother as I pointed out the area indicated. "It will be larger than the camp at Shittim. It will be from line of trees near the brook to the road we just came on."

The old woman nodded. "It will be good to have some space. For too long, we have put tent to tent in our camp."

I almost missed the next exchange while listening to my mother.

"Your people are welcome to trade with the merchants of Gilgal for food and other items you need." The Canaanite leader waved to the city. "All are sworn to offer as fair a price as they do to the people of the city."

"It is good." Joshua again saluted the chief. "Truly the blessing of God is on you and your people. We are in your debt."

"I am your servant." The words from the leader of Gilgal were part of the ritual welcome.

The Canaanite raised one hand in signal. A convoy of carts wheeled from the city. They were piled with barley loves. The sight made my mouth water.

An expansive gesture indicated the food. "Gilgal brings bread for your meal."

"Sacrifices will be offered to seal our covenant and give thanks for the generosity of Gilgal," the general announced. "Our tribal elders and priests will participate in the ceremony."

Twelve leaders stepped forward to stand beside Joshua. The younger priests were already busy constructing an altar and erecting the tabernacle on a low rise in the center of the area.

"Set up camp," Caleb ordered before he joined the tribal chiefs.

Some of the people hurried to claim a share of the bread. Others located a spot for their tent. Before evening, the encampment resembled the myriad other camps over the years. Fires were lit, and pots appeared from baggage as women set about the preparation of the meal.

"Go get our bread." I sent Mahlon and Chilion on their errand.

Elimelech unrolled our tents. With swift movements born of long practice we had our home erected before the boys returned. Our site was not far from the brook.

"You will not have to walk far for water or to get supplies," my husband informed me with a grin, gesturing to the nearby walls of Gilgal.

"You are a good man," I teased in return, slicing the barley bread onto a platter.

"Already we are eating of the bounty of this land." I relaxed after consuming the bread with cheese. "It is good to eat fresh bread and a treat to not have to make it myself."

I joined the man in our tent after banking the fire. All around, other families were doing the same evening chores.

"This is a good land," I mentioned. "Already the people welcome us."

"We have much to do before we can claim this as our home." The rumbled caution might have made me sad except he followed the words with a kiss. "Together, we will make a home in this land. My sons will have a heritage in this place."

His gentle kisses became more urgent until we were lost in the wonder of one another. Eventually, Elimelech lay back, satisfied. He fell asleep rapidly. I lay listening to the celebration for a short time.

The covenant meal went on long into the night. Fire on the altar lit up the camp. Even the sounds of chanting and later laughter did not disturb my sleep. Safe within my tent, I curled close to the man who was my husband.

7

MORNING DAWNED COOL AND a little cloudy. Trumpets from the city walls announced the dawn and awakened the camp.

"Wear your cloak and veil," Abital urged when I picked up the water jar.

I nodded and wrapped the wool around me. Other women and girls made their way to the brook. I was thrilled by the beauty I saw as I looked up the stream toward the mountains. Spring flowers carpeted the ground beside the water as far as we could see. We chatted as we filled our containers.

"It is lovely here."

"God is gracious."

"This is indeed a land of promise."

"We have waited so long."

I was reluctant to leave the shade of the sycamore trees near the water. Only the responsibility to my family dragged me back to camp.

"I believe this is a good place. The hills are green and verdant. Even under the trees, the flowers grow thickly," I told Elimelech when I returned.

He had news of his own and barely heeded my enthusiasm.

"All the sons of Israel who have not been circumcised will be made members of the covenant this night." My husband did not sound happy.

"But . . ." In horror, I realized that this ceremony would include both my sons and my husband.

"It is in obedience to the covenant of Abraham," he explained briefly. "Now that we are within the Promised Land, we shall ratify that pledge."

"Where? When? Tonight? So soon?" I tried to comprehend.

"There is a tent set up near the ark. We will all gather there. The Levites will perform the ritual. Then we will return." "Our sons will be fine. It is only a small thing the man insisted."

I accepted his attempted reassurances. Still, he winced slightly at the thought of the ceremony. My husband was not interested in food when he returned after dark. Stiffly the man walked straight into our tent. Mahlon and Chilion followed. Despite the tear streaks on their faces, the boys were trying to act as men in front of me. My sisters' husbands and my brother disappeared into the seclusion of their tents and blankets.

"We have obeyed the law," Elimelech told me in the morning. He seemed satisfied although he was careful when he moved. "By this sacrifice, the nation of Israel is made acceptable to inhabit the land. We will celebrate the Passover as a holy people. This will be a great festival to the Lord."

"I must go to the city to purchase things for the feast," I told the man.

He nodded, rose stiffly, and entered the tent.

With a basket full of blankets, I started toward the city. My heart pounded in apprehension. I wondered how the citizens would treat strangers in their midst. Leah and Hephzibah caught up with me.

"Can we join you for a trip to the market?" Hephzibah asked.

"The Passover begins in two days," my youngest sister stated as we strolled toward the city. "There is much to purchase and prepare."

At the gate we all paused. The imposing high wood doors almost looked like they could trap us inside.

"The market is straight ahead to the house with the red painted door, then right until you see the booths," a lounging guard told us.

I felt the stares from doorways and windows as we walked into the city. I was glad that I was not alone.

Later when Elimelech asked, I was glad that I could give a good report of my bargaining in Gilgal. "The people of the city are fair."

"It is as Joshua said. The hand of God is on us for blessing." The man was pleased.

His face still had a slightly pinched look; however, his dark eyes glowed with fervor. I had never before seen my husband so ecstatic.

"The One God will give the cities of the land into our hand. We have been faithful." The man held the tent flap in one hand and looked beyond Gilgal to Jericho. "All the inhabitants will fall before us. After the Passover, we will march against Jericho. When the queen of cities falls, everyone will know that Israel comes in the power of *I AM*."

"War, so soon?" The idea of assaulting the nearby city frightened me.

Even from our safe distance, the walls looked formidable. Such an edifice must have many armed men.

"Naomi, do not be afraid," my husband urged, trying to put my fears to rest. "Our spies say that the inhabitants and leaders are terrified already."

I shook my head. "Why can we not just move into the mountains and find a home? Then no one would have to fight."

"No matter where we settle, the people of the land will fight," Elimelech explained, making me feel like a foolish child. "Once Jericho falls, the rest of the cities will melt before us. Men will flee from the Children of Israel. We will live in peace."

As he spoke, the man became more and more excited. In the face his enthusiasm, I lowered my head.

"May it be as you have said." My response was as much a prayer as an agreement.

Sensing my disquiet, my husband drew me close. "All will be well. We are the chosen of the Almighty. We obey the laws of God. *I AM* will not fail us."

"Yes." I turned to the task of putting away my purchases, hoping that he would not be punished for my doubt.

The man changed the subject. "We will keep this Passover with your sisters, brother, and mother. There is much to celebrate."

"Yes, my husband." Again it was an obedient response.

I sought out Leah, Hephzibah, and our mother after Elimelech limped away to check his flocks.

"We are to eat the Passover together," I told my family.

"Yes, that is what Terah says," Leah nodded.

"It is a good thing," Abital agreed. "By the next Passover, you will each have your own houses. Who knows if we will be living near one another?"

The thought gave me pause. I had not considered the idea that we might settle in different areas. My sister's husbands were from the tribe of Benjamin. Vaguely, I remembered Moses designating the land for each clan before his death. Now I regretted my inattention.

I turned to Mother. "You must stay with us."

"I will live, God willing, where my son settles. That is the way of life," the old woman stated and smiled at me.

"Isaac would go where the tribe of Manassah is to live," I argued. "That may be far away."

"We will go to the lands given to the house of my father," agreed the old woman. "You will go to the lands of Judah with your husband."

Even as I worked beside my sisters to prepare the herbs for the lamb, the dough for the unleavened bread, and the many other details, I worried about the coming separation and if my family would remain faithful without my guidance. Platters and bowls were scrubbed, then polished with sand. Water jars stood ready to be filled for the feast day when no work could be done.

Hephzibah looked up from her work. "This will be a special Passover. We are camped at the very entrance to the Land of Promise. Our men ratified the contract with Abraham, Isaac, and Jacob in their own flesh and blood."

"This year, it will be the same and yet different," I mused. "Each man will offer a lamb for sacrifice. We will make the unleavened bread. Everyone will gather at the tabernacle to hear the saga."

Leah looked around the camp. "We will eat the meal of remembrance in this new land. It is a new life."

"That I have lived to see this day is a blessing." Mother sighed deeply.

By the time the sun descended behind the unfamiliar landscape, our Passover preparations were complete. The *shofar* blast summoned the entire congregation in the morning. We stood before the

Levites while they recited the story of the Children of Israel. The inevitable climax came.

"God does not abandon the Chosen People. *I AM that I AM* called to Moses from a bush that burned but was not consumed. God sent Moses to Pharaoh with one command."

No longer able to restrain ourselves, we all joined in. "Let my people go!"

"Pharaoh was stubborn. So the One God sent plagues against the gods of Egypt. The priests of the Black Land were not able to stand against the power of the True God. Still, Pharaoh refused to release us from bondage. The Holy One sent a final plague against the firstborn of Egypt. To the Children of Israel was given the ordinance and covenant we keep. 'The Angel of Destruction will pass over the house of each one who obeys.' Moses taught our fathers what to do."

Again, I found my mind wandering. While the priest droned on through the night with details of the sacrifice and marking the doors, I shuddered and drew my sons close. In this new land, they might face a different kind of death. I had no assurance of their safety. Even blood on the doors would not stop the swords of Jericho. Mahlon shrugged off my hand, too conscious of his manhood to bear my caress in public. Chilion looked at me curiously but did not resist the hug.

"We celebrate the remembrance of our God's deliverance. Before us is the very land promised to our fathers. We will enter in and possess our homeland! God does not abandon the Chosen Ones!" Exultantly the priest ended his recitation.

"Amen, Alleluia, El Elohim Israel!" All around the response resounded. I felt the solidarity of my friends and kin in their response.

"To your tents, Israel," Joshua spoke for the first time. "Give thanks for the wonderful providence of our God to those who keep the commandments. *I AM* will lead us in victory. Eat this Passover with grateful hearts for the Lord has given the land into our hands! When we next assemble, it will be to march against Jericho."

The general pointed south. In the morning light the city looked imposing and impregnable. I imagined the walls lined with armed men. It was impossible that such a fortress would fall to our army.

"Naomi," Elimelech interrupted my reverie. "I have the lamb for the feast. Let us go."

"Yes." With one word of assent I followed my husband and sons to our tent.

Tasks waited. My sisters and I finished preparing the bread, vegetables, and herbs for the meal. Mahlon and his cousin took turns watching the roasting lamb. Elimelech sat with his brothers-in-law. I overheard bits of their conversation around my banter with Leah and Hephzibah.

". . . attack the city is foolish . . ."

"God has spoken."

". . . advisors' plan to . . ."

"Surprise . . ."

Much later, after the meal was consumed and the last of the lamb consigned to the fire in obedience of the stricture 'nothing will remain until the morning,' I sought my blankets. Elimelech was already on the pallet, but my husband was not asleep. On the opposite side of the tent, low snores told me that both my sons were sleeping soundly.

"My husband." I sought for his big hand in the darkness. Tightly, I gripped the calloused palm. "Will all the men go against Jericho?"

"All those consecrated at the circumcision ceremony that are of the age to be considered a man will fight," my husband affirmed. "We obey the Lord our God."

"You could be killed." Fear overwhelmed me, and I had to grit my teeth against tears.

"Naomi," my husband crooned my name.

The man sat up and took me into his arms when I did not respond. I hid my face against his broad chest, trying not to cry. Gently, he stroked my hair.

"My wife, do not be afraid. Joshua and his counselors have a plan. They say it is from God. In the morning, all the congregation will hear how we are to defeat Jericho. Everyone will take part." The tone was implacable. "We will obey God."

The explanation seemed to satisfy my husband but did not ease my concerns. Elimelech kissed my forehead and lay down.

I did not dare say anything except, "Yes, my husband."

"All will be well, Wife," he stated. Through obedience, we will gain a homeland."

Soon he was snoring. I lay sleepless, struggling with a God who would demand my husband and even my sons.

Do not leave me bereft. You stole my father's life when he spoke against Moses. Must I now offer to you those I love? My thoughts raced hysterically in my mind. *What if I have done something wrong? God, please do not punish my family for my failing.*

The *shofar* announced dawn and the end of Passover. Obedient to the summons of the ram's horn, we all gathered at the tabernacle. Already the priests had kindled a fire on the altar. Incense rose above the entire hillock in the center of the camp. Joshua lay prostrate before the altar.

"Why is our leader laying on the ground?" Leah leaned close to ask.

"I do not know." I was as confused as my sister.

"Maybe he is praying," Hephzibah suggested.

"That could be," I agreed.

There was no time for any more speculation. The *shofar* sounded again. Joshua rose and faced the congregation. I could see purpose and confidence gleaming in the eyes that scanned the people.

"Today we will begin to claim our heritage," the general announced clearly.

Something between a gasp and a sigh came from thousands of throats. It was what we had waited for. Now that it was here, I wondered if anyone else was as frightened as I was.

"Our God has given instruction for the conquest of Jericho." I leaned forward slightly. "If we obey **I AM**, he walls will fall down at our advance."

A communal intake of breath accompanied many heads turning to peer at the imposing city only a few miles away.

Joshua ignored the disbelief. "This is what the God of Abraham, Isaac, and Jacob commands. We will all march from here in formation behind the ark. Priests and trumpeters will lead the way. We will march in silence. For six days, we will make a circuit of the city. On the seventh day, the Sabbath, we will circle the city seven times.

Only then will we shout and charge forward. Jericho will be defeated. *I AM* will give us a mighty victory. The entire city will be an offering to God as a sacrifice in blood and fire."

As the general spoke, he became more and more passionate. I felt myself caught up in the excitement. All around, I felt a ripple of anticipation.

"Amen, Alleluia, El Elohim Israel!" When the priests burst out in the chant, I heard my voice responding with everyone.

"Amen, Alleluia, El Elohim Israel!" We could not stop the acclamation.

Joshua waited patiently until the cheers ceased. An exalted expression remained on the bearded face. Each priest had a litany to add.

"We go forth in the name of the One Living God."

"We go forth to receive the promises of *I AM*."

"We go forth in the protection of the Most High."

"We go forth to victory."

"Let the ark be brought forward," the High Priest ordered.

To the blasts of the ram's horn, the ark was lifted from its place within the tabernacle by white-robed attendants. They marched straight ahead until they stood between the altar and congregation. I fell back a step. The proximity of the holy box frightened me a little.

Joshua raised the staff of Moses over his head. When he brought it down with a thump on the ground, the priests moved forward. An aisle opened through the congregation.

Priests followed the ark as the bearers began to walk toward Jericho. Trumpeters fell into line. As if drawn by ropes, we all formed a column and set out along the road. Joshua mounted his horse to ride back and forth from one end of our march to the other. The big animal was a tribute from a sheik in the Negev. Although I admired the sleek bay stallion, I was nervous of his size and never allow my sons to approach the creature.

The only sound was our bare and sandal-clad feet on the hard packed road and the brisk rhythmic thud of hooves along the edge of the highway. Once, a sneeze and giggle broke the solemn march. It was quickly hushed.

Jericho loomed larger and larger as we approached. Close up, the walls towered above the plain. At each corner, watchtowers faced the surrounding area. Awe and not a little fear kept us silent as we began our circuit of the city. I could see men on the walls watching our progress. The morning sun glinted off the spears as the men on the wall watched lazily. Then the taunts began.

"Jericho will never fall to desert rabble."

"Go back to the snakes and lizards."

"You have no future here."

"Come and taste our swords."

I felt Elimelech stiffen in outrage. Most of the other men also frowned and directed angry grimaces toward the speakers. Joshua rode between the walls and our column. His hand was held up in a calming and silencing reminder. It took all morning to circle the city and return to our camp. When the ark was safely behind the curtains in the tabernacle, Joshua dismissed the congregation.

"Return to your tents. Remember: the Lord has given the city into our hands, if we obey."

Most of the men remained near the tabernacle. I guessed they were grumbling about the rudeness of the soldiers. Over our jars of water, some of the women discussed the adventure.

"Did you see the height of the walls?"

"I heard that homes are built into those walls because they are so thick."

"Imagine all those people watching us."

"No one raised a sword or fired an arrow."

"They were too busy laughing at us."

"How will we destroy that huge city?"

"The Lord God will give the victory." Even the faith-filled response from Sarai only elicited shrugs.

The woman sighed in a discouraged way. She picked up her jar and walked away.

Hastily I trotted after her. "How can you be so sure?"

With a wry smile, the woman turned to me. "We have the promise of God. God has never failed us."

"You make it seem so simple." I heard my complaint as I struggled to understand my companion. "What if we do something wrong? There are so many laws. If someone fails, God will turn against us."

"Naomi, I can only tell you what I believe," Sarai replied patiently. "The laws are for our protection. They are not meant to trap us. First and from the beginning is the relationship of God with each of us."

"No." I drew back almost in horror at the thought of being too close to such a fearsome God. "The laws are to keep us safe from the anger of God. The Holy One demands perfection."

Sarai sighed. "Too many in the camp believe as you do. They cannot see that God is in our midst."

I agreed with an eager nod, as if reciting a lesson. "Of course. The tabernacle represents God and reminds us of our duty."

The smile in response was tender. It was the look a mother gives a confused and stubborn child. I bristled and spoke angrily.

"The priests and Joshua give us orders. We obey, and God blesses us. We fail and are punished. It is simple. I cannot understand why you would think otherwise."

Before Sarai could offer any more confusing explanations, I turned on my heel and hurried to my own fire. The woman's ideas were too troubling. I did not dare risk not obeying God. My family would suffer. It had happened before. Still, a seed of longing for the serenity I glimpsed in her smiling eyes was planted in my heart.

I told myself, "It is safer to obey all the laws than risk trusting a God who strikes men dead."

Morning saw us marching around Jericho. The next day was the same and again on the fourth dawn. Each afternoon, the men sharpened swords, daggers, and spears or prayed near the tabernacle.

"Look, Mother, I have a dagger! Proudly, Mahlon held aloft the sharp weapon.

"Who gave you that?" My tone was sharp.

"Father." The boy did not seem to notice my agitation. "He said that every man needed a weapon."

I dropped to my knees beside my son. "Do you really want to fight and kill?"

A pout appeared. "I am not a coward."

"No," my reassurance was swift. "You are a brave young man."

Young hands tightened on the dagger. "It is the duty of every man of Israel. Joshua said so."

I would have argued further, but Mahlon stood up to strap on his weapon. Then he strutted over to where his brother sat beside Abital.

"Look, Chilion. See what Father has given me." The young man pulled the knife out of its sheathe. "When you are a man, you will have a dagger, too."

Impressed by the weapon, the younger boy held out his hand. "Let me see."

"Be careful. It is very sharp." My warning was unnecessary. Chilion was using great care in handling his brother's prize.

"I wish I was old enough to fight." I was appalled to hear the longing in the voice.

Somewhat condescendingly, Mahlon offered his brother hope. "Father and the men say there will be other battles. Maybe you can fight in them."

Later, I confronted the man. "Why did you give Mahlon a dagger?"

My words were no less emphatic for the whisper I spoke in. We lay side by side, but I held myself stiff and unresponsive even to the stroking hands of my husband.

"Every fighting man needs a weapon." I felt the shrug in the darkness.

"What if our son is overcome by the exertion and smoke? Will you be there to help him?" I hissed the questions.

"I will watch out for Mahlon." The man tried to console me, but his tone was cross.

Fear made me reply heatedly. "So you say."

Elimelech became angry. "Mahlon will not be considered a coward, nor will he disobey God. All men will fight!"

With his ultimatum, Elimelech rolled away from me. I lay fuming long after the man began to snore.

Another silent march around the city began the day before the Sabbath.

"Tomorrow, Jericho will fall to the power of the Living God," proclaimed Joshua on our return to camp. "All the inhabitants will see that the Lord is greater than all the gods of this land."

"Amen, Alleluia, El Elohim Israel!"

"Our orders are from God. We will march seven times around the city tomorrow. On the seventh circuit all the trumpets will sound. Each man will shout. We will rush forward. Jericho will be ours." The man paused to look at the expectant faces all around. "Remember the ordinance of the Lord. Keep nothing for yourself from the spoils. All the gold and precious metal is an offering to God. The city itself will be burned with fire."

There was another pause while the leader looked deeply into the eyes watching him.

"Rest well, O Israel." When he spoke, it was a soft dismissal. "Tomorrow all the people will witness the power of *I AM*."

"Amen, Alleluia, El Elohim Israel!" I could barely join in the shout.

The words stuck in my throat, caught in the terror that God would turn against my husband and sons as against my father.

"Women and children are to stay in camp tomorrow," Elimelech told me as we walked to our tent. "Only the fighting men will march to Jericho."

"Even our son?" My voice cracked.

"I will go," Mahlon raised his chin in obstinate pride.

"You have never fought. Even the marching makes you gasp," I bent close to the boy to argue.

"My son will be in the assault tomorrow." Elimelech frowned angrily at my interference.

There was nothing I could say. With a lump in my throat, I turned to lay out bread and cheese for a meal. We ate slowly. My husband stared past the fire. Mahlon stroked his dagger. A small frown puckered his face. Chilion was subdued by the seriousness of the two men. My mind raced while I tried to think of a way to keep the boy from going with the army.

"You cannot have my son." Tight-fisted, I spoke to the dim shape of the ark representing the distant and demanding God I feared.

I did not think I would sleep, but exhaustion claimed me and I dozed. Agonized gasps startled me awake. Mahlon struggled to breathe.

"What is it?" Even Elimelech was roused by the sound.

"We must get Mahlon outside. The night air will help him breathe." My voice shook with panic.

The boy had not been so ill for years. Elimelech carried Mahlon into the moonlight. Chilion crawled after us to watch his brother. Each rasping breath chilled me. The young man could get enough air. Desperately Elimelech and I took turns rubbing and pounding his chest and back. Chilion sat very still watching with wide eyes.

"That is good, my son," his father encouraged with a strong hand on the heaving shoulder. "Breathe slowly now. It is well."

Mahlon still flung himself back to draw in air. His hand gripped my arm fearfully.

In the coaxing tone I always used at such times, I tried to infuse rhythm into the gasping. "My son, look at me. Breathe with me."

Pleading brown eyes stared into mine. The young man was frightened by the severity of the episode. I tried to hide my own fear. To me, it seemed someone was strangling my son.

I sent frantic prayers from my heart while I worked with Mahlon. *God, do not punish my son. It is my fault. I am a foolish woman and tried to prevent his obedience to you. Ease his breathing. Help Mahlon! Do not take him from me. Strike me instead.*

His attack was just starting to ease as the sky lightened to gray. Chilion was asleep on his father's lap.

Elimelech stood up. "I must join the men."

Gently, he laid his son on a nearby blanket. The man moved into the tent to don a leather breastplate and belt for the battle. In a moment, he was back. I caught my breath, for my husband looked sternly handsome arrayed for battle.

"May the God of Israel grant you victory." I watched him, hoping for a farewell kiss.

Instead, Elimelech strode away toward the tabernacle.

"Bring my husband home in safety." I added the final petition to my ongoing prayer for Mahlon.

The men of Israel looked grand as they strode from the camp. Trumpeters and priests led the way. In the center of the march was the ark. The army of God headed along the road to Jericho. By the time my sisters returned from waving their husbands away,

Mahlon's breathing was almost normal. Each inhalation still rasped, but the boy no longer clawed at his throat in an attempt to draw breath.

Leah patted her nephew's hand. "How disappointing that you cannot go with the army."

My son nodded. He did not speak. From long experience, he knew that talking would bring on anther attack. Worn out from his nightlong fight for survival, Mahlon fell asleep beside Chilion near the fire. The grip of fear on my throat lessened with each normal rise and fall of his chest.

"God of Israel, forgive me. I let my fears infect my son until he was ill." Overcome by guilt, I whispered a plea toward the vacant tabernacle. "Spare my son. Bring my husband back to me. I did not know. I am so afraid."

Hephzibah returned to find me still kneeling beside my son in prayer.

"Sister, Joshua has promised that our army will triumph. Do not worry." The young woman patted my arm. "Elimelech will return. So will Abrahim."

"Yes . . . no . . . it is . . ." I stopped just before blurting out my secret. There was no one I could trust with my dread of the Holy One. With effort, I took a calming breath. "I will be fine. My sons will be fine. Elimelech will return."

8

ACROSS THE MILES TRUMPET calls were heard. Everyone faced the south. We could see that small figures surrounded the city. Distance and the size of Jericho dwarfed our men. Suddenly on the wind came a shout. Like ants, the army of God moved against the fortress. The sound of sword-on-sword was not loud enough to carry over the incessant trumpets. Shouts drifted dimly to our ears.

"They are inside the city," Leah announced. "They must be. I do not see the men any more."

"Yes," I nodded slowly. "Look, there is a fire within the walls."

Smoke was rising. Soon, more and more columns of black and gray began to fill the sky.

"They are burning the city as Joshua commanded," Hephzibah sounded almost excited.

"I cannot watch." The sight made me ill.

Even if our men were safe, I could not feel anything but pity for the women and children inside the city who would die in the flames.

I bent over my sons. Chilion breathed normally, and Mahlon appeared to be much better.

"God, help my son," I breathed, hoping that I would be heard and forgiven.

I was still watching my sons when a stir of excitement swirled through the camp. All around were exclamations.

"Look, on the road, someone is coming."

"It is soldiers!"

"That is too small a group for warriors."

"Who can it be?"

"Is it refugees who escaped from the city?"

"I see red turbans." My sister identified the approaching group. "It is the spies. That must be the harlot of Jericho with them. I wonder which one she is."

Curious about the arrivals, I joined my sisters and several other women to watch the approaching people. Soon it became obvious that it was a large family. I saw the spies and their companions escorting several women, a trio of men, and numerous children to the refugee tents erected beyond the camp.

"I remember she hid Salma and Jamal. They swore to save her life," Hephzibah shaded her eyes to see. "You are right Leah! The red turbans are the insignia of the men who were chosen to bring out the woman and her family."

From behind us, Abital spoke. "I am glad that the foreign women are kept outside the camp. The law forbids mingling with those who worship alien gods."

Barely had the newcomers vanished into their tents than a shout turned attention to the road. Toward Gilgal marched the army of Israel. Triumphant trumpets announced the returning heroes.

"I want to find Abrahim." Hephzibah betrayed her fears by the speed with which she ran toward the men.

Leah rushed after her without a word of farewell.

Mahlon awakened at the clash of instruments and cheers. "Mother."

I hurried to his side. The young man struggled to sit up. At last, his breathing sounded normal, even to my fearful ears.

"They are back?" The question set my son to coughing, but the spasm eased in a moment.

"Yes," I affirmed.

"I did not get to fight." He sounded disappointed even as he struggled to catch his breath after another fit of coughing.

"There will be other battles," I reassured my son with a sinking heart. "You will be well. Something made you ill last night. It is not your fault."

All eyes were on the victorious warriors now in the camp. Women joyfully hugged husbands and sons. I stood up to strain for a glimpse of Elimelech and my brother. The milling crowd did not allow much opportunity to spot one man. Then my husband was crossing the space between the crowd and our tents.

"Are you hurt?" I scanned the man for signs of blood.

"There was little fighting." Elimelech sounded disgusted. "All resistance melted away as we scaled the walls. The armed men of Jericho ran like rabbits. See? The city burns as God commanded. The plunder will be offered to God."

I looked beyond the man to see smoke pouring up from the city in the distance. Heavy black clouds dimmed the afternoon sunlight. I could smell the burning wood and other odors I did not want to identify.

"I hope the smoke does not drift this way." A frown furrowed my forehead. "It would make your son cough again."

"Is he well?" A father's concern edged into the deep voice.

Mahlon tried to suppress the cough brought on by the exertion of scrambling to his feet.

"I am fine," he insisted after taking a deep breath.

"He is better," I tried to infuse enthusiasm into my voice, instead of apprehension.

"There will be other battles," unknowingly, Elimelech repeated my assurance. "This was hardly a skirmish."

He gripped the young man by the shoulder.

"Did the walls really fall down?" Chilion squinted toward Jericho.

"They might as well have." "We were able to march into the city with barely a sword thrust. Fear of our God made the people throw down their swords and plead for mercy."

My husband looked again at the smoking ruin that a few hours earlier was a proud city.

"The walls did not fall down?" My younger son was disappointed.

"No doubt they will fall apart when the fires cool," explained his father. "The God of Israel has won a great victory."

Elimelech's comment was repeated by Joshua and the priests when we gathered.

"*I AM that I AM* has triumphed!" Joshua gripped the staff of Moses and raised it above his head in elation.

"Amen, Alleluia, El Elohim Israel!" exulted the priests.

The entire congregation repeated the chant. There seemed to be no end to the exuberance of the people. Joshua spoke only after the cheering died down.

"Fear of the Living God will travel ahead of us. We will conquer and settle this land in the name of the God of Abraham, Isaac, and Jacob. God will receive our offering of the tribute of Jericho tomorrow." His final announcement was greeted by more roars of acclamation before we dispersed.

The celebratory feeling lingered over each campfire. I was relieved that as the evening progressed, Mahlon coughed less and less often. When we sought our beds, the boy seemed entirely recovered. I lay awake listening to the sounds of my sons and husband snoring.

In the night I let the gratitude well up. "Thank you God for hearing my prayer. You spared Elimelech in battle, and you have healed Mahlon. I see that you are a mighty God. Forgive my fears and doubts. I will no longer try to prevent my sons from serving you."

Comforting warmth and serenity filled my heart. I slept dreamlessly.

Hephzibah stopped me in the morning before we gathered at the tabernacle.

"I must be in the women's tent this week," she announced softly.

With a smile, I agreed to her unstated question. "Eglah may stay with me."

Only after she left did I realize that I had not needed the monthly cloths nor visited the tent in over a moon turning. The excitement of the move must have driven the thought from my mind.

"I visited the tent just before the new moon at Shittim," I mused softly. "Then there was the new moon of the Passover after we crossed the river. That is a full cycle and the moon is decreasing again. If my flow does not come with this new moon, I will have missed two cycles."

My heart beat with hopeful anticipation. Perhaps God would send me anther son now that Mahlon was almost a man.

I later could not remember any details of the morninglong ceremony. Piles of tribute were brought forward by tribe until there was a mountain of gold, silver, and bronze. Fine cloth and gems in-

creased the size of the hill. I spent the time calculating and recalcu-
lating the chances of my pregnancy. On my fingers, I counted the
possible birth time of the child.

"The baby will come around the time of the longest night," I decided. "It will be cold. I must be sure to have plenty of blankets. By
then, we should be in a house."

Then my dreams changed to imagining a real home with walls.
I guessed it would be like the ones in Gilgal and Moab. Bricks of
mud and straw were covered with a layer of thick mud. Some of the
wealthier residents had homes with a coating of finely ground limestone that made them white rather than brown. The temple within
Gilgal was painted with many colorful designs. My sister had been
delighted by the vibrant colors and designs on a recent visit to the
city for supplies.

I recalled my conversation with Leah. "The Law of Moses de-
crees no representation of any living thing."

"But look at how beautiful the paintings are," the young woman
insisted.

"We probably should not even look at such pictures," I admonished, even though I could not stop admiring the art work.

"I will have colorful designs on my walls," Leah announced.
"They do not have to be of anything—just lines and circles. It will
be beautiful."

"Who will paint your walls?" Hephzibah entered the conversation.

"Terah of course."

"He will not have time," my sister chuckled. "All the men will be
busy in the fields."

"I will have painted walls." For a moment, Leah looked like
Mahlon when he was pouting.

"It will be a treat just to have walls rather than a tent." My longing sigh distracted my siblings.

Soon we were chatting happily as we made our purchases. Leah
never referred to the idea again.

The ceremony dragged on, but I was content imagining my
home and garden and the baby that I would watch playing in the
dirt. I was surprised when the congregation dispersed. It seemed a

short time as I daydreamed. The sun was moving toward the hills in the west, however.

"The One God must be pleased with so great an offering." I was awed by the number and variety of things piled near the tabernacle.

My husband shrugged. "The priests are pleased. I am sure that God is as well."

My niece, Eglah, helped me spread a sort of feast on the blanket in front of the tent. There was the regular diet of bread and cheese along with beans and newly gathered herbs. A few carrots and radishes purchased in Gilgal completed the presentation with bright color. Hearty appetites made short work of the food. There was nothing left to wrap in cloths for the next day. Elimelech belched satisfaction. Both boys imitated the man.

My husband patted his stomach. "That was good."

We all sought our blankets as darkness settled over the camp. Only the priests remained awake, offering still more sacrifices of thanks to the One God who gave Israel the victory over Jericho.

9

I MET MY SISTERS at the stream early one morning a few days later. "Have you seen the refugees? There are the three brothers and the father of the harlot as well as their families."

"One of the strangers delivered a son." Eglah could not wait to tell her mother the exciting news of what happened while she was secluded.

"Yes, Sarai and the midwife assisted her. It was her eighth child. I feel sorry for her most of all. It would be hard to leave your home and care for that many children. They have to look at their burned city every day." Leah sighed sympathetically.

"Did you know that Sarai has taken the harlot into her own tents?" I whispered the news so that my niece would not hear.

In the distance, I saw Caleb's wife with the foreign woman. She was graceful and taller than Sarai. Her fair skin was very different from anyone I had ever known, as was the small nose. I saw red hair when her veil slipped back. It was rich-looking in the sun, and I was envious of the fascinating color.

"I think she is rather pretty," Leah suggested, "in an exotic sort of way."

"She is welcome because the woman was brave enough to save the spies," Hephzibah added. "It is sad that even her own family does not welcome her."

Leah peered toward the newcomer. "She does not dress like a harlot."

We watched furtively as the woman and Sarai approached. I had to agree that the clothing was not seductive. Except for the striking red hair, she could have been one of us. Sarai said something and the newcomer lifted her veil to cover the flaming locks.

"Can you believe that Sarai welcomed the harlot into her tent?" I wanted my husband's opinion later. "How can Joshua allow such a thing? Caleb is his closest lieutenant. Is it not against the Law of Moses to have a foreigner in our midst?"

"I do not know," the man confessed with a shrug. "Our leaders say Rahab is to be welcomed for saving the lives of Jamal and Salma. I hear that Joshua himself has met her."

"Rahab is honored?" I spoke with distaste. "If she tries to ply her trade in the camp, we women will have something to say."

"Joshua has given the woman of Jericho a new name. She will be Rahab the Faithful," he told me.

"Faithful?" I repeated in bewilderment.

"The woman was faithful to the will of our God, even though she was a servant of Astarte, the goddess of Jericho." The explanation brought up more questions.

"A servant of the goddess?" The conversation was full of surprises.

"Well," my husband muttered, "we have all been wrong. It is true that she ran an inn. It was not a brothel. The priests of Jericho used information from travelers to spy out our plans."

"So this woman is a spy, as well as a priestess of foreign gods?" I still did not see how the new revelations made her occupation any better.

Patiently, the man repeated what he knew. "Even though she was a spy for Jericho, Rahab did not betray our men. Salma and Jamal were helped to safety by the woman. She told them that she knew God had given Jericho into our hands. Joshua and the priests call her faithful because she believed in the One God before we crossed the Jordan. Who knows? Perhaps the Almighty even uses foreigners."

Doubtfully, I nodded. "I guess so."

The news gave me much to ponder. I did not have time to worry about whether the woman was a harlot or a spy. Joshua made an announcement in the morning.

"The Living God will go before us. We will sanctify ourselves to march up the pass to Ai. That city will fall like Jericho."

Our response was bold. "Amen, Alleluia, El Elohim Israel!"

We scattered to our tents and daily tasks. My thoughts were not brave. I was grateful to be alone so I could attack my grinding as if God were under the stone.

In my heart, I railed at my unseen adversary. *How dare you command that my husband and my sons face battle? You ask too much. Do not punish me through them.*

Strangely, it was the memory of the story of Abraham and his son Isaac that finally calmed my rage.

You demanded that Abraham to sacrifice his son. Then you provided a ram instead. Slowly, I turned the idea over in my mind. *Will you protect my sons and husband in the same way? Elimelech says that we are obeying the command. If that is so, you must keep them safe for they are sanctified.*

I fell asleep to dream of my sons turning into the rams of our flocks with their thick, curled horns. My fears returned in the morning when the men assembled. My son stood proudly with the army. I bit my lip to keep silent. Mahlon marched beside his father as the army strode out of camp. I knew he had to go, but when the men were out of sight I fled to my tent.

"God, do not let any harm come to my son. I have let him go in obedience to you." In the shadowed covert, I wept until Abital hobbled in.

"Naomi, stop this grieving. The boy is of an age to join the armies," my mother scolded. "My son has gone as well. If your brother is killed, I will have no status at all. Yet you do not find me sobbing."

"Isaac is healthy and strong. There is no reason for you to fear," I shot back passionately.

The woman tried to offer sympathy. "Daughter, it is a frightening thing to let your son grow up. Men go to war. It is their nature."

"Yes." With an effort, I set aside my fear and emerged from the tent.

The sun was high. Chilion sat disconsolate beside the fire. Absently, the boy poked a stick into the flickering flames.

"Mother, I am hungry," my son complained when he saw me.

"We will have warm bread and cheese with some of our share of the honey from the hives between Gilgal and Jericho," when I did not respond my mother answered.

"Yes," at last I moved. "I will get it."

The reminder of the defeat of the nearby city gave me hope that the coming battle would have the same result.

I busied myself unwrapping a misshapen loaf of bread and un-sealing the pot of honey. "Learning to cook with this barley and wheat is a challenge. It is not like manna."

Chilion did not mind that the slice was not neatly rounded. He slathered cheese and honey on one slice and then another. "This is good."

"When will Mahlon and Father return?" The next day my son raised the question on many lips.

"I do not know," I admitted.

The boy was bored without his brother, even though Eglah came with Hephzibah when we sat spinning. Leah joined us with six-year-old Mattan. Baby Beriah slept nearby as we worked. Mid-way through the third day, straggling groups of men arrived. They were not returning in triumph. Our men were fleeing in defeat.

"We were trapped."

"The men of Ai are strong."

"Arrows rained on us from the walls."

"Only the rocks and trees kept us from greater injury."

Appalled by the reports, we waited for the main body of troops to return. By afternoon, all the men had arrived. Tents were erected for the injured. The dead were laid reverently in front of the taber-nacle. Wails from bereaved wives and mothers filled the air. I was ashamed to feel nothing but relief when I saw Elimelech and Mahlon. Both men were filthy, with dirt caked on their tunics. Grass and twigs tangled in their hair, but no stain of blood was seen. They straggled into camp after nearly everyone else had returned.

"You are back!" Joyfully, I hugged son and husband, too relieved to be angry at their tardiness.

"Yes," growled the man.

"You are not injured!" My eyes scanned the pair.

"No." This time, I noticed that my husband scowled at his son. "We were nowhere near the fighting."

My face must have showed my confusion.

"We will talk later." It was a clipped statement.

I was not sure if he addressed Mahlon me or. The boy cringed away from his father.

As soon as the man stalked away, the young man began to whine. "I am hungry."

"What happened?" Chilion asked while I unwrapped bread to slice for my son.

"It was stupid. I did not get to fight," Mahlon complained through a mouthful of food. "I did not get food at all today. Father said we had to return to camp."

"What happened?" I wanted more detail.

My oldest son shrugged. "I do not know. I am tired. We walked and walked. Then we came back."

With the brief explanation, the young warrior crawled into his blankets. I had to wait until Elimelech returned to get answers. He appeared at sundown. The man refused to address Mahlon. Rage seethed from the figure. The young man lowered his head in a sub-dued fashion. Chilion did not dare approach his father. Both boys crept away to the tent as quickly as possible after snatching their food.

"Your son has made me look the fool and coward," my husband growled finally.

His response surprised me as much as his unrelenting attitude of ignoring his oldest son.

"How?" I was not sure I wanted to know the answer.

"Mahlon is a whining laggard." The harsh indictment was spo-ken with anger.

Before I could argue, the man continued.

"His complaints held up the march until I was ordered to the rear of the column. Even then we fell further and further behind. I decided to try a path that looked like a shortcut to the road above. It turned out to be a dead end into a steep ravine. By the time I dragged your son back to the highway our men were fleeing toward camp. I did not get to fight. Worse, my motives are now suspect. I have spent all this time attempting to justify my actions to Joshua and Caleb.

"Everyone knows Mahlon has been ill." I tried to placate my husband with excuses.

The man was not appeased. "Woman, your son will not be included in the count of soldiers when next we march. I will be in the rear guard as well, until I can prove myself."

I was left alone when he threw aside the tent flap and entered the darkness. Even though Elimelech was angry, I could not resist a quiet prayer.

"Thank you, God, for preserving Mahlon and Elimelech from the fight. Could it be you led them from the path to keep them safe?" I knew that my husband's pride was hurt and hoped that he would soon forgive his son; however, I could not be too upset because my family was safe.

"Someone transgressed the commandment of the Lord at Jericho." Joshua shocked us all with his announcement in the morning. "A man among us has kept something dedicated to the Living God for his own. The man who is at fault will be burnt. All his possessions will also be cast into the fire."

The edict was harsh. I shuddered to think that such a punishment was necessary. It awakened all my fears again.

"Only a harsh God would demand such retribution," I gasped.

Elimelech laid his hand on my shoulder and whispered an explanation. "We must cleanse the people in order to have a victory."

It did not ease my horror. I held my breath as each tribe stepped forward. Achan, son of Carmi of Judah, was chosen.

The man was unrepentant. "I took silver and a fine robe. It was not fair to withhold booty from the soldiers."

Only when the man stood with his wife and children in a small valley beyond the camp did I see bravado turn to fear. Already, his tents and animals were aflame. The men of Judah stood poised to cast stones in order to wipe out the contagion in the midst of the congregation.

A panicked look at the hillside and a final "No" were the last acts of Achan. After the family fell, we all took a turn throwing stones until the bodies were covered. My heart pounded with excitement as rock after rock pounded the cairn covering the bodies.

Joshua called a halt to the barrage with his decree: "The place will be called the Valley of Achor. Here lies buried Achan, who brought evil upon this camp."

I was sickened by my own bloodlust as we walked back down the hill to the camp. My sons were excited by the event.

"Did you see the rock that hit Perez in the face?" Chilion took a kind of gleeful delight in recounting the tragedy. "Blood spattered all over."

"I wish it was my stone," Mahlon, too, was excited. "He used to tease me for not tending sheep. It serves him right."

"Mahlon; Chilion, I do not ever want to hear you say such things," I reprimanded angrily.

"The stones could have been aimed at us just as easily. The God of Israel does not allow fools to live." Elimelech faced his sons. The look he directed at Mahlon was full of condemnation.

"I am sorry, Father." The boy cringed away from the man and hurried to our camp.

"Did you have to be so severe?" I snapped.

In a low tone, my husband shared his fears. "Wife, the lot could have fallen on us, if Mahlon's lagging had been counted as reason for the defeat."

"Oh . . . I . . . oh," the thought left me gasping.

It was a silent camp that ate the evening meal. Elimelech gradually relaxed. He lounged beside the fire just after sunset. This was the husband I loved—not the angry, frustrated warrior of the night before. I almost shared my secret hope. Before I could speak, the man leaned forward to pull me against his chest.

"Come to me," he urged with a kiss and caress that drove all thoughts of secrets from my mind.

I was glad we shared the intimate night. In the morning, Joshua had another announcement.

"We will sanctify ourselves in order to defeat Ai," the general announced confidently. "Our congregation is cleansed from the evil that kept us from victory. All men will consecrate themselves by sleeping before the tabernacle for three days. After the Sabbath, we will march against the city. This time our assault will not fail."

"Amen, Alleluia, El Elohim Israel." The acclamation was loud.

"You will remain with your mother," Elimelech told his son. "You are not ready to act with the men."

"Do not go." Suddenly afraid, I clung to my husband.

"Naomi." Gently the man disengaged my clinging hands. "God goes with us. We obey the Living Lord by this time of dedication."

Three days of prayer and sacrifice left the army of Israel impatient to fight. I stood with my sisters as the troops marched past. Trumpeters and banner bearers led the way past Gilgal to the nearby pass.

"May they all return in safety." I was not sure if my words were a prayer or just a hope breathed after the army.

Long days of no word followed. We tried to keep busy with the daily tasks of washing and baking. Priests took turns offering ceaseless sacrifices that were meant to inspire confidence. As the second and third Sabbaths came and went, I thought they signaled desperation. On the hills, lambs frolicked in the greening pastures, unaware of the tensions in the camp. It was the shepherd boys who first glimpsed the troops.

"They are coming."

"Our men return."

"Are they victorious?"

"I see the dust cloud from many feet."

The news raced through the camp. One of the youngest priests was sent to peer toward the approaching horde.

"They need to determine if it is the army of the Living God," I explained to my mother.

The old woman frowned. "Who else could it be?"

"I see the banners of Israel!" His reassuring shout was greeted with a cheer.

A sudden bustle of activity spared me from answering her question.

"There is Hephzibah," with a brief explanation, hurried to my sister's side.

She held Beriah. Together, we pressed close to the line of priests arrayed in welcome.

"They have returned at last." Rather unnecessarily, I stated the obvious.

"What could have taken so long?" Now that our men were near, Leah could voice her nervousness when she joined us.

"There must have been a lot of booty to divide," Hephzibah guessed. "I told Abrahim to bring me a fine gown."

"I asked for a jeweled comb," admitted Leah. "What did you want?"

"I forgot that the soldiers got to keep the spoils this time." With a shrug, I sighed. "Maybe Elimelech will bring me something anyway."

Now the column of men was close enough that everyone could see the tribal banners. Trumpet calls from the returning heroes were answered by ram's horn blasts.

"Amen, Alleluia, El Elohim Israel!" Loud chants from the troops were greeted by our treble response.

The army fanned out through the camp. Each man sought his mate. I glimpsed Isaac hurrying toward our mother's tent and sighed with relief.

"Naomi." At Elimelech's call, I spun around.

My feet left the ground when the man lifted me in his arms.

"You are safe!" Just to be sure, I tried to examine my husband when my feet found the ground again.

"Not a sword touched me," he affirmed. "Israel has won the way to the highlands. We marched all the way to Shechem and offered sacrifices on the altar build by Jacob. The land lies before us!"

Belatedly, I glanced back when we were nearly at our tent. Leah and Hephzibah were walking toward their tents. Both my brothers-in-law were safe and uninjured as well.

"We suffered few losses," Elimelech saw my worried look. "Those that were injured will be cared for. The dead were buried in the sacred ground at Shechem."

"The dead?" Sadly, I repeated his words.

A grim look briefly passed over the bearded face. "We had a few men struck down. Thanks to Caleb's plan, it was only a few." Then he grinned and teased, "Our family is safe. Leah has her gown, and

Hephzibah a fine comb. My wife did not ask for anything . . . Perhaps she did not want a gift . . ."

I waited when the man paused.

"Still, I found this for her." With the air of a conjurer, a layered gold chain with many bangles appeared from a pouch on the sword belt.

"Oh . . ." I could not find words to express my delight. It was a gift for a queen.

"Perhaps you do not like it." With a mock sigh, Elimelech started to coil the necklace into his hand.

"No!" My hand caught his. We held the gift between us.

"What do I get for such a prize?" Still teasing, my husband grinned and bent for a kiss.

"I will tell you my secret." I glanced at the man from the corner of my eyes.

In the past weeks, I had become sure of my pregnancy. My sisters guessed, but I refused to admit the truth to them.

"Do you have a secret?" Elimelech draped the heavy jewelry around my neck.

Briefly, I wondered if it was some woman's dowry and where she was. Then I brushed the guilty thought aside.

"What is your secret?" the man repeated.

"I will tell you . . . later," I teased in my own turn.

A downcast look appeared. I giggled because my husband looked like a woebegone puppy.

"Very well, I will tell you now." Suddenly, I wanted to tell this man that he would again be a father.

Elimelech drew me against him. I had to lean back and look up to see the bearded face.

"I am . . . you are . . . we will—" I had to start over. "You will be a father again, when the cold days begin to lengthen."

Amazement and then delight shone in the eyes looking down at me.

"I am sure." With a firm nod, I attempted to erase any lingering doubt.

"Soon after the longest night?" he asked in awed tones as he bent to kiss my forehead.

When the man raised his head with a faraway look, I hesitantly asked him, "Are you happy?"

"You make me very happy," the reply was sealed with another kiss. "Our son will be born in this Promised Land. He will not know the nomad's life. I am most blessed."

"Our child will play in the yard of a real home within a town. You will have your own rich land." Secure in my husband's arms, I joined his dreaming. "Mahlon and Chilion will help till the fields. We will not know want."

The man nodded, and his lips brushed my hair. "It is true."

ॐ 10 ॐ

ONLY A SABBATH LATER, distraction came in the form of three dusty visitors. Rumors raced through the camp.

"I heard that they traveled for a long way."

"The bread with them is dry and hard."

"They must be from another country."

Joshua and the leaders met with the trio. The men sought a treaty of peace. After a night of feasting, a covenant was ratified. Laden with fresh bread and on rested donkeys, the visitors left with the morning light. A new report set whispers in motion.

"Did you hear?"

"Rahab says that the men were from Gibeon."

"That is only three days travel from here."

"Joshua was tricked by the emissaries."

Everyone in the camp was outraged.

"The men of Gibeon will be taught a lesson." Elimelech was angry, although he was not the one tricked.

Our army marched up the pass to punish the town. A week later, they returned.

"Forever will the men of Gibeon be servants of the children of Israel. The people of the town groveled and begged for mercy which Joshua granted for a price," my husband reported to me. "We agreed to protect them, if it is ever necessary. They are a town of wine-growers. I do not think they will need protection. Who would attack such a place?"

Too soon, we learned that the enemies of the sons of Jacob were using Gibeon to draw out the army. A desperate appeal sent our men to their defense. I was not happy to see my husband march away. The women were left to plant and harvest the gardens. Young boys tended the flocks. Only the old and infirm men remained in the camp. Summer was ending when the troops finally returned.

"The chiefs of the south are defeated. The God of Moses and Joshua fought for us. Joshua buried the leaders in the cave at Makkedah. They chose that as their hiding place. It became their grave," Elimelech announceed grimly.

"How did the Lord fight?" I was curious about his vague statement.

"Great hailstones came from heaven. Many men were destroyed." My husband spoke grudgingly, almost afraid to tell the events. "The sun and moon stood still over the Valley of Aijalon until Israel had victory. Joshua said that the Amorites will never again trouble us. There has been much death."

He would not tell me anything more of the fighting. I worried about the new lines and bits of gray in my husband's hair. The battles were taking a toll on all the men. An assault to the north was undertaken against another alliance of chiefs before we had peace. I fretted at Elimelech's absence.

"Why are the men gone at this time?" I complained to my mother. "Joshua has left the women to harvest the crops."

"We must deal with the threats, or we will never be safe." Her reply was similar to what my husband told me before he left.

Still, I sighed. With my growing belly, I tired easily and did not relish the idea of the harvest work.

To my sisters, I confided, "I do not remember being so listless so early in my previous pregnancies. There are still at least four moon turnings before the birth."

"Let me do your share in the vineyards," Hephzibah suggested. "If you watch Beriah, I will be able to do twice as much work."

Happily, I agreed to her suggestion. "I would love to play with your son."

The baby was beginning to crawl. He was interested in everything. I was kept busy keeping my nephew out of danger in his explorations. Before long, other children were left in my care while their mothers joined the tramping of the grapes. I watched from the shade nearby. The young women stopped their work to nurse the babies and then returned to the task. It was fascinating to watch the juice run from the huge barrels into smaller vats. The men of Gilgal collected juice. Through some secret process, the liquid became a wine prized in the area.

Our men returned in triumph. Joshua made the announcement we all longed to hear.

"Arise, O Israel! Behold, the land promised to Abraham, Isaac, and Jacob is our possession. From the Negev to the Sea of Chinnereth, and from the Jordan to the coast, God has given us our heritage. We will go in and settle as Moses the Prophet foretold."

He had to pause for the cheers that rang out. I was sure that it could be heard as far away as Moab.

"Each tribe will be given the area outlined by the Deliverer." The graying leader grinned at our response. "Cities of refuge will be established. Indeed, they are being designated now by those give the task of mapping the country."

One event caused great discussion around the camp. Rahab, called Faithful by Joshua, was betrothed to Salma. The young man was one of the spies.

"Is it right to have a foreigner marry an Israelite?" I asked Elimelech when the announcement was made.

"Remember, the woman is no longer counted as a foreigner," he answered. "With her brother and his family, she was made a member of Israel."

My mother entered the discussion. "Moses himself had a Kushite woman as wife."

"That is true," Elimelech nodded.

"There was gossip then, too," mused Abital. "It died down after Zipporah accepted the girl."

"This woman, Rahab, has led a good life among us," my husband added, thinking out loud. "I have heard from the injured men that her touch and herbs healed them quickly."

"So you think this marriage is good?" I wanted a definitive answer.

"What I think does not matter. Joshua and Eleazar have agreed to it." My husband shrugged. "I see nothing against it though. The wedding will be after the harvest, before we begin to settle the land."

I had to be content with the response. When Salma took Rahab as bride the entire congregation bore witness.

"The wedding was lovely," I reported to my mother. She stayed at her tent, rather than joining the crowds.

"I am sure it was not any better than the marriages of my daughters," the old woman insisted proudly. "You are fortunate in your husbands."

We smiled at her reminder that we were all loved by our husbands. Tears brimmed as a wave of sorrow followed quickly.

I voiced my thought, "We will soon be separated. My sisters will be going to their homes."

"It is the way of the Lord." Abital took my hand in her gnarled and roughened ones. "We must trust in God."

Even though I nodded, I inwardly railed against the God who separated me from my family. *You killed my father. Now my sisters will be taken from me. Soon Isaac and Mother will also be gone. I know if I fail to obey, you may strike Mahlon and Chilion instead of me.*

I was six months into my pregnancy when Leah and Hephzibah set out for their new homes. They were in one of the first groups to leave the encampment at Gilgal. The people of the tribe of Benjamin planned to settle in the area of Bethel.

Leah held me and cried. "It is three days from here. I do not want to leave you. I may never see your child. God grant that he is healthy."

"I am sorry that I will not be here for you," Hephzibah whispered as she hugged me. "May your son be strong."

"This is a good time to move into the land," Elimelech told me. "They will be settled in time for planting and before the snows come."

Isaac and my mother left soon after. Isaac would live in Shechem because of our mother's ties to the tribe of Manassah. Elimelech was of the tribe of Judah. We would settle in Bethlehem near the tomb of Rachel.

"You will find a lovely woman who will make you happy," I told my brother. "I am sorry that I will never meet her. May the Living God give you many sons."

The man surprised me with a fierce hug. "Naomi, I will miss you."

"Take care of our mother." I glanced at the old woman.

She looked slightly forlorn as she accepted the farewells of Mahlon and Chilion.

With an effort, the woman forced a smile. "My daughter, may your sons grow to be blessings. May the child in your womb be strong and healthy."

I watched the small caravan disappear through a mist of tears. Elimelech laid one broad hand gently on my shoulder. I felt his comfort and turned to bury my face in the warm robe he wore. When I looked again all that remained was the drifting and settling dust raised by the feet of humans and animals.

"I will never see my mother again. She will die without me at her side to close her eyes." My voice choked, and I hurried away to grieve in solitude.

Daily, more and more families left to find homes. The tribes of Dan and Issachar set out before the Sabbath.

"There are so few left." I looked around at the shrinking encampment before the sun set to begin the holy day.

Finally, my husband gave me the news I anticipated. "We will leave at the moon rising. Samson and Salma are leading our caravan."

"They are good men." I was comforted by the fact that at least one of our leaders knew the land well.

Salma had traveled the length and breadth when mapping and planning for the settlement. He was one of the men who established the cities of refuge where an accused person could seek sanctuary until the case was decided by the priests and elders. Samson was uncle to both Salma and my husband. Nashon, Salma's father, was the oldest son of Amminadab bar Ram. Elimelech and Samson were the other children of his first wife, Esther.

"I have much to do in the next few days," I told Elimelech. "The next Sabbath will see the new moon. There is bread to bake, our clothing must be rolled, and the tents prepared."

"Mahlon and Chilion will help me separate my beasts from the larger flock." The man interrupted with his own list of tasks. "The animals that are going will be pastured on the south side of Gilgal."

It was a busy time. The morning of our departure was cold.

"Drink this." I handed my sons goat's milk for the morning meal.

They yawned after gulping down the creamy liquid.

"Hurry up," Elimelech called us.

"Blessed be the God of Israel who has given us rest. May the families of Judah prosper in the Promised Land that you go in to possess," Joshua spoke the same words to our group that each previous caravan heard.

"Remember the commandments of the Lord our God. Do not worship the gods of the people around you. Keep holy the Sabbath of the One Lord and respect the dignity of all," Eleazar admonished.

With a flourish, incense was cast onto the brazier. Sweet-smelling smoke billowed up.

"You are a holy people, chosen by *I AM*. Remain faithful. The Living God will bless you. Fail in obedience, and the Lord will turn away."

I shivered, but it was not from the cold. Dread of fulfilling the demands of the God of Moses rippled through me.

How can we hope to obey all that the law commands? I did not dare speak the thought aloud.

I glanced around guiltily, half-afraid that someone might read my mind. My gaze rested briefly on the wife of Salma. An almost ecstatic look was on her face. Her lips moved in prayer. I felt a jealous twinge. The woman of Jericho trusted in the God of Israel. During the long days when the army was at war, the foreigner encouraged us.

"The God of Abraham, Isaac, and Jacob wants to offer blessing to you," she insisted. "Has not the hand of God been with you? The Holy One provided food. Your garments did not wear out in all the years of wandering. Your God will not abandon you now."

Rahab's words sounded like empty prating. I tried to ignore her.

"How can a foreigner understand the will of God?" I asked my sisters.

Now Leah's answer came to mind. "Maybe the woman sees a different aspect of God. She has not learned all our laws. Perhaps there is truth in her words."

The tall woman looked serene, while my own thoughts and heart raged in turmoil of confusion and fear.

"Amen, Alleluia, El Elohim Israel!" The chant warned me that I missed hearing yet another blessing or admonition.

My face flushed. It must have been the final farewell. Samson and Salma bowed toward Joshua and the tabernacle. The pair faced the road past Gilgal to the hill country. We lifted our packs to follow. In a bleating of sheep and tramping of feet, we set out.

"This is so exciting!" I heard little Miriam giggle.

Rahab smiled at the child. "Do you want to walk with me?"

"Mother, may I?" The eager question received a nod of assent from Tamar.

The young mother was busy with six other children and an infant in her arms. Mahlon and Chilion walked behind me as we fell into line. The flocks were driven at the end of our caravan. At first, we walked close together, but soon the dense column turned into a snaking line. Far ahead, I could see Salma and Samson scouting the way. My sons trudged more slowly with each step.

"Mother, this hill is too steep," complained Chilion.

His brother added, "My feet hurt."

"We are all out of practice since living at Gilgal." I tried to be encouraging.

Elimelech frowned when Mahlon dropped his pack. "Keep up."

"There is too much to carry," the young man grumbled.

Although I tried not to show it, the whine grated on my nerves. I saw Rahab glance back. Embarrassment spurred me forward.

"Come on, let us see who can make it to that outcropping of rocks first." As I had when the boys were young, I tried to make a game out of our travel.

For a little while the ruse worked. My sons' budding manhood would not let me win so they forged ahead each time I offered a challenge. The sun was high when we paused for water and a bite of food.

"I cannot walk another step." Chilion flopped onto his pack in the shade of a small tree.

"The youngsters will watch the flocks so the shepherds can take a break and eat." Samson summoned the children. "All you have to do is keep the animals from straying up or down the hills."

It sounded like a simple task.

"Elimelech, are your sons going to avoid their duty?" The stern question brought angry color to my husband's face.

"Mahlon, go with Chilion to watch the sheep." The tone showed that only obedience would be tolerated.

I opened my mouth to argue but shut it again, realizing that the man would not appreciate further embarrassment.

"Go." I nudged Chilion with my hand when he hesitated to follow the other boys.

Mahlon frowned and plodded after his brother.

"I am not a child," I heard his low complaint.

When the troop of small shepherds was gone, the adults were able to rest tired feet and repack some of the bundles. Our peace was short-lived.

"The sheep . . ."

"Running away!"

"Stop them!"

Cries from the children alerted us to a problem. Every man sprang up and ran toward the flocks. The animals were no longer grazing happily. Instead, they were running blindly toward an incline and ravine.

"Is it a wild animal?"

"What frightened the flock?"

"Are the children safe?"

Only one of the questions was easily answered. Boys and girls ran to their mothers, wide-eyed with fear.

Mahlon and Chilion slunk to my side.

"What happened?" My concern increased when neither boy would meet my eyes.

Two pairs of shoulders lifted in twin shrugs. "We do not know."

We watched as slowly and barely in time the stampede turned from the dangerous drop off. Gradually, the animals were herded back to the area near the camp. Gentle calls and whistles from the shepherds calmed the creatures. I was relieved when they began to graze and drink from the stream.

The men were grim when they returned. Salma was frowning and talking earnestly with his uncle. Elimelech strode toward me. Both Mahlon and Chilion backed away from their father's look.

"Your sons have caused the entire herd to panic and run," my husband hissed low and angry.

"How?" I did not have time to hear an answer.

"Elimelech," Samson called above the murmur of the people. "Bring your sons."

Talk ceased as everyone held their breath. With a rough hand on their shoulders, Elimelech propelled his sons to stand in front of our leader.

"Even the smallest child knows how easily sheep are startled." The big man frowned at Mahlon and then at Chilion. "Yet one of you was thoughtless enough to throw a stone into the midst of the flock."

Samson waited for a confession. The silence stretched out. I gripped my hands together in front of my mouth. Even so, I could barely prevent a cry of dismayed denial.

Finally the leader spoke. "Have you nothing to say?"

Mahlon squirmed in his father's grip and looked at his brother.

"He did—" my older son began.

"Do not lie. You did it," Chilion interrupted angrily.

"Did not!" The denial was fierce.

A futile fist was aimed at his brother. If Elimelech had not been holding his sons, a fight would have erupted.

"It does not matter which of you is responsible." Samson looked more sad than angry. "Your actions have cost us the rest of this day's travel. I have the right to send you back to the camp for Joshua to deal with."

Elimelech frowned, and his eyes narrowed into slits. I saw his nostrils flare when he stared at his sons.

After a moment of silence, our leader continued. "Salma has asked for leniency."

"As the one who has born the loss of a ewe, I offer pardon," the former spy spoke up.

My heart pounded at the realization that my sons had caused the death of one of the animals belonging to Salma. The man was important and to be reckoned with. His friendship with Caleb, lieutenant to Joshua, was well-known.

"The guilty ones must still be punished." Samson looked from his nephew to my sons and husband. "We are family. Elimelech, your mother was my sister. Amminadab, my father, is grandfather to both you and Salma. It would be unfair to burden Joshua with such an issue."

I held my breath. Everyone in the group leaned forward to hear the verdict.

"Mahlon and Chilion, you will gather wood for the fires we need this night. That is your assignment every night on this journey." Samson took a deep breath and added, "You will walk at the end of the column of march, and you will carry the packs of the shepherds."

The punishment sounded harsh until I considered the alternative was to return to the encampment at Gilgal as exiles from Elimelech's only kin.

"Go and collect wood for our fires. We must camp here tonight. There is not light to continue up the road to a more comfortable spot. The animals are weary as well." The big man pointed to a grove of trees not far away. "We will need ten good bundles for cooking fires and watch fires."

Salma handed an ax to Mahlon and a rope to Chilion. Elimelech propelled his sons toward the trees by the grip on their arms. Then he strode out of camp in the opposite direction. The pair disappeared into the woods across the highway. They did not return for so long that I grew worried. With a glance around to be sure no one was watching, I slipped away from the camp to find my sons.

"It is your fault," I heard Chilion before I saw the boys.

"You dared me," a defensive reply was followed by the sound of fists on flesh.

I hurried forward to intervene.

"Boys, where is the wood?" I did not see any piles of branches for our fires. "Samson is expecting you to bring fuel for cooking."

"He is a mean old man," complained Chilion, wiping a bloody nose on the end of his tunic.

"This is really hard work," agreed Mahlon in a whine. "We have to bring ten loads, too!"

"What you did was wrong." I tried to be rational despite my frustration. "We are fortunate that Salma is willing to let us stay with the group. He could have sent you to Joshua for punishment."

Mahlon still pouted. I felt disappointment and anger building in me. Firmly, I suppressed it and tried encouragement.

"Come on. The sooner you get the job done, the sooner you can eat." I hoped that holding out the promise of a meal would inspire them.

"We have to do it," Chilion groaned resignedly. He began to scavenge for fallen branches.

"Look, there is a big dead tree trunk." I pointed across the open area in the center of the grove. "Mahlon, with your ax, you can cut that into smaller chunks for our fires."

"I suppose so." the young man plodded to the log and began to hack at it.

Slowly, the pile of wood grew. Chilion dragged a load to camp and returned for another. I helped pull dying branches from the trees. Before the sun was ready to disappear behind the hills, all the wood was piled and ready to carry to camp. I gathered a load in my veil.

"I must begin the meal for your father. Bring the rest of the logs, and you will be done." A trickle of sweat ran into my eyes.

I hoped I did not sound as tired as I felt. The baby barely stirred. I worried that he was tired as well. Mahlon and Chilion were trying to tie all the remaining wood together when I left the trees.

Feeling alienated from the rest of the travelers, I built my small fire near the edge of the camp. Nearby was the stream that ran down the mountain and fed into the brook by Gilgal. I took time to splash water on my face and wash away the dirt and bark that was evidence of my activity among the trees. Then I filled a small pot with water. Into the pot, I put vegetables. With the flat bread I brought, the thin broth would make a decent meal.

Elimelech arrived as the sun disappeared. "We will join in the prayers."

I followed the man to the circle. Samson offered praise and thanksgiving to the Living God. Each family turned to their meal.

"Tomorrow will be better." I tried to encourage my family. "The first day of travel is always the worst. You have said so yourself."

Elimelech ate in silence. He barely looked at his sons. Mahlon and Chilion sat sullen and subdued. Each of us chewed our bread, lost in thoughts of the day. When I lay on my blankets looking at the stars above, I felt a tear run down my cheeks. Quickly I wiped it away.

Have I failed again? The query was not voiced aloud. *How can we hope to settle this land if we cannot fulfill all that you expect of us? My family is outcast because of an accident. My sons are punished for their deeds. Elimelech is humiliated. Why must I suffer the shame?*

I fell asleep still questioning the heavens. Morning light awakened us all.

"You will load the remaining wood onto the cart with the tents," Salma told Mahlon.

The young man looked mutinous. He did not move until Elimelech struck his cheek. The blow made my son stagger. I gasped.

"Listen to the man, and save yourself work. Have I raised a fool for a son?" Low and enraged, the man added with a shove for Chilion, "Help your brother."

We set out with the sun lighting the road upward. Mahlon and Chilion struggled to keep up under the double weight of their own and the shepherds' packs. I saw Mahlon stumble and catch himself on a low-hanging branch. My heart ached.

"It is too much," I whispered after glancing back again and again.

"It must be hard to see your sons punished." The compassionate comment caused me to turn and frown at the speaker.

Rahab walked beside me. She looked back at the boys. Chilion was struggling on the incline. The road was now beginning to climb even more steeply. I felt the slope in my back and legs.

When Mahlon stumbled again, I stopped. "I must help them."

The foreigner linked her arm through mine. "It would be better if you allowed them to deal with this punishment on their own."

Even though part of me knew that she was right, I still repudiated the advice. "Wait until you have a child!"

Bitterly, I pulled away from my companion. She looked at me sadly. After a moment's hesitation, she moved up the road. I stared blindly away with my lips drawn tightly together. It did not seem fair that the woman from Jericho had every blessing showered upon her.

"God, you save her from a burning city, but I still wander without a home." I began a litany of my abuse while I stood beside the road. "Then she married Salma and is already carrying his child. I was patient for years before my womb was opened."

The rest of the travelers moved past. I fell into step with my sons. Together, we trudged after the caravan. I carried their bags so that they could carry the heavier packs of the shepherds.

"It is the least I can do." I rationalized my actions to Elimelech when he confronted me at the midday stop. "Their punishment was to carry the shepherds' packs. That does not mean they have to carry their own as well."

"You should be careful." My husband sounded more concerned than angry. "I would not want you to tire yourself too much. It would not be good for the baby."

"I am fine," I insisted, even though my feet and back ached.

When we set out, Elimelech had repacked our bundles. His own was heavier, but mine was lighter. I did not know what he had done with the clothing and blankets of his sons until we stopped for the night. Then he produced them from his own pack.

"Here is a blanket," the man spoke to the young men for the first time since the incident.

Chilion was respectful. "Thank you, Father."

"Thank you." Mahlon was subdued when he accepted the wool covering for the night.

Only when I finally lay down did I feel a stirring from my baby. It reassured me, for I had not felt movement during the long day.

The next day we tramped up and up. The hills were endless. On the fourth day, we paused near the ruin of Ai.

"Bethel is further along this road another few miles," Elimelech told me.

I looked longingly toward the place where my sisters now lived. A great desire to see Leah and Hephzibah welled up.

"Can we not stop there for the night?" I wondered.

My husband shook his head. "We turn south."

"Would it be so bad to camp near Bethel?" Rahab surprised me with her question. "I would like to see the altar my grandfather tended."

"I am sorry. It is a difficult climb and would be dark by the time we arrived." Salma slipped an arm around his wife's shoulders. "We will camp here at the fork in the road. Tomorrow we must reach Jerusalem."

"I understand." The woman gave a disappointed sigh but turned to her evening tasks.

"I will send a boy to Bethel. Perhaps your brother will come to meet us here," her husband offered.

He was rewarded with a radiant smile. When the woman looked up, her veil slipped back to reveal the always-unexpected red hair. Perez was the only one of Rahab's brothers who settled among us. He accepted the invitation to live at Bethel. His grandfather had kept the flocks dedicated to sacrifices in honor of Jacob's long-ago visit to the city.

"He hopes to learn if the God of his grandfather is the same God of Israel that he has now accepted," Elimelech explained when the man and his family set out with the families of Benjamin.

"It is not fair," I muttered slapping bread onto a tray as darkness gathered. "That woman has everything. Elimelech did not even think of having Daniel inquire about my sisters. Even if they cannot come, it would be nice to have word of them."

With a frown, I watched the son of Abel run down the road toward Bethel.

We all gathered at the fire in the center of the camp. Over the trek, we had evolved from the use of individual cooking fires to one central source for cooking and heating. The strangeness of the land encouraged us to group together. I was secretly happy to have only one fire. It meant less work for Mahlon and Chilion.

"Jerusalem has markets. You will want to purchase food supplies," the scout explained after we ate. "We will camp at the gates tomorrow. The following morning, all can visit the bazaars."

"We are almost to the end of our journey," Samson announced. "We will remain at Jerusalem for the Sabbath and leave the city with the next dawn. Before evening we will arrive in Bethlehem."

I found myself clapping with joy along with everyone else.

"In Jerusalem, you will see the great threshing floor of the Je-

busites. The harvest festival is reported to be an unmatched orgy of
Canaanite worship," Salma remarked. "We will use the smaller
threshing area in Bethlehem. In that way, none of us will be enticed
by the ways of the people around us."

"It might be interesting to see the festival." My whispered wish
was motivated by curiosity.

Elimelech frowned and hissed, "It is not the harvest time."

"I know that." My teeth ground together in irritation.

Samson pointed to a movement at the edge of the camp. "What
is that?"

Each man gripped his sword or dagger. Daniel bar Abel trotted
into the camp.

"Perez bar Hamash could not come," the boy reported. "He told
me to say, 'May the God of Israel bless you, my sister. I have reclaimed the altar of our grandfather, blessed be his memory.' He
gave this to me for you."

We all leaned forward to see what the gift was. I was disappointed to see a stone. Rahab, however, closed her hand around
the item.

"It is the one thing our mother had from her father." Tears
choked the woman's voice. "He gave her a stone from below the altar at Bethel so she would always remember her home. My brother
found it among her treasures when she died. He kept it in honor of
our grandfather."

I was not the only one to be openly listening to the explanation
meant for Salma.

"Perez sent this to me as a token that he no longer needs any reminder of the past. He has made peace with the One God." Although Rahab wept, I was sure that she was happy.

During the morning walk toward Jerusalem, I joined a discussion about Rahab's brother. The woman herself rode a donkey provided by Salma because of her pregnancy, although she usually
preferred to walk.

"I wonder what Rahab meant about the altar," I heard Tamar
muse to her daughter.

Miriam shrugged, more interested in the flowers she gathered
than her mother's curiosity.

"Did you know her grandfather was some kind of priest at Bethel?" the wife of Abel asked eagerly.

"What god did he worship?" I drew close to ask.

"She claimed it was the God of our father Jacob," Tamar replied.

"Jacob did visit Bethel," I remembered the story. "He slept on a stone."

"I know!" Little Miriam bounced up and down in excitement. "There was a ladder to heaven and angels."

We all smiled at the child's enthusiasm.

Again, a bit of a story surfaced in my memory. "It was at Bethel where the patriarch received the name Israel."

Tamar frowned. "How can a foreign woman be related to a priest at Bethel?"

It was the wife of Abel who supplied the answer. "He was one of the local elders charged with keeping the memory alive."

Our conversation drifted into silence when we topped a rise. Across a broad valley, we saw a city. Jericho had been inspiring with her thick walls. Jerusalem was smaller, but dominated the vista from a plateau.

"There is the threshing floor," Salma told Rahab. He pointed across the valley at the flat expanse on one end of the hill.

"It is huge." The woman sounded awed. "Even the threshing ground at Jericho cannot compare to that place."

"The city is not so large," commented Abel.

"It is the largest in the area," Salma explained. "The markets are busy. We will find the supplies we need there more easily than in Bethlehem itself."

"What are we waiting for?" Elimelech was impatient. "If we hurry, we can reach the gates before they close."

Samson scowled. "Our camp will be outside the walls. There is no need to rush the animals. However, we will move on."

At his signal, we began the descent. The valley held patches of green grass even so late in the season. Our sheep were allowed to graze slowly toward the city.

"From here, we climb up to the gates," Salma pointed out that the road led upward.

Beyond us was a camp already occupied by other travelers.

Camels and donkeys used by traders were tethered outside the camp itself. The number of beasts amazed me.

"There must be a large market here," I told my sons. "We will find salve for your shoulders and feet."

The heavy packs and long miles had produced blisters not just on their feet, but mine, as well.

"I will be glad to put down this load." Chilion had been less demanding in the past couple of days.

"It is not fair," Mahlon still grumbled. "I wonder if we have to gather wood tonight."

"You will continue your punishment until we reach Bethlehem," Elimelech answered before I could offer hope that there might already be wood available.

The flocks were herded into a field not far from the city. I saw Samson and Salma negotiating with an official at the gate. A sack of silver changed hands.

"I wonder how much it cost to have grazing and a place to sleep," Chilion spoke my question.

Mahlon returned to his whining refrain. "Too bad they did not buy wood."

"Look, there are branches right here." I pointed to a mound of wood between the camp and city. "It looks like that is where everyone is getting their firewood."

As I spoke, a boy about Chilion's age walked to the pile.

I nudged my son. "Go and ask him."

The hope of getting out of their appointed task was incentive enough for Mahlon to rapidly approach the stranger.

I rubbed my back as I watched the interchange. The young man shrugged and nodded when Mahlon pointed at the pile of wood.

"We will camp along the stream." Samson pointed to a trickle of water near our sheep. "There is grazing and water. We will be away from the main body of the traders."

"That is good." For once, Elimelech seemed to approve of our leader's decision.

"I am glad to be away from those staring men," I overheard little Miriam tell her mother in a loud whisper

She pointed to a camp of dark-skinned men whose long hair resembled thick, black yarn. One of the merchants bowed to the child. His teeth gleamed white when he smiled at her.

"Yes, it is better to have nothing to do with foreigners." Protectively, Tamar drew her daughter close and pulled the errant veil over brown curls. Even at ten, the child was dainty and pretty enough to attract interested looks from men wherever she went.

❧ 11 ❧

MAHLON AND CHILION RETURNED with their new friend. Each young man carried a load of wood to the camp.

"May we go with Abdul to see his camels?" Mahlon surprised me by showing an interest.

"Be back before the sun sets," Elimelech agreed after a moment.

"That is not long," the young man started to argue pointing to the sun already starting down to sink out of sight behind the nearby mountains.

"It is enough time to see camels," his father stated ending the discussion.

A slight pout appeared, but he made no further complaints. The trio trotted off toward the main camp. I was torn between concern and surprise.

"Is it safe?" I asked my husband, in the same breath adding, "I am glad that they have found a friend."

"Mahlon and Chilion will be fine if they do not do anything foolish. Your sons have to leave your side eventually." In the words, I sensed criticism.

"I have only tried to keep them safe from disobeying the laws of God," I replied in an undertone.

When I looked up, Elimelech had moved away to talk to the other men of our group. I blinked back hurt tears and joined the women in preparing the meal. No one except Rahab appeared to notice my emotion.

"Is everything alright?" Bending close, the woman of Jericho patted my hand.

I pulled back as though burnt. "I am fine."

It would never do to let this foreigner know that my husband scolded me. I knew that Rahab saw through my pride and understood my response. She turned to help Miriam stir the stew. I kept one eye on the sun and the other on the road from the merchant camp, even while I prepared cheese and onions for our meal.

It was dark when Mahlon and Chilion arrived, panting, in the camp. I was beginning to worry. Elimelech frowned when the boys rushed in. Mahlon wheezed slightly from the excitement and running.

"Abdul's father has six camels and four donkeys. He is rich," Chilion reported. "One of the camels spit at Mahlon. Abdul says it happens to him all the time."

"It was a big slobbering thing." My older son grimaced. "I liked the donkeys better. They are bigger than ours. Abdul let me pet one of them. He said it was his own beast."

"This is the first time Abdul has gone with his father to Jerusalem. We will see him at the market tomorrow if we look for the booth with the mark of his father. They sell spices and rugs and weapons from the Land of the Two Rivers. Can I get a dagger, Father?" Chilion sounded hopeful.

Elimelech pretended to ignore the question.

"Abdul told us that news of the One God has traveled to the Euphrates and beyond. He said he expected us to be huge giants. Stories of our military prowess surprised even his father." Mahlon breathed more easily now that he was not running.

I pressed gourd full of the thick soup into each son's hand. "Eat your stew."

"Did this Abdul say anything about the armies of Israel?" Salma overheard the last sentence.

"That we are undefeatable." Mahlon gulped down the bite in his mouth.

"He said his father is glad that we turned west rather than east to claim our land," Chilion added. Then he took a huge bite of bread.

"It is good that we are feared." Elimelech sounded proud.

"We must remember that our victories are from God, not due to our own skill." A warning was in the spy's reply.

"It was still our arms that wielded the swords," grumbled my husband.

"The battles we waged were not for gain or vengeance," Samson entered the conversation. "Our hands are made strong in the service of the Living God to claim the land promised to Abraham, Isaac, and Jacob."

"Without God, we would still be a captive people in Egypt." Salma's voice took on an exultant ring. "By the hand of the Holy One of Israel, we go forth in peace to settle in homes."

"I know." Abashed, Elimelech mumbled, "Praise God who has given the victory."

Salma and Samson left to see that sentries were posted against wild dogs or marauding neighbors.

"I still say we had the harder part," my husband told me privately. "The battles were won at the cost of our blood."

Fearfully, I put a finger to my lips. "Do not anger God."

Sometimes in my dreams, I still saw the snakes that killed my father and the other rebels in the mountains of the desert. The man turned away, dismissing me and my fears.

My lips moved in a softly spoken prayer. "Please, God of Israel, do not hold his words against my husband."

My sleep was restless. I wakened when the twining serpents in my dreams opened their mouths to scream at me. The sound was like a trumpet. Then I realized that it was the sentries on the walls announcing the morning. I sat up relieved that the night was over. With great creaking, the gates swung open, and the crowd of men pressed forward.

"Merchants are already entering the city," I mentioned in surprise.

"They want to get the best spots," chuckled Elimelech wryly. "Every trader knows that we will be visiting the market. You will have to watch for unfair prices."

I nodded, even though I did not need the warning. Already, I was reviewing what I needed to purchase for our new home.

Samson reiterated my husband's warning after we ate. "We will visit the city. Some of the merchants will have raised their prices because they know we must buy supplies. Do not let yourselves be cheated by unscrupulous men."

"Does he think we are fools?" Tamar grumbled as we started toward the city.

"My Elimelech said the same thing." I shrugged away my earlier irritation. "I can hardly wait to see the market."

Most of the men remained in camp or with the animals. Mahlon and Chilion were still asleep. I doubted that their father would let them sleep long. I noted that Salma held his wife's hand and helped her over rough places in the road.

"I think he must love her very much," my companion indicated the couple. "It was courageous to approach the priests and Joshua for permission to marry the foreign woman."

"Maybe." I hated to admit the jealousy that crept into my heart watching Rahab laugh at something her husband said. "Of course, it could be that she bewitched him with her foreign arts."

Tamar stared at me, aghast. Hastily, I laughed to make it seem like a joke. "I am sure that he really does love her."

Our small group reached the gate. I looked up, amazed at the height of the opening. Probably three men could have stood on one another's shoulders without touching the top of the entrance.

"We wish to go to the market," Salma spoke to an elder seated just inside the gate.

"Salma of Judah, you are welcome within our gates. May your God prosper your endeavor." His formal reply was accompanied by a lazy salute and gesture to the interior of the city.

Our guide bowed in a *salaam* of homage. "You are most gracious, elder of Jerusalem."

The man moved briskly down the street. He seemed to know where to go. We trailed behind. I tried to see the houses we passed. My impressions were of mud brick dwellings similar to those in Moab and Gilgal.

"Look at the size of that home." I was struck by the three-story building that loomed over its neighbors.

"It is almost as tall as the temple we saw in Gilgal," Tamar marveled.

Little Miriam stopped in the middle of the street to stare. I saw the reason. The market was larger than any I had seen in Moab or any town in the Sinai. Booths stretched beyond us in each direction. The only familiar thing was the booth where we could barter items or trade silver for a counting stick.

"It is good that we brought silver," I remarked when I saw the small amount being given for the merchandise offered by the women of Jerusalem

"Did you see how little she got in return for that handsome blanket?" Tamar was appalled as well.

Salma approached the trader. I could not hear what was said. The conversation went on for several minutes. The man kept shaking his head. Salma held firm.

Finally, the trader threw up his hands in agreement. "You will beggar me!"

"What you may lose in profit, you will gain in blessings from the Most High." The former spy looked satisfied. He gestured us forward. "We will be treated fairly now. This man will trade your silver."

One by one, we drew close to the table. Salma stood nearby. He appeared completely relaxed. He calmly watched each transaction. Once, he coughed and shifted his weight. Hastily, the merchant added another notch to the stick he was preparing. I held the precious token tightly.

Tamar ran one finger down the number of notches on her stick. "I think we got a fair exchange."

"With Salma watching, the man did not dare cheat." I smiled my thanks at our guide.

The noise from the booths offered a counterpoint to our conversation. From all sides came the cacophony of shouts as each merchant sought our attention.

"Buy my rugs."

"Jewels from beyond the Great Sea."

"Freshly ground wheat for sale."

"Damascus leather goods."

"Get your fresh fruit here."

"Vegetables grown in the finest soil."

"Tyrian cloth fit for a princess."

"Local olive oil, best to be had."

"There is so much." Tamar gazed around, stunned by the displays and sounds and smells.

Not far away, I heard Miriam call her mother. "Mama, look at the beads."

Immediately, a wheedling tone entered the seller's voice. "Pretty beads for the pretty lady."

I was glad that I had thought about our needs. Even so, I was overwhelmed by the choices.

I ticked off the things I had decided on. "Grain, oil, wine, salve for blisters, some dried dates, maybe a new blanket or basket, and of course, honey, if there is any."

"Look at this cloth." My companion held up a length of smooth material. It shimmered slightly in the sun.

Our interest was not unnoticed. "The wise lady has an eye for beauty. This is the finest of silk from the lands to the east of Asshur. It is just the color to enchant a husband."

"It is beautiful," I had to agree. Gently, I stroked the cloth and put temptation aside. "I am sure I will not need such a thing."

"Ho, Abdul, how much for this camel's hair blanket?" Behind me, I heard someone call the name of Mahlon's new friend.

Curious, I turned to see the boy I had glimpsed briefly the evening before. Competently, he flipped out the blanket in question.

"See how even the weaving is. You do not see such quality in blankets from the Negev. Only those from the East have such careful workmanship." Professional pride could be heard in the young voice. "My father would have my hide if I let you have this for less than four measures."

I drew closer to observe the bargaining. The customer was not one of our caravan. I assumed he was a local resident.

"One measure and not a notch more. Look here, the dye is uneven," the man held up an edge of the blanket.

"Why, sir that is a natural variation of the yarn. We do not dye our blankets. The wool is too fine to ruin with color." I had to admit that the boy was an expert trader already. He paused just slightly. Then with a sigh he appeared to relent. "I could perhaps lower the price to three measures."

"Three," the customer blustered. "It is not even dyed. How can you justify such prices? I might be willing to give you a little more than one, but never three notches."

"Ah, then it is your loss," Abdul rubbed the blanket against his still beardless cheek. "Such soft weaving cannot be had for less than three. It is a pity, for you would have gotten a bargain."

Seeming to be unconcerned about the loss of the sale, Abdul began to fold the blanket. I watched the customer. He was obviously not pleased with being out-bargained by a stripling. He did not turn away. Noticing that the man still hesitated, Abdul again unfurled the blanket.

"Perhaps you would like to see the product one last time before you decide?" Even without touching the blanket, I could tell it was soft by the way it flowed over the boy's hands. "You are welcome to feel it if you want."

"Three, you say?" Slowly, one hand reached out to finger the lovely tan material. "I will give you two."

"Two . . . it is worth much more." Still the young merchant played with his customer.

I sensed that he would sell for that price. However, the local man was not as certain.

"Very well then, three it is!" He snapped suddenly. "You are no doubt a robber and a thief."

"You are most generous," Abdul grinned at the disdain while carving off three notches. "Will you take this with you or pick it up later?"

The boy held out the folded blanket.

"I will take it now. Likely you would sell it again to someone else and claim I had not purchased anything." It was not clear if the man was truly irritated.

"My father and I are honest. We have no need for such tricks." A proud tilt to the young chin ended the conversation.

I saw a smile spread over the young face when the Jebusite turned away. The boy turned to his father.

"Good job, my son," the cloth merchant nodded proudly. "I, too, have made a sale."

"I bought it." Tamar was at my side. "Do you think Ezra will mind?"

"When he sees you in a new gown, he will forget any anger." I refrained from asking if she could still buy the supplies needed for her home in Bethlehem.

I need not have worried. We were treated fairly by nearly every merchant. At the end of the morning, I walked away from the spice trader when he refused to meet my price.

"There will be other times to purchase nutmeg and pepper," I shrugged.

The man hurried after us. "Surely you misunderstood. The price was for all the weight you asked for. Perhaps it was my accent that led you to think it was for each spice."

"I do not think there is time to discuss it." With my head, I indicated Salma waiting on the street leading from the market to the gate.

"Only a moment while I wrap up the purchases," the small man pleaded.

"Quickly, then," I relented.

"That is the last of it." I dropped my final measure into the outstretched brown hand and accepted three small packets of spices.

"I will seal these in pottery jars I have." With a smile, I fingered the carefully folded in linen squares. "The flavor will stay fresh much longer that way."

"Hurry," Miriam called as she trotted ahead of us.

I took just enough time to tuck the three little packets into my full basket. We hurried to catch up with the others who were slowly starting for the camp. Along the way, we compared purchases.

"The cloth is gorgeous, Tamar," Rahab enthused. "I wish I had seen it first."

"What did you get?" My companion looked curiously at the large bundle that Salma carried.

The woman smiled tenderly at the man who strode ahead of us.

"My husband insisted that we get several pottery jars and a grinding stone." A blush colored her cheeks when she admitted, "He also got me a few trinkets."

I did not enter the conversation, but I was satisfied with my purchases.

ॐ 12 ॐ

THE FINAL LEG OF our journey to Bethlehem did not take long. We skirted Jerusalem. The road led along the valley and then back up a hill south of the city.

"It is an afternoon's walk to our new home." Samson set a brisk pace over the rocky route.

"Look at the sheep," Chilion laughed as he pointed to the small beasts. Instead of lagging behind to graze, they kept pace with our march. "They must know that we are nearly home."

"Sheep do not know anything," his brother mocked. "They are dumb. It is the shepherds who are hurrying them along."

"I saw your friend Abdul in the market," I hastily interjected. "He was selling a blanket to a local man."

"Really?" Mahlon looked interested. "He was not sure if his father would let him help at the market."

"I think his father is glad he did." A smile came to my lips as I remembered the expert bargaining I observed. "He convinced the customer to pay more than I would have."

"Tell us," Chilion asked.

I recounted the sale to my sons. It made the miles go faster. Before we knew it, Salma shouted, "We are almost to Bethlehem. It is just over the next rise."

Our cheer resounded from the nearby hills. We all stepped out eagerly only to stop at the top. Like excited children, we spread out to stare at the goal of our travels. Bethlehem nestled against the hills. Terraced fields, bare after harvest, waited for spring. Sheep grazed among them. No walls surrounded the town. I could see people on the street. Children's shouts drifted to us. Some of the buildings seemed to vanish into the rock behind them.

"Are the houses built into the hills?" I peered at them.

"It looks like some are," Elimelech shaded his eyes to stare at our new home.

"The oldest part of Bethlehem is built into the caves," Salma affirmed. "Newer structures are not."

"I want to live in a cave," Chilion sounded fascinated.

"You would make a wise choice." Our leader grinned. "The cave homes are cool in the summer. However, in the winter they are not easy to keep warm."

I shivered in distaste. "They would have bats and insects."

"Who cares?" My son was eager to try it out.

"We will live in the newer houses," Salma explained, coming to my rescue. "The caves are now used for animals."

"I still think it would be fun." With a disappointed sigh, the boy shrugged the pack into place on his back.

Samson stepped out and led the way. "Let us go forward in the name of God."

We fell into line. My heart pounded in anticipation. We had not gone far before we drew to a stop again.

"What is that?" Miriam asked her mother.

"It looks like a shrine of some kind," Tamar answered.

I strained on tiptoe to see. A cairn stood to the side of the road. Drying flowers and even a few copper bangles adorned the pile of stones.

"Why have we stopped?" Mahlon let his pack fall to the ground.

"An elder of Bethlehem has met us," I stated and indicated the old man bowing to Salma and Samson.

The first words I heard explained the monument. "We meet beside the tomb of Rachel, beloved wife of the Patriarch Jacob."

"This is where Rachel is buried," I whispered in awe to my sons. "We are standing beside a piece of our heritage. Remember that Jacob worked many long years to wed her. She remained barren for years. Joseph was her first son, and she died giving birth to her second child, Benjamin."

"And Moses designated Bethlehem for the sons of Judah,"

Chilion supplied for his brother who shrugged, uninterested in the history.

"Rachel, wife of Jacob, let me bear a healthy son to bring happiness to my husband." Instinctively, I joined generations of women who sought the aid of the well-loved wife of the patriarch.

My mind wandered. I imagined holding my baby and exploring the area. When I listened again, the welcome speeches were complete.

"We will join you." Samson was offering a low salaam to an elder of Bethlehem.

We slowly followed the pair toward the town that would be our new home. I stared around as we entered the village. From doorways, I saw a few women watching. Mostly the street was deserted.

"I wonder where everyone is." Abigail drew close to me.

"It is odd," I agreed.

Salma and his cousin did not appear concerned. I noticed that Abel and Elimelech kept a hand on their daggers. When we reached the center of the town, I understood why the streets were empty. A feast was laid out. Residents, however grudgingly, were welcoming us to their town.

"We will live as neighbors. Our God is the God of Jacob," Samson announced to the gathering. "We come in peace."

Our cheer was greeted with scattered applause from the villagers. They seemed prepared to withhold judgment until a later time, even though the leaders offered welcome.

The feasting went on until evening. I found a seat under a sycamore tree. Earlier, I had seen Rahab resting there. When Salma escorted his wife away from the festivities, I sought her seat to ease my back. Darkness crept down the mountain. Salma and Samson directed each household to their house.

"Come wife," Elimelech ordered when he found me. "We will go to our new home."

It was a short walk. Mahlon and Chilion trailed behind. The house we entered was not large. Out of habit, I stooped to enter, although the door easily cleared my head. I stared at the ceiling over my head.

"The house is sturdy," I commented, touching the mud brick wall.

Elimelech looked around. "We will sleep on the roof except in the coldest weather."

I followed my husband up the outside stairs to the flat roof. A low parapet kept us from falling off. Drain holes cut into the wall would be for the rains, I decided.

"Keep back from the edge," I somewhat nervously cautioned my sons who rushed to look down at the street.

They raced from side to side staring at our neighbors to the south and north.

"Does everyone sleep outside?" I indicated the man and woman watching us not far away.

"It is cooler here," my husband stated. "I will erect a covering, tomorrow. See how some of the roofs have shelters?"

I looked where the man pointed. Nearly every roof had at least a canopy. Some of them even an elaborate room with windows that opened. I saw one that looked like a garden with vine covered latticed walls.

"That would be nice," I had to agree.

Without answering me, Elimelech instructed his sons, "Go bring our blankets."

Almost willingly, the boys ran down the stairs. Soon they were back. I noticed that even though they were panting, their breath did not have the dreaded gasping I feared.

"It will feel very unprotected, lying here so far above the ground." I arranged our mats and blankets close to the center of our roof.

"Soon it will be too cold to sleep outside," mused Elimelech. "I heard from some of the local men that often snow falls within a moon turning of the grape harvest."

"I suppose when that happens, I will be glad to have a house. Right now, it feels strange to be inside," I admitted as I cuddled close to my husband.

"Yes." I felt the man nod in agreement beside me. "I barely re-member the house I was born in. We left Egypt when I was still young. We will need to get used to four walls rather than a hide tent."

He lay silent and then I heard soft snores begin. A duet of snores came from my sons.

"God of Jacob." It seemed appropriate to name the deity by the old name here in this place. "You brought us safely through the desert. Now we are settling into homes, just as you promised. I want to be grateful. It is all very strange. Tents were good enough for Abraham, Isaac, and Jacob. How will we know what is right? What if I fail in some part of the law? Please do not strike down my family for my failures."

There was no answer. The clear sky spread from horizon to horizon, dotted with the same brilliant stars that Abraham observed. I must have slept, because the rising sun wakened me.

"Mahlon; Chilion, get up." My husband was already awake. He was eager as a boy. "We will get wood to make a shelter here on the roof."

I barely had time to hurry down the stairs and roll cheese into flat bread for each one before they headed from the house. They were gone all day. I spent the time trying to understand how to live in a house. Even the round oven in the yard was a mystery.

"Please stay lit," I begged the flickering fire.

Tears of frustration ran down my cheeks when again the little flame disappeared. At midmorning, a strange face peered in at the gate.

"Hello," said my visitor.

I looked up and tried to dry my eyes. All I succeeded in doing was spreading soot on my face from my hands.

"The ovens are hard to manage when you first use them." The newcomer moved forward.

She was a short, plump woman. I guessed that she was younger than me, only because her face was smooth and unwrinkled. My eyes had crow's feet at the corners from squinting into the sun. I recently noticed that my hair was not as glossy as it once was. I expected that I would find a strand of gray before too long.

"Can I help?" When I did not respond, the woman stopped.

"It will not light." The fact was obvious from the pile of barely singed wood in the mouth of the oven. I was embarrassed by the sob in my voice and glanced away.

"They are tricky," the young woman reiterated. "I will show you."

Briskly, she moved to the dome-shaped object that had frustrated me all morning.

"I am Rachel." The information was tossed over her shoulder with a giggle. "It is a common name here in Bethlehem."

"I suppose so." It seemed an answer was expected.

"Now, watch." Plump hands arranged the wood into a cone inside the oven. "You have to stack it like this. Then the smaller wood beneath will catch quickly. By the time the larger pieces are on fire, it is hot enough to sustain the blaze."

I watched the fire spring to life as she spoke.

"With these ovens, you do not cook with flame, but with the heat of the coals," the woman continued to explain. "It is very different than what you must be used to."

"Yes," I agreed with a nod. "It is nothing like an open fire."

"Do you have your bread ready?" My visitor looked around.

I had to shake my head. All my energy had been focused on getting the fire prepared.

"I can help," she offered hesitantly.

This time, I remembered to be appreciative. "Thank you."

"Have you been to the well?" Rachel glanced at the scant water remaining in the nearby jar.

"No," feeling very ineffective, I shook my head.

"How could you?" The woman scolded herself. "That was a foolish question. No one has shown you the way, have they?"

"Um, no." I had no idea where the well was located.

"Use this water to wash off your hands and face." Efficiently, the young woman splashed the stale water into a bowl for my ablutions.

As quickly as I could, I washed my filthy hands and sooty face.

Rachel smiled in a friendly way. "Come, the well is not far. Some say that it was dug by the one you call Isaac, father of Israel. We call him 'The Shepherd'. It is said that he pastured his sheep near here before his sons were born. Esau the Red came through this area on his way to Jerusalem. Of course, you know how Rachel, wife of Jacob, came to bear her son here."

"I saw her grave." Memory of my brief intercession brought a flush of color to my face.

My companion did not notice as she chatted on. "We all ask Rachel the Desired for help at childbirth. She watches over women in their labor because hers was so hard."

In a short time, we reached our destination.

"Here is the well. In the early morning, it is quite a hive of gossip." The woman lowered a bucket down the hole. "Just this morning, we learned that the wife of your leader is from Jericho! We thought everyone died in that city."

I had to smile at the astonished and curious expression.

"Well, that is true," I had to admit. "Rahab and her family survived because of her kindness to our spies. Salma, her husband, was one of them."

"How exciting! To think, we have a real heroine among us!" A bit of awe was mixed with the enthusiastic words.

I was sure that my brief tale would be elaborately embellished by morning as it circulated in the town.

"Let me." Feeling useless, I took the full bucket and filled the water jar carefully.

"Now we can make your bread. The oven should be hot enough soon."

I followed my guide back to the house I could not yet consider a home. For a short woman, she moved swiftly, and I had to walk rapidly to keep up.

"You can tell how hot the oven is by your hand." The Bethlehemite signaled me close. She demonstrated as she explained. "If you can put your hand inside, the coals are not hot enough for anything. If you cannot put your hand close to the opening, the wood is too hot, and you will have to drag some out of the fire with a stick and add fresh sticks to cool the heat."

I held my hand toward the round oven as my mentor spoke. "Feel now. When you can hold your hand this close for as long as it takes to chant 'Abraham and Sarah, Isaac and Rebecca, Jacob and Rachel,' then it is just right."

I looked at the foreign woman in surprise. Her use of the names I had learned as a child was unexpected. "We say the same thing over a campfire to see how close to put the stew pot!"

"We are not so different then." My companion smiled. "Many paths intertwine."

I smiled back. Together, we held our hands close to the stove and recited the names of our ancestors.

"Now we have to hurry and make your bread," Rachel said. "It will have to be flat bread today. There is not time for the leaven to work."

I agreed. It was the work of minutes to mix, knead, and pat the rounds for baking. We put them on a flat tray.

"The part that takes practice is getting things in and out of the oven," admitted my new friend. "The tray rests on the bricks inside. You push the coals to one side, or if you need a cooler oven, pull them out entirely."

I watched as she demonstrated.

"Yes, I see," I nodded and asked. "How do you put things in without getting burnt?"

"The easiest way is to balance the tray on this flat, long slab of wood. My husband made me a utensil with a handle. It is very nice."

Rachel demonstrated by sliding the bread into the oven on the wood paddle.

"Will it catch fire?" I held my breath expecting flames to shoot up. It was reassuring when the bread was safely in the oven without a conflagration.

"No," was the reply. "There is no flame inside to start a fire."

Rachel laid the wood aside. "Now we will cover the entrance."

In amazement, I watched the ease with which the flat stone nearby rolled into place. "I wondered what that was for."

"It does not take flat bread long to bake," the woman commented. "We will have time to slice vegetables if you want to roast them."

"Thank you." I caught the helpful hand in mine for a grateful squeeze. "I would never have figured it all out,"

Ignoring my gratitude, the woman continued her quick lessons. "Turnips and thicker vegetables take longer. Meat is best if done on a spit over an open fire. You can cook it in the oven if it is not a thick piece."

"There is so much to learn," I inserted quickly when she paused.

"I will come for you in the morning to go to the well." A few minutes later, my new friend left with a final admonition. "Remember, the bread will cook quickly. It will be done soon."

It was not long before the smell of toasted bread called me. I rolled aside the stone door. Inside, my first attempt at bread baked in such a way was ready. Using the two sticks, I drew out the tray very carefully. I was almost more excited about my success than years earlier when I made my first manna patties with my mother. It was when Mother was just delivered of my sister.

"Abital, my wife, we will name her Hephzibah." My father was proud of the baby.

"Her name means 'my delight'. My sister is my delight." I proudly share my six-year-old wisdom with everyone. "My brother is named Isaac because we all laughed when he was born."

"Naomi," my mother called me to her side. "You will prepare the Sabbath meal today."

"The Sabbath meal?" I was not sure what she meant.

In my childish way, each day was like every other day, except for the difference in where we camped. In the heat of the summer, we traveled along the foothills to find some grazing for the flocks. More often, we stayed near some low-lying oasis fed by the streams from those rocky heights. During the cold times, we camped until the weather warmed or the pillar moved on.

"You need to help me prepare stew and make a bread of the manna," Mother instructed.

"Won't the manna go bad? Abigail told me that their jar of manna turned to worms once when they forgot to burn the leftovers." I did not want to see that happen. Her horrified story made my shiver.

"Only for the Sabbath may we keep manna overnight." Mother's explanation sounded impatient. "We can do no work on the Holy Day. Our food must be prepared ahead. You are old enough to help."

Lowering her voice and glancing in fearful awe toward the column of smoke and fire lingering near the camp, the woman added, "The Living God gives us the Sabbath command. We obey by preparing ahead. The manna will not spoil in the bread and stew for tomorrow. It is a promise from the great *I AM*."

I followed the woman's instructions but still looked doubtfully at the bread in the morning. It looked like any bread, and when I tasted a piece, I was pleasantly surprised to find that the food was good.

"Naomi, did you think that just because you made it, our bread will not be any good?" my father teased when he saw my amazed expression. "We have been having a Sabbath rest for fifteen years."

My face still turned red at the memory of being caught in my wonder. Now, I carefully piled the warm bread in a basket. I could hardly wait for my husband and sons to come home. They returned with lumber for our rooftop room.

"Do I smell fresh bread?" Elimelech entered the yard sniffing the air in anticipation.

"I am hungry." Mahlon's comment was easy to predict.

"Me, too." His brother hurried through the door.

My husband stopped his sons. "Let us thank the Holy God for this food."

Two pairs of hands dropped away from the bread and cheese. We stood quietly while their father prayed.

"Blessed be the Lord God of all. From the Living Lord comes all food and all life. May this bread feed us and strengthen us for service to the Almighty."

"Amen," we all repeated piously.

Three pairs of masculine hands reached for bread. Cheese was spread over the surface. Grunts of satisfaction were the only sound.

"I used the oven to make this bread," I volunteered the information. "A woman from Bethlehem showed me how to make the fire in it."

"Um, good." Absently, my husband nodded. His mind was elsewhere. "The men of Judah are meeting this afternoon to determine allotment of the fields. Mahlon and Chilion will come with me. I must be certain that our lands are big enough for large fields and growing flocks."

"Will we have our own?" Chilion did not seem excited about the prospect.

"Until you are a man and wed, the land of Elimelech will be worked by us all." His father's answer was not entirely reassuring.

"I thought this was a rich place, and we would not have to do anything," grumbled Mahlon.

"It will be different than raising sheep. We will have to learn to plant and harvest," the man explained. "The local men will help us."

After a brief rest, my husband and sons walked up the street to meet with Samson and the other men in the center of the town. He was satisfied when they returned.

"I did not get the field we first wanted," the man told me. "The ones we got are better because they have been planted already. Our sheep have decent pastures."

"That is good." I was glad my husband was happy.

"The fields are a long walk." Mahlon sat down on a cushion and pulled off his sandals to rub his feet.

"You will get used to it." The statement was a promise of many trips to the land.

"Salma has decreed tomorrow as a day set aside for thanksgiving. It will be like a Sabbath celebration. We will do no work from now until sunset." The order caught me by surprise.

"But . . . but . . . I do not have food prepared or water drawn for a Sabbath celebration!" I was dismayed.

"You can do that after we gather for prayers in the morning," decided Elimelech. "The most important thing is to take time to thank God for our safe arrival."

I barely heard my husband. My mind raced ahead to figure out if we had enough bread for another day. It was fortunate that Rachel and I made so much.

"Maybe I will not have to make bread," I muttered with a frown. "There are vegetables and some fruit left. The cheese will last, as well."

Unconcerned about details, my sons wandered up the stairs to sleep when darkness fell. Elimelech followed soon afterward. I hastily filled the Sabbath lamps with the last of the oil I had before joining my family for sleep. Although I tried to sleep, I roused to remember details.

"The dishes were not scrubbed with sand in preparation." The thought struck me late in the night. I crept down the stairs to complete that task in secret before the men awakened.

Sunrise was welcomed by the call of the *shofar.*

"How often we have obeyed that summons," I mused aloud. "Always before, we have gathered at the tabernacle, but there is no ark here."

Elimelech ignored my comment. "We must not be late."

Heavy-eyed, I plodded after my family to hear Samson offer long-winded prayers of thanksgiving. I turned my head to stifle a yawn with my veil and noticed we had an audience. It looked like every inhabitant of Bethlehem was watching us. My face burned at their curiosity.

"My friends, this celebration is a thanksgiving for God's care of us on the journey. You may draw water and prepare food." Salma announced before we dispersed. "However, in honor of the Almighty, we will do no labor this day in the fields or on our houses."

My husband nudged me. "You see, even our leader agrees with me. You may draw water and prepare the meal."

"I see." Even though I nodded, I could not stop a rebellious whispered statement. "This day will be restful for the men of Israel. The women will do the same number of tasks."

"It is good that we have permission to draw water," I heard Tamar laugh nervously. "I would have needed to break the law. My water jar is empty."

"Mine, too," Hannah agreed.

"It is getting late. Miriam, run and get our jar." The child ran into the nearby house at her mother's order.

I had to hurry back to my house for my water jar. Rachel met me at the gate.

"I waited for you." She smiled. "We heard that you were all meeting to pray. It seemed rude to interrupt by carrying water to our homes and going to the market."

"Thank you." The consideration touched my heart. "I noticed that there were few people in the street."

We walked together to the well. I was happy that I remembered the way. Many of the women of Bethlehem waited their turn to draw water.

Rachel introduced me to her friends. "This is Naomi, wife of Elimelech. She is one of the newcomers to Bethlehem."

"Thank you for your welcome," I heard myself mumble. "These are my friends Hannah and Tamar, with her daughter Miriam."

"We are glad to meet you."

"Pray blessings on Bethlehem for us."

"It is kind of Rachel to bring you."

After a few comments, the women returned to the conversations our arrival interrupted. I filled my jar, uninterested in talk about people I did not know.

"How was the bread?" Rachel asked as we walked homeward.

"It came out well, I thought." With a wry grimace, I added, "My husband and sons did not even notice."

The woman grinned. "Then it must have been good. If not, you can be sure a man will complain."

I laughed with my new friend.

"I will not interfere with your holy day." The local woman left me at the gate. "Tomorrow, if you like, I can show you other ways to use the oven."

"That would be nice," I agreed as we parted.

I found myself already looking forward to her visit while laying food out for our meal. Mahlon and Chilion dozed under a tree. Elimelech leaned against the side of the house. He did not open his eyes as I passed back and forth making final preparations. I felt a sense of contentment. The child in my womb stirred, eager to join the family. After the final prayers, we made our way to the rooftop.

"Have you noticed?" I observed, "Mahlon and Chilion are not having as much trouble breathing now that they are away from the dust and heat."

"That is good." The man yawned.

"Thank you, God of Jacob, for making my sons stronger," I spoke softly to the unseen deity.

Somehow the God of Israel did not seem as intimidating away from the visible reminders of the presence of the Holy One. Even without the pillar to remind us, the ark in the midst of the camp was an ever-present and slightly frightening reminder of the One God. Amid these people who worshipped one that they insisted was the same God, I hoped to find a faith like Sarai, and even Rahab, had.

❦ 13 ❧

IN THE MORNING LIGHT, Elimelech and his sons left the house.

"We will be gone all day," I was told.

As soon as the men were gone, I began to prepare fresh bread. My carefully guarded horde of leaven was brought out. The little pot always fascinated me. I was the proudest girl in the camp the day Mother let me measure out the portion and stir in the flour and water to replenish our supply.

"For every measure you remove, flour and water in the same amount must be returned to the jar, or the leaven will be used up," cautioned Abital. "Measure carefully. Too much flour or water will overwhelm the mixture, and the leaven will die."

Leah used to stick her tongue out in concentration when she was first learning about the precious leaven.

Mother had other warnings as well. "If you do not make bread for several days, you must still stir the leaven and add a little flour and water. Once in a moon turning, add a spoon of honey."

Her words came to me each time used the supply. I could never understand how plain flour and water became a bubbling, almost alive, mixture that made our bread fluffy.

"You already have a pot of leaven." Rachel entered the yard. "I brought you some in case you did not."

I smiled a welcome. "Yes, I have been able to keep this going since my mother gave it to me."

"We were not sure if you would use leaven. . . ." My visitor blushed and tried to cover her blunder. "There are women here who have to borrow a supply regularly because they are not careful."

"My mother taught me how to keep it. We had to be very careful with our jar." Suddenly, I missed Abital very much. A sigh of loneliness slipped out.

"Where is your mother?" My new friend sounded interested.

I gathered my thoughts and summoned a half-smile. "She settled with my brother in Shechem. My sisters went with their husbands to Bethel."

"It would be hard to leave my family. You are very brave." The woman gave me a quick hug.

"I . . . yes . . ." I rapidly blinked back tears, embarrassed to let this stranger see my emotion.

Rachel pretended to be interested in the water jar as she changed the subject. "Let us go to the well. On the way, you must tell me more about Rahab. You said she was from Jericho, yet her husband is a leader among you."

I was thankful for her thoughtfulness. With a final pat of the freshly kneaded bread dough, I covered it with a cloth. When we returned from the well, it would be ready to form into loaves.

With a shrug, I began to explain. "I do not know the whole story. When we were in Moab, Joshua sent spies into your land."

A flush spread over my face. It seemed rude to tell this kind woman that her people were spied on.

"Anyway," I plunged on without waiting for a reply, "they came to Jericho. The men had to find a place to hide. Rahab had an inn."

"A woman ran an inn?" Rachel was surprised.

"It is true. We once thought that it was not an inn. Now everyone knows that she served her gods and the city leaders to ferret out our plans." I paused and added suddenly, "I think she was very daring."

My companion hung on the tale. "I do not understand. How . . . ?"

"How could she be the one rescued?" I finished the question when the woman stopped. "It was because she did not betray our men to the officials of Jericho. She hid them and sent the soldiers away."

"How brave!" An amazed intake of breath came from the small figure beside me.

"Yes," I had to agree, even if grudgingly. "Because of her

courage, the spies promised that when Jericho was defeated she and her family would be safe. Salma was one of the spies. He married Rahab after she joined our congregation."

When I finished my brief recital, we had reached the well. I looked up and saw the object of our discussion filling her jar. The veil covered all but a few renegade strands of the red hair I both admired and coveted. My own brown hair looked dull next to her radiant curls.

Rachel followed my glance and read my mind. "She is very pretty. I can see why men would tell her secrets."

With a grace and confidence I wished I could emulate, Rahab hefted the jar to her shoulder. Someone spoke, and she turned to respond without spilling a drop. Then she was gone, moving up the street toward her own home.

"Was that Rahab?"

"Have you ever seen such hair?"

"She does not look like the rest of them."

"Her husband is very kind."

Around me, comments swirled about the woman until she turned a corner. Then gossip turned to familiar ground.

"I saw Elisa-bet back from Jerusalem?"

"Do you think her father will take her back?"

"He did!"

"That girl needed a mother."

Rachel explained the story on our walk back to our houses.

"Elisa-bet is daughter of old Abner. Her mother died in childbirth, but the man never remarried. He insisted he would never find another like his wife. Elisa-bet is her namesake. She has only seen thirteen summers but took it in her mind to travel to Jerusalem with merchants from the Negev when they passed through recently."

"By herself?" I was shocked that such a thing would be permitted.

My friend nodded. "It was a scandal." A sad smile curved her lips. "The girl has been gone for three moon turnings. Poor Abner went to the city to find her. He came back alone and refused to talk to anyone. All he would say was, 'She will return.' It was heartbreaking to watch."

"How sad. Her poor father must have been grief stricken."

"Then just yesterday, the girl appeared. She held up her head and marched back into town. Of course, no one is surprised that Abner let her come home." Rachel sighed. "He loves her and cannot believe any evil of his daughter."

"How sad," I repeated, not knowing what else to say.

"It is," agreed my companion. "Let us talk of other things. When is your baby due?"

"Well . . ." I paused before answering. "The child should be born around the time of the longest night."

"That is an auspicious time," affirmed Rachel. "Any child born as the days grow longer is destined for great things."

"I hope he will be healthy," I confided to my new friend.

The rest of the morning passed quickly. Rachel watched me prepare the fire and gave more instructions in cooking the bread.

"You learn quickly." She nodded with approval after I removed the warm, round loaves.

There were also lessons in caring for the house.

"In the spring, we plaster all the walls. After the spring rains, a new layer is usually needed. The men are most often busy in the fields, but it is not too hard a job when several women work together." Rachel smiled and added, "Women are good at getting things done."

"I guess so." I was diverted by thoughts of the many things my mother and sisters would no longer share with me.

"It is time I went to my house." The woman stretched and drew her veil over her hair.

"You are like a new sister," I blurted out the thought born of my sudden feeling of isolation.

"What a sweet thing to say." My friend looked moved. "I never had any sisters."

We embraced, and I had to hold back tears. Rachel did not bother to keep hers suppressed. My tunic was damp when she drew back.

"The sun is high." She glanced up guiltily. "My husband and yours will be back soon. There is still a meal to prepare!"

"You must take some of the bread." I held out a warm loaf. "By helping me, you left no time to bake your own."

I thought she might refuse, but then a broad smile appeared. "You are right. It is what one sister would do for another."

Rachel wrapped the loaf in the end of her veil and hurried away. I turned to my own preparations. The roasted vegetables would soon be ready. I could smell the peppers and onions. Beans that simmered all night were now hot, as well.

"Tomorrow, I will visit the market," I decided. "We need more grain and chick peas so I can make humus and lentils for stew. I can make the sweet cakes Chilion likes, if they have some dates."

"What smells so good?" Mahlon was barely through the gate before he sniffed in expectation.

"Where is your father?" I asked when Elimelech did not immediately appear.

The older boy shrugged. "He was talking. Can we eat?"

"No, we will wait for your father to offer thanks," I insisted.

"But I am hungry," whined Chilion. "All the men do is talk. It is so boring."

"Listening made you hungry?" I could not resist teasing the boy.

"It was hard work to stay awake," Mahlon complained.

"You would have done better to pay attention." Elimelech sounded displeased. He entered the gate in time to hear the final comments.

"Yes, Father." Neither son argued.

Their father gave one last bit of advice while splashing water on his hands. "If you ever want to be taken seriously as men, you must learn to take part in the councils." Then he prayed, "We praise you, God of our Fathers, for this bread you give us. Amen."

Mahlon and Chilion barely waited before grabbing a chunk of bread.

"We were warned that the nights will be getting colder soon. Then everyone sleeps inside," my husband mentioned what he learned. "The people use braziers to keep warm during the cold months. I will purchase one from the smith."

Not many days later, the prediction came true. A heavy frost on the ground drove us inside to sleep. At first, I felt stifled by the walls. Soon, I was glad for the warmth and protection they offered.

My days were spent hovering near the small bowl of fire in the center of the room.

"I did not know I could be so cold," I confessed to Rachel one morning.

The woman kindly brought my water, for I suddenly bulged out to an ungainly size. It was all I could do to waddle around my house and prepare food for my family. Trips to the well and market left me cold and exhausted.

"It will be better when you are delivered." Her hopeful statement made me smile.

"I hope so," I tried to agree, even as I reached for another blanket to wrap around my shoulders. "Elimelech says he is cold, too."

"It has been chilly," agreed my friend. "After your baby is born, the days will be getting longer and then the warm weather returns. It is lovely when the fields sprout and lambs are born."

I tried to enter into her enthusiasm. "That will be nice."

"You will see. Spring is a lovely time." The woman smiled in anticipation.

I remained inside when the congregation gathered to celebrate the Day of Atonement.

"No one will expect you," Elimelech told me. "Everyone knows you are near your time."

"Naomi, you are blessed that your child will be the first of the children of Judah to be born in Bethlehem," Rahab spoke kindly on one of my last visits to the well.

"I thought you would want yours to be first," I blurted out my surprise.

"My child will be born during the heat." She smiled. "I will pray for a healthy delivery for you."

Time dragged. Each day, a new twinge in my back made me wonder if my labor had started. Then one morning, there was no doubt. The cramping pain that rippled around my body was familiar.

"Send for the midwife," I told Elimelech when he appeared for the midday meal.

"I . . . oh . . . Naomi," For a moment, the man was stymied. Then he turned and hurried away.

Rachel arrived soon after he left.

"It is time." Her words were not quite a question. "Your husband stopped me to ask where a midwife was."

"I am glad you are here." Resting between contractions, I could smile a welcome.

"Dinah will be here soon," my friend soothed when I gasped as another pain gathered strength.

"I hope she arrives soon. This baby will not wait much longer," I panted when the wave ebbed.

Even though it was not many minutes later, Dinah barely arrived before I told her, "I think the baby is coming."

A quick look confirmed my prediction.

"Help her up," the midwife ordered Rachel. She turned to me, "Bear down. Not so hard. Again. Here comes the baby."

I felt the infant slip from my body in a last effort. A healthy cry filled the room.

"You have a daughter," announced Dinah proudly.

"A daughter?" I could not believe that she was right.

"She is a healthy little girl," Rachel assured me as the newborn wails rang out. "You have two sons. Your husband will not begrudge you a girl now."

"I . . . no . . . he . . . she . . ." My mouth refused to form coherent words.

All my prayers for a healthy boy were ignored. I realized in the same moment that I had secretly hoped for a girl. I held out my hands for my child.

"Here she is." The midwife laid a warm bundle in my arms.

Brown eyes looked up at me briefly; then with whimpers, the infant began to nuzzle for my breast.

"She is beautiful!" Tears welled as I gave the tiny girl suck. "Look at the little curls all over her head."

I stroked the soft cap. The baby slept in my arms, exhausted from her entry into the world.

"You are blessed by your God." Dinah smiled. "To be delivered of a strong daughter after all the travels and changes is to be commended. Not all women would be able to do such a thing."

"She will be a joy to you." Rachel smiled as well. "What father will be able to resist her big eyes and curls?"

After I was ensconced in clean blankets, the midwife moved to the door. "I will tell your husband he may come in."

I nodded.

Dinah and Rachel left me alone. My friend gave me a quick squeeze on my hand before she exited. Elimelech entered softly. He was at his most endearing when I was just delivered of a child. At both previous births, the man had been just as awestruck.

"We have a daughter." I glanced down at the sleeping infant then at my husband.

"Yes." He knelt beside my pallet. "I was told."

"She is healthy and strong," I added, still unsure if the man was pleased or not.

"A daughter." When he stretched out one hand and touched her gently, I knew he was content. One curl tangled around his finger like a caress. "She will be a jewel for Israel. We will name her Adah."

"It is a lovely name," I agreed.

Mahlon and Chilion were hesitant when they came into the room.

"She is so small." Chilion sounded astonished.

I had to grin. "You were once just so tiny."

"I remember you cried a lot." Mahlon frowned. "Will she cry too?"

"Babies cry when they are hungry or when they are uncomfortable." It was hard not to laugh at the unhappy expression on the young man's face. "Your sister will cry sometimes."

I did not add that I hoped the little girl would be spared the tears of pain and shortness of breath her brothers experienced.

"Please keep her safe and healthy." Every time I took the baby into my arms, I breathed the same prayer.

Adah grew, and I rejoiced in the health of my daughter. My days of confinement finally ended. There was a ceremony after three moon turnings to welcome me back into the community. After the ritual bath, I was greeted with cheers. Elimelech carried his daughter to Samson. I barely listened to the words.

"The Living God has shown favor to the house of Judah," Samson announced to the congregation. "A daughter has been born. She will grow up in our midst like a fruitful vine. May she be graceful and wise. The Almighty will make her a blessing to your house."

"A man desires sons and forgets that it is daughters who bear the next generation. Truly, God is wise to remind us of this with your daughter," Salma added.

Despite his words, I was sure the man desired a son. I saw him look toward his wife. Rahab would bear her child sometime after the summer heat set in.

"The Holy One of Israel has blessed me," my husband responded to the leaders. He held the child high for all to see. "This is my daughter. She is an ornament for the nation."

I was surprised by the shout of jubilation that greeted my daughter. Many wishes and congratulations followed my family as we strolled to our home.

"Blessings, Naomi."

"God be praised."

"The Lord shows favor to us."

"May your daughter be strong."

I paused to inhale the fresh air. Soon, it would be time for Passover. I could see the early grain in the fields. Our first barley harvest would follow the Passover celebration. It would be time to plant a garden for fresh vegetables, as soon as the ground warmed a little more.

"It is good to be outside." I leaned against my husband briefly. "Our daughter will play in the sun and grow just as the gardens and fields do."

The man hugged me to his side. "God is gracious."

☙ 14 ❧

"HOW WILL WE CELEBRATE the Passover without priests to recite the saga?" I asked Elimelech the question in the evening as we lounged on our rooftop. "At the next full moon, the great feast will be here."

"We will gather for Passover prayers as always," the man told me. "One of the priests has been appointed to lead the remembrance. Bethlehem is the center for the area near Jerusalem, because it is too far to travel to Hebron, even though that is one of the cities given to the Levites. Bethlehem was chosen because our father Jacob stopped here, and his wife is buried nearby."

"Will people travel to Bethlehem?" I wondered how the arrangement would work. "Will my family come here?"

My husband shook his head. "Each tribe has a central location. A Levite is assigned to Gibeon for those of Benjamin. One will go to Shechem, where Jacob built an altar. Those of the tribe of Ephraim and Manassah will worship there."

"This year will be very different." I felt a touch of sorrow. "For the first time, my family will not keep the Passover together. My sisters will travel to Gibeon, and my brother will stay at Shechem."

"We will remember them in our prayers," Elimelech answered. "I am sure they will do the same. Passover is celebrated all over the Promised Land."

A few families did come to Bethlehem. They stayed with friends and relatives. The streets were full, and the market was busy. I was glad that my purchases were done well before the week of the feast. Elimelech returned from the fields as dusk fell.

"Tomorrow is the start of the Passover feast." My husband looked at the full moon just rising in the east.

"All my preparations are complete. The festival foods are in these baskets. Just this morning, I carried my pot of leaven to Rachel. She was happy to keep it when I explained our laws. I told her, 'We are forbidden to have leaven in our homes during this time.' She is a good friend."

"In the desert, you would all put your jars in a special tent outside the camp," Elimelech remembered absently.

I ran one finger along the edge of the lovely cupboard my husband created. "The carved wooden platters you made are ready and safely stored here. This is the perfect place to keep them from year to year. The new pottery lamps Mahlon and Chilion fashioned are filled with oil for the festival."

"We will honor the Holy One by having special dishes." The man could not keep a proud smile from his face.

I nodded absently. For one last time, I reviewed the various items I had ready. "It is good."

When the *shofar* summoned us at dusk, I gathered Adah into my arms.

"Passover will begin outside the city on the rise overlooking the town," Elimelech stated. "An altar has been prepared there."

"I am ready." I drew a veil over my hair and followed my husband to outskirts of Bethlehem.

"There is the altar for the sacrifice," Mahlon announced and pointed.

"We all helped build it," Chilion added.

"The younger children brought wood. Others carried the stones. Only a few of the men really erected it," corrected his brother.

"You did what you were told." I was distracted by the strange and familiar faces in the group that gathered. Few greetings were exchanged. We all focused on the ritual.

"Hear, O Israel, the Lord our God, the Lord is One." Loudly, the young priest drew our attention.

Our response was equally strong. "The Lord our God, the Lord is One!"

"This is the first of all nights," the Levite reminded us. "Sanctify yourselves to keep the Passover holy."

We all responded, "Amen."

In near silence, each household returned to their home. In the morning, we gathered at the altar to hear the story of the mighty acts of **I AM.**

"Our fathers went into Egypt seventy men. There they became a great people. Then arose a king who feared our strength. Our fathers were made to toil in hard bondage until the fullness of time."

On and on, he chanted the words. I listened with half an ear because Adah began to squirm and whimper. I moved to the edge of the crowd to find a seat on a rock to nurse the baby.

"Our God made a covenant with Moses and our fathers." As always, the words of the promise gave me a chill. " 'Take a lamb and mark the doorposts of your house so the Angel of God will pass over you.' "

I looked up when someone joined me. It was Rahab. We were not close friends, despite our husband's kinship. I was still slightly in awe of the woman because of her boldness in hiding the spies of Israel.

"I wish I had the courage to visit her house and hear more of her story," I had told Elimelech soon after we settled in Bethlehem.

He discouraged any visit by reminding me of the accident during the trek to Bethlehem. "We should not intrude on the household of the son of Nashon bar Amminadab and remind him of the loss your sons caused. Salma could have been the judge and chief of Bethlehem. My cousin allowed his uncle Samson to take that role, but he is still an important man."

Rahab settled onto the stone with a grateful sigh. With one hand, the woman supported her back.

"It will not be long," I whispered what I hoped were comforting words.

"The child will be born in two or three moon turnings," she responded.

Seeing the weary smile from my companion, I resolved to make a soft blanket for her child. I knew just the yarn I would use. It was finely spun of camel's hair. Elimelech purchased it in Jerusalem as a gift for me so that I could make our child a blanket. There was plenty left for another coverlet.

"Your daughter is growing quickly," the woman remarked softly when I lifted Adah over my shoulder for a burp.

"Babies do grow fast." Already my daughter could hold her head up. She stared at our companion then smiled and cooed. "Adah will be sitting and then crawling before too long."

"Amen, Alleluia, El Elohim Israel!" We both turned when the cheer rang out.

"We are being watched." I indicated the curious villagers watching from their houses and standing in the street.

"They are trying to understand our faith," Rahab replied. "The experience of the Children of Israel in Egypt and the desert has made us different from those who remained in Canaan, but claim to worship the God of Jacob."

"I had not thought of that." My eyes opened wide at the idea. "The God of Moses has always been what I knew."

"The God of Jacob is the same God," the foreign woman continued to explain. "However, the ways of worship are different."

"That is true. I guess." Uncertainly, I nodded.

"The people of Bethlehem worship the same God, but they have not had the same experience of the imminence of the Almighty," Rahab elaborated.

I wanted to stay and hear more, but there was no time. The priest stopped talking. Men moved forward to choose their lamb from the nearby pen. One by one, the bleating was silenced by a swift knife.

I saw Elimelech and his sons lift out our sacrificial lamb. I had to look away when he held the little creature toward the altar. A moment later, my husband started down the road. Mahlon carried the carcass.

"I must go." Adah slept in my arms.

"Passover blessings," Rahab murmured.

"Blessings on your house," I replied over my shoulder.

I hurried to catch up with my family. It was short work to light the fire. Chilion held the animal on the spit while Elimelech laced it in place.

"You will take turns with the spit," Elimelech directed, as every year.

While the boys rotated the meat so it would cook evenly, I finished the preparations for the feast. Little Adah nestled in the sling formed by an old veil tied over one shoulder.

"By next Passover, you will be too big for this," I told my daughter while I busily worked.

Only when the ritual prayers began was I able to relax.

My husband began the familiar words. "Blessed be the Lord God who has delivered us from bondage."

I sat back with the baby in my arms. With my family around me, I was happy. Mahlon and Chilion, at thirteen and eleven, waited patiently for the long prayers to conclude.

"It is good to be here in this land," I told Elimelech later as we lay together.

"God is good," he replied leaning over to kiss me and caress my hair. "The land is harsh, though. It is hard to learn to farm this rocky soil."

The words troubled me, even though I allowed myself to be soothed by his embrace and love.

In the morning, life resumed the normal routine. One afternoon, I visited Rahab with the blanket I made. She was delighted. Conversation drifted from children to religion.

"How can you understand our worship? It is different than you experienced . . . before . . ." My question stumbled to an embarrassed halt.

Rahab smiled and replied confidently, "My mother always insisted that all the gods are shadows of the True God. *I AM* that we worship is that One. The God of Abraham, Isaac, and Jacob gives us all that we need. We cannot fail to prosper."

I envied her faith in the Living Lord. Even though I nodded in agreement, I knew that I did not understand. This foreigner did not seem to live in fear of a God who destroyed the lives of any who disobeyed. Her faith made me uncomfortable, just as Sarai's similar statements had bothered me years before. Quickly, I changed the subject.

"Elimelech and my sons did not expect it to be so difficult to work the land," I confessed. "He says that the land is poor and that we might starve if the rains fail."

"The Almighty One has blessed us with all that we need," she insisted in surprise. "We cannot fail to prosper."

The woman's gentle rebuke ended my confession, and I left soon afterward.

Nearly three moon turnings after the great Feast, Rahab was delivered of a son. Salma outdid even Elimelech in his pride at the birth.

"My son will be called Boaz, a pillar for Israel," he proclaimed the Sabbath after the birth.

The child was circumcised, as ordained by the Law of Moses. I saw how tenderly Rahab cuddled her son after the ceremony. Her face had the serenity of one who had no fears or doubts.

Why does the foreign woman have such faith, while I struggle to obey the Laws of God? I turned away with the question burdening my heart.

Time slipped by almost unnoticed, except for the change in the seasons. We grew adept at planting and harvesting. The first and second year brought more forays into the surrounding areas to extend the territory of the Promised Land.

"Joshua has called out a levy from each town." The messenger from our leader was unwelcome.

When I heard the order, I was angry. "Why do you have to go and fight? Is there no end to risking your life?"

"There is still a threat from some of the natives of the land," Elimelech explained. "Mahlon and Chilion will remain here. There is no need for those who do not know battle to fight. I will be back before the harvest."

My husband was grayer when he returned, but I was glad to see he was uninjured. Tamar's husband lost use of his arm in the fighting. I gave thanks to God for Elimelech's safety.

"Blessed are you, Lord God, for you have spared my husband. Be with Tamar so that she can find comfort in her husband still," I prayed.

Rachel continued to be interested in our rituals and feasts. I wished that I could invite her to join our Passover feast. Neither her husband nor Elimelech would have approved. I was glad that they did not know of the many times we discussed the similarities and differences of our beliefs.

"We call the God of Jacob, *El*," she explained. "Before all things, there was *El*. Our ancestor Jacob himself knew God by that name. He renamed Luz, calling it Beth-el."

"I forgot, Bethel does mean House of God," softly I pondered her comment. "I never thought of it that way."

"There are sacred groves here," Rachel admitted, "and some people keep teraphim. That does not mean that we worship the trees or the figures, like the Canaanites do. They just remind us that *El* is all around us. Some of the household idols have been in use since before Abraham herded sheep through this valley on the way to Hebron."

"Your *El* seems less demanding than *I AM*," I confessed a little hesitantly.

"We have many rituals to help with the fertility of the land." My friend smiled. "You have great ceremonies of remembrance of the mighty acts of the Living and Holy One. Someday, maybe you will tell me of some of the great deeds you have seen."

"I think that we do worship the same God, as Rahab once said," I concluded. "It is our experience that is different. Those who live here remember the God of Jacob as *El*. The Children of Israel have received the covenant from *I AM* at Sinai. That makes our responsibility greater, perhaps."

Three years later, Chilion surprised me by offering to turn the spit without being asked. The sixteen year old was very different from the whining boy who arrived in Bethlehem. His muscles were strong, and I no longer thought of him as weak. My son appeared especially serious this Passover.

"You have to take the first turn because you are the youngest. Adah is still too little and cannot be trusted near fire." Mahlon sneered and stroked his thick beard to emphasize his age.

"I will do it," his brother stated calmly.

My youngest son appeared to be thinking deeply as he methodically turned the roasting lamb. I bustled back and forth with my usual final preparations, watching the young man's thoughtful expression.

"My husband, the meal is ready." With relief, I was able to light the special oil lamps just as the last rays of sun left Bethlehem in darkness.

"Come my sons, we will bring the lamb." The man walked toward the fire. Mahlon hurried to the spit.

The older boy pushed his brother away. "It is my turn now."

I almost laughed. Elimelech shook his head and lifted the spit from the fire.

"It is done, my son," he said.

Chilion held the platter. Smoothly, the meat slid off the spit.

"Bank the fire," I called a reminder.

"Mahlon, you can do that since you are anxious to help," his father ordered and turned away.

I saw a mutinous expression cross the young face before my oldest son bent to his task.

"Wash your hands." I held out a basin full of water for the men.

"With this water, we are reminded of the passing through the sea to freedom," Elimelech stated. "It is the culmination of all we remember this night."

"Why do we remember? Why is this night different?" Chilion spoke the words of the liturgy.

"On this night, the Lord God passed over the homes of the faithful. The Angel of Death smote the Egyptians, but no one of the house of Israel died," Elimelech recited his reply.

The young man frowned in concentration throughout the meal. I knew something troubled my son.

"What do you believe, Mother?" Chilion sought me out after the Passover. I was not too surprised.

"About what?" I hedged while I tried to form a response.

"God." In one word and a gesture, the young man encompassed all and denoted frustration at the same time.

My first reply was feeble. "The Holy One led us all the years in the wilderness."

"Here there is no pillar of fire or cloud," argued my son. "How can we know that God is still present?"

"The Living One who brought us safely to claim this land would not abandon us now." It was a hope that I kept reciting to myself when life became difficult.

"Do you have proof?" The challenge expressed my own heartfelt desire for certainty.

"Why do you need proof?" I could understand the confusion in the eyes that studied me. With a heavy heart, I knew my son would not be easily satisfied.

"The God of Israel is invisible, yet we are told that God is everywhere. If the Almighty is everywhere, then there must be some kind of sign." A stubborn set came to the young man's chin as it lifted in defiance.

I struggled to respond. "There is the cycle of growth and harvest. The One who created all renews it each year."

"The Jebusites say that there is a separate deity for each season, for the sun, and for the moon," he argued. "The people here say that the God of Jacob is the same as our God, but they do not have the commandments and the law. Some even have teraphim in their homes."

"They believe that all is subject to *El*." I remembered my discussions with Rachel. My mind raced to find a way to convince the boy.

"Then is *El* the same as *I AM*?" A considering frown came to the young face.

"That is it," I nodded, perhaps too eagerly. "The people here know the Holy One as *El*. Moses heard the Living God proclaim the name of *I AM*. All others are shadows of the truth."

My answer silenced the young man. It was several more years before the subject was raised again. I continued to mull over the questions in my heart. There was no satisfactory answer, and no one I could ask. Memory of my father's death at the hands of the Almighty remained in the back of my mind to trouble my thoughts. I still worried that we would be punished for some infraction and sought to propitiate God with avid prayers and observance of the laws.

𝕒 15 𝕓

THE YEARLY CYCLE OF festivals did not help me find an answer although I was reminded of the never-ending action of the Holy One. Our year started with the Passover celebration. Early harvests of barley were followed by the long, dry, hot season. Just before the cooler days, the wheat was harvested. Fall brought rains and ripe grapes. Gathering and pressing the purple clusters was always an exciting time. Almost immediately, we faced the Day of Atonement. It was a solemn time of rededication to the Living God. Each year, I examined my conscience to find some fault that might anger the Holy One.

"We have kept the commands of the Almighty," Elimelech always stated proudly. "That is why we prosper. My flocks are increasing. Mahlon and Chilion are learning to plant and harvest."

"Yes, my husband," I agreed. "Everything is going well."

Even when a year came when the harvest was small, we were not concerned.

"There is plenty to keep us until the next harvest," Elimelech was not the only one to make the claim. "We have been faithful. Our God will bless us."

The next year, the wet season passed without moisture. No snow or rain fell on the hills around Bethlehem. Passover arrived with the same preparation as in years past. At twenty, Chilion was no longer a chubby child, but a broad-shouldered and handsome figure, very proud of the beard he oiled in imitation of passing traders. The young man frowned at the lamb and other foods. He spoke up when the prayers started.

"Why do we continue to remember the events of so long ago? We are in a new land. Should we not worship as the people around us?"

I gasped. My son's words sounded blasphemous.

"You must not speak so!" his father growled. "We worship the True God. We worship the God that Abraham, Isaac, and Jacob followed long before the Children of Israel were slaves in Egypt. We worship the Almighty who rescued us from our slavery."

"Yes, Father." Chilion drew back from the angry man and lowered his head. I guessed he was not convinced.

A pall lay over the remainder of the meal. Even though we all recited the appropriate prayers and responses, there was no pleasure in the evening. The next afternoon, my son confronted me.

"Have we failed in obeying the law? Is God punishing us?" Chilion found the one question I had no answer for.

"The law is given so that we can flourish." It was a weak response. "Moses told us 'I set before you a blessing and curse.' The blessing comes if we obey the commandments; the curse will fall if we turn away and go after other gods."

"You say that there is only One God," the boy argued. "Yet all around, I see many ways of worship."

"We call God by many names," I reminded him. "*I AM* is called Holy One, Living God, El Elohim . . ."

"Yes, and *El*, who our neighbors claim is the same as the God we worship," Chilion interrupted impatiently. "They use many ways of seeking the favor of the God of Jacob. There is no answer. *I AM* does not listen to my prayers, either."

"Oh." Suddenly, I thought I understood. "Often, it seems that the Lord is silent. I prayed for years before your brother was born. Then I prayed again that he would grow strong. Again, I waited for you and prayed when you were ill."

I held up a hand when the boy opened his mouth to argue.

"At last, you and Mahlon are well." I could declare with relief. "It took over sixteen years for my prayers to be answered."

"I do not want to wait so long." My son was impatient.

"What have you prayed for?" I was curious about what crisis would have brought on these questions.

A rush of color darkened the tanned face. I thought he would not answer.

"I have prayed that the crops will not fail this year," the man blurted angrily.

The specter of the previous year's small harvest rose in my mind.

"We all pray that," I agreed.

He frowned. "The fields are not turning green, and rains do not come."

"It is early yet." I tried to be optimistic.

"Simon, son of Eli, suggested praying to the pillar in the grove near the crossroads," he confessed quietly.

"We are forbidden," my appalled whisper slipped out.

"If the God of Abraham, Isaac, and Jacob is worshipped there, why can we not visit the shrines?" His argument left me with no answer.

"It is the law." I fell back on the old excuse. "God punishes those who disobey."

The memory of my father fleeing from the serpents rose in my mind. The frown on Chilion's face told me that he was not convinced. I grasped the young man by his broad shoulders.

"My son, you must remain faithful." Fear made my voice hoarse. "I could not bear it if you died like your grandfather."

My emotional outburst was greeted by silence. Chilion drew back slightly from my grasp.

"Very well. I will not visit the shrine." The promise appeared to be given grudgingly.

I had to be satisfied, for my son turned away.

"Wait for God." I hoped that he heard my final counsel.

I stood watching the empty gate after Chilion stalked away.

"It would have been easier to let him go to the grove, but I know you would strike my son down for such an action," I whispered sadly to the invisible God I reluctantly defended. "Why must you demand such hard obedience? When will you send rain?"

"There is little need to work in the fields," my husband mentioned the next day. "We men of Judah will keep vigil near the altar outside of town until the rains come."

"Do you think that the Holy One will hear and respond?" Chilion lifted his chin in challenge.

"You will take your turn praying to the One God for rain," Elimelech ordered gruffly, instead of answering the question. "It is the lack of faith of a few that brings punishment on us all."

"Yes, my father." The young man lowered his eyes.

Chilion faithfully visited the altar. I was the only one who knew of his doubts. Mahlon watched the flocks. It was hard to believe that the boy who was once too sick to fight was now a burly young man, lazily leaning against a sycamore tree. As Mother predicted, he outgrew the gasping breaths that tormented his childhood.

"I will pray to the Living God as I seek pasture for our animals," he informed us. "Someone has to find the small remaining patches of grass, or we will have no sheep."

Elimelech gave his permission.

Another year passed without rain. Carefully, I tended my little garden, watering it sparingly with water left from washing. I looked across the yard one spring morning. Adah smiled at me. In her hands was a fresh loaf of bread.

From an early age, she was fascinated with baking. I was transported back to our second summer in Bethlehem. That morning, I had been hurrying to get everything done before the heat set in.

"Mama," my daughter, called distracting me from my tasks.

She was covered in mud but proudly presented me with a dirt patty topped with a flower.

"For you," she lisped happily.

I turned my attention to the toddler. "How nice. Wipe off your hands. We must go to the well. Then you can help me make real bread."

A happy smile appeared. Her hands were cleaned by a rapid swipe down the already-dirty tunic.

"I ready." She grinned up at me.

"We will use water when we get back," I promised the child. "You do not want to get mud in the bread."

"Yes, Mama." The cheerful agreement was so different from her brothers' whining at the same age that I found myself being more lenient than I should have been.

The visit to the well was not accomplished without stopping to exchange greetings with many friends. Rahab was filling her jar when we arrived. Ever since the birth of Boaz, we had been more relaxed around each other. Our children were friends.

"Boaz." My daughter left my side to tag her friend. "Look."

I glanced down to see that the girl had carried her mud creation with her.

"What is it?" The boy stared at his slightly older companion.

Proudly, she stated the obvious. "My cake."

"Oh." Uninterested, Boaz turned back to his mother.

"Boaz will be a handsome man." It was not the first time I made the comment.

I was always astonished at how closely the boy resembled his mother. His hair was only a shade darker than hers. It was reddish in the bright sunlight. The child stood out easily in any group. Like both parents, he was taller than the others youngsters as well. It was the startling blue eyes, like his father's, that first caught everyone's attention.

"Hello, Naomi," Rahab smiled a greeting as she gracefully balanced her jar. "I see Adah has been busy this morning."

"Yes," I grinned.

"She will make someone a fine bride in a few years." Tamar nodded a greeting. "My Miriam used to do the same thing. Now, she is betrothed."

"Mama." Adah brought my attention back to the present. "Do you want me to roast vegetables while the oven is hot?"

"Yes." I watched the girl deftly slice the onions and carrots onto the tray.

"Adah is becoming a pretty and talented girl," I whispered to Elimelech that night. "Before too many seasons, you will need to find her a husband."

"There are other things to be more concerned about," the man replied. "We have become used to rich harvests. This year, there is little grain in the fields. The rains do not come as they should."

"Next year will be better."

"I hope so." My husband looked discouraged.

A fourth year of no rain caused grumbling among the entire community. Around the well, the women shared a growing disquiet.

"The God of Jacob is angry."

"We must make propitiation to *I AM*."

"How can we live if there are no crops?"

"There must be some sacrifice we can make to *El*."

"Each day that passes without rain lessens the chance of a good harvest."

"God gives us a homeland and then withholds rain. What good are fields that do not produce?" I heard the complaint more and more often from my husband.

I sent prayer after prayer to the One God. "Please send rain. Show us our transgression so we can make atonement."

It was not to be. Another season came and went without rain. My prayers, as well as those of Chilion and the rest of the community, went unanswered. It appeared that God, by whatever name, was deaf. I knew that many, both Hebrew and Bethlehemite, prayed to the gods of the groves. There was no response.

"The God of Jacob has turned away," Rachel told me soon after Passover. It was the thirteenth year since we crossed the Jordan.

"It does seem that the Almighty is not listening," I agreed.

"The barley harvest is scant again this year. If the latter rains do not come, the wheat will fail as well. We will have to conserve what grain we have," the local woman warned. She looked worried. "This has happened before. I have never seen it last more than three years, though."

"I hope Elimelech will be patient," I confessed to my friend. "He is ready to leave if the crops fail this year."

"You must tell him that the rains will come again," Rachel urged.

I did not need to bring up the subject. The man was pacing when I arrived home.

"God is angry with us. We have only enough barley to fill one basket from all my fields. In years past, there have been mounds of grain. Too many of the sons of Israel visit the Canaanite groves."

My husband was implacable. "We must leave and find a better place."

"Rachel says the rains will come," I repeated her promise.

"I will not wait to be beggared," the man snarled. "Samson and Salma also counsel waiting. They can say that because their fields are close enough to the stream from the heights. Some of their plantings are green even in this drought."

I did not dare remind my husband of the offer made by our leaders the year before.

"We can dig channels from the water course to all the fields." I remembered the suggestion clearly.

Elimelech had been one of the most vocal in repudiating the idea.

"Why should we sweat in the sun to get a trickle of water? How much good will those few drops do?" To me, he added, "The only gain will be to our leaders when they claim our lands."

Some of the men took advantage of the plan, but most opted to wait for the rain. Clouds formed and vanished before a drop fell. The fields watered by the ditches were greener than the rest of the terraced hillsides but still grew too little grain.

I tried to divert my husband's attention from his despair. "The lands of Salma and Samson produce poorly, too."

"There is even less than last year." Elimelech shook the insignificant amount of grain with a sigh.

"We still have the wheat harvest," I tried to sound cheerful.

My husband frowned. "There is no need to wait. God is angry. My sheep die from lack of grazing. There were few perfect lambs for the Passover."

The man strode away from the house. He was resolute when he returned.

"We will seek land along the far side of the Jordan." I was not terribly surprised by the announcement. "I remember that it was green. The mighty Jordan waters the land. There are no mountains, like here, to stop the rain. Surely we can find a home among the tribes that settled the eastern side of the river."

All his arguments seemed logical. I was sad to leave behind my friends and the home I had come to love.

"When do we go?" I was half-afraid to ask the question.

My husband had an immediate answer. "The caravan of Joseph has come from the Negev on its way to Jerusalem. Then it will head east to the Land of the Two Rivers. We will join them in Jerusalem when the moon is full."

"The moon is just new! That is so soon!" I had hoped for a longer time to prepare and pray for rain.

"Why should we wait longer when it is obvious that God is no longer with us here?" my husband asked scornfully.

Chilion looked startled by his father's emphatic words.

"God cannot have abandoned the Children of Israel." I tried one final argument. "This is the land promised to Abraham, Isaac, and Jacob."

His argument remained unchanged. "The Holy One is punishing us all for the falling away of a few. I will not be ruined by the transgression of those who visit the local shrines and forsake the Living God. We will find a home where we can be faithful."

The harsh words sank into my heart like stones. It was true—we were being punished. Even though I had tried to push the thought away, I knew my husband was right. With a sigh, I set about deciding what to take and what to leave. It was hard.

"Once I was content with a tent and a few baskets," I ruefully told my daughter as we sorted and resorted into smaller and smaller piles.

It was surprising how much we had accumulated during the years in Bethlehem. Adah peered into a deep leather trunk. In it, I was packing the blankets and platters I could not take. I sighed when I rubbed oil into the cabinet Elimelech made for the Passover platters. The child did not understand my sorrow.

"Mama, why are you sad?" She patted my hand where it rested on the wood.

I tried to smile for the child's sake. "It is not important."

Rachel came to help me with my tasks.

"Will you take this for me?" I pointed to the nearly full trunk.

Tearfully, the woman nodded. "I will keep this until you come back to your home."

Salma and Samson tried to convince Elimelech to change his mind. I heard them pleading with him in our yard late in the afternoon.

"Elimelech, God has not abandoned us. We are not being punished," Salma argued.

Samson tried to persuade my husband. "It is a test of our faithfulness. The Holy One will visit us, and your fields will prosper. Meanwhile, there is grain stored for the entire city.

"You are not Joseph," mocked Elimelech. "If God does not want us to leave, there will be rain."

I gasped and covered my mouth with both hands so that I would not cry out in fear at the challenge to the Lord of All.

"How can you threaten God?" I asked the man in the night.

"We will see if anything happens." There was a grim tone in his voice.

Nothing occurred. Rain did not fall from the cloudless sky. No plague attacked my husband. The moon grew fatter each night. It appeared that God did not care. My days were spent in final packing and farewells.

Rachel pressed a gift into my hands one morning at the well. "Take this to remember us."

I unfolded a beautifully embroidered veil. The women of Bethlehem wore similar head coverings on special occasions.

"It is for your festival days," my friend explained.

"Thank you." I could barely choke out the two words. I found myself held tight by my neighbor.

I drew back. "When did you find time?"

"We all helped." My friend gestured to the other women nearby.

I looked around at the group I had come to know so well. Friendly smiles greeted me.

"We hope you will not forget us," Dinah, the midwife, said.

"I could never forget you, even without this lovely gift." My voice was choked with unshed tears.

It was midmorning before we returned to our homes. I carefully folded the veil and packed it amid the blankets so it would not get dirty.

"Hamar and his son, along with old Elam, will join us," Elimelech told me the night before we left Bethlehem. "I am not surprised. Their fields were not doing well even before the drought."

I felt sorrow that more people were leaving the town and could not think of any response to the news. It was hard to sleep during our last night in my home. The moon shown brightly, and I kept thinking of things that I needed to check. I crept up and down the stairs many times.

Elimelech had purchased a donkey to carry our possessions. In the early morning light, we loaded the little beast. She had soft brown eyes that I thought looked at me with sympathy.

"It will be easier than the packs were carried here," the man stated. "Our sons will take turns leading her and helping me with the sheep."

I did not argue. If I spoke I knew I would begin to cry. Mahlon and Chilion were delighted.

"She is your charge," the father expanded his sons' role. "You will see that she has food and water. The loading of her saddle will be your responsibility. If she goes lame, you will carry her burdens."

Mahlon frowned, but unlike the child of years earlier, he did not whine. Chilion looked happy as he stroked the soft nose. Already my younger son was making friends with the beast. In a short time, our donkey was piled high. I felt sorry for the creature.

"Are we loading her with too much?" I asked with concern.

Chilion studied the arrangement. "It looks like more than there is. There are many baskets that do not weigh much."

Final farewells were wrenching. Most of the residents of Bethlehem went with us as far as the grave of Rachel, wife of Jacob. I walked slowly beside my friend of the same name. She hugged me and turned back to her home too overcome to speak.

"May *El* be with you," I breathed a farewell after her.

Hamar and Elam spoke briefly to Salma and Samson. I saw them stride off up the hill away from the town. Their small flocks of sheep moved ahead of them. Then it was time to bid farewell to those who traveled with us to Bethlehem not so many years before.

Rahab handed me a small bundle, "This is for your meals today."

I was surprised to see tears in her dark eyes. Her sorrow at our departure seemed sincere. Boaz waved to Adah. I wondered if either child understood that they would not see their friend again.

"May the Living God of Abraham, Isaac, and Jacob be with you and bring you peace," Salma offered a farewell benediction and salaam to my husband.

"You and yours are always welcome." Samson looked sad. "The fields of Elimelech will be retained as his possession."

My husband was surprised by this generosity. His head jerked up.

"You are kind," he stammered.

"It is just," the chief of the city half smiled at the disbelief. "You are a son of Judah and will always have a possession in this land."

"I pray the God of our Fathers will visit you and give you blessing." My husband bowed to his kinsmen.

"God be with you Elimelech." Samson rested one hand on my husband's shoulder. He looked at me and my sons. "God protect you all. Mahlon and Chilion, you must never forget you are the Sons of Israel and servants of the Most High."

It was a solemn moment. A lump formed in my throat. I wished Elimelech would change his mind.

"Let us go." The man signaled to his sons to start.

The small, brown beast trotted up the road ahead of us with Mahlon at her halter. Chilion whistled to our sheep. The small flock started up the road. I took Adah by the hand. With my husband's arm around my shoulders, we started after our sons. At the top of the rise, we looked back. Samson and Salma remained watching our departure. Small groups of our neighbors could be seen walking slowly back to Bethlehem. I remembered my first view of the small town from the same spot. When I looked back again, rolling land hid the town. The men did not even pause. I felt bereft.

"Will we ever see Bethlehem again?" Hesitantly, I broached the question.

"This Promised Land is too unpredictable, and the people turn from God." The answer saddened me. "On the far side of the Jordan, we will find prosperity. *I AM* will bless us for our faithfulness."

I was silent until we reached the camp outside of Jerusalem. From the south, the vista was not as dramatic. I felt chilled, even in the late afternoon heat, by the looming presence of the city.

"Where will I find Joseph and his son Abdul?" Elimelech asked the first man we found in the trader's camp.

The dark-skinned man pointed. "They are on the far side of the gate, near those palm trees." His words came out in a difficult to understand singsong. "I will show you."

I would not have known how to negotiate between the many close-packed tents and tethered animals. Our guide knew a route. We passed smoothly through the odd assortment of people and beasts to reach the shelter of the palms quickly.

"Joseph and his son are in the market," our guide remarked. "You may wait here or seek him there."

"Blessings on you for your help," my husband saluted the man. "We will wait for him. Joseph is expecting our arrival."

"We heard that there were some men from Bethlehem that would join the caravan." Openly curious, the dark face peered at us. I could see that he was especially interested in my presence. I drew my veil over my face and pulled Adah close.

"I am Elimelech bar Judah, with my sons and family. This is Elam. Here is Hamar and his son Simon." My husband indicated the small group. "We travel to the Jordan to escape the drought here."

"Then it is true that your God turns away?" His prying and singsong voice made me grit my teeth.

Elimelech shrugged. "Who knows the mind of God? I am only thinking of my family. We cannot survive without crops for food."

"You are wise to travel with Joseph. He knows many people. I bid you safe travel." The black-skinned man bowed and moved away.

I blinked, and he was lost to sight in the maze of tents.

"Do you think that he is honest?" Hamar asked with a frown.

"Joseph?" Elimelech squinted at our neighbor, now seated on his pack rubbing his feet.

One hand indicted the direction our guide vanished in. "That man."

My husband shrugged again. "I suppose so." He turned to me. "Naomi, you and Adah can sit under the trees. There is shade. We will eat, and then I will go into the city to find Joseph."

"Here is food." I produced the packet Rahab gave me. Inside

was fresh bread rolled around a savory cheese and olive mixture. "There is water in the skin on the donkey. It will be warm, but we will not have to pay to draw from the well tonight."

Elimelech proudly smiled approval. "My Naomi remembered that the water at Jerusalem is not free and has provided!"

We shared our food and drink with our companions. Privately, I begrudged the water, but the long-ago lessons from my mother surfaced.

"Always give bread and water when asked by friend or stranger," she said often during our journeys. "Someday, you will need to have a cup of water, and the blessing will return to you."

Chilion unloaded the donkey and led her to graze near where his brother watched the sheep. Elimelech strode toward Jerusalem in search of the merchant Joseph. Hamar and his son went with my husband. Elam dozed under a tree.

"Adah, help me clean up," I called my daughter. "Wrap the rest of the meal in these cloths while I move the water into the shade."

My daughter quickly did as she was told. Then we sat down in the shade. Soon, the girl dozed in my lap tired from the excitement of the journey.

"God of Jacob, be with us. Do not cast us away in anger," I addressed the deity in the way I had become comfortable with. The elaborate titles used by the priests belonged to the ark and fiery cloud, not to a self-imposed exile.

It was very lonely in the trader's camp outside Jerusalem. Shouts and the smells of cooking drifted on the breeze when some of the men returned to the area. More and more merchants strode to their tents. A few looked curiously at our small group. The sun began to descend without a sign of my husband.

I pulled Adah closer to my side. Eventually, I saw Elimelech. He was walking beside a man who looked vaguely familiar. Only when he arrived did I recognize the merchant as the man who sold Tamar the fine material that she wore for every festival.

His son was a young man that I barely recognized. He was taller than his father now, with a full beard and thick, black hair. I knew this handsome man was a favorite with the women when he grinned at something his father said. The even teeth gleamed in the disappearing light.

"Abdul, stir up the fire. Our guests will be hungry." I heard a hearty laugh. "More importantly, you father is famished."

The grin appeared again, briefly, "Hard to believe that you have missed any meals," Abdul joked, glancing at his father's broad midsection.

It only took a few moments to stir the fire to life. Abdul was efficient. I admired his speed in chopping vegetables into a pot over the fire. It was strange to have nothing to do. Soon, a tempting smell emerged. With the sun dropping out of sight in the west, we gathered for the meal.

"Blessed be the God who gives us our food." I was surprised that Joseph's prayer was similar to our own.

"I could not have said it better," Hamar spoke. "How do you know our way of praying?"

The merchant shrugged. "Your ancestors came from Ur, it is said. Perhaps that prayer has been handed down from generation to generation in the Land of the Two Rivers, as well as to the sons of Abraham."

"Yes, that must be so." The man was satisfied.

There was little conversation as we ate. The stew was delicious.

"Your wife and daughter shall have my tent," Joseph offered in a low tone to Elimelech when the men belched and stretched in preparation for sleep. "Among so many men, they will want privacy."

My husband offered a salaam of thanks. "We are in your debt. Blessings on you." He seemed to slip easily into the old nomadic ways learned in the desert.

"Naomi, you will sleep in the tent of Joseph," the man informed me although I heard the conversation. "Mahlon, bring your mother a blanket and one for Adah."

It was the work of a moment for Joseph to remove his sleeping blanket from the small hide structure. Elimelech spread blankets for Adah and me.

"I will sleep outside." My husband did not surprise me with the decision.

I was comforted to see him flip his blanket neatly across the entrance to the tent. It was difficult to sleep on the ground again. For much of the night, I tossed restlessly. Trumpets from the city jarred me awake with the dawn.

ᴀᴇ 16 ᴈᴀ

Iᴛ ᴡᴀꜱ ᴏʙᴠɪᴏᴜꜱ ᴛʜᴀᴛ most of the camp had awakened before the trumpets. As once before, I saw a line of merchants awaiting entrance into the city. Slowly, the gates swung open. The men poured in to set up booths and barter their goods.

Joseph and his son were busy harnessing camels and tying on loads. I watched their efficient movements briefly.

I poured a cup of goat's milk from the jar standing nearby. "Adah, come and drink this."

I folded our blankets and gulped down a drink of the milk myself. Elimelech strode across the campsite.

"Chilion, get our donkey." The young man did not need his father's order. He was already securing some of the bundles to the saddle.

"Mahlon, you will start the sheep onto the road," Elimelech motioned to the road north.

Before the entire line of traders was inside Jerusalem, we were moving off in the opposite direction. I looked back once. The city gleamed in the bright morning light. I did not see a cloud anywhere, although I shaded my eyes and looked at the sky hopefully.

"It will be hot later." At first, I thought Abdul was speaking to me. He was addressing Mahlon.

"This year, heat is all we have had," the young man answered.

I realized my sons were renewing the brief friendship from thirteen years earlier. The trio walked beside the donkey. Behind us were a dozen camels and drivers. Joseph, with Elimelech and the other men of Bethlehem, strode beside the sheep. The animals moved steadily along the road. The scant grazing barely slowed our travel. Feeling rather alone, I began to eavesdrop on the conversation ahead of me.

"Tell me, why are you leaving this land?" Abdul sounded confused. "When we met before, everyone was full of anticipation. You said 'God has given us this land!' I remember being so impressed, because I did not care about any of the gods."

"Well, the priests say that this is the land promised to Abraham, Isaac, and Jacob," Mahlon began.

"It seems that God has now forgotten us, though," Chilion interrupted, despite a frown from his brother. "There has been no rain for the past four years. The crops have failed."

"Our father decided it was safer to go where the fields are watered by the Jordan," Mahlon added when his brother paused for breath.

"Moab is nice." Abdul seemed to be considering options. "Not as pleasant as my home between the two rivers. The Tigris and Euphrates never fail. The land floods every year."

"Our father hopes to find a home along the Jordan," explained Chilion with a shrug, indicating location made no difference to him. "I hope the girls in Moab are pretty, though."

"Ha! Ha!" Abdul roared with laughter. "Do you seek a bride already? Be like me, and enjoy what is freely offered before you settle down."

"Easy for you, the handsome trader who is passing through," Mahlon laughed back. "We, however, will have to live in some town."

"True enough." I could tell that the merchant's son still grinned. He lowered his voice so I only caught two words. "Maybe . . . journey."

I guessed that he was offering to introduce my sons to women by their surprised and delighted expressions.

Joseph called a halt when the sun was high. "We will stop here for a meal and rest."

Camels fanned out onto the sparse grass along the edge of the road. I drew my veil close against the eyes of the men, although nearly all tried equally hard not to look in my direction. Abdul was the one exception. He joined my sons lounging on the ground nearby.

"Do you remember this road?" The young man looked at Mahlon and Chilion.

My older son nodded. "Vaguely. I know I was miserable and angry because of our punishment."

I remembered the plodding steps up and down the hills. I could almost hear my desperate encouragement of the boys.

"Why were you in trouble?" The trader asked curiously.

"There was an episode with the sheep at our first stop," my firstborn looked down with a grimace of regret. "We caused a stampede, and one of the ewes died."

"By the beard of Baal! I would have been whipped senseless if I did something so foolish!"

"It almost got our family ejected from the caravan," Mahlon admitted. "As it was, we had to carry wood for the entire trip and lug the packs of all the shepherds."

"It was good for us," Chilion interjected. "We were at fault and deserved punishment. Salma was generous in allowing us to continue to Bethlehem."

I tried to hide my gasp of surprise with a cough.

With a chuckle, my son gestured in my direction with one hand. "Mother never thought she would hear either of us admit that we were wrong."

Abdul flashed his grin. "I rarely give my mother that satisfaction, either."

"Do you see your mother often?" I heard myself join the conversation.

"Only during the winter months." I thought I detected a sad longing in the deep tones. "The camels are rested during the cold season. Equipment is fitted and repaired."

"It must be an exciting life," Chilion burst out. "You get to see new places and strange people all the time."

"Not really." Our companion sighed. "It is the same route, year after year. You have probably seen more places than I have."

The observation left my son silent.

"Still, you *do* travel." Mahlon sounded envious. "That has to be better than living in the same place all the time. I remember traveling before we crossed the Jordan. Every time we moved, there were new sights. Even if it was the same oasis from a year earlier, everything felt different."

Abdul looked away and spoke so low that I barely heard the words. "Travel is not always exciting. Especially if it means you are away from your family."

"Do you have siblings?" I was curious about who the young man missed.

He looked up with the grin back in place.

"I have three sisters. Esther is twelve. Rebekka is eleven, and Lilith is just a little older than your daughter. It is odd that I would miss them, because we fight when I am home." The grin turned sheepish, and the young merchant shrugged. "Still I suppose I do love them all."

Abdul looked past my shoulder. Then he scrambled to his feet. "It is time to move. I see the drovers tightening saddle girths. Here comes my father."

I turned to see Joseph and Elimelech walking in our direction.

I held out a hand to my daughter. "Come, Adah."

Progress was steady. My daughter and I followed the men. Joseph did not appear to be in a hurry, but much ground was covered.

Elimelech waited for me to catch up. "We will stop near Bethel tonight."

"Do you think we will see my sisters?" Immediately, the question sprang from my lips.

"I will ask about them. Joseph plans to trade all day tomorrow." My husband considered the idea. "If they can be found, you may see them."

The promise made my steps lighter. I did not even mind the cold stew we ate after making camp at dark.

"Bethel is an hour away," Joseph told the group. "Before first light, we will be on the road. It is best to arrive at the city at dawn, before the residents start their day."

My heart beat eagerly when I saw the town in the morning light.

We had roused before the sun even turned the horizon gray. In the strange predawn light we loaded the animals.

"We will stay here with the sheep," Elam offered.

"That is wise," Joseph approved.

"Watch your step," Elimelech and Abdul both cautioned me when we set out.

It was hard to see the track, although the animals appeared to know where it was. I stayed close to my sons. The road became more and more distinct as the sun drew closer to the rim of the world. It was barely peering into the valley when we arrived at Bethel.

"There is the altar built by Jacob." Abdul pointed to the hillside opposite the city. "At least, that is what everyone here says."

"Do they still use it?" Chilion wanted to know.

"I suppose so." The young trader was not interested. "I have heard that there is a cult that has maintained the rituals since Jacob passed this way long, long ago."

"Rahab's grandfather served that sect," I interposed. "Her brother was hoping to find evidence of it when he settled here, too."

"Then it is true." Abdul nodded satisfaction and changed the subject. "We usually have good luck trading here. Before Ai was destroyed, many caravans passed through here. Now, not so many come by. Gilgal and Jerusalem have become the centers of trade. My father always makes an effort to stop."

The town looked about the same size as Bethlehem. It lay one on side of the narrow valley that formed the pass through the mountains from Gilgal to the coast.

"I hope we will find your aunts," I told my sons. "They will be excited to see Adah. I wonder if there are any new babies in their homes."

Mahlon and Chilion nodded at my babbling excitement. I fell quiet when Joseph halted the caravan. Without a wasted movement, each driver set up a shelter. With the ease of long practice, they laid out a display of the rugs and pottery and tools that each beast carried.

"What are they doing?" Adah asked, fascinated by the traders setting up their booths.

"They are going to sell things to the people here," I explained. "You know how traders come to Bethlehem sometimes."

Already the booths were becoming busy. At first, there was a trickle; then a flood of residents busy searching for bargains. I did not recognize anyone. Abdul was still a master salesman, and I admired the way he coaxed the customer into a purchase if even the slightest interest was shown.

Elimelech found me standing near the stall displaying rugs. "Come, I have learned where Leah lives."

"My sisters are here! You will meet your aunts!" I took Adah by the hand. "Mahlon, Chilion, come with us."

Somewhat reluctantly, the young men joined us.

"Are they well? Are they happy? What did you hear? Do they have more children?" I bombarded my husband with nonstop questions.

Elimelech stopped in front of a mud brick home that looked like every other one in the town. "Here is the home of Terah of Benjamin."

"You are sure?" Suddenly, I was nervous and hesitant.

"This is where I was told." The man raised his eyebrows at my doubt.

I took a deep breath. "Then it must be."

My hand shook slightly as I pushed open the gate. The yard looked almost like the one I left in Bethlehem—It, too contained a round oven, a garden and some chickens. One thing that caught my eye was the colorful design decorating the wall nearest the garden. While strictly in obedience to the law that forbade the representation of anything created, the lines and swirls were delightfully brilliant.

"Leah did paint her wall." I smiled to myself, remembering the girl's insist comments in Gilgal.

"Is that you, Hephzibah?" a familiar voice called from inside the house.

"No, it is Naomi." My reply was almost inaudible.

"Who?" My sister appeared in the doorway.

She looked the same. Dark eyes widened in amazed astonishment. Then she smiled. I was almost knocked over when she rushed to me.

"Naomi! How? When? Why?" Half-crying and half-laughing, my youngest sister clung to me. "Let me see you. Who is this?"

The woman stepped back briefly. That was when she spied Adah trying to hide behind me. Her exuberant aunt made her nervous.

"This cannot be your baby!" Before I could respond, Leah dropped to her knees in front of the child. "You are a pretty girl!"

Adah decided that anyone who called her pretty must be nice. She released her grip on my gown. With tentative steps, she moved toward my sister.

"This is Leah, your aunt," I told my daughter.

"Leah," she repeated solemnly.

My sister smiled. "What is your name?"

"Adah." She grinned back.

"That is a pretty name. Do you know that it means that you are a lovely ornament?" Leah tried to be formal, but her eyes danced when my daughter smiled brightly.

Mahlon and Chilion stepped forward when I signaled them with my head. "Aunt Leah."

"These men are my nephews?" Still kneeling by Adah, the woman looked up.

"Yes, my sons have grown-up," I laughed happily.

My sister stood to embrace each young man. "Look at you. I would never have recognized my nephews as such handsome men with beards. You will be wed soon yourselves."

I indicated to my husband. "Here is Elimelech."

"The husband of my sister is always welcome." Leah nodded her greeting with a slightly formal tone before explaining. "Terah is not here today. He has taken the flocks to the upper fields. Hephzibah and I were going to spend the day washing and gossiping. This is even better!"

"Do I hear my name?" I turned to see a plumper version of my sister enter the yard.

She stopped and stared, her mouth open in surprise.

"Hephzibah, it is Naomi!" Leah practically danced to the new arrival. "Look at Mahlon and Chilion. They are men. Here is little Adah."

Hephzibah stood staring from one face to another. Then she trotted to me with tears streaming down her face.

"Naomi, how I have longed to see you!"

We held one another for a long time.

"Wife, I will return to the caravan," Elimelech finally interrupted our reunion. "My sons will go with me."

"You must come for a meal tonight," Leah begged.

"Only if the traders camp overnight," the man agreed reluctantly.

We barely noticed that the men departed. Our day was filled with sharing the experiences of the past thirteen years. There was happiness and sorrow. I learned that Hephzibah was soon to be a grandmother.

"How can this be?" I could barely comprehend the news.

"You know my daughter is only a year younger than Chilion," the woman reminded me with a smile. "She became a woman and wife several years ago."

"Does she live near here?" Suddenly I wanted to see my niece as well.

"Her home is not far," nodded Hephzibah with a smile. "She will be joining us soon. Eglah wanted to visit the traders. I never saw such a girl for seeking bargains."

Her words seemed to conjure up the young woman. Despite her advanced pregnancy, I could still see the child I remembered in the graceful woman. She reminded me of Hephzibah.

I held Eglah as close as a full belly would allow. "Your grandmother will be pleased to see how lovely you have become."

"You do not know?" Leah interrupted. "Word came from Shechem the second winter. A chill took hold of our mother when the weather turned cold."

"Oh!" A cry of grief wrenched from my heart. "No one told me."

"The messenger said he was going on toward Bethlehem." Hephzibah took my hand in hers. "I am sorry you did not know."

"If my child should be a girl, I will name her Abital." A small smile crept through my niece's glistening tears.

"We pray for a son," Leah remarked. "However, it would be a pleasure to have our mother's namesake nearby."

"Where is Beriah?" I noticed the absence of my nephew. "He is not old enough to be with his father, is he?"

"The boy is fifteen," his mother chuckled. "He is nearly grown. It has always been impossible to keep him from the men's activities."

Leah smiled. "Our nephew is with his father nearly every waking minute. He was a herdsman before he left the tunic of a child. The boy has such a talent for handling animals that even the oldest shepherds are amazed. Even the most obnoxious ram grows calm at his voice."

"How amazing." I did not know what else to say.

There was much other conversation. We shared stories about learning to live in our homes.

"If it had not been for Rachel, my neighbor, I would have been totally at a loss." My admission was greeted with nods.

"We had Eve here," Leah remarked. "I suppose everyone found a mentor."

"Or struggled very hard," Hephzibah guessed. "Remember how Deborah, wife of Benoni, refused any help?"

"That was very sad," agreed Leah. "Her family might have starved if Benoni had not continued to build a fire each morning in the yard."

"Eventually, she did come to us for help," my younger sister noted. "It was very embarrassing though, because she was so angry."

"Why was she annoyed?" I could not understand.

"I suppose because she felt foolish and had to blame someone," Leah guessed. "We were happy to help, even though she made it difficult."

"Tell me why you are here now," Hephzibah finally asked the question I half-dreaded.

"We have left Bethlehem because of the drought. Elimelech thinks that we will be prosperous if we find land near the river." I briefly told the story.

"Then you have not come to stay here?" My sister was sad.

"I wish it was so." A wave of sorrow washed over me. "It would be comforting to be near family again."

"Can you not ask Elimelech to stay here?" Leah wanted to know.

"Even though we have not had rain, our fields are watered from the heights."

"He is set on this course." I shook my head and tried to explain further. "My husband blames those in Bethlehem who have abandoned the God of Moses for the old ways of worship. They call on **El**, saying it is the same as the God of Jacob. Some even visit the Canaanite groves.

"We must seek prosperity away from such abominations." The object of our conversation spoke from the gate. A dark frown indicated that he had overheard.

"We must return. The caravan is ready to leave," the man announced, looking at the sun beginning its descent toward the mountains.

Leah clasped her hands together in supplication. "Will you not eat with us tonight? Terah will be back soon. He will be sorry to have missed you."

"We must remain with the caravan." My husband tried to look apologetic. He only succeeded in looking stern.

"I am sorry." I felt a great wrench at leaving my family again.

Only with an effort was I able to keep my voice from cracking. Adah sensed my grief and ran to me. When I held open my arms, my sisters and niece flew into them. We held one another tightly. I felt tears soaking my gown. I choked back my own sobs. Elimelech cleared his throat. We drew apart only to cling close again.

"Naomi." My name firmly spoken by the man finally made me draw back.

"We must go," I stated the obvious in a choked voice.

"Will we ever see you again?" Leah sobbed openly.

"Who knows?" I tried to be hopeful. "The God of Israel may yet bring us together again. After all, we did not expect this meeting."

"I will pray for you." Hephzibah stood beside her daughter. The two women held hands for mutual comfort.

"May your grandchild be a blessing, whether you bear a boy or a girl." I swallowed my tears. It was unlikely that I would learn if my mother had a namesake or not.

Leah swallowed hard. "My sister, blessings on you and yours."

"And on yours." I was barely able to speak.

The man held out his hand to Adah. "Come, Daughter."

The little girl waved at her aunts before obeying the summons. I let Elimelech guide me through Bethel. With my veil tight around my face, I did not see whether there were curious eyes or not. My heart was with my family. I barely cared if anyone saw my misery.

"Here we are," I heard Elimelech call out.

"Let us be going." Joseph's order sealed my distress.

Camels complained. I heard the plop of their broad feet on the road. I still held Elimelech's hand. Each step took me further away from my sisters. Tears blinded me. I was glad that my husband remained at my side. He did not say anything. I would not have accepted any comfort. Too soon we reached the camp at the crossroads, I crawled into my blankets without even eating the bread and meat Hamar had waiting for us.

"It has been a tiring day." Everyone accepted my excuse.

From inside the tent, I could hear the talk around the campfire.

"We made these today," I heard Adah tell the group.

"What are they?" Mahlon asked.

"Honeyed cakes." The child sounded offended that her brother did not recognize the delicacy.

"They are smashed," he remarked.

I smiled sadly in the darkness, sure that the sticky treats were flattened together after being carried all the way from Bethel by my daughter.

"Let me try one," Chilion offered.

He loved the sweets. I was certain he would eat them, even if they were covered in mud.

"They are good." His approval was all that was needed.

"See?" Adah challenged the rest.

"I will have one, then." I could almost hear Abdul grin. "You are right. These are very good."

Before long, everyone had a sample and agreed that they were delicious. I was glad the little girl brought the cakes with her. It gave her a happy memory of the day. I fell asleep with a smile on my lips.

⤙ 17 ⤚

WE JOURNEYED DOWN THE mountain road in the morning. I barely remembered the route.

"Look at the pretty butterfly." I pointed out the bright-colored insect flitting past as we rested after the midday meal.

"Come here butterfly!" Forgetting that she was almost a woman, Adah ran after the creature in an attempt to capture it.

I laughed and wished I dared join my daughter. She returned panting and flushed.

"You should stay with Mother," Chilion scolded his sister.

"I did not go far." She made a face at the man. "Go help with the donkey or camels."

Her brother scowled. "You are a spoiled child. I think you are scared of the animals anyway."

The girl flared at the challenge. "I am not. It is just not woman's work to load camels."

I hid a smile when Adah flounced away to pat the donkey as proof that she was brave.

"I think camels are funny looking," she confided in me when we started out again. Each box and bundle swayed with the odd rhythm of the humped beasts of burden.

"Yes, they are. Maybe someday you will ride on a camel," I dreamed aloud. "Your husband will give you jewels and gowns. There will be camels and donkeys and servants to answer every need. A fine house in Moab will be yours."

Elimelech startled me when he spoke from behind me. "You have great plans."

"Our daughter deserves the best," I defended myself.

"I do not deny that, Wife." There was a smile behind his beard.

"You are teasing me." I thrust out my lip in a mock pout.

The man laughed. "Naomi, why not dream? We will have a new beginning. Without unfaithful neighbors, we will find happiness."

The words brought an end to my pleasure. A chill of fear gripped me.

"What if God punishes us for abandoning the Promised Land?" For the first time, I shared my secret terror.

"The God of Israel does not care where we are." The response sounded callous until he added, "As long as we obey, the Almighty will be with us."

He walked on to speak to Joseph. Our conversation had to wait. All afternoon, I plodded in the dust wondering if Elimelech was right.

"Would it be better or worse if the only God I know abandons us instead of bringing punishment?" I whispered the question to the hot wind that blew in my face.

Stinging dust that whipped in a spiral was my only answer. I shivered, wondering if God was trying to stop us. I was glad when Adah distracted me.

"Look at those flowers!" The child hurried to pick a bouquet of wild daisies.

"Even in the drought and heat, there are plants blooming," I marveled, inhaling the scent.

The plants reminded me of something Rachel said during one of our discussions.

"I have always thought of the God of Jacob as the lingering scent of a lovely flower that clings even after the plant is gone." The woman had smiled dreamily while she explained. "We have never seen the evidence of the Almighty as you have, yet I feel the care all around me. Seasons and sunsets and even difficult times are all chances to find the Holy One."

At the time I shook my head. Longingly, I confided, "I have never felt that the God of Israel is comfortable or caring. I wish I could believe like you and others do."

"Like Rahab." The Bethlehemite's insight surprised me.

I nodded, but not even to my friend could I confess, "**I AM** is more likely to punish than to care for me."

For the rest of the afternoon, Adah carried the flowers. By the time we made camp they had wilted, although the delicate fragrance lingered on her hands and clothes. I smelled it when I tucked her into her blankets.

Later, I addressed the God who seemed as distant as the stars above the camp. "Are you like the little stinging whirlwind that punishes for no reason or like the flower with sweet-scented comfort?"

I fell asleep with the scent of the wildflower in my nostrils. It was soothing. I awoke rested and briefly unconcerned about our destination.

Morning brought us to the descent onto the plain in front of Gilgal. The smell of water and hint of green along the stream encouraged the sheep to move almost rapidly. Hamar and his son herded the animals to a safe place near the town.

"There is nothing to show that an entire nation camped here," I marveled softly to Adah. I pointed to the walls we were approaching. "That is Gilgal, where we are going."

We walked behind my sons and the donkey. As he often did, the son of Joseph strode beside them.

"There is the Pillar of Consecration," I heard Mahlon tell Abdul. "The local men called it Gibeath-haaraloth."

"I have heard that and wondered why it bore such a name," the young trader responded.

"All the men and boys of Israel were circumcised before the sack of Jericho," Chilion explained.

"*All* the men and boys?" Abdul sounded stunned. "Every one of you was circumcised before a battle?"

"It does sound crazy," admitted my son. "We followed the command of God. It is the covenant made with Abraham."

"Your God must be with you," the man from Asshur stated in awe. "If the men of Gilgal or Jericho had attacked, we would never have met. You would have been defeated without being able to raise a weapon."

"I suppose so," Mahlon admitted. "It is not something I really thought about at the time."

"I would think not." I saw the young man shudder.

Camels and donkey strained at their harnesses to reach the cool shade of the trees. The trio had to step out more rapidly. They walked on in silence until we made camp. Elimelech found me when the camels were being unloaded.

"We remain here through the Sabbath," the man told me. "You will have time to visit the market tomorrow if you want. We will rest on the Holy Day. It begins at sundown tomorrow."

"We will keep the Sabbath?" I was surprised.

"Why would I change my habits?"

"It is just . . . that . . ." My words trailed off when Elimelech frowned. "I will see that the meal is prepared."

"Joseph and Abdul will join us," the man added as he turned away.

I was left to ponder the actions of my husband and to consider what foods I should purchase in the morning.

Trumpets from the walls announced the dawn. It had been many years since I heard the brazen trumpets from Gilgal, but immediately, I was transported back in time. For a moment, I was disoriented and expected to see the encampment around me.

"Mama." Adah was startled. "What is that?"

"It is the signal to open the city gates." I leaned over to comfort my daughter. "They are sounding the trumpets from the walls of Gilgal. We heard trumpets at Jerusalem, too."

"They were not as loud," she complained.

"We are closer to the walls," I said. "Get up. We need to go into the city and get Sabbath foods."

I arranged my veil over my hair and crawled from the tent. Already, the air was warm, hinting at the scorching heat to come. The campsite was deserted. Joseph and his men were inside the city. I guessed that Elimelech and my sons were with them.

"There is much to do to prepare the Sabbath meal for tonight," I told Adah when she appeared. "Let me comb your curls, and we will go to the market."

The girl looked confused. "It is the Sabbath?"

I nodded. "Yes, we will celebrate the Holy Day even as we

travel. We need to get barley flour and fruit. I hope your father will bring some meat to roast."

"On a spit over a fire?" Her small face lit up. "Will I get to turn the meat?"

I grinned at her eagerness. "We will have a fire to make the bread and cook the meat."

"Hurry," she urged, dancing toward the city.

I trotted to catch up to my daughter. The guards at the gate barely gave a glance at the woman and child from the trader's camp.

"Last time I was here, my mother and sisters were with me." Remembering the sorrow that none of us would admit then, I sighed.

"I like my aunts," Adah confided and slipped her hand into mine.

"They like you, too. I am glad you got to meet them. The market is this way." My feet remembered the way past the mud-brick homes.

Adah stared around in amazement. "Look how close together the buildings are."

"Some of them have gardens in the back. There are some really large houses on the other side of the city," I explained. We turned a corner. "Here is the market."

"Fresh berries for the little lady."

"Flour, ground this morning."

"Buy your wine here."

The cacophony of merchants struck my ears. It had not changed over the years. I produced the weight in silver Elimelech gave me. The moneychanger took the pouch and weighed it carefully. He squinted at the scale then nodded and produced a stick. Into it, he carved that appropriate number of notches.

"Do I know you?" The man peered at me. "Your face seems familiar."

"I am not from Gilgal." Brief honesty was better than a long explanation.

"Still . . ." The trader frowned and tried to see my face clearly.

Instead of answering I held out my hand for the counting stick. "I have much to purchase."

"Yes, yes, of course." I felt the man watching me as I walked away from his booth.

Adah stared in awe at the many stalls. Gilgal replaced Jericho as the hub of trade. Merchants of many nationalities shouted their wares in accents known and unrecognizable. Local craftsmen and farmers ran the bazaar in Bethleham. The rare caravan was an event.

"Who is that?" The girl drew back from a tall dark-skinned man who held out some exotic animal pelts.

"He is from south of Egypt," I replied. Nodding to a pair of men hawking shell jewelry, I added. "Those men are from the Great Sea."

Odd turbans proclaimed their nationality. I took a firm hold of my daughter's hand. I did not want to lose her in the crowd.

"There is Joseph." The girl pointed to a familiar face. She tugged me in the direction of the man and his booth of blankets.

The trader nodded at us. "The wife and daughter of Elimelech are welcome."

"We are purchasing flour and fruit for the Sabbath meal," I explained.

"My son and I are honored to be included." The man indicated his pleasure with a grin that almost resembled Abdul. "Elimelech tells me he is getting a goat for the feast."

I was relieved to learn that my husband was going to provide meat without being reminded.

"We have much to do. Come, Adah." I turned to leave.

"We will join you at sunset." With a slight wave, Joseph bid us farewell. "You will find good flour and other reasonably priced foods on the north side of the market."

I hurried in the direction indicated. A few minutes later, Adah and I had a measure of flour and more than enough fruit for our meal. Wine and some vegetables were added to the basket. On impulse, I added a bag of dates and a small jar of honey.

"We will make a special treat," I promised my daughter on the way back to our tent.

Mahlon was ahead of us. My son had just finished lacing meat onto a spit. He waited beside the freshly kindled fire for the flames to diminish.

"Father sent me with this." The young man indicated the roast. "Chilion is bringing water and more wood."

The young man arrived as we spoke.

"Here is wood enough for today," he announced, dropping a huge mound of branches near the fire.

"That is good." I put down my bundles. "I will mix the bread to be baked."

"Chilion can watch the meat," Mahlon stated. "I am meeting Abdul in the market."

"Can I turn the spit?" Adah offered, moving close to her brother.

"Sit beside me," Chilion offered. "We will turn it together. You have to keep the spit moving at an even rate."

With lips pursed in concentration, the girl rotated the meat. I briskly set to work mixing the bread. When it was formed into loaves, I turned to prepare a fruit platter.

"Adah, will you help me?" I asked. All that remained was to make the honeyed dates.

"If Chilion can turn the meat by himself," she teased.

The young man pretended to be offended. "I have turned more roasts than you have curls on your head."

"I will put an almond in each date," I explained. "You roll them in this dish of honey. Then put them to dry in the sun."

"I remember making these before." My daughter set to work efficiently. We were both soon sticky.

"Chilion, will you set the bread around the fire to bake?" I called. "We are making a special treat."

The young man's face lit up with interest. "What are you making?"

"Honeyed dates," Adah replied with a conspiratorial smile at me.

"We have not had them for so long." My son licked his lips in anticipation. He winked at me. "I do not think Adah likes them. I will eat hers so they will not be wasted."

"They are mine," his sister defended her share loudly, causing the man to break into laughter.

"It is time to turn the bread." I found myself smiling as well.

Adah hurried to the fire. "I will do it."

I watched the competent way my daughter rotated the baking bread so it would cook evenly. She was growing up quickly. I turned to finish my tasks.

"I think our meal is almost ready. We just need water for the men to wash their hands."

"It smells good," confirmed my son. "Soon, the men will come from the city."

A glance at the lowering sun confirmed his observation. The flavorful, toasted scent of hot bread mingled with the roasting meat. It made my mouth water.

"Adah, come and help me with the rug," I called to my daughter.

Together, we flipped and smoothed the wool carpet in front of the tent. It made a colorful place to put the food.

"Here are cups for the wine." I held out the mugs used each Sabbath, glad that I had packed them.

I did not have to give further directions. The girl was used to arranging our Sabbath table. A torch was lit in place of the pottery lamps left in Bethlehem. Approaching voices signaled that our guests were arriving. I placed the tray of fruit in the middle of the rug.

"Put the platter of warm bread and the bowl of cheese beside the fruit," I ordered, admiring the way it balanced the arrangement.

Space in the center was left for the tender roasted meat that Chilion slid onto the platter.

"Hold the jar steady," I ordered Adah. "I will fill it with the wine."

I smiled at the way she concentrated so hard on keeping the pottery jar from spilling that her tongue was gripped between her teeth.

"Here is water to wash." Elimelech held the bowl to his guests.

"Come, we will go into the tent." I held open the flap until the girl entered.

Adah looked back, longing to be part of the gathering, though we both knew that women and children did not eat with the men unless it was just a family gathering.

"Here is bread and cheese," I offered. "I am going to have some, too."

We ate slowly, savoring the quiet time. Outside, Joseph and Abdul received a lesson in the Sabbath protocol. I braided my hair and combed Adah's curls. Her hair was long, but still formed ringlets around my finger. The men continued to feast and talk long into the night. I yawned and dozed against the piled blankets. Adah fell asleep long before the men sought their beds. When I heard movement outside, I roused.

"We will remain here at Gilgal for three sunsets," I heard the announcement from Joseph with relief. "With the dawn, we will again enter the city to trade."

"My sons and I will obey the command of our God and remain in the camp tomorrow." Elimelech surprised me with his obedience to the law.

"I understand," the trader replied. "It is wise to follow your heart. The gods I serve are more lenient, but there are feasts we are commanded to keep."

Footsteps moved away. For a moment it, was quiet. I lifted the tent flap and stepped into the night lit by the flickering torch and the dying fire.

"My wife, we did not leave much." The man indicated the remaining meat, bread and fruit scattered on the platters.

"You were hungry," I agreed. "There is not much to put away."

"We will remain in camp to honor the Sabbath," my husband repeated his ordinance. "It is the least we can do for the God of Israel here, where we first encamped in the land given to the Patriarchs."

The men turned to their pallets. Almost before I started cleaning up the remnants, I heard snoring.

"I wish I could believe as easily that God will bless us, even if we leave this land behind. How can you be so certain that we will not be punished?" I whispered, shaking my head at the sleeping man. "I do not understand you, Elimelech of Judah."

After three days, we resumed our journey. Well-fed sheep had to be herded away from the water and green grass. The camels were loaded again. Our donkey was piled with our possessions. Adah and I repacked our supplies so the little animal was not loaded with so many bulky bundles.

"Last time we crossed the river on dry land," I told Adah as we drew closer to the water. "Those rocks came from the center of the river."

I paused in my walk to stare at the altar of twelve stones erected when we entered the land. It brought back memories of sitting be-

side Sarai. Her belief that God wanted relationship more than obedience was something I still could not comprehend.

"How will we cross this time?" Mahlon stopped beside me.

"I do not know." I tried to hide my uncertainty.

We were rapidly approaching the river. I could see that it was
flowing steadily but not flooding.

Abdul led the way. "Here is the ford."

He splashed into the water at an angle to head for the far bank.
Water came to his ankles, and then his knees. The young trader
stopped and turned back. He struggled back to our side of the river.
It looked difficult. I realized he was working against the current.

"Father, can we allow the wife of Elimelech and his daughter a
place on one of the camels?" Abdul grinned at us as he made the
request.

"Well-thought-out my son." Joseph called a halt with one up-
raised hand.

Quickly, bundles were rearranged, one camel was make to kneel.
Elimelech lifted me onto the creature and set Adah on my lap. She
squealed when the beast rose to his feet.

"This is so high!" I gasped, grabbing the saddle as the caravan
moved forward.

Abdul grinned up at me. I thought I saw him wink. All he said
was, "Hang on."

"This is fun," Adah whispered. She appeared to enjoy the rocking motion.

I was grateful we rode safely above the water that came to my
husband's knees when we reached the center of the river. The sheep
paddled through the deep water, and then struggled onto the dry
land. Their soggy wool made them look pathetic.

Abdul looked up again. "Nearly there."

I saw Chilion reach the shallows. He scrambled up the bank,
dragging the donkey. Mahlon followed. My camel started up the
slight incline.

"Lean forward," Abdul cautioned when a squeak of fear escaped
me at the tilting ride.

It helped us balance. In a moment, we were on the dry, level
land. The men busied themselves with checking all the packs to be

sure nothing got wet. Elimelech lifted me from the camel. Tears threatened to fill my eyes when I looked back at the land that was my home for so many years. I wanted to cling to Elimelech and receive some assurance, but he was busy. Neither Mahlon nor Chilion felt any loss at leaving our home. They were too busy helping Abdul and the other traders.

"Do not forget us, God." I wondered if the Holy One, or indeed anyone, heard my plea amid the racket of setting up the camp and building fires to dry clothing and equipment. "What will happen to us far from our people and the only God we know?"

"Why would God forget us?" Adah asked innocently. "We are the Children of Israel."

I tried to smile for the sake of my daughter.

"I am sure that the Living Lord will not forget us." My assurance sounded firm. I wished I believed it myself.

A fire was built near Joseph's tent. I imagined Rachel and my sisters preparing their evening meals safe in solid homes. A wave of loneliness caught me.

"Come help make our food," I called to Adah, glad for a distraction.

The men talked on the other side of the camp. I guessed that they were discussing the direction of travel. Elimelech gestured north. Joseph pointed to the south. Elam and Hamar stood nearby offering an occasional comment. The sun set over the hills we had come from. Once again I was a wanderer.

"This time there is no pillar of cloud or fire to lead the way." I longed for the leadership of Moses and Joshua.

After the meal was prepared, Elimelech and my sons strode to the fire. Abdul, Joseph, and our fellow travelers were with them. They continued the conversation while eating.

"The half-tribe of Manasseh is to the north," I heard my husband argue. "We might find a welcome among my mother's kin."

"We have seen Moab," Elam stated. "It is closer."

"The river valley has land to spare," Hamar inserted. "We could have rich fields."

"The land is less fertile as you travel north," Joseph mentioned casually.

"You say the land is not as rich in the north. I know near Shittim and Beth-peor, the fields are fertile." Elimelech said slowly. "I do not know the welcome we might receive from the sons of Manasseh. We parted with angry words."

"The sons of Gad and Reuben settled between the river and the desert toward the land of Ammon," Hamar remarked.

My husband frowned. "The land near the River is a wiser choice. I do not want to live in a desert."

I could tell that the man was leaning more and more toward settling on the fringes of Moab.

"It is your choice," Joseph shrugged. "I have traded in the area around Shittim. There are men I can introduce you to."

My husband nodded decisively. "Then we will go south."

"We leave in the morning." Joseph bowed his agreement and strode across camp to where Abdul oiled a harness dampened by the crossing.

"I remember Habbukuk of Shittim offered to find us a plot of land if we stayed." Elimelech turned to me. "It would have been better to have done so."

He did not seem to want any answer. I doubted the wisdom of returning to the town. Habbukuk had seemed a sly and untrustworthy ally, and I doubted he had changed. I swallowed my arguments. My husband would not listen to my fears. The morning routine of loading camels and setting out kept me from brooding. We traveled south and east, away from the river. I took a deep breath and looked down the road disappearing in the distance. Each step took me further from the people I knew and the God I tried to obey.

"We will reach Shittim today," Abdul told Chilion.

"I do not remember much about the area," my son replied.

The young trader explained. "Shittim and Beth-peor are twin cities on the watercourses from the Heights of Ammon. The river that runs into the Jordan waters the Plains of Moab. There are rich fields there."

"I pray we will find a welcome there." No one heard my comment in the excitement of meeting a caravan coming from the south.

"What news?" Joseph hailed the lead drover.

"All is well, Joseph of the Two Rivers. I am glad to have left before your arrival. My meager offerings from Canaan are no match for the things you carry in those packs."

"You mock yourself." Our guide guffawed loudly. "I have seen the fine beadwork and baskets you sell."

The newcomer laughed in his turn. "Perhaps. I have always felt myself fortunate not to compete with your woven goods from Egypt and Asshur."

"It is true that I carry only the finest." The trader tried to look modest and failed. "Where are you headed?"

The man gestured up the road with a tilt of his chin. "North, to deal with the sons of Jacob living there."

"Is that a useful trip?" Elimelech asked. "I considered going in that direction to settle."

For the first time, the Canaanite appeared to notice that Joseph was not alone.

"I would not encourage you," he frowned. "The sons of Manasseh are a fierce lot. They are tight-fisted and dark of hair and mood. It is only the need for profit that sets me on the road north to their territory."

"May the gods give you good trading," Joseph saluted his friend.

"And to you as well," responded the short man before giving the signal to continue.

With complaining grunts, his camels moved out. Joseph motioned to Abdul. Our caravan set off again, only to stop a short time later at a small oasis.

"We will pause here during the heat of the day," Joseph announced.

I was grateful for the rest. Adah ran to the water. She dipped her hand in and splashed it on her face with a giggle.

"Our daughter is still a child. You do not need to worry about a husband for many seasons." Elimelech smiled as he came to my side. "Did you hear what that trader said? I was wise to turn south, away from the harshness of people and land to the north."

"It will be hard to remember the ways of the One God in Moab," I muttered.

"Is that what worries you, Naomi?" The pitying chuckle made

me flush. "The God of Abraham, Isaac, and Jacob will bless us because we separate ourselves from those who go after idols. We will find prosperity in Moab. My family will continue to serve the Living Lord."

The man strode away to talk to Joseph. I stared after my husband, questions circling in my mind like vultures.

"What of the manna and the fall of Jericho and the dividing of the water? God was with us because we were a community." More softly, I whispered. "What of the punishments of Kibroth-hattaavah and the Wilderness of Shur, when God struck down those who turned from the congregation?"

When travel resumed, my husband walked beside me.

"Joseph knows the chief of Beth-peor. He will help us find a home." The words were meant to be conciliatory.

I nodded, even though in my heart, I wept for the loss of my home. Faith seemed to be slipping away from my grasp the further we moved from Canaan. My feet dragged.

"Come, Wife." Elimelech was excited. "We will camp beyond Shittim this night. Soon you will start a new life."

"Yes, my husband." Obediently, I walked faster.

As promised, we reached the city by midafternoon. Joseph approached us.

"My friend, Abdul will set up camp. Come with me. We will visit the chief in Beth-peor." The men strode off together and had not returned by the time the evening fires were banked.

I stared toward the town, anxious about my husband.

"Father will have news in the morning," Chilion tried to reassure me. "It will be good news to have taken so long."

"Yes." I tried to not show my concern to the young man.

Finally, I crawled into my bed. Adah already slept. Elimelech and Joseph were in camp when I awakened.

"All is well, my wife." The man caught me in an uncharacteristic hug near the fire. "We have a home and our choice of fields. Mahlon and Chilion will accompany me this morning."

Some of his enthusiasm seeped into my heart. I felt a smile grow on my lips. Perhaps all would be well.

"How?" I still wanted to know the details.

"We will talk later." The assurance left me wanting more. "My sons must come with me."

The man turned away to find his sons. Joseph and Abdul had already disappeared into the town to display their wares. I found myself alone with Adah.

"Your father says we will have a house." I tried to infuse my voice with enthusiasm.

"Like in Bethlehem?" the child asked.

I nodded. "I am sure it will be very nice. Just like the one in Bethlehem."

It would have been easier to relax if I had not been so nervous about my husband's plans. As it was, I was unable to even settle to spinning. The yarn kept tangling because of my shaking hands and distracted thoughts.

❧ 18 ❧

"YOU WILL FIND THAT everything is ready." Elimelech was like a child with a special surprise.

He escorted me to Beth-peor. We passed many houses before he stopped beside a gate. The house was smaller than we left in Bethlehem.

"This will be our home," my husband proclaimed happily. "The well is not far. I am sure you will soon make friends. The people are friendly."

"It is nice." I tried to find something positive to say. "The carving over the door is quite fascinating."

"Here, we will prosper." My husband swung open the door. "You will be able to have many carvings done, if you want."

I followed the man inside. Adah immediately began to explore the room.

She peered into a covered basket and then a jar. "Here is flour. And some milk."

I stared around the room. Baskets with various foods awaited my arrival. There was even a jar of water, ready in the corner.

"You have gotten me all this?" I heard the choked sound in my voice and cleared my throat.

"Joseph has friends in this place." Elimelech shrugged sheepishly. "They did all this."

"I will prepare a meal for the trader and his son here tonight." Impulsively, I made the offer.

"They will be delighted. I will go and tell them."

"Adah, we have a lot to do," I told my daughter. "First, we must light the oven and make bread."

Adah hurried to my side. The round oven looked like the one in Bethlehem. I stacked the kindling and wood carefully. With a bunch of straw, I lit the fire from the firepot my husband set beside the door.

"That should heat nicely." I nodded complacently.

"You are new," a young voice called from the gate.

"Yes, we just arrived." I looked up to see a girl of perhaps ten standing just inside the yard.

"Hello." Adah crossed the yard to greet our guest.

"My name is Ruth. It means friend. Will you be my friend?" The Moabite tilted her head and looked at my daughter. They were of similar height because the visitor was tall for her age.

"Uh-huh." Adah nodded. "Your hair is pretty."

She reached out to stroke the thick braid of hair that fell over one shoulder. It was not brown, but neither was it black. The color reminded me of the velvet of dusk, just before night.

"You have beautiful hair, too." The newcomer smiled. "I have never seen so many curls. What is your name?"

"Adah," my daughter replied. "It means that I am an ornament."

"Maybe we can play sometime," Ruth suggested. "I have to carry this water to our garden now."

She picked up the jar standing just outside our gate. Competently, if not gracefully, the water was placed on her shoulder and carried down the street. Adah watched until Ruth turned the corner.

"Come on, we have to make the bread and slice vegetables," I called my daughter.

The rest of the morning was a frenzy of activity. I formed the bread into loaves with a sigh of relief.

"There is not much left to do," I told Adah. "Are there onions and radishes left in our supplies?"

"Here are some." My helper produced a bunch of radishes and one onion from the bundle I carried to the house only that morning.

"I am glad that I brought what was growing in our garden." The comment did not merit a response from Adah.

"I will put the bread in the oven." My twelve-year-old daughter was competent and quick.

The scent of the baking bread drifted into the house as I finished the tray of vegetables and sliced the onions to roast in the hot oven.

"Taste the bread." I tore a chunk off the hot loaf when I carried it to the house.

"It is good," the girl mumbled around a mouthful.

"Nothing like freshly baked barley bread," I agreed, taking a bite of my own piece.

I looked around the room, deciding that everything was arranged as well as possible in the short time.

I sighed with relief. "We are just in time. Here comes your father."

"You must let me honor you for all your assistance," Elimelech responded to an unheard comment from Joseph. "What you have done has given me new hope."

"It was the least I could do," asserted the trader.

I enlisted my daughter's help. "They are at the gate. Help me put out the platters."

"Here is water." Elimelech offered the basin to his guests.

Mahlon and Chilion trailed after their father and Abdul. I wondered at their sullen expressions. It was not until after the meal that I learned the reason.

"I will walk with you to the city gate," my husband offered when the food was consumed and the jar of wine emptied.

Barely had the trio disappeared when Mahlon faced me.

"We did not come here to work as slaves." His tone was angry.

"What do you mean?" I was at a loss to understand the complaint, even though my heart caught with fear.

"The land we own has to be irrigated," Chilion explained unhappily.

"That means we have to open and close the levees. Dirt has to be shored up nearly every day to keep the entire field from flooding. It will be back-breaking work," Mahlon expounded on the complaint. "In Bethlehem, all we had to do was wait for the rain."

I tried to coax my sons into a more cheerful frame of mind. "I am sure that when you learn how, it will not be hard."

"You and Adah have it easy." The young man was not interested in my suggestion. "All you do is bake bread and draw water."

"We also prepare the fire, clean the house, whitewash the walls, do your laundry, cook meals for you, weave blankets and rugs to trade, bear children—" I was appalled at the venomous tirade pouring from my lips and covered my mouth.

"Mother . . . I . . ." My son was struck silent by my reaction.

"Your father brought us here to prosper." I heard irritation in my tone. "That will take some work, no matter where we live. We all have to make sacrifices."

"Yes, Mother," Chilion nodded his understanding. Meekly, he added, "We will do our part."

Mahlon looked abashed and nodded silently in agreement.

"I know you will." Impulsively, I stepped forward to hug each sturdy young man. "Go to your beds. Tomorrow will bring brighter thoughts."

I hoped I was right. Elimelech returned after I sought my blankets. The man smelled of strong barley beer when he drew me close.

"Let us celebrate." The words were slightly slurred.

I did not resist. After he began snoring contentedly, I lay wondering what the future would bring.

"We are far from your land," I confessed to the unseen God of my people. "I hope you will not abandon us and that we will not forget you."

Exhaustion claimed me. Bright sunlight streaming across the eastern desert awakened me to my new life.

"We will go to the well." Adah and I set out after the men left the house in the morning.

"There is Ruth!" The girl spotted her new friend before I did. She darted away from my side.

"Hello, Adah!" The Moabite smiled a welcome and introduced me to the women gossiping at the well. "This is Naomi and her daughter."

"Are you are from Canaan?"

"I heard that the newcomers were Hebrew."

"Why did you come?"

"Probably their God told them to move."

"Will you be staying?"

Between the questions and speculations, I could not answer everyone. Ruth took pity on me.

"The family of Elimelech is from Bethlehem, in Canaan. They came to Moab because there is drought in the land. Our chief has made them welcome."

"How do you know so much about us?" I bent close to the girl to ask after she gave a brief history of our lives.

Ruth blushed and admitted, "I listened when my father was talking to our chief last night. I hope you do not mind that I told the women."

"No, it made it easier." My sigh was from a wave of loneliness. Even though they smiled, none of the women offered friendship. I found myself remembering Rachel's welcome.

"They will soon come to like you," the girl tried to reassure me, sensing my sorrow.

We walked home together. Over the next few days and weeks, Ruth came to visit often. My daughter and the Moabite girl became good friends. Even though two years separated their ages, neither was a woman yet. Adah was not interested in meeting other girls in the town. I, too, was reserved about my friendship with the women I met. Their unveiled hair was often dyed to imitate the goddess Astarte. The garish red reminded me of Rahab, even though she never had to color her naturally beautiful locks. I found myself missing the wife of Salma, as well as Rachel and my other acquaintances in Bethlehem. It was not long before I learned that Ruth had no mother.

"That must be very hard for you," I sympathized. "I just learned that my mother died several years ago. She was living with my brother in Shechem."

Ruth loved to sit beside me while Adah and I were spinning or carding wool.

"I have never learned to weave," she admitted longingly one afternoon when the men were harvesting the barley.

"You must learn," I insisted. "It is a skill no bride should be without."

My companion blushed and giggled. "I am too young to think about being a bride."

"Some man will find you a lovely bride," I prophesied.

The child shrugged. "My father will chose a husband at the right time. It is a long time away."

"Will you let me teach you how to weave?" As soon as the idea came to me, I asked the question.

"You do not mind?" Eager but cautious, the Moabite looked longingly at my loom nearby.

"I will teach you and Adah together." I drew both girls close to me. "It will be like having two daughters."

The plan was implemented after the Sabbath. Ruth and I had many conversations as the days turned into months and the hot season slid by.

"Has anyone spoken to your father about a bride price?" One fall day, I raised the subject again. The girl was beginning to have a woman's form.

"There is no hurry. I do not want to marry." The girl shrugged. "My older sister was wed the year before you came. These two years have brought her no joy. Even the birth of a boy child has not made her husband happy. Hiram is a strong-willed man. Elsbet is worn out with trying to please her husband. I could not live that way."

Weakly, I tried to offer a defense. "Not all men are like that."

"I think they are all thoughtless." A frown grew on the young face. "Look how you had to leave your home."

"Elimelech thought it was for the best." I did not sound convincing, even to myself.

"Naomi," the girl said as she laid a hand on mine, "your husband did not ask if you wanted to move, even though he cares for you."

"How do you know he cares?" I could not resist hearing the answer. The man had never spoken of love in all our years together.

"He looks at you when you do not see. I have never seen Hiram even smile at my sister." Ruth sighed.

"You will find a good man," I said encouragingly.

"If the gods are gracious. Maybe it is the One God who has blessed you with such a husband." The thoughtful comment made me pause before replying.

"I do not know if God cares for such things," I mused aloud.

"We keep the Sabbath as commanded, but it is not the same. No one in Beth-peor is interested in learning about the ways of the God of Abraham, Isaac, and Jacob."

The girl did not respond directly. "My father has told the other men that it must be a blessing from your God to bring about such bounty from the fields."

"Yes," I said slowly.

"Astarte and Baal do not hear me," the nearly twelve-year-old girl whispered a moment later.

"What have you prayed for?"

"For my sister's happiness." A flush of color rose over the high cheekbones at the admission. "Hiram is still Hiram. He does not care."

"I am not certain if my God listens either." The confession was low. "I have prayed for many things that never happened."

"But some did?" Eagerly, the young girl pounced on what I left unsaid.

"I suppose so," I admitted with surprise. "My sons are now healthy. I had to pray for a long time, though."

"Then there are all the miracles your God performed." Ruth became animated. "My father remembers seeing the Jordan stop flowing. We all saw the smoke from Jericho. Only a powerful God could defeat the city of Astarte."

"Well . . . I . . . God . . ." My words fumbled to a stop.

I found myself unable to explain the dread that kept me from approaching the invisible God. I was not even sure God was present in Moab. Ruth ignored my silence.

"Tell me how to pray to your God," the girl begged suddenly.

"Well . . ." I stammered. "I . . . I . . . do not really . . . know . . . how."

"Please, Naomi, if your God can help my sister, I will believe." The child sounded earnest and eager.

After a long stretch of silence, I replied. "I guess you could just ask God. It may not help, but I do not think it will hurt."

"Thank you." I was caught in a hug before my friend darted out the door.

I stared after the lithe young figure that ran from the yard. She barely missed running into Mahlon. My son stared after the slender girl. Raven locks flew behind her as she ran.

"Was that Ruth?" The young man peered after my friend.

"Yes." Absently, I nodded, bending over my weaving to tease a knot loose.

"Ruth is my friend," Adah told her brother.

"That is good." The man grinned down at his sister.

I glanced up in time to see my son look at the gate where our visitor vanished. He smoothed his beard, but I thought I glimpsed a smile.

Ruth did not mention if she actually prayed to the One God. I did not ask because I was afraid to show interest. Summer passed to fall, and the air held a chill.

"It will soon be time for the Feast of Atonement," I told Ruth and Adah a few Sabbaths later. "It will seem odd to have no ceremony and sacrifice to remove all the transgressions of the people. The gods of Moab are appeased at the Longest Night, when you light the new fire. I do not know if the God of Israel even hears our prayers here."

"Naomi." My name was barely a whisper on Ruth's lips. "I think that your God has heard my prayers."

I faced the girl. "Why do you say that?"

"Hiram has changed." The simple statement brought a gasp to my lips.

"What do you mean?" I could not comprehend why she thought her brother-in-law was different.

"Elsbet told me that he brought her a fine gown when he went to Gilgal. He is excited about the coming baby and does not care if it is a boy or girl." A smile broke out along with the torrent of words.

"You think that the God of Israel did that?" I was slightly incredulous and a little shaken by the report.

Staunchly, the girl defended her conclusion. "It happened after I prayed."

"I am glad." My mind was in turmoil, but I summoned a smile at her delight. "Your sister deserves happiness."

"Your God has brought her peace." Simple faith was in the statement.

Adah and Ruth began to discuss the next color to use in the blanket. I barely listened.

"Do you think that the God of Abraham, Isaac, and Jacob still hears our prayers?" I asked Elimelech that night. "We are not in the Promised Land. Is the Living God present?"

"Why do you ask, Wife? Have you not seen how we prosper here? That must mean that we are blessed." The man sounded annoyed at my question.

He stamped away before I could explain.

"It does seem we are blessed," I had to admit to Adah.

"Yes, even my brothers are happy," the girl agreed.

"It is time for our sons to marry," I told Elimelech a few moon turnings later, when the air began to warm.

"It is true." The man's brows drew together as he considered my comment. "There are no unwed daughters of Israel here. They would have to marry local girls."

The observation made me gasp. "God will punish us if we allow our sons to wed foreign women."

"Naomi, God will provide," I was left with the assertion to ponder when my husband strode away. "I must tend the sheep. The ewes are getting ready to lamb."

I watched the man head west toward the fields. Beyond was the river, and past that, the land of promise we deserted. There was no sound. Even the birds were silent.

"Are you even there?" I dared confront the empty silence. "If you are really God, you would not be bound to a land. Ruth believes you answered her prayers. I am not even sure if you are present. If you are really God, send wives for my sons."

I ended my challenge when I heard giggles.

"Is God mocking me?" My heart almost stopped with fear.

The giggles drew closer. It was Adah and Ruth returning from the well.

"We will make sweet cakes today," I decided. "It will be time to prepare Passover foods before too long, if Elimelech decides to keep the feast again."

"I remember watching you last year. You had just barely arrived," Ruth confessed. "It was fascinating to see all the different things you made."

"It is a lot of work," I agreed. "Each thing we eat is a reminder of how the Holy One acted in Egypt."

"I will slaughter a lamb for our Passover," my husband told me that night. "We will honor God, as always."

"It is lonely keeping the feast without others," I mumbled. "The celebration does not mean as much if there is no one to share the story with."

"Then you will be pleased that I have invited Hiram and his kin to share in our feast." The announcement left me open-mouthed in astonishment.

"He is not Hebrew," I gasped after a moment.

"The Law of Moses says that any stranger may keep the Passover with the Children of Israel. The man has been of great assistance to me since we arrived. Inviting him to our feast is a good gesture."

"You . . . he . . . when . . ." I struggled with the unexpected news. "How many?"

"There is Hiram, his father and father-in-law with their wives. He has two more brothers and one sister. Also Hiram has a sister-in-law yet unwed and a child."

I counted on my fingers as he spoke. "That is a dozen people plus the baby." I was outraged. "The feast is at the full moon. That is only a day away!"

"Yes." The man seemed unconcerned. "I will see that we have a large lamb."

"Passover is more than a lamb," I sputtered. "Bread and vegetables and herbs and . . . and . . . all the rest have to be made!"

"It will be a grand celebration," Elimelech assured me. "Hiram has promised that he will provide a fine wine."

"I am glad of that." Angrily, I spat the response before turning to survey my supplies.

The man patted my shoulder before leaving me alone. "You will do well."

Still fuming, I checked to see what was needed. "There is not enough flour. I really will have to purchase more vegetables, even though they cost dearly this time of year."

Too upset to rest, I spent my frustration on cleaning. Every speck of dust was swept from the house. The lamps and platters gleamed in the moonlight after the brisk scrubbing with sand they received.

I was curt with Adah in the morning. "We must get things for the Passover. I hope the market has what we need."

Help came from an unexpected source. We had barely returned to the house when Ruth stuck her head in the door.

"This is so exciting! I am to share the . . . the . . . what is it called . . . 'Pass . . . by' meal with you. Hiram was invited with all his family." My friend glowed with anticipation.

"Passover. It is Pass-over." I relaxed in response to the enthusiasm.

"Passover," Ruth repeated slowly. She seemed to be committing the name to memory.

"Elimelech told me that he invited Hiram and his family. I forgot that the invitation would include you." I was pleasantly surprised.

"Now I know that your God has heard my prayers. Hiram is a changed man. Even my father was surprised by the invitation. Will you let me help you? Please. I want to learn all about his feast!" My friend skipped with eagerness, and her words tumbled over each other.

"I would be happy for help. There is much to be done. First, we must remove all leaven from this house."

The little pot was already wrapped in a linen cloth.

"I will take it to my house," the girl from Moab offered. She returned in a few minutes carrying a clean dress for the feast.

"Where do we start?" Adah looked at the pile of food waiting to be prepared.

"A new fire must be kindled. Then we will wash and roast these eggs in the coals. There is unleavened bread to prepare. Elimelech will bring a lamb that will be roasted whole over the fire. All these vegetables and herbs must be chopped properly." My tongue was racing as I listed all the items to be accomplished by sunset.

"What can I do?" Ruth looked a little overwhelmed.

"You and Adah must take these jars to the well. With all the cooking and washing, we will need more water."

"Come on, Adah." Cheerfully, the young woman picked up the containers. "I will carry this jar if you carry that pitcher."

I smiled after the pair. Ruth was showing more and more promise of the woman she would be. Her form was filling out, and her walk was graceful. Adah was still not a woman, although my daughter also had a feminine shape. I sometimes worried because she was past thirteen, but then I reminded myself that my mother and I both started our cycles at that age.

"Perhaps Adah and Ruth will be women together," I told the pile of sticks Mahlon arranged before he left for the fields at dawn. "God, will you hear me and send a husband for my daughter?"

I regarded the flaring of a small flame as proof that my words were heard. Carefully, I built up the fire to a nice blaze.

"Here we are," Ruth announced a moment after I heard the returning giggles.

"Here we are," Adah echoed. She laughed merrily.

"Here you are!" I joined the laughter as I dusted my hands.

Both girls settled to work, washing and chopping vegetables. I sighed with relief and rapidly washed the eggs, trying not to think about the cost of each brown oval.

"It is early in the year. The hens are not laying much yet. Most of the eggs, I save to hatch." I replayed the excuses from the farmer as I gently wiped away the barnyard filth.

Carefully nestling the clean eggs in a basket, I moved to the fires. The shallow hole just inside the ring of stones waited. With care, I set each egg in place, added the damp palm leaves, and then a thin layer of dirt. Finally, I nudged part of the fire over the location and added another log to the blaze.

"These are all clean," Ruth announced, shaking the water off a final bunch of radishes.

"Good." I rinsed the ash from my hands. "Pour the dirty water on the garden. We will begin to prepare the platters."

Adah grabbed the pot I washed the eggs in. She squealed when some of the liquid splashed on her legs.

"Some of the water got to the ground," Ruth laughed. She playfully splashed some of her water on her feet.

I smiled at their antics. Anything seemed possible, so I repeated my prayer. "Please send wives for my sons. If Mahlon and Chilion wed, I will have other women to help me. That would be wonderful, and I could believe that you are not angry."

"What do we do next?" My two helpers stood waiting for directions.

I opened my mouth to reply, only to be forestalled by the arrival of husband and sons.

"We have a fine lamb this year," Mahlon stated.

"It was from our own flocks. 'Take a one year old, without a blemish' as required by the Law of God," his brother recited.

"Who performed the sacrifice?" I asked with concern.

"As the eldest representative of the Children of Israel, I did," Elimelech explained defensively, if not proudly. "There is no other way."

"Yes, my husband." I hoped it did not matter.

"You have the fire ready, I see," the man remarked. "Mahlon, see that the lamb is secured. We will watch the meat and recite prayers until the sun sets."

"Yes." My son moved to the task.

"It is right to observe the ritual," I mumbled to myself. "The tabernacle is far away, and we are strangers in this land. Perhaps God will still hear your prayers."

"God has been with us," my husband responded sternly, close to my ear. "We do well to remember the ways of our people."

I felt my face flood with color and bent low over the food to hide my embarrassment.

"We will finish preparing the food inside so we do not disturb the men at their prayers." As I spoke, I picked up the pile of platters.

Adah picked up a basket with herbs. It tilted precariously but did not spill. I glanced at Ruth. She was watching my oldest son tie the lamb in place. The young man looked up, caught her eye and grinned. A wave of red flooded the pretty face. Hastily, the girl turned, grabbed a basket of vegetables and fled into the house.

Could it be that God has heard me? I felt my heart leap with hope, although I dared not voice it.

The remainder of the day was spent in chopping and mixing.

"I will take the bread to bake," the Moabite offered when it was ready.

"That would help," I nodded.

The girl started for the door, but then turned back. "May I borrow a veil? I would not want to interrupt the men at their prayers with uncovered hair."

"Here." The excuse was transparent, but I pretended oblivion and hid my smile until the young woman was gone.

I could not resist watching the graceful figure cross the yard. Mahlon looked up. I saw a smile lift the edges of his mustache.

His softly spoken words floated to me. "Thank you for helping my mother."

Ruth ducked her head in shy acknowledgement. She did not reply. I watched my son casually turning the spit. His eyes kept straying to the slender girl baking bread on the hot stones.

"There is just time to arrange the final platters," I told Ruth when I met her at the door. The sun was preparing to slip behind the far hills of Canaan. "I will take this tray to my husband for the lamb. Your family will soon be arriving."

I crossed the yard. Elimelech dozed at his prayers. Deliberately, I shuffled my feet on the ground. As I hoped, the noise roused the man.

"Amen." His resounding conclusion was meant to convince us all that he had been in conversation with God.

Chilion coughed to cover a chuckle. Mahlon squinted at the meat with his lips pressed tight against a grin.

"Is the lamb ready?" I had to bite my lip to prevent a smile when the man stood and stretched before he took the polished bronze platter.

Chilion scrambled to his feet as well.

"You can unearth the eggs," I told my youngest son, pointing to the spot.

It was easy to identify. Singed ends of the palm leaves protruded like a crown from the ground. While Mahlon and Elimelech slid the lamb from the spit and Chilion dug out the eggs, I returned to the house.

"What a lovely display." With unfeigned pleasure, I admired the platters arranged on the wide carpet. "You girls have done well."

"Welcome, my friend." I heard Elimelech call the greeting, even as Chilion entered the house with his basket of eggs. Mahlon followed with the heavy platter.

"Hiram has arrived," my older son announced.

"Come, Ruth, Adah. We must change our clothes," I caught both girls by the hand and ran up the stairs.

I was grateful for Adah's curls. They never needed much, except to be pinned back from her face with a wooden comb. My own had to be brushed and braided. I threw my festive gown over my head.

"Now let me look at you." I turned my daughter around with an approving nod.

"Is this alright?" Ruth questioned shyly.

"It is lovely." My hand reached out to feel the soft Egyptian cotton of her gown.

Like me, the Moabite girl had braided her hair. A veil that matched the gown framed her face.

"It is perfect," I reiterated. "Now we will join the others."

In the short time it took me to change, Hiram and his entire family had gathered in our home. Elimelech was indicating where each person should sit.

"Women eat with us for this special feast. The God of Moses brought freedom to all Israel this night," he explained to the man. "You will sit at my right hand with your kinsmen beside you. My sons will be at my left hand."

"Come," I led Ruth to where her sister stood nervously twisting her veil tassels. "Elsbet, welcome to our home. We will sit here."

With a gesture, I indicated the cushions arranged across from the men. The women looked uncomfortable at sitting in the presence of the men and only sat down after Hiram and his father both nodded permission. Adah was fascinated by the baby. She crouched beside Hiram's wife, staring at the small boy.

"Blessed are you, Lord of All." Elimelech began the prayers and recitation of the mighty acts of God from the beginning of time.

"Why is this night different from all others?" Chilion asked the requisite question after the first cup of wine circulated.

Elimelech began the saga. "On this night, the Holy One frees the Children of Israel from bondage in Egypt."

I looked at our guests. Ruth was listening with parted lips. Her sister and other women talked in low tones. I guessed from their curious glances that they were comparing my home with theirs. Adah held Ruth's nephew in her lap. Hiram and his kin appeared to be listening closely to the story.

The prayers, recitation and eating continued, as it had for over forty years. I felt myself relaxing. There was something comforting in keeping the ritual remembrance even in this foreign land. God no longer seemed distant. Perhaps it was possible for my prayer to be heard and answered.

I pray you send a wife for Mahlon. The secret intercession had nothing to do with the feast.

I could not help but notice how my son kept stealing glances at my companion. She did make a pretty picture in the light from the oil lamps. Her soft gown emphasized the fact that she was almost a woman.

I could be happy here. The feeling of contentment surprised me. It lingered long after the oil burned away and our guests departed.

Hiram offered a low salaam in parting. "Thank you, Elimelech for sharing this special feast with me. I can see that you truly believe the One who has no name is holy. Many are the wonders I have heard tonight."

"It was wonderful." Ruth hugged me tightly before following her family.

"I am glad." My whisper followed the girl into the night.

Adah slept like a kitten, curled on one cushion. Elimelech bent and gathered his daughter into his arms.

"You are tired; I will carry her." The man surprised me even more when he added, "Naomi, you have made me proud."

I stifled a yawn and followed my husband to our bed.

"I am content here." We lay hand in hand. I shared my revelation. "It does seem that God has blessed us, even though we left Bethlehem."

"My wife, you make me happy with those words." The man drew me into his arms. I forgot my exhaustion in his rekindled ardor.

❧ 19 ❧

WE DID NOT SEE as much of our friend after the Passover.

"My father says I should be concerned about his house and spend less time playing since I will soon be a woman," she sadly explained one afternoon.

"That is not fair," insisted Adah.

I tried to be encouraging. "Ruth must obey her father. I am sure she will still visit sometimes."

It was the full heat of the summer when the girl surprised me with her announcement.

"I am a woman," she whispered on one of her infrequent visits. "My father will offer sacrifices to Astarte. All will know that I am marriageable."

"That is good news." I hugged the girl close. "Who will he choose?"

"I do not know," confessed my friend. "Someone who will provide well for me, I guess. That is how Hiram was able to marry Elsbet. He has many flocks and fields."

"Your father will find you a fine husband." I hugged the slender girl close again.

"Ruth." Adah held her friend's hand. "I am happy for you."

"I wish we could have the celebration together," Ruth confided to my daughter.

Seeing the girl nod, I challenged God, *Why will you not let my child find happiness as woman and wife.*

"My sister is waiting for me," the young Moabite explained a moment later. "Elsbet wants to talk about my party and the procession through town. Every young girl has a celebration when she becomes a woman."

"I will clap for you and throw a coin for luck. This is not the first coming-of-age feast we have seen since leaving Egypt, but it is the first I have had any interest in," I admitted, smiling at the dreamy look that crossed Ruth's face.

"Thank you." Ruth hugged me quickly before running back to her sister's home.

"We will have to tell Mahlon when he comes home," I told Adah.

"Yes." The girl watched her friend with a longing expression.

"I saw Ruth today." In the cool of the evening, I brought up the subject to my family.

"Who?" Elimelech frowned in the dusk. "You mean Hiram's sister-in-law. Was she the young girl who helped at Passover?"

"Yes," I confirmed.

My husband lost interest, but Mahlon leaned forward when his father did not speak.

"She is well?" He tried to sound casual.

Chilion's chuckle showed he was not fooled by his brother's nonchalance.

"More than well," I smiled in the deepening dark, gratified by the interest. "She is a woman. Her father will soon seek a husband for her."

"She . . . bride . . . I . . . but—" My son lost his tongue.

"Why do you not ask Father to speak to Hiram on your behalf?" teased Chilion. "Or should I say, speak to old Hosea, her father?"

"Be quiet. You do not know anything." Almost fiercely, Mahlon turned on his sibling. For a moment, I thought they would end up wrestling on the ground like children.

"What is this?" Elimelech heard the teasing.

"Mahlon desires Ruth as a wife." Chilion ducked out of his brother's reach.

I put a hand on my older son's shoulder to stop him from following.

"Is this true?" I could not tell if my husband was surprised or appalled.

"Yes, Father." Mahlon straightened proudly. "I would be happy if I could wed Ruth, daughter of Hosea the Moabite."

"She is not of our people," Elimelech stated the obvious.

"What does it matter? I will never meet a woman of the tribes of Israel here." A mutinous tone crept into the answer. Then he launched into arguments that showed he had thought much about my friend. "Think of how Ruth has shown interest in our ways. She already has helped Mother with the Passover. You yourself invited Hiram of Moab and his family to join the Feast. We have kept ourselves away from the local rituals. If Chilion and I do not marry, the line of Elimelech will die out."

Elimelech raised his hand to stem the torrent. "My son, I see you have given this idea consideration. It is possible that Hosea will not want to join their family to ours."

Mahlon sighed deeply before responding. "I know that. How will we find out if you do not ask?"

"You have given me much to think on." My husband rose. "Pray God will give me guidance."

The young man watched his father climb to the roof where we slept. Adah looked at her brother; then she smiled thoughtfully. I followed my husband.

The man held up a hand before I spoke. "Naomi, I must think. I have to consider the future of my sons and my heritage. Our possessions have multiplied. Mahlon is right to say that unless he marries a Moabite, the lineage of Elimelech will die."

"The God of Jacob has given you rich fields and increased your flocks. You have said that is proof of blessing." I sought to ease the torment by reminding the man of his own words.

"Dare I disobey the word of Moses?" His big hand ran through his hair, causing it to stand up in front, instead of lying in neat square bangs similar to all the men of Moab.

"My husband." Kneeling beside the man, I tried to smooth the hair. He pushed me away. "Ruth wants to know more of our ways and leave the gods of this land."

"Do you know that?" Hopeful eyes looked at me across the short distance.

"Yes." I did not know if he could see my nod in the meager light of the sliver of a moon rising in the east.

The man made no reply.

"She has prayed to the God of Abraham, Isaac, and Jacob." I hoped the girl would forgive any breach of confidence. "It was Ruth who helped with the Passover. She hung on every word of the story."

"I will think on it." My husband did not sound convinced.

Three full days passed before Elimelech spoke of the matter again.

"Hiram tells me that his sister-in-law is to have a grand procession to their temple in honor of her womanhood," my husband announced after the evening meal.

"It is at the full moon," I mentioned.

"We are invited," the man said, dropping another crumb of information.

"Why should I attend and torture myself if you will not speak to Hosea?" Mahlon challenged his father. A nearly full moon lit the discontented pout on my son's face.

"Have I said that I would not?" Elimelech looked at his son leaning against the house.

Mahlon leaned forward, hopefully.

"Will you?" The young man sounded eager.

Elimelech remained silent for so long that the pout reappeared. The young man slumped back against the wall.

Very slowly and seriously came the reply. "God has shown me that if the young woman is willing to accept our faith, we may approach Hosea about his daughter."

The elation on Mahlon's face made me smile with relief.

"We will go to him in the morning," my son proclaimed.

Later, I snuggled close to my husband. "How did you decide?"

"God reminded me of the woman Rahab. Joshua himself made her a member of Israel when she renounced the gods of Jericho. She was wed to Salma bar Nashon, as well. How can I do less for my own son?" The explanation was simple.

"I am glad." In the moonlight, I smiled to myself.

"It still remains to convince Hosea and Hiram," the man reminded me before bending over me with a kiss.

I held my breath when Elimelech and Mahlon left the house at midmorning. They would approach Hosea and the other elders of Beth-peor at the gate. Like Bethlehem, it was where all important business was conducted.

"Old Hosea was more than willing to accept a field and a few sheep for his daughter's happiness," Elimelech reported when they returned. "The announcement will not be made until after the festival of her womanhood, however."

The procession and feast at the full moon was a grand affair. We all attended. I saw Mahlon watching the young woman in her dance with the other maidens. His were not the only eyes. I saw him frowning jealously at some of the other men.

"The betrothal will be at the moon before the harvest," my husband told us after he met with Hosea again. "You will be wed in a year."

"That is so long," complained my son.

"There is much to do," his father reminded the young man. Counting on his fingers, he enumerated the tasks. "An addition must be built for you to live in. Deeds are to be drawn up. Ruth must learn more of our ways. The dowry will have to be paid. Plans for the wedding feast have to be made."

"Time will go quickly," I assured my son with a pat on the muscular arm. "You will see her often."

"I suppose so." Mahlon did not look happy.

When I was alone I could not stop the prayer of thanksgiving. "Thank you God of Israel. You have heard my prayer. I see that you have not deserted your servants, even here in Moab."

Ruth approached me shyly the day after her ceremony.

"Come in, my daughter," I greeted my young friend.

"Are you happy?" The tentative question surprised me.

"I could not be happier." My hug was all the proof she needed.

"It is what I dreamed of. I prayed to your God," the girl confessed. "The Holy One has heard me again."

I heard myself say words I was not sure I believed. "The Living God hears all who truly seek for faith."

Ruth answered with a radiant smile and fierce hug. "I want to learn about your God, not just because that is a requirement of my marriage."

Chilion surprised us a moon turning after his brother's betrothal. We rested in the evening from the exertions of the harvest.

"I have found a girl I wish to marry," the young man announced.

"Who is this, my son?" His father leaned forward.

"Orpah, daughter of Daniel the woodcutter. I saw her when I purchased the logs for Mahlon's house. The girl is a woman now. Will you speak to her father?" Chilion ended with the pleading question.

"If she is willing to learn the ways of our God, and if her father is willing to let her wed a foreigner, she will be your wife," Elimelech promised.

At the harvest festival, Chilion was betrothed. Orpah, a short, plump sparrow of a girl looked almost afraid.

"I will obey Chilion bar Elimelech as my duty." Her response was barely audible.

Orpah came with Ruth the afternoon following the betrothal.

My friend led the younger girl by the hand. "Mother Naomi, Orpah has come with me to learn of your God."

"I am pleased with the women my sons will marry." My sincere smile eased some of the girl's fear.

"Thank you," she whispered softly.

We spent that afternoon, and many others, in conversation about all that the God of Moses demanded and promised. I found myself remembering things long forgotten from the stories of Miriam.

"Why did the serpents come?" Adah asked when I finally told of the attack of the snakes.

"It was punishment from God for rebellion." I swallowed hard at the memory of my father's death.

Orpah shuddered. "How horrible."

"The creatures attacked and many died that day," I remembered. The shudder that ran through my body was an involuntary reaction to the memory of my father's limp body.

"Why did the people die?" my daughter asked.

Ruth had a wiser answer than I could summon. "Because they

tried to take the power from God and do things their own way. A God as mighty as *I AM* deserves to be obeyed."

"It is true," I agreed. "Not everyone died that was bitten. God told Moses to make a bronze serpent. It was carried through the camp. All who looked on the image lived. It was too late for your grandfather and some of the others."

"You have had much sorrow." The insight from my young friend jerked my head up. "It is fortunate that you have your faith in the Living God to sustain you. The God of Abraham, Isaac, and Jacob provides healing, even in the midst of death."

I gave the expected answer. "Yes."

Many times in the next weeks and months, the comment returned to haunt me.

"Does God really bring healing in the midst of death?" The question was still not answered to my satisfaction when the seasons turned to harvest again.

"There is so much to do to prepare for your brothers' weddings." I brushed a straggling hair out of my face and adjusted the yarn on the loom for Adah. She had started a blanket for her brother.

"Here comes Chilion," the young woman warned. "He probably has another plan for his Orpah."

I was delighted by the protective way my younger son acted toward his bride. Her short, plump figure and round face made her appear a child still, although I knew she was a year older than Ruth.

"Mother, will you make the honeyed dates that you used to give us in Bethlehem?" The young man almost licked his lips in anticipation. "I know that Orpah would like them."

"It would take many, many dates to supply the entire town," I shook my head, thinking as much of the work as the expense involved.

The young man wheedled until I gave in. "Mother, I will only get married once."

"Very well. If you can find enough dates, we will make the treat." My reward was a hearty hug.

"I will find the dates." With that promise, the man was gone.

"Why do you let him beg you?" Adah conveniently forgot all the times she pouted and wept until I let her buy a new comb or length of cloth.

"Maybe he will not be able to find the dates," I suggested, though I did not answer her question. "Anyway, we will do what we can for Ruth and Orpah. A wedding is a special day."

Chilion did find the little oval fruit. Ruth and Adah helped me prepare the delicacy. Adah's agile fingers stuffed a piece of almond inside each one after Ruth carefully cut it open to remove the seed.

"This is going quickly," I rejoiced while rolling the dates in honey and lining them up on a tray to dry in the afternoon sun.

The sun was only halfway down the sky toward the mountains when we finished. Elimelech sauntered in from the fields as I set out the final tray. Ruth snatched her veil and hurried from the yard. She remained in awe of my husband and rarely stayed long when he was home.

"The harvest is gathered. It is a good omen to be wed amid such bounty. God is blessing us. Mahlon and Chilion will prosper in this place. They will be leaders in Moab." My husband had grand plans.

"God is indeed gracious," I agreed absently.

"When the moon is full, our sons will be wed." The man bent over to kiss the top of my head. "We will offer prayers and sacrifices to the Holy One."

The day of the weddings dawned gray.

"I hope the sun comes out," I told Adah as she braided my hair.

The girl had a gentle way of tugging every strand in place so that it did not come undone. My own hasty work too often started straggling by midmorning. I tried not to think about the few gray strands I noticed when combing the brown locks.

"It will be a lovely day," my daughter answered confidently.

She was right. Soon, the sun melted the clouds to light the road through Beth-peor. Mahlon and Chilion set out with their attendants along the shining ribbon to claim their brides.

"Come to the wedding of Mahlon and Ruth," one group of young men chanted.

"Join the celebration with Chilion and Orpah," the other groomsmen called out.

They processed all around the town.

"We have to hurry and set out the festal foods," I told Adah.

She was already piling the myriad breads on platters to put on the benches along the front wall.

With a worried frown, I surveyed the mountain of food. "I hope it is enough."

"There is a bounty to feed all the armies of Israel," laughed my daughter. "Father has purchased so many jars of wine that we will be washed away if they break."

"Laugh if you want." I pretended to be angry, although I was sure the girl was right. "Your father and brothers must not be shamed."

"I can hardly wait for them to get here." Adah danced from one foot to the other.

She popped a honeyed date into her mouth. A minute later, she darted across the yard to look out the gate. Elimelech emerged from the house. He bent to add a stick to the fire in the center of the yard.

"It is good," he said, nodding at our preparations. The man laughed at his daughter's eager dancing. "You will know when your brothers approach. The music will get louder and louder."

"I know." Still, the girl impatiently moved to stand in the center of the street. "They must have found Ruth and Orpah. The music has changed."

A moment later, I hurried to the gate, almost as excited as Adah.

"The drumming has changed," I agreed. "You can hear the pipe and cymbal, as well."

Elimelech could no longer wait. He joined us at the entrance. "Here they come."

We could hear clapping from many hands. The music grew louder as the crowd approached.

"Here they are!" Adah clapped with delight.

"Welcome my friends." Elimelech stood in the gate. "This is a happy time. I came among you, a stranger seeking a home. You welcomed me. My God has given me blessing among you. Like my ancestor Jacob, who traveled to Haran, my sons have found wives among your daughters. This is a time for all in Moab and in Israel to be as one."

A cheer greeted my husband's words. Hosea tottered forward, balancing on Hiram's arm.

"Your God has brought blessing to this city. We are glad to join our daughters to your sons." The speech ended with a wheeze and cough.

Not to be outdone, Orpah's father stepped up. "Elimelech of Israel, we worship differently. I rejoice to give my daughter to you. All see how your God has blessed this place on your behalf."

Elimelech bowed to both fathers before he spoke. "Let Mahlon and Chilion bring their brides."

Mahlon lifted Ruth from her litter. Although covered with the thick veil and heavy, bangle-covered headdress, I guessed that the young woman was poised and calm. Orpah clung to Chilion, again reminding me of a small child. Her bridal finery seemed to overwhelm the small figure.

"Mahlon you have made promises and signed the marriage contract. Will you abide by the terms to gain Ruth of Moab, daughter of Hosea, as wife?" Hiram spoke for the old man who was still coughing hoarsely.

"I will abide with Ruth as my wife." The young man tried to speak solemnly. His blissful grin betrayed him.

Daniel the woodcutter faced Chilion.

"You signed the marriage contract and made promises to care for my Orpah." The man's voice broke when he said his daughter's name. "I charge you to hold to those vows."

My younger son looked down at the small figure. She did not even come to his shoulder.

"I will honor her with all that I have promised."

My heart swelled with pride. No longer were my sons weak and sickly. They were healthy, strong men who were now responsible for wives of their own.

Elimelech spoke a benediction: "My sons and daughters, may the God of Isaac our father who brought us from bondage in Egypt make you fruitful and bless the work of your hands."

Silence fell after my husband finished his prayer. He raised his hands and spread them wide in welcome.

"Come, my friends; let us celebrate with the young couples."

The invitation was greeted with loud clanging, clapping, and cheering. Mahlon, with Ruth, led the way into our yard. His father and brother followed. Then the entire town tried to surge in. The celebration spilled into the street and lasted long after the sun had set. Torches lit the faces of my sons after the brides were whisked away by their bridesmaids.

"They are anxious to join Ruth and Orpah," I edged close to my husband to whisper. "Send them on their way."

"Go to your brides," Elimelech announced at last.

Great applause and shouts of encouragement followed the men. Both my sons tried to pretend nonchalance.

"Give courage to Ruth and to Orpah," I prayed, suddenly remembering my own bridal fears.

A few guests continued to linger after the torches burned low. All the food and wine was consumed, before Hiram and Hosea stumbled through the gate. Elimelech finally joined me on the roof to fall asleep almost instantly. I lay watching the moon disappear in the west.

"Truly, we are the chosen of God," I marveled, at peace with the Holy One. "I see that you do bless us here. You heard my prayers and have brought wives into my sons' homes. My daughter will find a husband, and I will hold grandchildren in my arms. May Ruth and Orpah be fruitful in your eyes."

The wedding week passed slowly.

I kept Adah occupied during the day with many tasks. "Let us finish this rug for Chilion and the blanket for Mahlon."

Graceful hands deftly worked the yarn so that the colorful blanket grew steadily. My own job was to complete the larger, heavier floor covering. I loved to watch the design take form. By the time the newlyweds emerged, both gifts were complete.

Adah ran to her friend with a hug. "I am glad you will live here."

Orpah hung back slightly until I held out my hand. "It will be wonderful to have two more daughters living here with us."

Before long, we settled into a routine. Morning was for baking or cleaning and washing. In the late morning, we prepared food for the men. After Elimelech and his sons returned to the fields, we would work in the shade. Weaving or sewing occupied our time.

"Tell us again of Joseph." Ruth often asked for a story.

Orpah occasionally made a request. "I want to hear about the creation."

Adah had her own favorite. "It is the story of the Exodus that is most exciting."

Again and again, I told the stories of Israel. We compared the creation saga of Miriam with the Moabite stories of gods who fought and died to establish the world. One story that we both knew told of a flood that covered all things.

"It was Noah who build a big ship," I explained. "In to it, he took two of every kind of animal."

"We heard from our priests that the hero Gilgamesh saved a few people on his great boat," Ruth countered.

"How could water cover all the land?" Orpah wanted to know.

I was glad that the young woman lost her shyness. The three girls were close friends. I rejoiced in their company and in my daughter.

"You are becoming more and more lovely," I told my fourteen-year-old daughter. "When I look at you, I see the same beauty that my sister Leah has."

It was true that the dark curls surrounded a face that looked similar to my sister.

"You will be much sought after as a bride," I promised.

My words proved prophetic.

"Hezik, son of the chief, has asked for a betrothal contract with Adah," Elimelech told me one night before the Passover arrived. I could not tell if the man was pleased or distressed.

"She is not yet a woman," I argued.

"He is willing to wait," responded my husband. A smile lifted the man's mouth. "What he said was, 'I desire Adah as wife, even if I must wait five years for her.' It seems that her beauty and youth have entranced the young man."

"Is he a young man? I do not want my daughter married to an old man. She need not know grief for many years."

"Hezik is younger than Chilion," my husband explained. "It is a good age for my daughter."

Feeling old and tired, I nodded my acceptance. "Do as you see fit."

Adah was nervous, as well as excited, when she was escorted to the house of the chief. There the appropriate documents were prepared. My throat tightened as I watched Elimelech press his seal into the clay.

Ruth leaned close to whisper an explanation. "They will bake the tablet. If either party fails in the bargain, the tablet will be broken."

"I am sure that the contract will not be broken," I whispered back.

The betrothal turned my daughter into a woman almost overnight. Only a few days later, she came to me.

"Mother, I think I have become a woman this night."

"It is time." Holding my daughter close, I let my heart offer a prayer of thanks. "You have taken away her shame. Blessed be the Living God."

Elimelech stared out the door for a long time after I told him the news. "We will not have a grand procession to the temple of the gods of Moab. My daughter will not be paraded through the streets. Besides, she is already betrothed."

I was a little sad that Adah would be denied the same experience as other girls in town. Even though I knew that their celebrations honored the goddess Astarte, I longed to celebrate my daughter's womanhood. My own procession through the camp from the women's tent to the ark had been a special time, even in the midst of my mother's grief.

Forcing a smile, I suggested, "Let us make this Passover a special celebration."

"We will keep the command of God," Elimelech agreed. "The Living Lord has blessed us for our obedience."

Mahlon offered one of the precious new additions to his flock. "I will find the best lamb. My sister deserves no less."

I did not find peace in the celebration. There was too much to think about.

"Adah will leave behind the faith of our people. Will God condemn us?" I sought consolation from Elimelech.

"What choice do we have?" the man reasoned with a frown. "The Almighty has not punished us for the wives of Mahlon and Chilion."

"My prayers for grandsons are unanswered," I argued weakly.

"The women are young." My husband shook his head. "We will have grandchildren."

≈ 20 ≈

MY SONS WERE HAPPY with their brides. Chilion rejoiced in Orpah. He loved to swing his wife high over his head until she squealed.

"I do not treat my wife like a child," Mahlon scolded his brother.

"Nor is she with child," countered my younger son.

"There is time enough." The answer was always the same.

It was nearly a full year after the wedding feast when Chilion announced that Orpah was pregnant.

"It is about time," joked Elimelech. "I want to hold my grandson while I still have hair for him to pull."

Fondly, I looked at my husband. Few knew that, beneath the turban, his head was almost bald. The gray beard was a reminder that my husband was older than me. I saw Ruth flinch at the words and lower her head. A few days later, my daughter-in-law shared her sorrow.

"I have failed Mahlon and I have failed your God," she wept as we walked in the fields together.

We were gathering a few stalks of wheat to roast the plump kernels for dinner. It was a special treat reserved for the time just before the harvest began.

"You are still young."

"Perhaps your God is punishing me for being so presumptuous and praying," she sobbed.

"No." I held the slim girl close while she cried. "Often it is the women who think that they are forsaken who are most blessed. Remember the lives of Sarah and Rebecca and Rachel."

I was not sure my words comforted my friend. We never spoke

of it again. Ruth helped me comfort Orpah when her womb cast out the child before the Longest Night.

"It is not fair," she sobbed. "Are the gods punishing me?"

"We will pray to the God of Abraham, Isaac, and Jacob that you will bear a child. Surely God has not forgotten us." My words did not ease the wailing.

Eventually, I mixed soothing herbs into a tea. Only then did she sleep. From that day, darkness descended on the house of Elimelech. It seemed that my daughters-in-law were right, and God had turned away. In my secret heart, I feared that the Holy One was angry because the young women were not of the Children of Israel.

Orpah began to gain strength as the fields turned green and days lengthened. Chilion sat close to his wife in the evenings. I rejoiced in the love that blossomed between my son and his wife. Ruth remained barren. Mahlon avoided her bed. The girl pretended to understand, but I was not fooled.

"The ewes must be watched," Ruth refused to meet my eyes when she repeated his excuse for not spending the spring nights with her. "They may have trouble lambing. There are few enough as it is. We dare not risk the loss of any lamb."

I opened my mouth to respond but shut it before I did so. Ruth turned to Adah. The Moabite taught my daughter the intricate and lovely embroidery I never learned.

"Please give Ruth and Orpah the comfort of children," I begged God, but there was no answer. I was sure we had angered the Almighty.

My dread increased when the fields did not prosper as in years past. Grasshoppers came from the south. All the men were kept busy beating the insects away from the grain. Every man in Bethpeor worked long hours under the hot sun.

"God is very far away," I confessed to myself in the darkness of the nights when Elimelech did not return to my side.

Then one day, when the summer heat was upon us Mahlon carried his father home.

My son did not attempt to hide his tears. "I found him in the field."

My death wail brought Orpah, Ruth, and Adah running from the house.

"Let me hold him." I fell on the man I had known all my life.

Adah clung to me, crying hysterically. After a long time, I forced myself to get up. With the help of Ruth and Orpah, I washed my husband for his burial.

"He must face the Promised Land in death," I decided. "Even if we can never return, at least my husband will look at the mountains."

Our burial procession to the highest point in Elimelech's fields drew most of the town. I walked beside my daughters-in-law. Dirt covered my unbraided hair, and my garments were torn. My eyes were dry. No one knew that I felt entirely alone and bereft.

My sons stood together "We will care for you," they swore. "Our mother will not know want nor have to spend a coin of her dowry while we live."

"You are good and faithful sons. Your father would be proud," I assured the men, finding small comfort in their strength.

The grasshoppers vanished as swiftly as they came. Despite their depredation, we had a decent harvest much to the chagrin of Hiram.

"My brother-in-law is jealous." Ruth's confession made me smile for the first time since we buried my husband. "His fields have always had the best grain. This year, the God of Elimelech has blessed us with a richer harvest."

My smile vanished into grief. "It is a harsh God who blesses by taking away."

"You still have me and Orpah, as well as your sons," she reminded me gently. "Adah will not be far, even when she is wed."

"Now that she is a woman, the wedding can be at the harvest," I spoke slowly. "My daughter will live in the house of the chief. She will be lost to the house of Elimelech. Adah will learn the ways of Moab and forget the ways of her father."

Ruth tried to ease my anguish. "My mother, we will still be close. At the Passover, we will invite her, along with Hezik, to join us."

"God has taken the one I love. The Almighty only blesses in order to snatch away my joy," I fumed to my friend. "All my life I have tried to appease *I AM*. Again I am bereft. What is left to me?"

Only later, did I realize that I should never have challenged the Holy One of Israel.

"Raiders from the south!"

"Bring your weapons."

"Hurry!!"

Adah started to her feet at the shouting in the street. Ruth dropped her spindle. Orpah put a frightened hand over her mouth.

"What is it?" I asked, seeing terror in my companions' eyes.

"I am not sure," Ruth hedged.

We ran to the street. Terrified sobs told the story as the news ran through the women gathered near the well.

"It is raiders from the southern desert."

"They have not troubled us for years."

"They are heading for the fields between the hill and the river."

Ruth caught my arm with her nails. We looked at each other in fear.

We spoke the name together. "Mahlon."

When the men returned, they carried six bodies. Among them were the forms of my two sons.

Hezik and his father personally brought our dead to us. "We were too late."

Adah hid her face from the blood. Orpah slipped to the ground in a faint. Ruth and I were left to wash and care for the savagely slashed bodies.

"We will bury them beside Elimelech." A strange calm kept me from hysteria, but only until my sons lay beside their father.

When Hezik finished filling the grave I heard myself scream as I fell across the newly turned earth.

"Come, Mother." Loving hands pulled at me.

"No!" My wail and struggle caused my daughter to desist. "God is punishing me."

Adah sank to her knees beside me, weeping loudly. I had no comfort to offer for her grief. Orpah and Ruth sat with us through the night and next day. Hezik approached us on the third day.

"My mother," the young man addressed me respectfully. "Allow me to wed Adah now, instead of at the harvest. Then you will all be under my care."

I looked numbly at the earnest young Moabite.

After a long time, I forced myself to speak. "It is for the best." The hoarse croak barely sounded like my voice.

Eager to reassure me, the chief's son explained. "You may remain in your house. My servants will care for the fields and flocks."

"It is for the best." The five words were all I could say.

I let myself be led back to town. We dressed Adah in a clean gown. At the last minute, I opened the small box that held my dowry and other jewelry.

"This is from your grandmother." I held up the tinkling necklace I wore on my wedding day. "You must wear the veil that Rachel gave me, too."

I refused to let myself cry, even when I fastened the tiny bells around her neck. She clung to me until I gently pulled her arms away. With a last kiss, I smoothed the lovely veil over my daughter's face. Silently, I watched a dazed Adah wed our protector.

~ 21 ~

"THERE IS A LAW in Israel that a near kinsman can act the part of *ga-al* and raise up sons for the line," I told Orpah and Ruth a few weeks later. "Hezik has done this when he married Adah and took over the lands of Elimelech. There is a chance another would do the same for you."

"We will stay with you," Orpah assured me. "I have no wish to marry another."

"Neither do I," Ruth slipped an arm around my shoulder.

"You are the only blessing I have left." It was a heartfelt comment. "My sons and my husband are gone. If not for you, I would be willing to die, as well."

Ours was a house of mourning. The only happiness came when Adah announced that she was pregnant.

"At the Passover, you will be a grandmother." My daughter shared her secret as if opening a treasure box.

The next months were full of hope. We planned and wove and sewed. One afternoon, just before spring, we sat together adding the final touches to the blankets we were making for Adah's child. I let the cloth fall to my lap and gazed out the door.

"It is spring. There is new life everywhere." Ruth pointed at the green touching the fields beyond the town. "Soon you will hold your grandson."

"I know." Summoning a smile, I added, "When I see a flower growing, I imagine holding the baby and telling him the name."

Hezik sent for me when Adah began her labor.

"My son will be here soon." My daughter smiled at me. "Your grandson will bring you pleasure."

With the midwife, I worked to make her comfortable. The labor stretched out. Adah no longer smiled.

"Do something," I pleaded with the midwife. "She will not have the strength to push the boy into the world."

"The child is not right," the woman muttered under her breath as she sweated over the writhing figure.

Adah's screams tore my soul. I cried out to the One I turned from when Elimelech died. "God of Israel, help my daughter!"

We struggled through the night and all the next day before a stillborn girl was delivered.

"A girl," Adah moaned. "I . . . can . . . not . . ."

Her head fell back against my arm.

"Adah, my daughter, wake up," I pressed a damp rag to her cheek and shook the young woman. "Do not leave me."

The midwife bent over her patient. "She is gone to the Land of Ancestors."

"No!" I knew that my only remaining child was dead. Still, I refused to relinquish my daughter until Ruth came to take me home.

"Hezik must grieve as well," she told me while gently lifting the body from my arms.

"How can I leave her? You do not understand. Your womb has never carried a child. Let me go to her." With fists and hurtful words, I struggled against my friend.

Ruth and Orpah let me rage. Others in the town were not as generous. One by one, the women quit offering comfort.

"They spout only empty words," I stormed. "God has taken everything I cared for. I am being punished by the Holy One. Does it matter if no one is concerned for me?"

Summer came. Still, I hid behind my wrath.

"We will sell some of our dowry," I overheard Ruth say to Orpah one day.

"Why would you do that?" My tone was apprehensive. "What of Hezik?"

Ruth struggled with the dreadful announcement. "He . . . he . . . he . . . will . . . not . . ."

"My mother, Hezik has broken the tablet. Since Adah died and there is no son, the man is justified under our law," Orpah explained in a monotone.

"Oh!" It was a cry of pain ripped from an animal in anguish. "Do not call me Naomi. I am no longer pleasant and desired. Call me Mara, for I am bitter and bereft."

My heart was empty of anything except hatred for the God who stole everything I cared for. Even grief did not touch me.

"Take my dowry. You should keep yours. Now you must leave me and seek husbands," I instructed the young women.

"I will not leave you," both of my companions insisted firmly.

Summer passed. Bit by bit, the dowry I was so proud of as a girl vanished. The necklace Elimelech brought me from Ai was first to go. It turned into flour and cheap barley beer and cheese. Even though we practiced great economy, the coins disappeared gradually.

"With the harvest, we will be able to sell grain and have money for next year," I told my friends as I stood, looking at the ripening wheat just outside of town.

Ruth and Orpah exchanged a glance.

Orpah broke the news to me. "Hezik and his father have reclaimed the fields."

For a moment, I was unable to speak. I could barely draw air into my lungs.

"How? Why?" I heard myself pant the questions.

"He sent word." The young woman looked at her friend.

" 'The gift was to Elimelech, not to his widow.' Those were the words," Ruth whispered. She bit her lip. Her dark eyes watched me with concern.

"It is not fair." I stamped my foot in frustration and despair. "A woman has no rights."

That night, I walked out of our house. My footsteps took me in the direction of the graves of Elimelech and my sons.

"What am I to do?" I asked the barren ground. With my teeth gritted, I looked up at the starry sky. "God of Abraham, Isaac, and Jacob have I not been chastised enough? I obey all your commands, even in this foreign land. You take from me all that I love, and now you make me abandon those I love as daughters. In order to spare them death from poverty, I should leave so they will look for new husbands to care for them. Do you offer no hope?"

There was only silence in the night. Far away, a dog barked. My heart was empty. I did not have the courage to walk away from my home into the barren desert, even to spare Ruth and Orpah. With plodding steps, I turned from the graves. At the edge of town, I paused. A trader's camp was set up ready for the morning business.

A tiny hope flickered in me. "I will do it."

For the rest of the night, I sat outside our small house. My jaw ached from my tightly clenched teeth. There were no tears—only a cold resolve fueled by anger at the God who abandoned me. My course was set.

I faced the two young women in the morning. "My daughters, if you did not have me as a burden, you could find new husbands. You still have your dowries. It is only your faithfulness to me that keeps you from returning to your families."

"You are not a burden," Ruth interrupted.

She frowned fiercely at me. Orpah nodded her head in agreement.

"Hiram would find you another husband." I looked at the face I loved, then at the round, childlike face of Orpah. "Your father is eager to see you wed so he can hold a grandson."

Orpah denied my anxious optimism. "Few men would consider marriage to me. I am a barren widow."

"With another husband, you may yet have children." Although the words almost choked me, I forced them out.

Still, the girl looked unconvinced. Ruth was visibly upset. She stood up and crossed the small room to my side.

"Mother Naomi, you must not speak this way. Your God will provide a way." She crouched at my side with one of her hands resting on my arm.

I looked straight at the worried young woman. "Ruth, I have decided to return to Bethlehem. The Law of Israel commands that a kinsman take on the support of a widow. When we left, Elimelech was told his land would be held for him. If no one comes forward, I will sell the land. When the money is used, I will die. My life has no meaning."

As I voiced the plan, I heard the misery in my voice.

"You cannot leave." Ruth gripped my arm tightly.

"It is decided. I have already made arrangements with the caravan driver from the East. When they leave for the Jordan and Canaan, I will be with them."

Seeing tears brimming in the dark eyes, I stood up quickly. "You can return to your families and be free to forget me and my sons."

"NO!" I paused at the emphatic denial from the young Moabite. "Your home is here now. Hiram must act as provider."

At the desperate words, I shook my head. "Your brother has enough responsibilities without adding the widow of a dead associate. If he could have, I am certain the man would already have taken us into his house."

I left my companions staring after me. Ruth looked frustrated. Her hands hung limply at her sides. Tears slid down her face. Orpah seemed stunned by my announcement.

"Let them see that this is best." My thought was not so much a prayer as a demand.

We spoke little during the day. Ruth watched me packing my few possessions into a small bundle. Her lips were pressed in a stubborn line. Her fine, black brows drew together in concentration. An occasional sniff betrayed her sorrow.

On the morning of the second day, I slipped out of the house before the sky was even gray. I had to meet Abdul and be on the road before either of my companions awoke. The young man had been astonished by my request two nights earlier.

"I could escort you to Bethlehem, yes," he agreed. "Our route takes us to the Jordan, then south. We pass the Salt Sea and then move into the hills. There we stop at Hebron before going on to Bethlehem and Jerusalem."

"How much is the cost?" I hated to haggle with the son of the man who brought us safely to Moab ten years earlier. I knew how few coins were left in my dowry. It had to be enough.

Abdul looked dismayed. "I could not charge the widow of my father's friend a fee."

Proudly, I lifted my chin. "I do not need your pity or charity."

Still, the trader would not set a price. "My father's spirit would never let me rest if I made you pay. He held your husband in honor."

"You cannot lose money." I insisted.

"If you will cook for us on the way, I would be satisfied." A smile flashed through the neat beard. "I remember the stews you made on the journey here."

"Do not flatter me," I warned, trying not to smile in return.

I knew I failed to hide my relief when Abdul grinned. "It is settled then. We stay here one more day. On the following morning, we will leave at dawn."

"I will be ready," I promised.

Now I hurried through the predawn streets. My small bundle of possessions was clutched in my hand. I felt like a traitor or thief.

"It is for the best. When Ruth and Orpah find me gone, they will have no choice but to return to their families. May their gods grant them kind husbands," I rationalized as I walked rapidly toward the camp.

The smell of camels and men carried me back in time. I almost expected to turn and see Elimelech talking to Joseph until I remembered that both my husband and the trader lay in their graves.

"Welcome, wife of my father's friend," Abdul greeted me with his grin. "You are prompt."

"Will we leave soon?" I was anxious to be gone before the young women discovered my absence.

The trader looked at me with a raised eyebrow. He asked no questions. With a wave, he indicated the busy camp.

"The men are almost ready. Wait here."

I stood where I was told when the man strode away. In a few rapid movements, packs were laced down with ropes. Fires were doused before the animals were roused.

"Hup. Hup." With relief, I heard the command.

The trio of beasts heaved to their feet with loud complaints. I faced the road with a sense of inevitability.

"I am in God's hands now," I told myself. "If there is a God and *I AM* is gracious, I will live."

"Come, my mother," Abdul addressed me kindly as he waved me forward with a flourish of his arm.

I took one step and then another. Each one carried me away from the life I had grown accustomed to.

"Mother, Mother Naomi!" At first, I thought Abdul was speaking to me.

I realized the voice was too high-pitched to belong to the young man. The sound of running feet made me turn around. I was astonished to see Ruth and Orpah racing after the caravan. It was Ruth who called again.

"Mother Naomi."

All the men in the caravan paused. Every pair of eyes looked at the disheveled young women. Oblivious, the pair caught my arm.

"If you are set on leaving," Ruth panted, "we will go with you."

Her loyalty broke my heart. "My daughters, what future can you have with me?"

"Do not leave us," Orpah begged.

I tried to be stern. "I must return to my kin. You must return to yours."

"I will go with you," Ruth insisted, pretending she had not heard.

"Ruth, Orpah." I looked at each dear face in turn and hugged both young women to me. "Even if I would marry this day and conceive tonight, would you wait for that son to be grown? No, my daughters, go back to your families. There, you can find the hope of happiness that is denied me."

Orpah began to sob. "I will miss you," she finally managed to say.

With dragging steps and her veil back in place, the young widow began to walk back to her home. I saw her glance back once to see if Ruth was following. The Moabite stood still. A stubborn expression matched the clenched fists resting on narrow hips. It would be more difficult to convince this friend and daughter to stay behind.

"Your sister-in-law has gone back," I pleaded. "You should also return. Hiram will find you a husband to honor you as you deserve."

The woman shook her head. Her usually smiling mouth was set in an obstinate line. "My mother, do not beg me to leave you. I will go with you. Where you go, I will go. Wherever you live, I will live. Your people are my people. Your God is my God."

As she spoke, the stiff determination melted until she was holding my hands. Tears ran down her cheeks. I had to blink rapidly to
keep from crying.

A final time I tried to dissuade the girl. "I have nothing to offer
you."

"My mother, I will go with you." Now she smiled as she made
the promise.

"Very well." My throat tightened with emotion.

Despite my rage and grief, Ruth still loved me. I knew that I did
not deserve her devotion. There were no words to express my gratitude. We clung to each other until Abdul cleared his throat.

The trader looked sympathetically at me. "We will go now."

22

CREAKING LEATHER AND THE crack of whips sounded as we moved down the road. Ruth held my hand. For the first time, she looked around at the curious merchants. Even though the men tried to look busy with their jobs, I knew that they were wondering about the two women who joined the caravan. She drew her veil over her hair and around her face. Even before she became Mahlon's wife, the girl adopted our way of wearing a veil. She rarely used it to cover her face. I realized that this was an unusual adventure for my friend.

"I have never been outside of my home this far," she whispered to me.

"These are good men." My assurance was answered by a hesitant nod. "Abdul is the son of the trader we traveled with when we came to Moab. He and Mahlon were friends. The caravan is from the Land of the Two Rivers. Some of our rugs have been purchased by these merchants over the years."

The history and chatter kept my mind from the rapidly receding town. I hoped it distracted Ruth as well. Camp was made where the streams north of Mt. Pisgah emptied into the Jordan.

"We will ford the river in the morning," Abdul informed us when he brought gourds of something I guessed was stew. "Rest tonight. Etan has already prepared the meal."

Ruth stared at her portion. I struggled not to betray my reaction.

"Now you can see why I asked you to cook," the trader chuckled. His broad grin broke out when he added, "Tomorrow I will see that you have what you need."

"Yes." I could not withstand the grin and found myself smiling up at our guide.

"What is this?" Ruth whispered after Abdul walked away.

"Our dinner, I think." My reply was a whisper as well.

"We are to fix the meals from now on?" There was a hopeful note in the question.

I nodded. "It is the bargain I made with Abdul."

"That is good." Ruth set aside her food. "I am not very hungry tonight."

"Think well on what you are doing," I cautioned as we lay down in the tent thoughtfully provided. "When we cross the River, there will be no turning back."

"I do not wish to turn back. You are my mother. I will go with you," the young woman insisted firmly.

She rolled on her side to end the conversation. I did not sleep well. The ground felt harder than I remembered. Ruth tossed restlessly all night. I was glad to see the hint of gray lightening the sky through a crack between the hides. There was movement from the men. I quietly slipped from our sleeping quarters to find flour and other items waiting. Ruth followed. Although she yawned several times in the morning, my friend would not admit that her night was sleepless.

"Will you make the unleavened bread?" I asked the young woman.

"Of course." She set to work near the fire patting out the rounds to bake.

I mixed a handful of finely chopped nuts into the soft cheese to add flavor. The scent of the fresh bread brought an interested audience. Only one man remained aloof.

"That is Etan from Egypt," Abdul explained when he saw me looking at the dark-skinned laggard. "He has been cooking for us."

"I thought so." It was the only explanation for his stiff demeanor.

Picking up a piece of Ruth's bread, I spread it with cheese. Rising, I crossed to where the thickset man lounged against a pack with his arms folded over his chest.

"Thank you for dinner last night," I opened the conversation. "I hope you do not mind that we are fixing breakfast."

His grunt did not encourage me, but I pressed on.

"You see, it was the only way Abdul would let me travel with your caravan to Bethlehem." With partial truth, I hoped to win the man's sympathy and support. "As a poor widow, I do not have enough to pay, so I must work."

"Said that, did he?" The big man shot a frown at the young trader. His face cleared when he took a bite of my offering. "I suppose I would not mind a break from cooking for these ungrateful stomachs anyway. It is to Bethlehem you travel?"

"Just to Bethlehem," I agreed and turned back to Ruth and the fire.

Abdul bent toward me. "You did not have to make peace. Etan will do as I say."

"Yes," I agreed, "but it will be more comfortable for us all if he is not upset."

"Still the peacemaker." The man smiled fondly. "I remember you doing that between Mahlon and Chilion on the way from Bethlehem."

His face clouded, and I felt my lips tighten at the reminder of my loss and the uncertainty of the future.

"If you need anything, let me know." Abdul moved toward the camels. "We will be going. You and your friend will ride a camel across the river."

"I remember doing that last time." I felt a thrill, followed by a twinge of sadness at the memory of Adah clinging to the saddle in front of me.

Almost before Ruth and I rolled up the last two pieces of bread with the remaining cheese, Etan had put out the fire. One of the other men stored the flour and other food in a pack. The tent was folded and stowed away as well.

"Here is your camel." The trader led us to the kneeling creature.

Ruth eyed the animal with concern. "Are we really going to ride that?"

"It is rather fun," I told the young woman. "I rode across the river ten years ago on a camel. Just hang on."

Carefully, Abdul helped us onto the beast. Ruth clung tightly to the leather straps on the saddle.

"Hup. Hup." Camels rose to their feet at the command.

"Oh!" My friend gasped when our mount moved forward.

The day had started. We soon accommodated to the slight

swaying of the hump. The river was not as deep as ten years earlier. We crossed without incident.

"I am glad to be back on land," Ruth whispered to me when we were safely across. "It was an interesting experience, but I do not think I would want to ride far. The ground is a long way down."

"We travel south along the Jordan until we get to the Salt Sea," Abdul informed me when we started out. "We will make camp beside the water tonight."

Ruth stared around at the changing scenery.

"The hills are closer and higher," she mentioned.

"Have you ever seen so much water?" I asked when we stopped at midday.

The Jordan emptied into a body of water that stretched away into the distance. A little farther south, I could see the land start to rise steeply both in Moab and Canaan.

"Is it true that if you throw something into the lake it will not sink?" I asked.

"You will see," the man promised with a grin and wink. "Here, the river keeps the water from being so thick. Farther along, near Middin, it is true."

"I have heard of the Salt Sea," Ruth spoke up. "I never dreamed I would see it."

"Then I am glad to be the one to show you this wonder," Abdul grinned at my friend.

The girl blushed and drew her veil around her face. I was sure that the Moabite had never encountered anyone like the man from Asshur.

"Tonight, we will camp close to the Sea, not far from Middin." Abdul turned to me. "Then you will see how the Salt Sea keeps objects, and even men, from sinking."

"How can water hold up people?" Ruth asked me when we set out again.

"I do not know," I admitted. "We will see soon enough."

There was an air of anticipation while camp was set up. Even though they had to pour water for the camels from the skins we carried from the Jordan, there was much laughter. No sooner were the animals cared for than the men stripped off their outer garments and hurried into the nearby water. We tried to pretend that we were not watching, but the sounds of laughter and splashing were irresistible. From behind our veils, we watched the revelry as we prepared a meal. All the drovers were bobbing on the surface of the murky water.

Ruth pointed in amazement. "Look at how they do not sink."

"Even Etan, big as he is, stays up in the water." I, too, was astonished that the bulky man floated as easily as the slender Abdul.

They all played like boys in the thick water. Ruth and I laughed at their antics. It was easy to forget the future until we turned toward the hills in the morning.

"Hebron and Bethlehem await," the young trader announced. He was unaware that his cheerful words caused my stomach to clench in dread.

"There, we will find cooler breezes." Etan mopped his face with the end of his turban. "I, for one, will be grateful for that."

"It will be nice to be where it is a little cooler," I agreed.

Abdul nodded. "It is an unusually warm for this time of year. I hope the weather holds fair until you are safe in Bethlehem."

Once again, the mention of our destination brought a wave of panic. I did not share my apprehension with Ruth, but I wondered if anyone in Bethlehem would care that Elimelech's widow had returned.

"Tell me about Bethlehem," Ruth begged the next day as she walked beside me.

"I have been gone for ten years," I reminded the girl. "Much will have changed."

Abdul overheard us. "Not so much. Bethlehem is still the same town in the hill country. Sheep graze on the hills between the fields. Harvests have been rich recently, and the people prosper."

"It sounds pretty," the young woman softly responded when I said nothing. "I have always admired the mountains. On clear days, I can see them from my window. Or, I could."

Ruth fell silent, lost in memories of the home she left behind. I walked on with my head bowed as I considered Abdul's words. Despite his assurance, I was sure that some things had changed.

The caravan remained at Hebron for three days. I was startled when an old woman sought me out in the trader's camp on our last morning.

"It is true!" The ecstatic exclamation caught me by surprise. "Naomi has returned to the Land of Promise."

I looked up into Sarai's eyes. The wife of Caleb, lieutenant to Joshua, smiled at me. We had not seen each other since parting at Gilgal over twenty-five years before. Caleb settled in Hebron where he became the chief.

Like me, white hair replaced the brown. Fine wrinkles etched her face, but the bright eyes held the same serene expression. I remembered her kindness to Rahab of Jericho and her attempts to help me find comfort, rather than fear, in my relationship with the God of Israel.

"God does seek not punish, but to love and protect." Her long-ago words rose up in my mind to mock my situation.

"How are you?" My response was guarded. I wondered if Abdul had told her any of my story.

The woman caught my hands. "My friend, it is so good to see you. I almost envy your adventures. Since Caleb built me a house, I have not wanted to budge from here."

Sarai looked around for a place to sit. I gestured to a leather stool nearby. Ruth moved quickly to bring it for our visitor.

"Thank you, Daughter." The woman smiled. "You are Ruth of Moab. I have heard of your loyalty to your mother-in-law."

The young woman flushed red.

"Ruth is a blessing," I stated. "She has forsaken all to accompany me, although I am only a dry husk."

"The Lord God will bless you, my daughter." Sarai smiled at the embarrassed girl.

Silence reigned. I guessed Sarai wanted to hear my story. I was reluctant to speak of my grief and loss.

After a minute, she brought up the topic. "We heard how the Holy One blessed Elimelech in Moab."

"Then God turned away," I hissed in a low tone. "My husband, my sons, and my daughter all lie buried in that land. I return to this land bereft. My name is now Mara."

Ruth rested a sympathetic hand on my shoulder. She knew the depths of my pain. I looked away from Sarai.

The woman leaned forward to speak earnestly. "The God of Israel is gracious. Trust, and all will be restored."

"How can you say that? I do not need your pity." Anger rose, and I glared at our visitor. "Has God struck down those you love?"

Sarai drew back. Instead of the angry response I anticipated, the woman smoothed the end of her veil. After a minute, she took my hand. The tear-filled eyes did not hold pity, but understanding.

"I, too, am a widow. Caleb died before the planting. Only the honor of my husband keeps me from being outcast, for I have no son left either."

"You are fortunate. Your heart has not been torn out by a God who kills your children." I did not dare respond to her compassion. My anger at the Almighty was the only armor I had against despair.

"Let go of your rage," counseled my friend.

"God has dealt harshly with me." It was a sigh of defeat that emerged from my lips.

"May you find peace in the hills of Bethlehem," Sarai rose to leave when we heard men's voices approaching. "May the God of Abraham, Isaac, and Jacob bring you peace."

I pretended to be busy at the fire so I did not have to acknowledge the kindness of the woman's prayer. "They are coming for the midday meal."

"Thank you." It was left to Ruth to bid our guest farewell. "May the God of Israel bless and keep you, Sarai of Hebron."

My breath hissed between my pursed lips. I wanted to scream my grief and ease the emptiness of my heart. With each heartbeat, sad truth drummed in my head.

Everyone around me has faith. I cannot find God anywhere. Truly, God has left me bereft.

I kept my face hidden behind my veil as I served Abdul and his men the thick soup made of lentils and carrots.

"We leave for Bethlehem with the morning light," the trader announced.

"That is good," Ruth responded when I did not.

I could not sleep. My mind raced in anxious circles. I imagined rejection from the elders of Bethlehem and scorn from the women. My feet dragged when we set out northward through the hills. In Moab, Bethlehem had seemed a sanctuary. Now, as each step took me closer, I wished I had remained in Moab. All that I loved lay buried there. The God I hoped to find in the Promised Land seemed even more distant than on the Plains of Moab.

"My mother, are you ill?" Ruth laid a hand on my arm as I plodded along.

"No, I was thinking." Not wanting to share my misery, I tried to summon a smile.

She was not fooled.

"Surely the God of Israel will honor your faithfulness in returning."

My head shot up, and I stared at my companion.

"What do you know of the God of Israel?" It was an angry challenge, born of my anguish.

Ruth stared at me. A frown appeared between her eyes. Then her face relaxed.

"My mother," she spoke tenderly, as if to a child. "I have found in your God compassion and hope that the gods of my people did not offer. Your God—"

"My God," I interrupted harshly. "I have no God. The One I trusted has taken all I loved."

Without waiting for a reply, I drew my veil tight around my face and body. I left Ruth watching me as I strode ahead of her down the road.

"Mother Naomi." The sorrowful call that trailed me did not halt my retreat.

I spent the day tramping blindly along the road. A lame camel made us stop early.

"We will reach Bethlehem tomorrow," Abdul spoke to my bowed back.

I nodded without turning from the turnip I was chopping.

Ruth tried to engage me in conversation. "It will be good to see old friends."

"If any remain," I shrugged.

After a few more attempts to interest me in dialogue, Ruth gave up. We ate silently. I lay awake most of the night. Now that we were so near the goal, I was terrified. The stars were as distant and silent as the God I repudiated. I could find no words with which to address the deity.

We set out slowly in the morning chill. The lame camel limped awkwardly. I could see the swollen knee and felt pity for the beast.

"How will you continue your route?" I joined Abdul when we paused near a stream so animals and men could drink. "That camel will slow you so that you will not get to your home before the weather changes."

"It is true." The young trader frowned in the direction of the creature.

The drover was soaking his turban in the chill water and wrapping it carefully around the swollen leg.

"If there is no improvement by the time we leave Bethlehem, I will be forced to leave him behind." Abdul sounded resigned. "If I cannot sell the animal, perhaps Boaz bar Salma will keep him until we return. He is a generous man. You might remember him. Salma has died, but his mother is still living. Rahab is her name."

"Yes, I know Rahab," I answered slowly, remembering the foreign woman. "We were never close friends. She was always kind, though. Her husband and mine were related. They had the same grandfather. Amminadab bar Ram was well-known in the camps of Israel."

The last leg of the journey was along a well-traveled downhill slope. By early afternoon we saw the town.

"It is nestled into the hillside." Ruth was delighted.

"Some of the older homes are actually caves in the hills," I mentioned briefly. "Most of them are now used for animals."

"What is growing in the fields?" The young woman turned her attention to the area surrounding Bethlehem.

"That is barley. It is nearly ready for the harvest," Abdul informed us before I spoke.

"There are many fields," my companion noticed. "This is a rich area."

"Yes." I did not want to discuss the fields.

A tiny hope glimmered in my mind. If the harvest was rich, we might be able to glean enough from the grain dropped by the workers to survive. I had little even thought to the future. The arrival of the caravan was a time of excitement. I heard shouts of welcome. Soon, we were surrounded by a crowd alternately shouting greetings and questions.

"Welcome, Trader."

"The caravan from the Two Rivers is here."

"I need a rug."

"Do you have new cloth from the Black Land?"

I was grateful to melt into the background. It was not long before one of the women noticed Ruth. I did not recognize her face.

"Abdul, have you brought a wife?" she teased.

The man turned red above his beard. He shook his head. In explanation, the man nodded toward me.

"My family remains at home," he responded. "This is Naomi, wife of Elimelech, and her daughter-in-law Ruth. They have returned to Bethlehem."

"Naomi? Can it be?"

"The wife of Elimelech has returned."

"Where is she?"

"Who is with her?"

Like wildfire, whispers spread through the gathered women. I clenched my hands into fists until my nails dug into the palms. Ruth laid a hand on my arm. I was not sure if it was for comfort or support.

"Welcome home, Naomi, wife of Elimelech."

I looked up when a soft voice addressed me. The woman who stood before me showed the beauty that won the heart of a Hebrew spy, years earlier. Although the red hair was streaked with white, I recognized Rahab.

"Do not call me Naomi," my voice was hoarse. "My life is no longer pleasant. Call me Mara, for the Lord has dealt bitterly with me."

The woman ignored my statement. "You are home and among friends. Come, the house of Elimelech awaits you."

The whispering women parted as Rahab escorted me past. Ruth

followed. I kept my head lowered so I would not have to see pitying or curious stares.

"I am sure you are exhausted." At the door I remembered so well, Rahab left us. "We will talk again. The son of Samson is chief now. He will want to welcome you himself when he hears you have returned."

As she spoke, the woman opened the door. Dust lay thick, but the furnishings Elimelech made remained in their places. Emotion choked me. I moved slowly into the room to touch the small chest carved for our first Passover in Bethlehem.

"Thank you." Again, it was Ruth who offered the salaam of gratitude to our guide. "You are kind."

"We will talk soon." There was understanding in the tone. "I look forward to hearing of your life in Moab."

I heard the rustle of garments, and the woman was gone.

"She was nice," my friend mentioned as she came to stand beside me.

"Elimelech made this." My voice was husky. One finger traced the vertical panel of dark wood that made the door. "It was where I kept the lamps for Passover."

Wondering if the clay containers were still be inside, I pulled gently. The hinges gave with a slight squeak.

"Mahlon made this one." I reached inside and lifted out one pottery lamp and then the other. "He spent days working until it was just right. I thought my son would never be satisfied. Finally, he took it to the master potter to be fired."

I was barely aware of the tears running down my cheeks.

"It is perfect." Ruth admired the handiwork of her husband. "The handle is so thin that I would be afraid it would break."

I nodded with a reminiscent half-smile. "I always picked it up from the bottom."

"Did Chilion make this one?" The young woman touched the similar-lamp.

"He tried to imitate his brother." I found myself smiling at the memory. "The boy did not have as much patience. Mahlon teased him about the crooked rim until Elimelech called a halt."

"It is a bit tilted." Ruth had to smile as well. "One side is higher than the other.

I turned around to survey the room. "Everything is as we left it. I never expected to see these things again."

"I will go to the camp for our bundles," Ruth offered. "Abdul will be expecting a meal, too."

"I will go with you." Suddenly, I did not want to be alone with my memories.

Side by side, we walked back down the street of Bethlehem to the trader's camp. All was calm. A few children played in the street, and two dogs darted across in front of us. We passed through the gate that even the elders had vacated for their meals.

Abdul welcomed us with a grin. "When your friend carried you off to your home, I thought you would not be back."

"That would have been impolite." Ruth sounded shocked, although she smiled. "We would not leave our fine guide to starve. You will have one last decent meal before we leave you to the mercies of Etan."

Abdul chuckled and leaned close to whisper, "You should not joke about such things. We will miss a woman's touch with the food. It will hasten our homeward journey."

It was bittersweet to prepare the meal of flat bread and warm the stew. While the men ate, Ruth and I gathered our few belongings.

Abdul set out beside us. "I will see you safe to your home. When I return next year I will retrieve a healed camel. Boaz bar Salma will keep the animal. No one wanted to buy him. I hate to lose the use of the beast for a season. Fortunately, there will be few trips until the weather cools again."

I was grateful for the inconsequential discussion of the camel. It kept me from becoming sad over the departure of my friend.

"We will meet again," the trader promised with a deep salaam at the door. "May your God watch over you to bless and keep you. May the Holy One of Israel be your strength and honor your loyalty with blessings."

"Blessings on you, Abdul bar Joseph." My voice broke on a sob. I turned away.

Even though the admonition was not for my ears, I heard Abdul charge Ruth. "Watch over Naomi. She is fortunate to have such a faithful companion. Take this, as well. Make it last until you are settled."

Sandals crunched upon the road as the man strode away. I stood in the center of the yard, torn between anger and affection at the trader's meddling. Without looking, I knew that Abdul had given Ruth the heavy bundle he carried down the street. I had no doubt that it contained flour and other food.

"Come, my mother." Ruth walked past me without mentioning the gift. "Do you want me to prepare your pallet?"

I took a deep breath and followed. In the morning, I would begin to clean the house that was once my home.

"There are still coins in my dowry, and perhaps the carved work can be sold, as well," I declared to the darkness after my companion dozed. "Ruth can glean in the fields until someone steps forward under the Law of Moses to redeem the lands of Elimelech."

✎ 23 ✎

"MY DAUGHTER, IT IS the Law of Moses that widows and orphans may glean in the fields." I raised the subject on the first day of the barley harvest. We had not even celebrated a Sabbath in Bethlehem when the work started. "Moses ordered all farmers to leave a portion of the grain unharvested for the widow, the orphan, and the sojourner," I recited the law. "In that way, the poor do not starve."

The young woman interrupted. "I heard about this custom at the well. In Moab, we leave the edges of the fields to the dark spirits. When they are well-fed, we are not troubled. This law is much better. Too many are destitute in Beth-peor."

I wondered if she was thinking of how we struggled to survive. Even the grain from the edges of Elimelech's fields in Moab would have been welcome. For the first time since we walked away from Shittim, I thought about Orpah.

"Daniel the woodcutter will have welcomed his daughter back." I tried to sound emphatic.

Ruth confessed, "Yes, she is likely a bride again. Her father tried to coax her to return many times. She refused because she loved you."

I had to blink back tears. Hastily, I returned to the subject. "Anything left on the ground after the sheaves are bundled is to be gathered by those who have no man to provide for them. We should—"

"You must let me glean for us both," the young woman interrupted.

"I am not so old," I responded half-affronted, although the

thought of bending over all day to gather stray heads of grain made my back ache.

Ruth dropped to her knees in front of my seat. "Mother Naomi, I want to spare you the embarrassment of such a task."

"Everyone knows we have nothing," I protested stubbornly. "We could gather more if both of us worked."

"Let me try," the girl offered a gentle solution. "If I do not gather enough for us both, then you can come with me tomorrow."

"Very well, go then," I nodded.

I watched the graceful figure move through the door with a flat basket in her arms.

"God of Abraham, Isaac, and Jacob, if you will listen to one who has turned away, for the sake of Ruth's loyalty, help her find a generous landowner." I prayed hesitantly.

I felt guilty turning to the One I hated and feared and was not surprised that I felt no comforting assurance. With a deep breath, I turned to making a small amount of bread to go with the vegetable broth I prepared for our meal. The sun was sinking in the west when I heard the workers returning from the fields. They called to each other.

"God give you rest, Abel."

"We will start the high field tomorrow."

"The work is going well."

"It will be a rich harvest."

"Your God has blessed us," Ruth announced in an awed voice.

I turned to see that my friend carried the basket awkwardly. It was mounded high. My eyes opened in astonishment.

"Surely you did not gather all this from the ground." It ran my hand through the bounty wondering what farmer was so wasteful.

"Some is a gift." A blush rose and retreated. "The man was kind."

"What man?" Instantly, I was fearful that someone had taken advantage of my friend. "What did he say?"

"It was Boaz bar Salma." Ruth emptied the grain into a deeper basket near the wall.

She did not see my eyes and mouth open and close in shock.

I found my voice. "The son of Rahab spoke to you?"

"He is a kind man," the young woman repeated her assessment.

"Tell me." Dinner was forgotten as I waited for the story.

"I followed the other women to the fields." Ruth sank onto the cushions and stretched. "There are other widows in Bethlehem."

"I suppose so." The lives of others did not concern me. "You followed them to the fields of Boaz?"

"Not right away." The girl from Moab smiled at my impatience. "The first field we came to was picked almost bare. We found only a few heads of barley. It was Suzanne, widow of Isaac, who suggested moving up the hill. 'Boaz has just started his harvest,' she said. 'He is rich and can afford to be generous.' So we joined ourselves to his group of dependents."

"What do you mean?" I was confused by her explanation.

"Suzanne told me that Boaz allows the wives of his servants to glean in his fields. Not because they need the food," she hastened to add. "It is so they can sell the extra and buy special things."

"I see." My astonishment must have been transparent because Ruth giggled.

"Even Suzanne says he is the only man in Bethlehem to do such a thing," she explained.

"If the man already has so many women gleaning, how did you get so much? Did he suggest . . . anything . . . ?" Suspicion continued to tease my mind.

Ruth's face turned bright red when she realized my implication. "Mother Naomi, Boaz is an honorable man. He did not even come to the fields until late in the day. The man spoke to me as I was gathering up my basket to come home. I had not taken much. It did not seem fair to the older women if I collected all the grain. The man is kind."

I waited when the young woman stared off through the open door. A dreamy smile came to her lips.

Finally, I said, "And?"

My friend turned to me. "What he said was, 'You are Ruth. I have heard of your loyalty to your mother-in-law. Naomi is fortunate to have you with her. You do not have enough grain. Here is another measure. Take it as a gift for your devotion.' Then he poured a whole container of grain into my basket."

"Is that all?" I was not certain that my suspicions were allayed.

"He told me to follow his women for the rest of the harvest. 'You will be safe. My workers will watch out for you,' he said. Then I came home." The girl smiled and added again. "He is a kind man."

I was silent. It was my turn to stare out the door. Boaz, son of Salma the spy and Rahab of Jericho was a wealthy man. I still did not dare trust what seemed like a wonderful opportunity.

"Why would such a man single you out?" I asked my companion.

"I do not know. I am sure he was just being kind to a stranger."

"Perhaps." I frowned.

The Moabite was unaware of her beauty and the innocent appeal of the thick eyelashes that framed her wide eyes.

"Mother Naomi, if I glean with the women of Boaz, we will be well supplied." Ignoring my distracted frown, the girl asked the question I was turning over in my mind. "Could this be an answer to our prayers? I knew that your God would provide help."

I hardly dared hope that the interest of Boaz might prove the answer to prayer.

"Perhaps," I replied slowly. "You may be right. If Boaz will let you gather with his women, you will be safe."

"Thank you, my mother," I found myself caught in a hug. "Now I will toast some of this fresh grain to go with our meal."

I watched Ruth strip the heads from several stalks. On the edge of the brazier, she spread the grain. Soon the delicious smell of freshly toasted barley filled the room.

I savored the crisp husk with tender center. "This is delicious. It is the perfect addition to my soup."

Early the next morning, Ruth gathered her basket and left for the fields. During the day, I spread the barley on the ground and beat it so that the grain would separate from the stalks. Carefully, I gathered the heads into a basket.

"Here is what I gathered today." Ruth showed me an overflowing basket when she returned to the house.

"Soon we will have enough to take to be ground." I indicated the basket, half-full with the grain from her first day. "This will fill the basket after I thresh it out.

"I think the men are leaving extra behind," Ruth confessed. "It looked like they were pulling clumps of grain from the sheaves if I was gleaning nearby. They shared their bread with me at midday."

"Really? You must have made quite an impression on the workers and their master." I raised my eyebrows.

Ruth blushed and insisted, "Boaz is just a kind man."

I did not push the subject. After the young woman left in the morning, I faced south. Somewhere in the far distance lay the holy mountain of my childhood. I could picture the cloud-covered summit in my mind and remembered my awe of the place before my father died. Miriam's sagas of a caring God seemed real then. I wished I still believed the stories.

"God of Israel, is this your answer?" I held out my empty hands. "I do not have any offering to bring. Do not allow Ruth to be shamed. I pray you, raise up a protector for her. Do not hold my sins against this innocent girl."

I felt better after my prayer. For the first time since Adah died, I did not feel entirely weighed down by a sense of condemnation. My heart and step were both lighter when I walked to the well. Several women greeted me with smiles and questions.

"What is it like in Moab?"

"I am sorry for your loss."

"Naomi, how does it feel to be home?"

"I . . . it . . . it is good to be back." With a little surprise, I realized that it was true.

"I heard that your daughter-in-law goes to the fields to glean for you."

I nodded. "Ruth is a great help."

"You are fortunate to have her."

"Yes," I readily agreed. "She has been fortunate in her gleaning. I need to thresh the grain she has gathered."

I lifted my water jar and hurried away before any further questions were raised. I wished that my old friend Rachel were alive. It would have been comforting to talk to her.

"She died last winter soon after the Feast of Atonement," Rahab told me when she returned the day after we arrived.

"Oh!" My cry of dismay was sharp.

"Rachel often spoke of you," the widow told me. "Her sons have cared for the fields of Elimelech, along with Boaz and the son of Samson. The heritage of your husband has been preserved."

"It will do me little good." The words were out before I thought of my audience.

"The Law of Moses declares that a widow is to be cared for by the nearest kinsman. Someone will step forward as *ga-al*." Her soft hand covered mine in an attempt at comfort.

"That is why I returned." I had to swallow my pride to admit the truth.

"The Living Lord will provide for you."

"I hope so." My response was lost in the folds of my veil when I bent my head.

Some of my loneliness and grief eased while I threshed the bounty of grain and ground enough for a loaf of bread as a treat for Ruth.

The young woman sniffed happily when she entered the house. "Mmm, that smells wonderful."

"I thought you would like it." I smiled to see my friend savoring the bread.

It was worth the bangle from my wrist to see her delight as she spread the fresh slices with the goat cheese and olives I purchased with it.

"This is the end of the first barley harvest. Suzanne says that the second harvest will begin after a couple of Sabbaths," Ruth stated the next afternoon. She arrived earlier than I expected. "Tomorrow, I will take what we have to be ground, if you want."

"That would be good. During the years in Moab, I did not need to grind my own flour. I forgot how much work it is."

My wrists still ached from the work of the previous day. I rubbed them absently.

"You should not have to grind," my friend stated firmly.

The young woman returned in tears from the miller.

"My child, what is it?" I closed the door and drew her close.

Between sobs the young woman tried to explain. "The man . . . he said . . . will not . . . ."

"Did someone try to hurt you?" I was more worried about her safety than the unground basket of grain she carried.

"No." Ruth took a deep quavering breath, dried her eyes on her veil and after another breath was able to speak.

"The man refused to grind our barley." Her voice was low monotone. "He said, 'You are a foreigner and have no inheritance in Israel. Take your grain to Jerusalem. The Jebusites will grind for anyone.' Then he spat on the ground at my feet."

"May God punish him!" I was enraged by the report. "I will take our grain. Let Ahaz tell me that I have no inheritance in Israel."

Ruth tried to stop me. "No, my mother. I will grind it here. There is not so much."

"I will take it." Stubbornly, I picked up the basket.

It was heavier than I expected, but in my rage, I did not care.

"Please." The girl laid a hand on my arm. "It is not worth the cost."

"Our grain will be ground." With that final statement, I marched out the door.

I was still seething when I reached the grinding stone. What I saw shocked me. A tall man with auburn hair stood over the miller. The man cowered away. Blood dripped from his nose onto the flour-covered apron he wore.

"What gives you the right to judge someone outcast or unworthy? May the Almighty so judge you." Boaz spoke low and intense. I cringed from the threat even though it was not directed at me. "The woman Ruth is widow of the son of Elimelech. Her loyalty is exemplary. If she returns, you will charge nothing for the grinding of her grain."

Pathetically, Ahaz looked up. "Nothing?"

Boaz's piercing blue-gaze impaled the miller. Ahaz sank back with a hand up to ward off another blow.

"If I hear of you acting rudely to her or any woman of this town, you will feel my wrath." The son of Salma bent toward the man who recoiled from the stern face.

"I did not understand." The unfortunate miller passed a shaking hand over his nose. "Lord Boaz, forgive me. The Moabite is special to you. I will remember."

"The woman is a widow and deserves your consideration as such under the Law of Moses. She is nothing to me." I was not surprised to hear the denial, though I wondered at his vehemence.

Quietly, I turned to leave with my basket of grain before either man saw me.

Why would a leader of Bethlehem confront Ahaz about a woman he barely knows? I pondered on my return walk. *Could it be that he cares for Ruth?*

"He would not grind for you either," Ruth sighed, when I entered the house.

"He . . . I . . . um . . . the man was . . . um . . . busy . . . with . . ." I stammered my way through an excuse.

"Never mind. I will grind it here." The young woman held out her hands.

With a shake of my head, I set the container aside. "I will go tomorrow. We will say our prayers and eat what we have. Here is the bread made with the last of the flour I ground."

It was a subdued meal. I was distracted by the idea that Boaz bar Salma was developing an interest in my daughter-in-law. Ruth stared at the basket of grain as though she detested the sight.

When she spoke, I realized that she thought my preoccupation was from anger. "My mother, forgive me for bringing such shame to this house."

"Oh, my child, no!" A wave of sympathy swept over me. "You have done nothing wrong. I was thinking about something. My daughter, truly: without you, I would not care to live."

Tears welled and slipped down her smooth cheeks.

Through sobs she spoke. "I am a foreigner. The *ga-al* you spoke of will not want to have the burden of two women. Why would anyone be concerned with what happens to a Moabite?"

"Ruth, my daughter." Compassion had me scrambling to her side.

I took the slender frame in my arms. Sobs shook her body. I held my friend tight.

"Ruth, you must forget what Ahaz said. He is wrong. You are a daughter of Israel." Comforting words flowed easily.

I felt the negative motion of her head on my shoulder.

"Yes," I insisted, "Your faith is greater than mine. I turned away from the God of Israel in despair and anger."

My own words convicted me. I stopped with a gasp. It felt like all my breath had been kicked from my lungs. Ruth drew back to look at me when I stopped speaking. I stared past my companion trying to draw air past the great lump that lodged in my throat.

"Mother Naomi?" I barely heard the question.

I lowered my head in despair. Tears welled in my eyes. Suddenly, I was sobbing. Whimpers of animal anguish wrenched from my lips.

"God! God!" It was all I could say. I rocked back and forth, holding my knees, as the truth rolled over me.

"My mother." Ruth tried to take me in her arms.

She had to be satisfied with patting my shoulder as I continued to rock and weep. A lifetime of pent up sorrow and grief flooded out in my tears.

"It is true. I rejected God." I spoke more to myself than Ruth. "God did not abandon me. I turned away from the Holy One. I would not let *I AM* comfort me."

The girl stroked my hair. "I did not know."

"I needed to blame the Almighty for my grief. Ever since my father died, I felt guilty. All my life, I have hated *I AM*. It was easier to say that God took those I loved because I did something wrong. I was sure that my father died because I wanted a house. I never dared trust that I would be cared for. If I failed in any way, I was certain that I would be punished. When Elimelech died, I knew I was right. I told myself that the God of Abraham, Isaac, and Jacob turned away when we left the Promised Land. Then my sons died, and I was certain that God was angry. After Adah's death, I knew that the Holy One despised me because I allowed her to marry a foreigner." I panted as the confession poured out through my sobs. "I hated my life enough to die."

"Mother Naomi," the young woman whispered as she held me close, unable to comfort me.

"I was wrong. The Living Lord did not desert me," I gasped as comprehension burst into my heart. "You once said that the Holy

One of Israel provides healing, even for death and pain. Ever since my father died from the bite of the serpent, I have been angry with God. Everything that went wrong was another reason to blame the Lord of Life. My rage only made me feel responsible for the bad things that happened. I was sure that I was judged guilty because I could not love God. I let my anger and the laws become a prison to my heart."

Tears I could not stop rolled down my face. My heart was breaking with sorrow and regret over the wasted years.

Ruth tried to comfort me. "My mother, you are not to blame."

"Sarai once tried to explain to me that the Law of Moses is a guide built on love, not a whip for punishment." I raised my head and took my friend's hands in my own. "It is in relationship with one another and with God we can all live in freedom, no matter what our circumstances. *I AM* wants us to freely offer our hearts."

I wiped my cheeks with the end of my veil. More tears streamed down my face. Tenderly, I looked at Ruth.

"Your loyalty and steadfast faith in *I AM* are all that kept me alive, even though I refused to be free. I preferred rage to belief in a caring God. The Almighty never stopped offering help and comfort. I was too blinded by my anger to see it. Even in the depths of my despair, a way was opened to return to Bethlehem. We have come here to the land of promise."

"Your God may yet be gracious," the young woman whispered hopefully.

"Yes." I took a deep shaky breath. My tears dried on my cheeks as I moved my head in assent. With my newborn faith, I asserted, "*I AM* will provide."

Ruth tilted her head to study me. She smiled suddenly. "You really do believe the God of Israel will help us."

"I do not know what will happen now that we have returned to Bethlehem." Tears began again, but they were joyful. Confidence enfolded me. I held Ruth's hands between mine. "Already we are being blessed. God is with us. I know that the God of Israel will yet bless you—bless us."

We sat together quietly. I felt peace enter my heart. There was no need to worry. Memory of an angry young man with auburn hair entered my mind. Perhaps Boaz bar Salma was the instrument of the Living God. Even if he was not, I knew that I would not fear any longer. My sleep was deep and restful for the first time since I buried Elimelech. I awakened still confident in the love of the One God.

In the morning, I visited Ahaz. I noticed the man had a swollen nose. There was no other evidence of the altercation I witnessed.

The miller came forward with a smile. "Welcome, widow of Elimelech."

On closer inspection, I saw that one eye was blackened.

"I have some barley to be ground. It is not much," I admitted. "Only what Ruth has gleaned."

The man winced slightly when I mentioned my daughter-in-law.

"I . . . yes . . . we heard that she returned with you." Rapidly, he recovered and held out his hand for my basket. Amid the piles of grain, it seemed a pitiful amount.

I held onto my basket. "How much will you charge?"

"For the widow of Elimelech, there is no charge." A lopsided smile appeared. "It is my honor to serve the widows of Bethlehem."

"That is kind." I relaxed my hold on the container.

Ahaz carefully weighed the barley before pouring it with the rest to be ground. My basket was filled with an equal weight from the barrel of flour nearby.

"You have gathered a great deal by just gleaning." The man sounded surprised.

I nodded and accepted my portion. "Yes, Ruth was fortunate in her labor."

Carefully, I folded a cloth over the top of the flour so it would not blow out during my walk home.

At the door, I paused. "May the Living God bless you for your kindness."

The man bowed in response. "And may the Holy One give you peace and provide a ga-al."

"Mother Naomi," Ruth greeted me with a smile. Outstretched hands took the basket. "What a lot of flour our grain made! I will make fresh bread right now."

I looked around the room. In the short time, I was gone a trans-
formation had occurred. Surfaces were polished and the floor
swept. New coverings even hung at the windows.

"You have been busy." I gasped.

Eagerly, the girl showed me her work. "I have shaken all the rugs
and blankets. Here is a soft pillow for you to lean on as you sew."

"What would I do without you, my daughter?" The hug I gave
did not begin to express my gratitude.

"Sit here, and let me make the bread," Ruth insisted. "I have not
had a chance to bake since we arrived. My fingers itch to knead the
dough."

"Very well." My assent was full of relief.

I found it easy to sink onto the cushions. Soon I was dozing
over my mending. The smell of fresh bread nudged me awake. Ruth
was just slicing the loaf.

Somewhat slowly, I got to my feet and joined my companion.
"That smells delicious."

"Yes, it does." Her happy smile appeared. "A woman from the
town brought us a lump of cheese and jar of milk to add to our
meal."

"Let us thank God for the generosity of that woman." I found
myself feeling very grateful.

"Thank the Lord for all that is provided," Ruth echoed my sen-
timents.

I was hungry and consumed two thick slices of the bread before
pushing away the offer of a third.

"No, we must not be greedy. The flour has to last." I smiled as I
said it.

"Before long, there will be more barley ready to harvest," Ruth
reminded me. "I will glean again in the fields of Boaz."

With a nod, I agreed, "Yes, my daughter, the man will watch for
your return with his women."

"It is . . . he is . . . there is . . ." my friend stammered. Finally,
she insisted, "He is a kind man."

I watched the slender figure hurry away with my head tilted to
one side. "Can it be that the son of Rahab is the *ga-al* provided by **I
AM**? His mother was a foreigner. Boaz bar Salma is a kinsman, al-

though not as close as the son of Samson. I will see what this harvest brings."

The fields turned white with the later barley as the weather warmed. Neighbors supplied us with milk and eggs. We made butter and cheese in return. Ruth became known rapidly for her delicate and lightly flavored cheese.

The young woman was ecstatic when she returned from the market one morning. "My mother, see how God supplies what we need. I was able to trade fresh cheese for a basket of newly picked vegetables."

"We are being blessed."

The garden I tended was slowly showing signs of life. We spent a day clearing out the old overgrown weeds and plants so seeds could be sown.

"You are enjoying this." Ruth smiled at my tender, almost caressing, mounding of the dirt.

"I have always loved to work in the soil," I admitted to my friend. "As soon as I see the first green, I know that God will bring a fruitful harvest."

Beans and carrots and melons began to grow happily. Even the grape vines I had thought dead sprouted leaves after I pruned and watered them.

Each day, I grew more and more sure of the providence of God. I could barely explain the feeling of confidence to myself. The anger I held onto for so long disappeared into the night with my confession to Ruth.

"The second barley harvest begins after the Sabbath," Ruth informed me one afternoon. "I will glean in the fields for us."

"Yes, my daughter, that will be good." I noticed the flush of excitement on the pretty face. "May God give you success."

My Sabbath prayers included a secret petition, "God of Jacob, let Ruth find favor in your sight and in the eyes of Boaz."

"Go to the fields of Boaz bar Salma," I urged in the morning. "It may be that he will again be kind."

A rosy flush covered the smooth cheeks. Ruth ducked her head so that the veil hid her face.

"I . . . yes . . . I will." Hastily, the girl slipped from the house.

"Be gracious to your daughter so that the house of Elimelech may serve you again," I prayed as I watched Ruth greet Suzanne and other women.

They walked off together toward the fields. I spent the day feverishly trying not to wonder what Ruth was doing.

"Well?" I barely allowed the young woman to remove her veil before asking, "How did your day go?"

Ruth giggled at my eagerness.

"I have a large basket of grain." She held out the evidence.

The flat basket was mounded high with broken heads of wheat.

"You have done well!" I sifted through the bounty with one hand. "There is little waste here."

"It seemed silly to bring home the stalks," my friend smiled.

"In whose field did you glean?" I was sure I knew the answer.

The quick blush that appeared confirmed it, even before Ruth answered, "Boaz bar Salma."

"Did you see the man today?" I probed when the young woman turned away to fold her veil.

"Only for a moment," she confessed. "He waved when he saw me and came to tell me, 'Remain with my workers for the wheat harvest.' He is a kind man."

The statement ended with a sigh.

"Yes, Boaz, son of Rahab, does seem to be a very kind man." There was a smile in my tone. "Who can tell what may happen?"

The harvest proceeded rapidly. Golden stalks of wheat fell before the scythes after the fields of barley were finished. Before a moon turning passed, the hillsides stood bare. Each night Ruth returned with a basket filled with grain. I knew she remained with the women of Boaz bar Salma even without asking.

"He is a kind man," was all she ever replied if I questioned my friend about the young landowner.

"After the Sabbath, all the grain will the threshed," Ruth told me when she came home at the end of the harvest. "There is a festival."

"All of next week will be devoted to threshing and celebrating the harvest." A thrill of remembered excitement ran through me when I explained. "The threshing time is more than a time to beat out the grain."

"That is what Rachel, daughter of Miriam, told me yesterday," Ruth agreed. "She said the men beat the grain with flails. Women follow to sweep the grain into baskets."

"Then two or three women hold the edges of a blanket and toss the grain," I interrupted. "It is dusty work. The chaff flies into your hair and the dust settles on your skin and clothing."

"It is the same in Moab," Ruth remembered.

I smiled to myself. "This is a happy time. The evening dances of the women and the men are the most fun."

"Do you want to go, then?" my daughter-in-law asked hesitantly. "I did not think . . ."

When her voice trailed off, I stared past my friend. Thoughts and memories ran through my mind.

"Yes, I think I would like to go, at least once." As I made the decision, I wondered if it was right. "Many widows attend."

"It will be wonderful!" Ruth was enthusiastic. "It cannot be too different from Moab. There, the widows have a special place."

"That is true." I thought of the row of black-garbed old women I used to pity. "You must not sit with me and the other aged widows, though. You are of marriageable age and should join the dances."

Ruth did not respond. She busied herself with slicing bread. I could not see her face but guessed it was red.

Late in the afternoon of the second day of the festival, I found myself walking beside the woman from Moab. After Ruth braided my hair and found my best veil, I hesitated.

I began to find excuses. "Maybe I should not go this year. We have only just returned to Bethlehem."

"My mother, I would be sorry if you do not attend. You were so excited about the idea." Ruth pleaded.

"Yes . . . well . . . me . . ." There was no excuse I could come up with.

The girl crouched at my side, and continued "My mother, I wish you would come with me. I am the stranger and will not go if you do not."

"You must go! It is at the threshing floor where men and women find love."

"I am not looking for love." The bright color in Ruth's face betrayed her.

"We will go." With the decision made, I stood up.

Hand in hand, we walked toward the sound of merriment. I remembered long years past when Elimelech and I found hidden corners in which to cuddle. An idea was born in my mind.

Ruth looked at me curiously. "What are you smiling at?"

"Memories," I prevaricated. "Just memories."

I did have a good time at the festival. One by one, old and new friends greeted me.

"Welcome, Naomi."

"It is good that you are here."

"The harvest is rich; no one will know want."

"Come and sit here."

Ruth insisted upon sitting with me and the other widows. Boaz escorted his mother to her seat among us.

"I hope you will enjoy the harvest festival." Even though the words could have been addressed to Rahab, the young man's eyes were on my companion.

"Go, my son. I am not so old that I cannot delight in the music and dancing." The woman hid a smile behind her veil when Ruth glanced up to encounter the look Boaz bestowed on her.

Rahab leaned toward the young woman when she hastily covered her face with her veil. "You are lovely tonight. You should be with the young women dancing."

"I do not know your dances," the girl from Moab murmured shyly.

I said nothing, but I watched her eyes following a tall man with blue eyes and auburn hair. Boaz joined in the celebration with abandon. However, before couples formed after the final dance, he was nowhere to be seen.

"My son has never found a woman that he cares for." Rahab sighed and stood up. "I had hoped that this harvest he would look for a wife, but he has left the festivities already. He will never find a bride. Boaz always leaves before the end. My son thinks that I do not know his habits. He has gone off to sleep among the grain. I am not interested in staying to watch the other men find wives."

Ruth, too, was suddenly bored. "Are you tired, my mother? We should go home."

"Yes," I agreed. "It is time to be in bed."

My friend walked silent at my side. Only when we were inside our house did she speak.

"My mother, why do you think Boaz bar Salma has never married?"

I pondered my answer. "His father was truly in love with Rahab. I suppose Boaz wants to also find someone just as special. Anyone that the son of Salma chooses would be lucky."

"I . . . I . . . did not mean . . ." Ruth stammered. "It . . . I . . . was just . . . curious."

"He is a kind man," I repeated her own words.

"Yes." There was a kind of sigh in her reply.

The girl walked away to climb up to the roof. In a moment, I heard her rustling movements above me.

"I will do it." With a decisive nod, I followed the young woman to bed.

❧ 24 ❧

"TOMORROW IS THE LAST day of the festival." Casually, I broached the subject at the end of the celebration.

"Yes." Ruth smiled. "Ahaz has given us credit for a good weight of grain."

Gradually I began to introduce the plan conceived the first night of the feast. "My daughter, now that the harvest is done, we must consider finding a *ga-al* to honor the Law of Moses."

"Mother Naomi, I have no wish to marry," the young woman argued immediately.

"I think that there is one . . ." I let the words hang in the air.

A bright red flush flooded my companion's face. She looked away for a moment.

"It is not possible." When the girl spoke, her voice was calm, although her cheeks were still rosy. "I am a foreigner."

"You must do as I tell you." My hand reached out to take hers. "Boaz bar Salma is a kinsman of my husband. He has shown interest in your welfare by keeping you close to his workers. As you say, he is a kind man."

"I . . . I . . ." Ruth had no answer to my observations.

"Tonight, the men will remain at the threshing floor after the last of the grain is winnowed out. They will eat and drink most of the night. Each man will seek a place to sleep."

My daughter-in-law was watching me with her head tilted to one side. A furrow drew her brows together. When she opened her mouth to argue, I hurried on with my instructions.

"You must bathe and anoint yourself with the scented oil we have. I have laid out your finest gown. You will go to the threshing floor. After the man has eaten and drunk, notice where he lies down. After all are asleep, go to Boaz; lie down under the blanket with him." In my eagerness, the words tumbled over each other. "He is an honorable man and will tell you what to do."

Ruth stared at me for a long time. At last, her face cleared and she slowly nodded. "All that you have said, I will do."

I hugged the young woman tightly. "It is for the best."

Never had I combed her hair so smooth. With ribbons and beads woven into it, she already looked the part of a bride.

"I wore this when I wed Mahlon," Ruth mused as she held up the gown I had ready for her. "It is fitting that I wear it to find a *ga-al* to take over his property and his wife."

The last words were so low I nearly missed them.

Suddenly, my conscience smote me. "Ruth, I will not force you to do this. If you do not care for Boaz bar Salma, I do not want you to take this step."

"My mother, I will do as you ask. The man is kind," she responded softly with head bowed so I could not see her face.

"Is that all?" I probed. "Do you not find him desirable?"

"Naomi, I . . ." The young woman paused. I saw her take a deep breath. "I do find the son of Salma handsome. He fills my dreams. Since the first barley harvest, I have not dared to hope that the man might find me attractive. However, I do not want you to think I am false to the memory of Mahlon."

Without hesitation, I reassured my friend. "My child, you have my blessing." With one hand, I smoothed a strand of hair out of her face. "All will be well."

It was almost dark when Ruth slipped from the house. I stood in the gate watching her slender shape until she vanished into the dusk.

"God of Abraham, Isaac, and Jacob," I breathed the fervent prayer into the sky. "Give her the courage to do as I ask. Let Boaz find her pleasing this night."

I spent most of the night pacing the floor and repeating my prayer to the Living Lord. It was not quite dawn when I heard the latch lift on the gate. I did not have time to rush to my bed. Instead I bent over the brazier, pretending to light the fire. My head pounded with apprehension. Such an early return could mean Boaz rejected my friend.

"You have returned already?" My surprise was not feigned.

"It is nearly daylight," she responded without a smile. "You have been awake all night."

"No . . . I . . . no . . ." My lie was hollow.

"You are still wearing the flour spotted tunic you wore yesterday." A small smile appeared. In a few short steps, Ruth crossed the room to gather me into her arms. "I know you waited and prayed for me this night."

"Tell me." It was easier to turn the conversation than offer explanations that were not necessary.

"I did as you told me." Ruth dropped her arms to her sides. "After all the men were snoring, I crept around the edge of the room to where Boaz was sleeping."

"No one saw you?" In case my plan failed, I did not want the girl named as wanton.

"Everyone was asleep," she repeated. "I stayed in the shadows. I almost ran home instead of doing as you asked."

My friend lowered her head as she confessed her fear.

"It was a difficult thing that I requested of you." Now I could admit the truth.

"I lifted the blanket and lay down next to the man. From that moment, I was afraid to breathe or move. A short time ago, Boaz rolled over and awakened." The girl paused.

My heart was beating so hard that I had to press my hands to my chest. Her next words would tell me our future. Ruth looked past me out the window.

"Then what?" When I could take the suspense no longer I burst out with a question.

"He sat up and stared at me. 'Who are you?' I was not sure if he spoke in anger or alarm." The woman from Moab mused.

"What did you say?" I had to prompt the recitation.

"Oh." She seemed to return to the present with a quick intake of breath. "I said, 'I am Ruth, your maidservant. Spread your garment over me, for you are next of kin.' Then he took my face in his hands."

Again, there was a long pause. I waited impatiently for my friend to continue.

"For what seemed like forever, the man looked at me. I was sure he was going to reject my claim. Finally, he said, 'May you be blessed by the Lord, my daughter. Your last kindness is greater than the first. You did not seek the young men. Do not fear. I will do as you ask, for all know that you are a loyal woman.' His fingers smoothed my hair away from my face." The soft voice was dreamy as she remembered the moment.

"That is wonderful!" I burst out with relief. If I had not been sitting down, I would have danced around the room.

Ruth held up a hand. "He said one more thing. 'It is true that I am your kinsman but there is a closer one. Remain with me tonight. In the morning, if he will act the part of *ga-al*, it is God's will. If not, as the Lord lives, I will be your *ga-al*.' Then he kissed my forehead."

"The man will not rest until the matter I settled." I was satisfied. "He will speak to the son of Samson this morning."

The young woman was not done with her story. "We lay together until the sky began to turn gray. He told me 'Return to your home before the men awake. It should not be known that you have come to the threshing floor.' I prepared to leave, but he drew me to his side. 'Bring the cloak you wore and hold it out. You must not go back empty handed to your mother-in-law.' When I did, he poured in six measures of barley. It is outside the door."

"We will wait, my daughter." I hugged the girl close. "You will see: Boaz bar Salma will be your husband. The Holy One of Israel is gracious and does not forget the faithful."

"Yes, my mother, your God has blessed us."

We sat together watching the sky turn rose red in the rising sun. After a while, I dozed. There was no doubt in my heart that *I AM* heard my prayer. It was after the midday meal when a knock roused me. Ruth rushed to the door.

"Hello, my child," I recognized Rahab's voice. "All is well. I have come to speak to Naomi."

I sat up rubbing the sleep from my eyes.

"Let me bring you a cup of water," my friend offered.

"Yes, a fresh cup from the well." There was a smile in the woman's voice.

"I will get it." Ruth snatched up the water jar and hurried out the door.

"Come in." I waved my visitor toward the cushions. "May I offer you some fruit?"

"Naomi, you do not need to stand on ceremony. We both know why I have come." The woman lowered herself to the seat I indicated.

"Then Boaz has spoken to Aaron bar Samson?" I knew the answer but needed to hear the affirmative reply.

"Aaron has renounced his claim to Elimelech's property and to Ruth," Rahab smiled. "My son seeks to wed Ruth of Moab, the widow of Mahlon son of Elimelech."

"It is well." I sighed with relief.

"We are widows together," my visitor replied. "Our happiness is buried, but we can still give pleasure to those we love. Boaz has found a woman to care for in your daughter-in-law. Ruth is a lovely young woman."

"She refused to leave me alone. Instead, she left her home and kindred to come here with me. I have prayed that the God of Israel will bless her faithfulness. Our children will rear sons for Israel," I asserted fervently. "Blessed be the God of Abraham, Isaac, and Jacob."

"Amen, Alleluia, El Elohim Israel." Rahab smiled as she repeated the old chant.

"Here, my mother, is the water." Ruth hurried in with a full jar of water on her shoulder. Carefully, she poured a fresh cup for Rahab.

"My child, let us bless the Living God of Israel. You have found favor in the sight of Boaz." I could not wait to tell my friend the news. "It is as I said; the man has not delayed to seek you as wife."

Rosy color flooded the young woman's cheeks.

"I only did as you suggested," she insisted softly.

"Rejoice, for the Lord has blessed your obedience," Rahab announced as she crossed the room to embrace Ruth.

I joined the pair. We three women stood together. My heart rang with praise to the God of Israel.

In a moment, I stepped back to face the practicalities. "We must make plans."

The rest of the afternoon was spent working on details of the event.

"At Passover, we will sign the betrothal agreement, and at the next moon turning, celebrate the wedding," Rahab announced when we started to make decisions. "You must let me help with arrangements."

I opened my mouth to protest, but the woman held up a hand. "It is best if we help one another. In that way, neither of us is over-burdened."

After Rahab left, I looked at Ruth. My friend stared out the door she held open for our visitor.

"Are you happy?" I needed to be sure.

The radiant face that turned to me was answer enough. "My mother, truly your God has become my God. The Holy One of Israel has given me more blessings than I thought possible. I will be the wife of Boaz bar Salma!"

"He is a kind man." I could not resist repeating her words.

My answer was a merry laugh. The girl crossed the room with a dancing step. She pulled me to my feet and hugged me tight.

"You are the mother I never knew. Thank you." Happy tears spilled down her cheeks.

We held each other as a peaceful prayer burst from my lips. Blessed are you Lord God of Jacob. It is true. You come to the aid of widows and offer hope. Thanks be to *I AM*.

Before it seemed possible, it was time for the wedding. The day dawned clear after a week of rain. All of Bethlehem attended the marriage of Boaz bar Salmon to Ruth of Moab, widow to Mahlon, son of Elimelech. Many blessings were showered on the couple.

"Peace on your house."

"May the Lord grant you many sons."

"God give you prosperity like Abraham, Isaac, and Jacob."

I whispered my hope to the young couple before they moved together to the room prepared by Rahab and me. "Your children will be a delight to the Lord. The Holy One seeks to bring in, not exclude, all people. Perhaps your children will bring about such reconciliation in the world."

⊷ Epilogue ᥟᴖ

"GOD IS GRACIOUS," THE old woman affirmed exultantly when she finished her recital.

She looked around at the other occupants of the room. Rahab brushed away tears. Ruth smiled lovingly at her friend. Boaz smoothed his beard to hide his emotion. Naomi bent to kiss the forehead of the infant she held.

"Now I hold the promise for the future in my arms. The Almighty has restored my life and renewed my faith. The God of Abraham, Isaac, and Jacob has blessed me beyond anything I expected. *I AM* never withheld love from me, even though I was blinded by my fear and hatred. It was not my fault that my father died in the Wilderness of Shur. I was wrong to think that the Holy One turned away when we were in Moab. Even in my grief for my husband and sons, I was never alone. The Living Lord showed me love in the loyalty of Ruth and in the circumstances that brought me home to Bethlehem."

"My mother." Ruth laid her soft hand over the wrinkled one of her mother-in-law.

Naomi smiled at the young woman. "Good has come from everything that I saw as punishment. You, my daughter, are the greatest of my blessings."

The girl from Moab repeated her vow of just two years earlier. "Wherever you go, I will go. The place where you live, I will live. Your God is my God."

"I can see now that even when we doubted, the Holy One did not abandon us in the wilderness," Naomi continued to muse. "I never understood that the Living Lord desires to cherish and bless each person. My own slavery was to my fears and rage. *I AM* has freed me as surely as the Sons of Jacob were rescued from Egypt. Even in my grief, I have found healing. You were right to say that God blesses us in all things."

Rahab smiled at her friend. "Thanks be to the God of Abraham, Isaac, and Jacob that you are restored to faith. The Living Lord blesses us, even when our faith is weak. When I was still the Daughter of Astarte, I was accepted by the Holy One of Israel."

Both grandmothers bent over the baby when he began to whimper. He opened blue eyes to blink at them. The old women smiled.

"My child, I pray that you will grow strong in the service of the Almighty." A wrinkled hand cradled the small head as Naomi held her grandson high. "Your inheritance will be blessing."

"Obed will grow up to be a pillar of strength in Israel," Boaz proclaimed with a proud smile.

"Yes," Rahab agreed with a fond smile for her only child. "Your son will be great in the land."

"Come, my Obed." The new mother held out her arms for the baby who began to cry loudly. "You are hungry. There will be time for greatness when you are fed."

In a moment, the child was cuddled against her breast, nursing happily. The young mother looked at her baby and then up at the tall man who was her husband. A smile lingered on her lips. The son of Salma kissed the top of his wife's head before turning to leave.

"I must return to the men." Boaz raised the curtain between the two rooms. "We will offer prayers for every Son of the Promise and all who believe in the God of Abraham, Isaac, and Jacob."

"We, too, will offer prayers," Rahab replied so softly her son did not hear.

"It is right to give praise to *I AM*," Naomi agreed. "The One God worked in all that I saw as misery. The Living Lord provided for our needs after my father died. Elimelech watched over my mother and siblings as if they were his own. The weakness of my sons became strength in time. Our journey to Moab was a time of learning that the Almighty is not bound by borders nor isolated to one people. *I*

AM blessed me with the faithfulness of Ruth even while I raged in my grief."

The young woman rested her cheek against the old woman's shoulder. "My mother, you showed me the way to trust in your God."

"I never expected to find such contentment and peace." A wrinkled hand caressed the infant's head. "Behold, God has raised up a son for the house of Elimelech and for the house of Salma."

Rahab smiled at the trio. "He will be a blessing for all Israel. I, too, am blessed. God has given me a daughter who makes my son happy. I have found a friend for my old age in the widow of my husband's cousin."

"The God of Abraham, Isaac, and Jacob is truly the God who gives blessing to all nations." Naomi lifted her hands in benediction. "In this child, we see the union of Canaan, Moab, and Israel. May the Living God make him great!"

From the next room, men's voices raised in praise. "Blessed be the Name of the Lord."

"Amen, Alleluia, El Elohim Israel!" the three women responded in unison.